Whispering Snowflakes

Whispering Snowflakes

Elke Chantil

Ivy's Publishing

Houston, TX

Published by Ivy's Publishing, LLC
15634 Wallisville Rd. 800 PMB 160
Houston, TX 77049 USA

Cover design by AK Organic Abstracts
Map illustration © 2026 Virginia Allyn
Interior illustrations © 2026 AK Organic Abstracts

Library of Congress Control Number: 2026900838

ISBN (eBook): 979-8-218-82665-9
ISBN (Hardcover): 979-8-218-82664-2
ISBN (Paperback): 979-8-234-06174-4

First edition, 2026

I was a reader, until I wrote.
This one is for my loves—V, A, and C.

Sneeuwvlok
Vampyre Isle
Crescent Moonz
Starfish Lagoon
Twilight Sands
Granite Mountains
Waitomo

POLAR ISLES
Glaycyr Falz
The Lost Queen
GLASS LAKE
FOREST OF
FROZEN DREAMS
WHISPERING
WOODS
Arkaik Alpynz
FOREST OF
SHADOWS
RIVER OF SPELLS
ALPYNE
FISHING VILLAGE

PROLOGUE

SNEEUWVLOK

The Forest of Shadows

The forest bowed to the witch as she entered, its branches dipping low in a slow, obedient arc. Frost clung to her cloak, hissing where it touched the fabric, as though the cold itself rejected what she carried.

"Welcome to Sneeuwvlok, Myst," Queen Frost whispered as the witch surrendered the small but powerful bundle.

The infant stirred in the queen's arms, her tiny fingers curling against the fur-lined cloak.

Then a single snowflake drifted between them—

shimmering,

twinkling—

before settling on the baby's cheek, soft as a mother's kiss.

Far beyond the forest, a mother's cry tore through the night.

In Queen Frost's arms, the stolen child—Myst—answered.

The forest went still as the curse began.

1

Arkaik Alpynz

Jealous Poison

NINE MONTHS EARLIER

Queen Frost

I pull the hood low over my platinum hair and select the smallest of my three cherished sets. The quiver settles across my back—holly-berry–tipped arrows ready.

Just in case.

I leave my chambers while the castle sleeps—

not as a queen, but as something far more dangerous.

At twenty-five, I rule without an heir.

And a crown without succession is an invitation to ruin.

At my touch, the hidden passage yields—frost surging into my palm, shaping itself into a pale sphere of light that drifts ahead, illuminating the narrow stone corridor.

The air is colder here, quieter, untouched by courtly whispers and watching eyes.

Tonight, I will do what a queen must.

Even if it damns me.

At the base of the passage, I lift the bar and ease the slender door open. Night greets me in a hush of silver and shadow. The cold slips beneath my cloak, threading through my breath as though it recognizes me.

Claiming me.

My wool-lined dress brushes the earth as I crouch, drawing the dagger from my boot. Behind me, the distant murmur of guards fades into nothing.

Ahead, the Forest of Shadows waits.

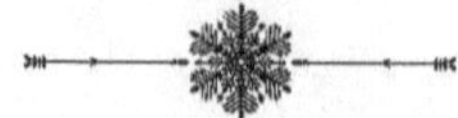

But the forest is not the only shadow I carry tonight. My secret walks with me.

It was a tension-laden choice when I said "I do" to the man I made king—one who repaid me with lovers and unwanted bastard children, yet left his bloodline unclaimed. I once believed that, in time, he might come to love me.

Foolish hope.

He gave his heart to another long ago. I loathe him.

And I hate her.

Mairi, clever witch that she is, knows I'm close. My presence stirs hushed secrets through the eerie forest as I move along the dirt path, moss thickening beneath my steps near the River of Spells, which demands hexed offerings for every favor the witch bestows.

A small stone near an aged willow catches my eye. I bind a dark spell to it and drop it into the clear water. It sparkles as it settles among the others.

The cottage comes into view, and the air, as though awakened, carries the scent of mystical herbs and forgotten spells.

"Veraminta, I see you." Agitation threads my voice as I confront the slinky black cat, her long whiskers twitching, her curious green eyes fixed on me. The gate creaks as I push it open. "Where is she?"

At my command, the familiar hops from the overturned flowerpot and begins her leisurely stroll toward the back. The stone path winds us through a garden of twisting vines and berries. At midnight, the moonflower opens, revealing heart-shaped petals that seem to glow just for me.

Right on time.

Eyes down, I notice three pansies dancing in circles. They sing a dark, whimsical song while insects burrow through mud and root, weaving over and under the ground. The full moon seizes my attention, and I bow my head in silent prayer to the Moon Goddess, Luna.

Formality has no place here.

I push the back door open and step into the confined space. A hearth hisses at damp wood while a large cauldron hangs over a steady flame, awaiting Mairi's spells and potions. Candles burn in abundance around her as she sits at her wooden table, surrounded by spellbooks and scrolls.

Finally, she lifts her head from an ancient tome filled with inscriptions and tucked-away pages.

"I've been expecting you. Are you prepared?"

Her greeting fades as she slips back into her thoughts. Absorbed in her incantations, she rises, crosses to her cupboard, and retrieves a goblet. I pull a chair from beneath the table, sit, and watch the preoccupied witch.

With a large dipper, she ladles the brew through the steam and sets the goblet before me.

"When you drink the potion to its end," she says, "the child's name will be revealed. Her birth mother—a powerful queen—has already chosen one. The goddesses will protect it, leaving it as her first, known only by an initial. The one you receive tonight is the name she will live by."

As the words settle, I begin to hear secrets in the wind, whispering through the stillness.

The witch leans closer and murmurs, "It's time. Drink, wicked one."

Every candle flame extinguishes at once, plunging the room into darkness as the second part of the curse unfurls.

"Those without magic will gradually forget the realm the child comes from. Its name will fade from maps. Memories will grow faint. Stories will lose their endings. If the curse remains unbroken, on the child's twenty-first birthdate, the realm will vanish entirely—sealed from thought and denied to memory—forever known as the Hidden Hybiscus."

Three moon phases have passed and the consequences of my choice begin to take shape. The elixir compels my body to experience the sensations and transformations of pregnancy, even though my womb remains empty.

My dark secret.

The long corridor to the west wing becomes a passage of shame, its whispers drifting toward me. Inside, the chamber my father once ruled from is unrecognizable. This king is surrounded by alluring women—none quite my age, none I recognize.

My purpose dims beneath his spectacle.

Glossed oils glide over his broad shoulders, shimmering along the lines of his sculpted chest. One woman settles at his hip, russet locks falling forward as her kisses weave secrets across his skin. Three brunettes sway near the bed. Their sheer winter silks cling to their bodies, catching firelight as their bare feet slide across the furs lining the floor.

Between his relaxed legs, ashen hair spills past her waist, her mouth filled, while his fingers wander across the breast of the woman with copper strands—his favorite.

Disgust coils in my throat.

The women notice me before he does, catching my movement as I step out of the shadows. The king jolts upright.

"Get out, now!"

Temptation urges me to send a cold lash of frost across the chamber, but I restrain it.

I will not waste my power on scurrying rats.

They scatter at my presence, laughter echoing down the

corridor as the last flees with a silk robe barely clinging to her silhouette. I take a chair near the windows and sit, the familiar stretch of untouched trees filling the view.

"There is news to share."

My husband slides into a thick robe, adjusts himself, and retreats briefly to wash.

He disgusts me.

We were intimate not long ago—but it was essential for my plan.

He returns, irritation masked by forced calm, and stops a few paces from me.

"I'm waiting, my dear."

I rise slowly and drift to his side. He keeps his gaze on the windows while mine stays on the door. I lower my head beside his, my breath grazing his ear as I whisper the lie.

"I am with child."

Before he can react, I walk toward the doors.

"Her name is Myst."

My fingers curl around the iron ring pulls as I open them. Frost blooms where my touch lingers.

He believes I carry his heir.

I can almost taste the question forming in him—how I could possibly know the child is a girl, when his beloved is the one swollen with a child that will never be his.

But she will be mine.

2

Arkaik Alpynz

ARRIVAL

NINETEEN YEARS LATER

Sage

"Please follow me, Sage. What did you say your surname was?" the man asks, having introduced himself simply as William.

"I did not, sir," I interrupt before he can press further.

He leads me through the rear entrance, and I follow closely, noting every detail of the regal yet stone-cold castle. A chill settles around me, and I pull my shawl tighter as my eyes roam. It has been decades since I last walked these halls, yet the air feels unchanged—heavy with memory, unwilling to give up its secrets.

The grand hall does not greet me. Instead, I face the towering backs of twin staircases.

What lies beyond those steps, waiting to be remembered?

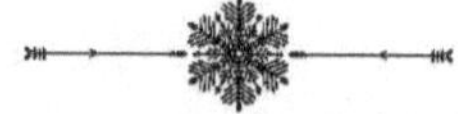

"This is urgent, Sage," William says. "Answer my last three questions: your town of origin, your family heritage, and your work historia."

I tread carefully, choosing my truths with intention. "A small village to the west, where my family once served at Crescere Moonz. Managing large events is my specialty—organization, records, expenditures. I'm meticulous."

Looking directly at him, I continue, "Keeping thorough records is another strength of mine. And last, William, if I may, this position has been open for several moon phases. I understand the urgency in filling it."

If this man only knew who he was speaking to.

One day, I will enlighten him with the truth of my heritage.

When we reach the kitchen, the air is thick with burning oak, seasoned meats, and a tea kettle begging for attention. Worktables crowd the space as kitchen hands prepare the day's meals, while servers move in and out like ants, carrying trays toward waiting guests.

"Dulce," William says, "allow me to introduce Sage, the temporary steward who will manage food purchasing, storage, and preservation. She will also oversee large events."

He continues, a brittle note in his voice. "Please handle things from here. We need Sage's references and complete working records. She'll also require a clean room." He turns to leave, pausing only once. "Sage, I will follow up with you in a few days to discuss how things are faring."

His voice fades as Dulce speaks, stern and clipped. "Let's get you settled in. Then we'll have something to eat and go over the responsibilities."

I nod and follow her to the far end of the kitchen, down a narrow hallway, and into a descending stairwell. At the bottom, she turns into a longer corridor lined with doors.

"We'll keep this brief," she adds. "I haven't had a moment for the noon meal."

"You'll be here. Room three." She inserts the skeleton key, turns it easily, and presses it into my palm before stepping aside.

What other doors might this key unlock?

I pocket the thought and move inside.

"Your steward's garments are in the bottom drawer. Make

yourself comfortable. I'll see you back in the kitchen shortly."

Dulce leaves, closing the door behind her.

The room is modest, with a single bed, a small armoire, and a wash basin with fresh linens.

No engagements here.

A quiet chuckle escapes me before the thought dissolves. The accommodation is clean; nothing else about it matters.

The only exit besides the door is a window above the bed.

I'll need to see where that leads—later.

My small sack is easy to unpack. I retrieve the simple black dress from the bottom drawer and slip into it. Lifting my arms, I draw a shimmering circle over my body, voicing the spell as it settles.

Much better.

The dress now fits as if tailored, and my ashen hair suits me perfectly. I gather it at my nape, twisting it into a neat bun and pinning it in place before it can betray a single loose strand. A charismatic laugh slips free as I wink at myself in the warped mirror.

On my return to the kitchen, I brace for Dulce's disposition and wonder how many of my lies she has already seen through. She is short and plump, likely from tasting every sweet treat and baguette that passes through her domain. I place her in her mid-sixties—hair more silver than brown, her scowl permanent from decades of running a kitchen staff.

This woman will be a fountain of information, with only a few sprinkles of personality. I need nothing more.

When I reach her, my suspicions are confirmed.

"I have managed this kitchen alone for well over thirty years," Dulce says tightly. "My capability has not waned. But if this is what they want, so be it."

She leads me to a small table near a window overlooking one

of the courtyards, where half-frozen men practice fighting maneuvers.

Is this how they train?

Two settings await us: warm bread and what appears to be root vegetable stew. Painfully, I allow Dulce to sit first, then follow, placing the linen in my lap as impetuous manners take over.

Softening my tone may be crucial.

I am already on thin ice with William.

Steam rises as I pour broth over the vegetables, unable to resist dipping a corner of bread into the fragrant heat.

"This is delicious," I say quietly as my thoughts drift to a forgotten place.

It has been a long time since I have tasted this.

Dulce outlines my responsibilities, then leads me to a small writing desk tucked into an alcove of the main kitchen. Manuscripts, merchant records, and guest lists await, including preparations for the many balls held throughout the year.

"With that, I'll leave you to it," she says, returning to her inspection of prepared meals.

"You know Myst doesn't like eggs. Why would you prepare that for her?" Dulce barks. "Redo it completely. Easy on the jam— Queen's orders. Apricots are running low, and the next shipment from the southern provinces won't arrive for weeks."

The name robs me of breath. I still myself, hands slipping into the pockets of my skirts, fingers curling there, hidden.

She tips the plate, letting its contents fall into the bowl kept for the small black animal.

I sit at the desk, take up a crow-feather quill, and face the records. Two ink jars wait before me—one black, one scarlet.

Annotations reveal a butler responsible for ale, wine, and champagne, as well as the pantry. A bakehouse on the castle grounds must also be accounted for. The complexity mounts as I read.

Sauce chef

Dessert chef

Wafer maker

Brewer—my favorite so far.

Slaughterer. Poulterer. Fruiterer.

And then those responsible for the dining experience: tablecloths, candles, silver flatware.

A low sigh leaves me.

So many people to meet.

I desperately need a beverage—perhaps two, likely three.

"Dulce," I call, "where is the wine cellar?"

No answer.

I rise, resigning myself to finding the butler.

Dulce steps out of the storeroom, color high in her cheeks, smoothing her skirt before tucking a loose strand behind her ear. She won't meet my gaze as she delivers exactly what I do not wish to hear.

"William was promoted to butler. You took his former position as steward."

An obvious question escapes me. "What was the butler promoted to?"

Dulce stills, fingers lingering at her waist as if deciding whether to answer at all.

I turn away, already done with the conversation, and head into the corridor to see where William has hidden himself.

3

Arkaik Alpynz

Velvet Dreadnought

Myst

My hand drifts across Midnight's silken coat—the ebony wind demon whose caramel eyes and twin horns give her a beauty born of ancient strength. My dreadnought, who blazes through snow daily, rests beside me on the lounge, attuned to my thoughts. A calm midwinter morning settles around us as a young maid brings the morning meal, her black hair loosely pinned, stray strands slipping free. Her full lips soften her features, though strain pulls at her movements.

Midnight, my sweetest girl, gently takes the pork I offer from my greased fingertips while I nibble toasted wheat spread with only a smear of apricot jam. I study the unfamiliar maid, and a loose strand of my thick, wavy chestnut hair slips forward, brushing my cheek. I tuck it behind my ear, the rest cascading over my shoulders and down past my waist. Only then do the tender snowflakes beyond the windows quiet my thoughts and soothe me.

The morning is pleasant—until footsteps approach. I already know the words that will shoot like stars from her sharp tongue before they flicker out. I slip the book I was engrossed in beneath a heavy covering, shielded by Midnight's presence.

Both heavy doors swing open, and she swans in through the center.

The queen holds her head high, exuding authority. Her

expression demands obedience, and her eyes watch it take shape. Her platinum hair is plaited into a lattice, the low bun threaded with gems. She is stunning—and people are gravely afraid of her. It is not effortless; she is never happy. Still, she is magnificent. Tall, with delicate yet striking features.

"Myst, why aren't you dressing for Tea and Cards?"

She is not asking; she is demanding. I cannot tell her that I was reading and deeply engaged, so I opt for the next best thing.

"Morning, Mother. I am breaking my fast."

She walks past me, through the bathing area, and into my dressing room, rummaging through gowns as she speaks to herself—and to me.

"The creature next to you is breaking its fast."

Midnight meets my gaze, and I console her in my lowest voice. *Creature? How dare she address you in that manner.* Unacceptable.

A soft huff escapes me as Midnight jumps from the lounge and stretches her long legs in one sleek movement. She pads to the door and nudges it open with her snout and paw—just enough to slip through.

Clearly insulted, she makes her exit.

Back in the bedroom, my mother turns her attention to the maid.

"Dear, what is your name?"

The pretty girl curtsies, her raspy voice trembling faintly. "Jessye, Your Highness."

The queen continues being the bitch she is. "Wonderful. Jessye, please take this half-eaten food and leave us."

A perfect day would be spent here beneath warm blankets, snuggling with Midnight while reading.

Sighing, I rise and move toward the space my mother dominates, drifting into daydreams of butterflies above frozen ponds and lilies trapped beneath ice while she fills the room with talk of what dress I should wear this afternoon.

The mirror reveals more of me than I invite, yet my reflection still softens into a smile—I love this gown. Since my eighteenth birthdate, my wardrobe has been entirely replaced—thank Valore, Goddess of Beauty. This gown suits my mischievous nature, and gifting the seamstress her favorite wine ensures her designs remain flawless.

The slate-gray fabric accentuates my eyes. Goodbye pastels; hello bold, desirable shades. The bodice fits tightly, the strapless neckline leaving my shoulders and upper arms bare, olive skin on display. Sheer arm cuffs sit snug at my wrists. The skirt flares modestly below my waist, and my velvet slippers are charcoal, just darker than the gown.

My long hair has been braided into several sections, pinned with tiny crystals resembling snowflakes. These designs, repeated day after day, are growing tiresome—but they will have to do.

The queen issues another command. "Shadow, assist Myst with her face powder and lip oil."

My handmaiden steps forward from her quiet post near the wardrobe as my mother's eyes sharpen on me.

"I will see you later for the evening meal in the great hall. Be on time—for once."

I fix my gaze ahead to avoid rolling my eyes as I sit at the dressing table and study my hair again.

Shadow powders my face lightly, dusting my cheeks with crushed crystal that leaves a soft, rosy glow. Her touch calms me despite her fussing.

"Child, keep your head straight," she scolds gently. "You are always late—to Tea and Cards, and everything else."

"Yes, Shadow," I reply sweetly. "But isn't that the point? To arrive late so my entrance is anticipated—and the guests delighted?"

Shadow purses her lips, unimpressed. "Hold still. This lip oil is difficult to remove and must be set."

She presses one finger to my lips, freezing me in place while she paints a soft nude hue onto my pout. A snap of her fingers releases me. Her ability to still me—even briefly—is something I endure most days.

She reaches for a pink silk muffler. I lift a hand, stopping her before she can take it. "There isn't a draft within the castle walls, and Tea and Cards will be set near the fire stream. Nothing should distract from this gown I will only wear once."

After settling the tiara atop my head, I rise and step closer to the mirror. When Shadow appears behind me, she looks at me as if I am a masterpiece and releases a quiet, "You are ready."

The truth rests in my smile.

"Yes. Thank you."

Her hand brushes mine—secretly comforting, as it does each day. Her kindness is the only balm against my mother's sharpness.

4

Arkaik Alpynz

Magical Kaleidoscope

Myst

"Guards. Please escort the princess to Frost Garden."

Shadow leans in with a small, knowing smile. "Krystelle is sitting in for Allysia today, so this should be a bit more pleasant for you." Her voice lowers, light as a falling feather. "But please extend yourself to Beatryx. Her father is important to the queen."

A sheepish smirk claims my lips—the best I can offer instead of a promise.

In the corridor, my guards await. I loop my arms through theirs, and together we move toward the main staircase.

"Let's skip," I say lightly. "I'm feeling daring and untouchable today."

Garrett laughs. "What are we so happy about on this fine afternoon?"

Shayn slips his arm free and leans closer, tone sharp. "Myst, seriously. Do you want us stripped of post? We've only been assigned to you for two moon phases, and already the queen watches us like hawks."

These two need their composure adjusted—and I am in the mood to play.

I loosen my stance, my arms falling easily to my sides. Pale mist coils from my fingertips, tracing soft paths through the air. I think of lust.

Both guards relax at once.

"Princess Myst, you look exceptionally graceful on this glorious day," Shayn says, smiling.

I lock eyes with him, and we chuckle. "Let me assist you further." He takes my arm and loops it through his own.

I glance lazily at Garrett and blow mist onto his chiseled jawline. He smiles immediately. "Yes," he agrees, "let us assist the most beautiful princess of all realms."

We descend the staircase together, passing guards who stare—confused, envious. Unable to resist, I wink at one, earning a ripple of tittering.

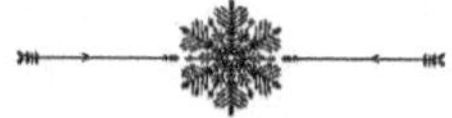

At thirteen, I began to understand my gift, though I had sensed it long before. Fear kept me silent until one evening.

On my way to my mother's chambers, I heard her door click. I hid in shadow, watching as she slipped away. When the passage cleared, I followed—through secret corridors I never knew existed—until she entered the Forest of Shadows.

How I was not caught, I do not know. Either she sensed me and allowed it, or she froze the forest itself, and I stood close enough to fall beneath her protection. Both seem equally possible.

An eerie cottage emerged from the fog. Staying hidden, I watched from behind a great oak as a toad hopped through a puddle and snapped up its dinner. Then singing drifted through the darkness.

we see you we see you
we tattle when we see…

When I looked down, nothing was there.

Eventually, the queen left, and I felt the forest bend to her as she walked away—wordless as she had entered.

I rose and, as quietly as possible, approached the cottage, hoping to explore. That's when the encounter happened.

A dark witch appeared and offered to help me understand my gift—for a price.

"On any three occasions, at any given time, you must honestly answer a question I ask you."

Easy.

I knew nothing of consequence. I agreed.

Her cottage was unlike anything I had seen. Cobwebs framed the doorway, one bearing a black widow dancing on silk threads.

Repulsive.

Beautiful.

Forcing the image from my mind, I took in the interior as we moved through a small room where a hearth warmed a wing-back chair. Maybe she sits there and unwinds in the evenings—if witches do that. In the kitchen, a larger hearth fed a cauldron, and a black cat with enormous green eyes brushed against my leg. It likely caught Midnight's scent.

My patience gone, I hardened my resolve and finally asked my questions.

"What is your name? Why does my mother visit you?"

The witch loomed close, her voice a mad whisper. "You ask too many questions, girl."

"I have more," I insisted.

Her cackle sent nearby creatures fleeing. "Sit. You are braver at this age than I expected—but it does not surprise me."

She made little sense but insisted I obey, so I did. Candles burned and the cauldron smoked before she turned, handed me a small glass, and offered her advice.

"Master your magic," she said. "Use it as your mind wills. But remember our deal. I will come, and I will collect. We will meet again."

I drank and left.

From then on, I practiced daily—shaping emotion into effect. But shame crept in. When Grandpapá alone marveled at my mist lifting dessert plates, the embarrassment was too sharp, and I withdrew.

Now, older, the mist returns when emotion surges. I know this—when its enchantment fades, memory fades with it.

As much as I hate control, I will not waste this gift.

No one has been harmed—yet.

As my guards and I enter the open courtyard, I stop at the small bridge. Beyond it, a pond lies iced over, flowers suspended beneath the surface, while a narrow stream curves in a protective loop. Fire rims the water, keeping frost fish alive and the air warm. The space always soothes me.

I cling to hopeful thoughts. I only need to endure what I cannot control.

Beatryx sits with the poise of her lineage, posture immaculate. Krystelle—my companion since childhood—draws my attention before I can look away. I force a smile, my mother's lectures on social order echoing whether I wish them to or not.

Once across the stream, I slip free of my guards' arms and release the spell at once. Garrett shakes his head, disoriented, which nearly makes me laugh, as both girls rise.

We sit. Gossip follows.

Honeysuckle tea with sweet cream—my favorite— accompanies cucumber bites and delicate cakes.

"Should we start the game?" Krys asks, tentative.

I nod, reaching for the cards. Nine in total. I shuffle without looking and place three before each of us, each painted with a bloom. The goal is to share a personal trait matching the first letter of your flower, then briefly expand. According to my mother, this is how one truly comes to know someone.

Beatryx laughs softly. "Jasmine."

"Tell us," Krys says.

"Jealous," Beatryx replies easily. "It's my favorite scent, and I envy anyone who still has access to it. Father says it hasn't been imported in nearly eighteen years."

"Why." I swirl honey into my tea, letting the warmth steady me.

"No one knows where it came from. What I have costs a fortune—and even more to preserve."

I sip my tea as she continues, her hands moving with the easy confidence of someone who's done this a hundred times. Her final bloom is a rose.

She is striking—full curves, thick brown curls pinned with care, hazel eyes that dare you to linger. Beautiful in a way that draws attention she never asked for. I suspect men have taken advantage of that, leaving her jealous not of affection, but of power. Her father, Lord Blake, appears kind, with a warm smile. Nothing else has been revealed to me about her family.

Privately, I turn my own cards.

Peony. My favorite.

The shy iris.

And then—

Hybiscus.

The bloom is amethyst, unfamiliar, unsettling. It feels as though it watches me in return.

"Did something happen in the training yard earlier?" Krys asks.

Before I can answer, Beatryx leans forward. "I saw Iyce speaking with your father, Myst. The conversation looked tense, but his icy blue eyes were piercing as ever. Have you spoken to him?"

Her cheeks flush.

I glance toward the frozen infinity pond, uninvited memories surfacing. Once, I admired Iyce—his body carved like the glaycyrs themselves, eyes cold enough to still you in place.

Now?

An arrogant ass.

I toss my cards face down. "Hot," I say lightly. "Iyce is doing well, I'm sure. I haven't spoken to him in days."

I rise. "The heat is getting to me. Most likely from this flame around us. But without it, the fish would die. I think I should go now—and they should live."

Both girls stand.

"Stay," I say, palms raised. "Enjoy yourselves."

At the stream, I pause, watching silver fish glide through firelit water, and think of the one person who understands me best.

Beatryx and Krys return to idle chatter as I cross the bridge toward Shayn and Garrett.

"We're going to the bakehouse in the western town," I say. "I'm craving something sweet."

"As you wish, Princess," Shayn replies.

Garrett sheathes the sword held low at his waist, and we walk on, the men a pace behind me. Neither notices the card I slip into the hidden pocket of my dress.

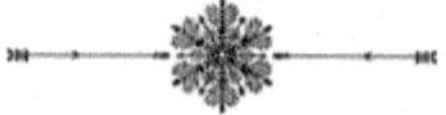

The bakehouse greets me with warmth and the promise of normalcy. Dough is kneaded at a wide wooden table, flour dusting the air. Shelves of cinnamon, nutmeg, and cloves perfume the space.

Shayn and Garrett remain outside.

I sit near the window as beeswax candles flicker against the fading light.

Lavender scones arrive, drizzled with honey.

"Warm milk, Princess?" the frail woman asks as she sets the teacup to the right of my plate, hands trembling slightly. "The extra vanilla bean and cinnamon you favor have been added."

"Thank you, Sara."

She moves away, returning moments later with treats wrapped

neatly for my guards. *A sweet woman.* I savor the moment. Tea and Cards has its indulgences—but solitude is sweeter.

With my quarters in the north tower, this western town remains hidden from most of my windows. Yet its invitation is always there. Today, I accept it. The air is warmer here. The people, too.

The door chimes.

"Hello, Calyx."

A young bakehouse girl looks up from dusting pastries with powdered sugar, her flaxen hair catching the light. She smooths her apron, cheeks warming as she meets his gaze. "The usual."

"Yes, please, Ella," the young soldier says with a small smile. "Same as yesterday. Same as tomorrow."

My thoughts drift again to the hybiscus.

There is a small library in town. *I'd like to find a book on that bloom.* As many times as I've played the game, I have never seen it. The monastery library holds spiritual tomes; the castle library is vast. This one—perhaps—holds something different.

I place my lace linen to the left of my plate with two coins, then rise. "Thank you, gentlemen. Please follow me."

Entering the library intrigues me. The air hums with promise, scented with parchment. Shayn moves ahead, hand on his sword, and announces, "Royalty enters!"

"For the love of all goddesses," Garrett snaps. "We're in a library."

"I appreciate caution," I say. "Stay by the door while I explore."

Their bickering fades as I round the first corner.

A lavish wooden desk commands my attention, reference ledgers rising behind it—until a quiet voice interrupts.

"May I help you?"

Startled, I flinch.

"I did not mean to disconcert you, Princess. This is a library; we speak softly." He edges closer. "Which is why I heard your approach."

A mischievous smile suppresses my laugh. He wears round wire glasses over curious brown eyes, a dark green suit tailored to perfection. Copper hair curls faintly at his temples.

"Browsing for a particular read?"

I glance everywhere but at him. "No. Never been inside. May I look around?"

"Of course, Princess."

He bows, gesturing theatrically. "The arts."

Then, "Historia and Geōgraphia."

Finally, passing me, "Lingua and Litteratura."

"I'll be at my desk if you need anything."

He clears his throat and points to an ornate object displayed near the entrance. "Be sure to look through our newly imported kaleidoscope. One silver coin. A glimpse of your future."

The temptation is there—but I am too focused on why I came.

"Possibly, if time permits. Thank you."

The staircase creaks as I ascend.

At the top, I veer toward the arts to mislead him, then slip into Historia and Geōgraphia. Leather-bound tomes surround me. One ancient volume perches just out of reach.

Rather than summon my guards, I browse books left on a reading table.

Carefully, I withdraw the card bearing the amethyst hybiscus.

Then something disrupts my thoughts.

Whispers.

Soft panting.

A pulse of breath that urges caution—and curiosity.

Peeking around the bookcase, I glimpse the source of the girl's purrs and the reason behind them. Heat floods my cheeks as I turn away quickly. Something unfamiliar stirs low in my stomach—unbidden, unnamed.

Unable to focus, I return to the stairs, fingers sliding along the rail. Below, Garrett and Shayn still argue.

"I am ready."

The walk back to the castle is quiet. In my haste, I never look through the kaleidoscope.

Perhaps for the best.

Someone else will gaze through its lens soon enough—and I suspect their future will be the one worth seeing.

5

Arkaik Alpynz

Shayn

I enter the banquet hall with confidence, my attention passing over the space by habit. Nobles gossip in tight circles; guards stand stiff as stone; the musicians balance on the edge of a single mistake. Nothing here requires my attention.

"Where is Myst?" the queen asks through her teeth, her gaze never leaving the guests.

I pause. "In her chambers, I assume, my queen."

The cold woman turns her head only slightly, pretending to observe the goings-on, one eye cutting toward me as she speaks again, her voice even lower. "Why don't you go and verify that, dear boy?"

Respectfully, I lower my head, careful not to draw attention. Steadying myself, I match her quiet tone. "As you wish, Your Majesty."

I take my leave.

Boy.

Is that how the wicked woman sees me? Perhaps I should invite her to my humble room and let her take a good look at what she calls boyhood. Maybe then she would change her tone—beg, even.

Ridiculous. I am not attracted to older women.

My thoughts press in as I consider Myst and her whereabouts.

Where else would she be? She does not attend every dinner. The girl prefers solitude—reading with that wild creature curled beside her, riding through the woods, or doing whatever else Myst does. Yes, I am her guard when she requires escorting. What I am not is a damn babysitter.

As I make my way through the castle, I pass the kitchen, hopeful for a glimpse of the new steward, Sage. Petite, keen-eyed, with shimmering cheekbones and pale hair always twisted into a neat bun at her nape. Her hourglass figure stops my heart.

Maybe an older woman is exactly what I need.

I adjust every crease of my attire, still simmering over the queen's remark.

By the time I reach the grand staircases, I have not caught so much as a glimpse of Sage. But another surprise awaits.

The moment my gaze lifts, there she is.

Leaning casually against the banister, the playful beauty spills from a scarlet gown painted onto her sculpted body. Fingerless gloves tease the handrail. Beatryx's curves seem endless, making it impossible to look away.

Myst is fun—witty, stunning, mysterious. A precious doll, admired but never touched.

As if I would ever have a chance with her.

She is royal, for fuck's sake.

I force my focus back to Beatryx and take the first steps up the staircase toward my demise.

With both hands extended, she takes mine. Before I can react, we are spinning—gone. Responsibilities vanish as we whirl through galleries, hiding in dark corners whenever guests draw near. Her innocent giggles soften into breathy whispers.

We reach a chamber—surely the one she occupies when her father is at court. Pressing against the door, she opens it and pulls me inside. The scent of flowers overwhelms me. I should resist. My body betrays the thought.

She closes the door just as I insist, "I shouldn't be here."

She huffs. "Stop. What is the problem?"

Her pout drives me mad. "If you must know, I was on a very important mission."

She tilts her head. "You have a new mission now. But tell me about the one you are abandoning."

Her inquisitive stare makes me stutter. "The queen—Your Majesty—well, *our* majesty—asked me to locate Myst."

Beatryx drops to her knees.

Any remaining thoughts evaporate.

Soft light spills from the wall sconces. Those ornate hazel eyes pin me in place. I am no longer concerned about Myst. This beauty may do with me as she pleases.

Spiderlike fingers unlacing her bodice free her breasts. She removes the pins from her hair, letting it fall like rain; the faint tap of metal hitting the floor is the only sound in the room. I stand there—helpless, obedient—while she toys with me.

Just as I relax, she crawls toward me on hands and knees. I press harder against the wall as her fingers work at my laces, slowly freeing—

…my boyhood.

Damn that queen.

Beatryx gasps, then pounces. The figurine is clearly pleased with the control she holds, conducting this orchestra with confidence. Her palms—soft as silk—move over me while her lips hum.

I may hurt this girl, despite rumors that contradict her innocence. Or perhaps she will hurt me. To say I am gifted is an understatement—but I want her.

I want to learn.

This is happening.

I place my hands at her neck as she takes me slowly. Her tongue dances; her lips prove capable. I do not believe a woman exists who could take me fully, so I allow the temptress to play a while longer before I claim control.

I pull her up, spin her, and begin unlacing the corset at her back. Why are there so many things to untie? Good goddesses above—how do women survive this? Buried in ribbons and fabric, it's worse than training with sweaty men.

She laughs at my frustration.

Finally undressed, she is breathtaking.

I hold her arms gently and bury my face in her neck. "What is that scent?"

She guides me to her bed and sits gracefully on its edge, hands returning to my parted breeches. Looking up, she answers, "Jasmine."

I undress quickly, leaving clothing scattered near hers. Need burns in her eyes, but beneath it, sadness flickers.

She is too beautiful to be sad.

I roll her over and notice deep brown marks scattered across her skin—adorable, despite everything.

"Do not move," I whisper.

Then I hesitate. "Wait—do you…?"

"Yes," she answers quickly. "I drink the potion daily."

Desire weighs heavy, but an inner battle rages. Every guard has warned me: once I take a woman, madness follows. My past lovers never crossed this line.

But brushing against her hidden flame decides everything.

I lose control.

With one hand, I guide myself; the other steadies her. Slowly— painfully slowly—I enter.

She feels incredible. Beatryx moans softly, breath quickening. "Oh my goddess, Shayn. Please don't stop."

I do not. I pull her closer, moving deeper, harder.

This is something I may crave daily.

What I do not need is the madness that follows.

I pull free at the brink, release spilling across her skin. She turns, breathless, touches my chest, and whispers, "That was the best sex I've ever had, Shayn."

There it is.

I was warned.

She pushes me onto the bed and climbs atop me as I brace for what comes next.

Later, I leave her singing in a steaming bath.

Relaxed to the point of stupidity, I head to Myst's quarters and knock hard.

"Guard!"

Nothing.

I pound on the door.

Still nothing.

Fuck.

6

Arkaik Alpynz

The Whispering Woods

Myst

As I approach my final hurdle—the stables—I touch the brooch pinned to my cloak, grounding myself in its familiar weight.

No one noticed me slip from my chambers.

I dressed in black riding breeches and a white tunic, gathered my hair back loose and secured it with a black velvet ribbon, and drew my cloak around my shoulders. With care, I fastened my favorite brooch to the left side—a snowflake pierced diagonally by an arrow.

My fingertips meet the jewel, and sadness rises through me. It is the crest of our kingdom. Grandpapá gave it to me when Grandmamá passed away, and I feel that loss every time I touch it.

The stables are unusually still this evening—until a girl startles me with a confident, "Need some help there?"

Aside from seeing her most days, I know little about her. Still, I accept the offer. I want to be as far from the castle as possible.

"That would be much appreciated. Thank you."

She strides over. "Aspen is the one you want, I assume."

She has noticed my preference. "Yes, please."

Once I am atop my stallion, she hands me the straps. "Girth is tightened."

With a soft kick, Aspen trots through the wide open doors, and we move soundlessly around the back of the grounds, heading north along a frosty path lined with berries and thyme as snow begins to fall at the forest's edge.

Aspen breaks into a powerful surge, the rush of cold air tugging my hair loose as the ribbon slips free and spirals away. My cloak darkens against his coat; we move as one.

He stops at a half-frozen stream to drink. I lean back and look up at the pitch-black sky, the full moon glowing as stars scatter and snowflakes fall. I trace constellations until I find the most striking of all—a great snowflake hunted by an archer.

A tiny silver snowflake was etched into my skin above the hollow of my left shoulder at birth. Each year, during Sextilis, another appears somewhere new.

On my eighteenth birthdate, an exquisite snowflake bloomed on my left hip—shimmering silver, with a soft pink undertone. If the legends are true, my secret will soon be revealed by one of the ice princesses drifting from the sky.

These woods are where I breathe.

The sound I have been waiting for finally comes—a flute's melody winding a spell through the trees. The scent of smoked cherries and pine nuts guides me deeper, toward the cottage nestled among towering pines, smoke lifting lazily from its chimney.

Aspen pricks his ears, eager, as I guide him toward the humble barn behind the cottage. He trots straight to Ginger, a deep-brown mare. They greet one another softly, breath mingling.

I dismount, draw my cloak close, smooth my wind-tangled hair, and step to the back entrance.

"Come in, my darling. What a pleasant surprise."

His voice alone steadies me.

"Grandpapá, I've missed you so." I fall into his embrace, and he catches every piece of me.

"Let me take this, dear." He reaches for my cloak, lifting it gently from my shoulders. His eyes linger on the brooch pinned to the fabric, his thumb brushing over the metal before he drapes the garment over a high-backed chair near the hearth. "The kettle's whistling. Wildflower and blackberry—your favorite."

Firelight catches a painting on the mantel. My mother sits as a child before my grandparents, anger already shaping her small frame. And beside Grandmamá stands an older girl I have never noticed until now.

"What brings you to the woods, my child?" Grandpapá asks, pouring boiling water into mismatched teacups.

"Space. And the need to escape the chaos."

He stirs honey slowly. "Ah—but chaos always finds us."

"How is Midnight?"

"Spoiled. Beautiful. She is my love."

He chuckles. "Sounds familiar."

I lift my teacup and burn my fingers. "Ow."

He gently takes it from me. "All right, sweetheart?"

I nod as a cool mist curls instinctively around my skin, easing the sting.

"Royal dinners aren't the same without you," I say softly. "You made them bearable."

He arches a brow. "You always know where to find me."

I close my eyes and smile through tight lips. *He is not wrong.* He had his reasons for leaving.

"You will be married soon," he says. "Have you begun preparing?"

"That will all be arranged by others. They can put a potato sack on me and a strand of pearls around my neck if they like. What a beautiful bride I would make."

His laughter joins mine until tears break free. He rises suddenly.

"I nearly forgot." Grandpapá walks to a table near the hearth. "Before your Grandmamá left this realm, she made me promise I would place this on you when you turned eighteen—so it is time."

He gestures for me to join him, his back still turned. I rise from the sofa, my eyes widening as he lifts something from a velvet-lined box. When he finally turns, he reveals a necklace—a delicate silver chain that shimmers briefly, but the pendant itself is extraordinary.

"My darling Myst," he says softly, "this snowflake pendant represents this realm. Wear it proudly."

As I step closer, the snowflake glows silver, sparkling like crushed diamonds—accepting me… or perhaps resisting. I lift my hair, and he settles the pendant against my neck, securing it with a quiet click.

Wanting to admire the piece, I move toward the modest mirror near the front entrance. The snowflake pendant catches the light as I turn slightly, then face forward again, lingering on its reflection.

"I love it," I whisper. Warmth gathers behind my eyes.

His voice lowers. "Never remove it, sweetheart. The pendant offers protection."

I turn back to him and fold myself into his embrace. "I miss Grandmamá."

"So do I," he says, holding me close. "More than anyone will ever realize."

He plays his flute while I lounge by the fire. Later, I retreat upstairs to a modest room—simple, quiet, waiting for me.

"Myst, darling," he calls, "I love you beyond the farthest star."

"Love you more than wildflowers and blackberries."

The sconces burn softly as I move to the wide window and watch snowflakes drift past the glass, desperate to reach the ground. As the night chill deepens, I wonder when the truth meant for me will show itself in one of those intricate pieces of ice art.

At the brush of my thought, tiny snowflakes form, and a light mist drifts from my fingertips—gentle enough to snuff out the flames around me.

I remove the robe encasing my body and free my feet from their slippers before settling beneath the blankets and quilts.

Sleep claims me.

I sit up, breathless, beads of water sliding down my neck. The dream clings to me.

In it, a child with honey-brown eyes, rimmed with darkness, offers three white blooms. She holds them out in her small hand before speaking.

"Princess Keiki, I picked these for you."

The image lodges itself deep—unshakable. The baby girl is precious, achingly so. *But who is she?*

I reach for the glass of water on the night table. After a few quiet moments, calm draws me back into sleep.

Morning rises to Grandpapá's humming and the sweet drift of pork. I knot my robe's sash and move into the narrow stairway, its close walls a stark contrast to the castle's vast, open flights.

"Come down, sweet child," Grandpapá calls. "Let's have hot tea while we wait for the pork to cook through."

My hair is a mess, and I do not care. The moment draws me backward—childhood rushing in. Grandpapá would take me to the kitchen and ask Dulce to set a small table just for us. Greasy pork, biscuits drowned in jam, laughter until our bellies ached. Then Shadow would arrive, and I would slip back into princesshood.

The past settles around me, warm and close, making the distance to the castle feel smaller. Berry jam and pork, Grandpapá's humming, the softness of my robe—it all wraps around me like a memory spell.

For a moment, I am only a girl in slippers, cradled by a kitchen where love is served in laughter and jam-covered biscuits.

If only I could stay a little longer.

7

Arkaik Alpynz

Vigil Lighthouse

Myst

"The beach is calling—let's go," I holler to Krys, who answers from deep within my closet.

"I'm nearly ready. I need a warm hat."

My closet is overflowing, so I join her and gently settle a simple periwinkle bonnet onto her head.

"Perfect. Seize your cloak. Shayn went to the kitchen to gather our basket and will meet us at the stables."

Krys and I love the beach. It lies far enough from the castle to feel like sanctuary—an escape we can claim as our own. Shyanne, my solid black mare, is my companion today. Krys rides with Shayn on his horse.

As we near the coast, the waves announce themselves, the air heavy with salt. We've done this for as long as I can remember. I hope we always will. At the shore, the breeze welcomes us.

Today is not as cold as usual, though the wind still demands respect. Little blue birds stand at the water's edge, slender legs half buried in damp, shifting sand. They ruffle their feathers as tall trees sway, keeping time with a low, hypnotic song the wind seems to play just for them.

"Shayn, hurry—come on! We don't have all day!" Krys hollers through the wind.

Shayn—being typical Shayn—takes his time tending the horses

and gathering our things.

"On my way, my lady," he calls, approaching with a blanket over one shoulder, a basket in one hand, and enough logs tucked under his arm to last the afternoon. He has been especially chipper these past few days.

He and Krys lay the blanket and anchor it with stones. Satisfied, he declares, "Perfect spot for our little gathering."

We watch the waves crash as the sun casts gold across the water, the moment slipping into something dreamlike.

Krystelle is striking, with hair and eyes the same shade of noir. Her olive skin is flawless, and we are the same age. She was introduced to the court as a ward—an orphaned noble girl entrusted to Queen Frost's care after a tragic accident in a far-off province. Her name was changed, her lineage erased, and she is treated as a quiet guest of the court. Perhaps her silence is grief. Perhaps it is something heavier.

While we are not permitted to spend all our time together, meals are one of the few moments we are allowed. She knows most of my secrets.

As I walk toward the water's edge, fear rises—but I push past it. Slipping off my slippers, I laugh as the cool water teases my toes. "I hope you've got corn and oats for the birds."

The wind lifts my dress. I hold it down with one hand, waving Shayn over with my hat in the other. *I should have braided my hair.*

Krys and Shayn join me. Shayn scatters corn, and I glance at Krys. "Did you bring ribbons?"

"What do you think?" she replies instantly. *Of course she did.*

Back on the quilt, I lift the basket lid, draw out the terracotta amphora of wine, and place the heavy clay vessel in Shayn's outstretched hand.

"Careful with the glasses," I say. Krys nods and sets them at the center.

I peer inside again. "Fresh cherries, date loaf, thyme-and-oregano baguettes, dried meats, cheeses—and wine. Sage remembered everything."

Shayn responds first. "Sounds amazing. This boy is starving."

"Boy?" Krys tilts her head.

I frown at him as well. "Why are you calling yourself that?"

Shayn laughs under his breath. "Your mother—the queen—calls me that sometimes."

Do I even want to know?

Krys grins. "Let's drink first. Then we'll get the story."

Shayn pours.

Krys pats the blanket in front of her. "Myst, slide in front of me." I shift forward, settling where she wants me.

She eyes Shayn. "Boy, should I tie yours too?"

We dissolve into laughter.

"I know all the women want to run their fingers through my hair," he says, far too pleased with himself.

Our eyes roll—though there's truth there.

Krys and I return to the sand, searching for shells. I keep my distance from the water this time. That unease still lingers. Excitement bubbles as I spot the perfect shell. "Gray and lavender! Let me know if you find more."

We collect several and place them gently inside Krys's bonnet.

Shayn begins building a meticulous fire in the stone pit he crafted the last time we were here. He scatters driftwood splinters across the bottom, adds a ring of smaller twigs, then builds a triangular frame, the longer pieces propping up the base.

The real magic begins when he draws his polished dagger from its leather sheath. I have only seen him reveal it a handful of times, and each time leaves me silent. *Where did he even find such a rare piece?* He angles it toward the waiting pit and strikes flint against the blade, sending the whole structure into flame.

Warmth draws me closer. Behind me, Krys has spread a handful of shells across a cloth, her fingers tracing their ridges as she reads them aloud in a low voice. Shayn leans in beside her, listening closely, adding quiet remarks about different individuals at court. The soft clatter of shells punctuates their hushed exchange— a rhythm of secrets unfolding in the firelight.

I close my eyes, lulled by the rhythm of the waves. My thoughts drift beyond the ocean. Not long ago, I was granted permission for a day's journey to the southern isles beyond the realm. The tea and spices were wonderful, and the people struck me as genuine.

Then Iyce intrudes on my thoughts.

Why wouldn't my father align himself with a powerful kingdom by matching me to a prince from another realm? I've seen the war maps. I know more than they think—yet I'm told nothing.

"Shh," Krys whispers.

I straighten.

"I hear voices."

I strain. At first—nothing. *Why does she hear it before I do?*

Then—

Light.

Breathy giggles.

They echo in my mind.

Shayn frowns. "Where?"

We turn together.

"The old lighthouse," I murmur.

Krys echoes me, and she and Shayn rise, beginning to walk in that direction.

"Wait," I say quickly. "Let me conceal us."

Mist coils thick around us as we move forward.

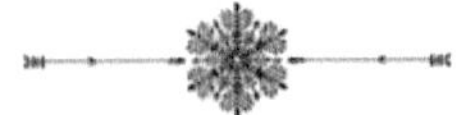

Shayn

I stare through the narrow window.

Garrett.

My friend. My equal. A fellow guard sworn to protect Princess

Myst.

He is shirtless, his broad chest framed behind the sensual woman seated in a chair. He moves in with a smooth, deliberate confidence, his fingers working at her corset laces. He lowers his head and sprinkles kisses down her upper back.

Then he wraps his hands lightly around her neck and whispers a lover's secret into her ear—an ear I know smells of jasmine.

She moans softly as the corset falls.

Garrett lifts her chin, kisses her, raises her from the chair.

He unlaces his breeches, releasing his boyhood from restraint. He's hard. Not as big as me, but still—he has the goods. He sits, lifts her skirt, and moves his hands to her hips, backing her directly over him. She lowers her soft curves slowly, and his head falls back.

Red floods my vision.

How does he know how to undo a corset like that? He didn't even undress her fully—just lifted her skirt. She really does get around.

And still—

Damn it, it's only been a few days since my cock was buried inside her. I thought she'd be driving me crazy for sex, yet the desire to fuck her hits me again, sharp and unwelcome.

I rip the ribbon from my hair and toss it onto the sand.

Myst's eyes are wide as she watches me. "What is your problem, Shayn? These two hiding out here in the woods is the best thing I've seen all week."

I feel sick.

"Don't be jealous," she continues gently. "Beatryx will be with as many men as she wants. One will never be enough for her. You deserve better."

The mist thins.

"We need to go," she adds. "It won't hold much longer."

8

Arkaik Alpynz

Shayn

The last two days weigh heavily on me. I shared something intimate with Beatryx… of course Garrett did it better. He and I spend ample time together—meals, training, and council meetings, side by side.

Fuck Garrett. The alehouses beyond the walls are calling.

Why wasn't I enough? The smell of jasmine lingers as I recall her soft voice. "Oh, Shayn, that was the best sex I have ever had." *Was she lying?* Garrett was gentler than I am, and he knows how to unlace that contraption around her bodice.

I land in the Dragon's Dungeon, a tavern in the fishing village southeast of the castle, near the harbor. I've never been here before and will likely never return; tonight is my private escape. One night to disappear—nothing more.

A young boy, his face dusty from the day, steps forward. I press a silver coin into his palm, and he spits lightly on it before wiping it clean against his sleeve as he takes my mustang's reins with pride. "You take care of ol' girl now, and you'll see a second coin."

"Yes, sir," he replies.

I head inside and make straight for the bar.

"Barkeep, tankard!" I shout over the soused men throwing knucklebones at the sturdy tables behind me. Where is the old man who surely runs this place? The thought lingers until a charming voice interrupts.

"Will a barmaid work for ye, love?"

A very ambitious redhead with bright green eyes retorts as she scoops up both coins I laid down, slipping one into the pocket of her apron.

She pauses at the second coin, considers it, then sets it back with a thoughtful little hmm. A subtle wink follows, and before I can process the exchange, she's already turned away—only to return moments later with my much-needed drink.

"I haven't seen you in here before, soldier." She lets the unspoken question hang in the air before introducing herself. "I'm Myah, by the way—and that is one large sword you have strapped to your back." She leans in closer, exposing more of her bosom, and with a sly smile asks, "Are we expecting something to happen in here tonight?"

Her charm has my full attention. "Nice meeting you, Myah. Name is Shayn, and the sword serves me in daily rescues of damsels in distress." Her laugh is soothing.

"One coin was more than enough for a tankard, Shayn," Myah says as she wipes down the bar, keeping her hands busy.

"Who said I was only having one?" I press. She is already turning her attention toward the stage.

"Coming right up, Frederik," she calls across the rowdy crowd to the musician. *She didn't hear a damn thing I said.*

An older man climbs the few steps to the small stage and begins setting up. "'Preciate it, little lady!"

Myah moves along the bar, tending to others before venturing out among the men and women scattered through the tavern.

I look around cautiously and am instantly captivated by a young woman sitting alone at a small table in the corner, her head buried in a book. She has porcelain skin and hair kissed by gold. *Why come here to read?*

I've been thinking too much lately. *Mind your business, Shayn.*

And there it is—I'm talking to myself again. I turn back to the bar and wait for Myah to return, swipe up that second coin, and bring me another ale.

Frederik tunes his lute, and shortly after, he begins to play and sing.

a magical kingdom of snowflakes
whispering into one's ear…
drink enough ale in one evening
the secrets will carry you here…

"You ready for that second one, big boy?"

Myah's playful voice pulls me from the lute player as she swings around the corner. All I notice is the adorable smile that makes her green eyes sparkle.

If one more person— I sigh and answer casually, "Yes, thanks."

"Coming right up," she chirps.

She's so damn happy—a burst of fresh air tonight. I turn back toward the stage, letting my eyes follow the rhythm of the song before they drift again to the bar, where Myah sets a peculiar drink in front of me. A tall, slender glass holds a blue liquid, red steam rising from its surface.

"This is our signature drink—Dragon's Breath!" she announces, delighted.

"Oh, is it now?" I study the strange concoction, starting to relax. Maybe this place could become my new den.

I drain the glass and thank her. Myah leans on the counter, chin propped in her hands. Those green eyes lock on me. *I need her to walk away.*

I shift on the stool, my breeches suddenly too tight.

Garrett's hands around Beatryx's throat flash through my mind—

"Don't thank me," Myah says, snapping me back. "Thank that doll in the corner."

I follow her puzzled stare to the small table—its only companion a book. The golden beauty is gone.

The musician's rough voice carries through the tavern like rustled leaves weaving an ancient forest, his tale of snowflakes in the Whispering Woods unfolding as he plays. The hymn draws the intoxicated patrons into his story. When the chorus fades, he lowers his lute and surveys the room, eyes lingering on drunken folk lost in thought before a knowing smile touches his lips. He passes his worn hat, and it quickly fills with coin.

A large hand grips my upper arm, followed by a sharp slap between my shoulders. "Look who I found!"

Damn it.

He's happy—same as I was. Escape had been the plan. Clearly, that isn't happening.

My jaw tightens. "Garrett."

Myah appears at his side, bright and eager as ever, and my thoughts darken despite myself. I pull two more coins from my satchel and slide them toward the bar. Garrett really should be buying my drinks. "One for my friend here."

"Hello, friend," Myah says warmly. "Do you have a big sword, too?"

Garrett chuckles at her wit.

What Goddess have I insulted?

Myah walks away, humming along to the lute player's next song, oblivious to the one-sided war raging in my head. She hollers back, "On it," before disappearing.

"Damn, she's a sweet thing," Garrett says, a grin forming on his face. Ignoring him is best. *Something is off.* I'm not fully in control of myself as he keeps talking. "I'd like to grab that sweet ass and take her to the loft." Then I do the unthinkable. When Garrett turns toward me, I punch him square in the jaw.

Frederik keeps playing from the bottom of his soul, as if nothing unusual is happening in this tavern. I'm done with this chaos. I walk out, and the much-needed cool air welcomes me. "Whew. That feels good." I should find the boy who tended my horse. I move slower than usual toward the stables.

"What about that second coin, mister?" a familiar voice hollers behind me. I turn—too slow. Too foggy. Instead of the boy, I catch sight of my mustang trotting along the dirt path, a rider already in tow.

"Hey—that's my horse," I slur. The golden beauty lifts her chin and flicks a coin toward the boy. "Paid." Then, to me: "I need a ride." She doesn't have to tell me twice. I barely manage the saddle behind her, clinging as she urges the horse forward. With a subtle kick, we vanish down the path as shouts rise behind us.

"Where are you taking me, my lady—and who are you?" I ask as we ride fast. She leans back just enough for fierce blue eyes to lock onto mine, pulling me deeper into a trancelike state.

We tear across the land until she brings the beast to a stop just outside the castle grounds, in a meadow of flowers frozen in timeless ice. She dismounts with ease, her hair spilling around her shoulders. My gaze drops to her legs before I drag it back to her soft face. She meets my eyes and gives her next command.

"Honey, follow me, now."

I obey.

"Where do you sleep—the dungeon?" she asks, giggling.

"My bed," I answer. "Why?"

"Take me there."

We pass through the castle gates, the guards watching a beat too long as she walks at my side, unbothered, certain. I lead her to my quarters, but she steps inside first, scanning every inch of the small space as if it already belongs to her. This is the most confident woman I've ever seen, incredible on horseback, impossible to keep pace with—even here, in my own room.

Goddesses, help me.

She partially undresses, then moves to the basin and washes

her face and neck, unhurried, at ease. "What is your name?" she asks.

I wake in the dead of night—witching hour—and something is horribly wrong. The room tilts, my head spinning worse than before, in a way I've never known. I lurch to my feet, fast but not fast enough. The beauty is gone.

She was stealing my horse, yet I yielded to her every whim. Shaking my head, my thoughts snap to Myah. Was this planned between the two of them? Last night, I breached the castle walls with someone I didn't even know—and now she's vanished.

At the basin, I splash water on my face and watch droplets trail down my chest, trying to shake the fog as instinct slams into me, urgent and unforgiving. *Find your weapons.*

They're gone. Including my cherished dagger. I grab my breeches from the floor and dig for my keys. Gone.

Fuck. Why can't I manage myself for just one night?

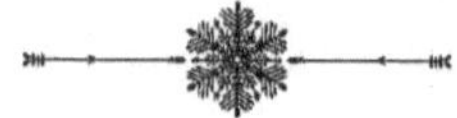

Sage

These people and this kingdom are exhausting. I make my way to the bathhouse; the basin will not suffice. I need to submerge myself in steaming water laced with herbal oils, to let heat do what patience cannot.

Fresh evergreen floods my senses as I enter the inner chamber. I cross to a stone bench and slip free of the heavy robe encasing me, then descend the steps into the heated pool like the queen I am—every movement deliberate, balanced, precise. Steam rises as my body sinks beneath the surface, my head tipping back while the day's strain finally loosens its grip. A gentle current carries me toward the center, warmth wrapping close as moisture seeps into my skin, soothing tension and mind alike until I am more relaxed than I've felt in days.

No matter the hour, couples gather at bathhouses for many reasons—though pleasure is most often the foremost.

Tonight, I observe the revelry and choose to align myself with its quiet cause. I know my needs, and I will claim them here, in this accursed frozen kingdom.

One couple draws my attention. The man towers over a petite woman, gazing at her as though she were made of petals. He trails soft kisses along her body—beginning at her lips, circling her neck, then continuing downward with care. When he reaches the waterline, he steadies her with strength, lifting her with ease as his devotion deepens.

A mirror illusion of a man forms before me, and then I am her. He touches me as he touches her, conquers me with the same unhurried devotion. Every breath he leaves upon her skin I feel as my own, until ecstasy overtakes me—swift, complete, unquestioned.

In thanks, I cast a spell. Flowers bloom in radiant bursts around them, unfurling through steam and water, shimmering with magic and gratitude.

Rejuvenated, I begin the frozen walk back to the castle, reflecting on who I truly am—and how I will make my move on the king. Once inside the main kitchen, I commit the goings-on to memory, then head toward room three when a tingling sensation brushes my ankles.

Sweet whiskers. A gorgeous black creature with caramel eyes gazes up at me, demanding attention. I've seen her before, slipping through the edges of my days like a shadow with purpose. Unable to resist, I run my hand over her soft fur as she sniffs me delicately.

"You are mistaking me for another, little sweet thing. Go along."

The pretty one blazes off.

When I reach my small room and open the door, I cannot believe my eyes. Lounging on my bed, sharpening a blade, is—

"Olyvia!"

"Hello, Mother. Did you really think I would be left out of this crusade?"

"How did you get in, Olyvia?" I demand.

She answers with a wicked grin, forefinger raised as she spins a set of skeleton keys. Then, with infuriating ease, she adds,

"Who is Shayn? And I love the new look—especially the hair. You've always wanted light hair."

I ward the room at once, then cross to her and sit on the edge of the bed. Focus.

"You're sure about this?"

Her smile lights her blue eyes as she nods. Good thing I had a proper bath, or I'm not sure I'd be handling this so calmly.

"There was an opening for a steward. At first, I managed only the kitchen, but now I'm doing much more—the advantage is gossip."

Olyvia listens as I continue.

"We're preparing for a summer solstice ball. Extra handmaidens will be needed to tend the noblewomen, and you'd be excellent with practical tasks—hair care especially."

Olyvia's eyes widen with excitement.

"I would love that."

I incline my head.

"Remember why we're here—to watch and listen. Myst is engaged to Iyce, and that wedding is set to take place in less than two years. Carefully, I am beginning to gain her trust."

Then, in a more serious tone, I add,

"Now, we must talk about Shayn."

Olyvia relays what took place.

"He was in a tavern in town—the Dragon's Dungeon—and he looked exactly like what I needed to gain castle entry: a man distraught and weakened by a woman. I struck. Getting into his room was easy after the little gift I slipped into his drink, leaving him witless until he passed out. I took his weapons and his keys from his breeches, then left. Night had already fallen, so slipping through the castle was no challenge. In the end, I traced your scent here—from a filthy bathhouse."

I roll my eyes, a quiet curse slipping free.

"Holy Goddesses above, Olyvia!"

She fires back immediately.

"I'm not implying you were at the bathhouse—it's just where I picked up on you."

I lean forward.

"Essentially, I'll create a spell—one that will obscure you from his mind. But for it to work, you must kiss him."

Olyvia jumps to her feet.

"My goddesses, no! Absolutely not!"

I stand as well.

"By the goddesses, yes—you will. Once he drinks the potion, you must kiss him and walk away. Then, the next time he sees you, it'll be as if he's looking at you for the first time. The boy is handsome enough; it's not as though you're kissing a creature. Besides, it sounds to me like you handpicked your prey all by yourself."

I let the weight of my words settle.

"This must happen before this moon phase ends, Olyvia. Tomorrow, I'll gather what I need for the spell. Once we handle this situation, we'll focus on your new role here."

Olyvia finally agrees, with little choice, and we settle our next steps.

Feeling faint with appetite, I ask,

"Are you starved after your little adventures?"

She nods, sleepy-eyed.

"There are plenty of things to nibble on in the kitchen. I'll fetch you something. Stay here."

I lift the ward from the room and slip out quietly, casting a protection spell over the door once more—because I refuse to take chances.

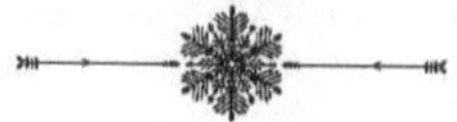

On my way to the kitchen, I hear voices—Shayn and Garrett. I pause long enough to catch anything useful. I linger in the hallway, listening.

Shayn has no idea who Olyvia is. He mutters that either she or someone named Myah tampered with his drink—and whatever it was, it worked. He remembers little, only that the girl is here, in the castle, with his weapons and keys. Garrett swears he didn't see her, insisting he went straight to the bar.

So. That's all I need. Easier than I thought.

Those two men guard the princess of the most powerful kingdom in this realm—oh my. That means one of two things: either she's being tightly managed by those in charge, or she can't protect herself. Shayn, undone by a young girl. Garrett, utterly indifferent.

When their footsteps finally fade, I slip into the kitchen and pull a glass bottle from the cupboard, its contents a dark amethyst liquid. I pour a small measure into a crystal flute, then spot the beaker Shayn left behind—the one he's been sipping water from, careless as ever.

Perfect. Thank you, Shayn. You've just made my hunt a little easier.

I cast a spell to bind his spittle to the rim, then wrap the glass in cloth and tuck it into my pocket.

"Hello," says a deep voice from behind—and my heart stumbles.

When I turn to face him, I freeze at the sight of his arm reaching past me. He takes a piece of fruit, and he's close—close enough that my breath loses its rhythm.

What I do next may very well kill me, but I do it anyway.

"Sire."

The soft word slips from my lips, reluctant as I bow low.

He responds by gently taking my hand and guiding me upright.

"That is not necessary. What is your name?"

His voice is cool, yet it brushes something warm inside me. I gather myself.

"Sage."

He takes no more than two steps back, and the space between us feels abruptly vast.

"Ah. Yes. I recall."

His eyes travel over me like a phoenix drifting through heat.

"William informed me that you would assume his position as steward. Is the stewardship maintained to your satisfaction?"

Time slows. A trance settles over me as he brings the innocent piece of fruit to his lips, then bites. A jolt runs through me as juice breaks across his lips—lips I once knew.

"Yes, Sire. All is in order, and I am honored to be here."

At this point, my body breathes on its own—barely.

He doesn't recognize me. Not through the glamour. Not through the years. And yet, something in his voice still reaches for me.

But I remember.

I remember who he chose.

I remember how she wove his strings around her fingers.

I remember that she was my closest friend.

Before he leaves with the shadows that ushered him in, he says.

"I do come down frequently for a small bite to eat, so please do not be alarmed next time, Sage."

I stand still until he's gone. Only then does the tightness inside me unwind, and I finish the liquid I had poured for myself.

By the time I return to Olyvia, she's in a deep sleep. I set the plate on the small desk and step to her side. Gently, I sweep her hair from her face and draw the blanket up around her shoulders, settling it with a careful tuck.

Afterward, I linger for a moment, nibbling at the bread and cheese while I slowly drink the second beverage I poured.

This is going to be harder than I realized—but it must be done.

9

Arkaik Alpynz

TEA HOUSE

Myst

In anticipation of my nineteenth birthdate, I must set aside time with Estelle, my seamstress.

She will need to order fabric samples from shops both local and abroad, as the gown must reflect a blending of summer and winter—surpassing every gown that has come before. Silver thread, drawn straight from a magical black widow's spinnerets, is what I want running through the seams.

Sitting up in bed, I stretch my arms high and glance around the room for my sweet girl.

Frozen kisses scatter across my face, stealing my breath. "Did you play in the snow all night, Princess Midnight?"

She nudges my shoulder once more before shaking herself free and leaping to the floor.

"You're done with me now?" I murmur, smiling.

A subtle knock caresses the wooden door. It opens a crack before Beatryx steps in, her presence as practiced as ever.

"Myst, I cannot believe you're still in bed. Time is of the essence; we need to begin dress preparations for the summer solstice ball," she announces, already halfway to the windows. Once there, she struggles with the heavy tapestries, pushing them aside enough to let in what little light this kingdom offers.

Falling back onto the soft pillow, I reply lazily, "I was just thinking about the perfect gown."

Beatryx continues contending with the stubborn layers of drapes as she huffs, "I enjoyed my time with Krystelle yesterday. She has a sharp wit and excellent taste in fabrics."

I lift one eyebrow. "She does."

Eager to be out of bed, I grab my heavy robe and stand. I pull it around me, tie the sash loosely, and walk toward the bathing chamber.

While I rinse my face with primrose oil, Beatryx opens the balcony doors and asks, "Have you been through those woods to the north?"

I don't answer right away. Instead, I walk to my dressing area and stare at the many gowns, debating how to respond. *Those woods offer me solitude. Those woods are my secret.*

Day after day, I stand here, weighing gowns like choices. Beatryx joins me and says, "Just close your eyes and choose one."

I let the world blur, reach out, and turn in a slow circle until my hand finds a gown.

Perfect choice.

Beatryx lightly shakes her head, a smile tugging at her lips.

At the dressing table, she steps forward and buttons the back of my gown. She reaches for an ivory brush, its pale handle gleaming softly, and begins to work it through my hair as I confess my desperation for new ways to wear it.

There's a softness in her voice when she speaks, and I realize we're both still learning about each other. "Since I was a young girl, I've always managed my own hair—which likely explains the simplicity."

I've only recently decided to give her a true chance at friendship—and I've been surprised by how much I enjoy her companionship. She's the first person, besides Krystelle, that I've allowed in. But I do feel like she has secrets, hopefully secrets she will share when the time comes.

Cautiously, I answer her earlier question—then offer a secret of my own. "The Whispering Woods are magical. I visit them often."

Beatryx meets my gaze in the mirror, then uses the backs of her hands to push my hair forward, letting it fall to my waist.

"There," she says softly. "Beautiful. Magical, how?"

Looking back at her through the mirror, I smile.

"Let's go for a walk."

Outside my chamber, Shayn and Garrett wait to escort Beatryx and me wherever we wish.

"Ladies," Shayn speaks first.

Beatryx gives him a strange look, nods, and continues walking. *That was… odd.*

She grabs my hand. "I think we should go into town—the shops are quaint, filled with rare fabrics and jewel-worked adornments. Then lunch near the harbor, and perhaps we'll find a potential hair artist. How does that sound?"

I think for only a moment. It sounds perfect. "Agreed. Let's prepare."

Turning to Garrett and Shayn, I tell them we'll need a carriage.

Once downstairs, I make a sharp turn toward the kitchen. *Maybe Sage baked her amazing shortbread today.* I've never tasted anything like it.

We step inside, and Midnight darts out of nowhere, catching me off guard. "Hello, pretty girl. Have you had a treat this morning?"

Dulce staggers from the closet and snaps, "This animal gets treats all day."

Sage is at her writing desk, her hand dropping to run through my sweet girl's soft fur. Midnight is rarely affectionate.

Spirited, Sage straightens. "Hello, ladies. Interesting plans today?"

Being around Sage is the best feeling; she brings beauty into even the smallest moments.

"Actually, we're taking a ride to the fishing village," I say, "in search of something rare enough to be worth keeping. The guards are preparing a carriage and will accompany us."

Beatryx chimes in, selecting a piece of dried fruit from the basket before adding, "We're also searching for a hair artist. Myst has grown weary of the same styles."

"That sounds like an excellent idea." Sage's eyes light up as she moves to the cupboard and lifts down a small basket. "Take this for your travels. A girl can never have too many refreshments."

She lifts a crystal flute of bubbling pink liquid and takes a pleased sip, as though such indulgence were the most ordinary thing in the kingdom.

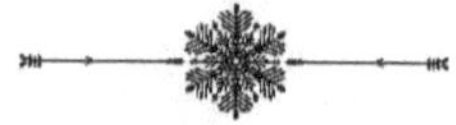

Olyvia

I'm barely seated on the bed when Mamá finds me, the window behind her casting a pale line of light across the wall.

"Myst and Beatryx will be leaving shortly," she says under her breath. "They're bound for the harbor district, with Shayn and Garrett beside them."

My chest tightens.

"Beatryx is searching for a new stylist," Mamá continues. "For Myst. For herself." Her gaze sharpens as it settles on me. "That stylist is you."

I release a breath I hadn't realized I was holding.

"If you leave now, you'll arrive ahead of them. Once in town, find the tea shop beside the boutiques. Ask for Liora—she'll guide your next step."

I hesitate. "What if Shayn sees me?"

Mamá doesn't pause. "He won't."

"I'm to ride into the fishing village to purchase tea for the castle steward. I'll need a horse," I say to a boy hauling a forkful of hay from a cart.

"Take Shyanne. She hasn't been ridden in a few days."

I glance away, biting back a sigh.

Naturally. Because horses reveal their names the moment you look at them.

A shift of movement catches my attention. A tall girl steps out from behind a stall, her eyes narrowing with suspicion. "Where's your badge?"

"I don't have one yet," I say, adjusting the leather apron so the monogram sits plainly in view. "I was told it would be issued."

She studies me for a moment longer, then nods toward the apron. "Even so, I see the castle's crest worked into the leather. That mark is enough—it tells me you belong."

Relief loosens something in my chest.

The boy steps away and returns leading a raven-black mare, her thick mane and tail shimmering sapphire when the light strikes just right. One ear flicks in my direction as she shifts her weight, calm and unbothered. "This is Shyanne," he says, handing me the reins.

I take them and slide my hand briefly along her neck, feeling the steady warmth beneath her coat as I gather the leather into my grip—silently thanking Mamá for insisting I wear the apron.

The beauty is built for strength—long, powerful legs, a proud arched neck, and a finely sculpted head that turns with quiet awareness. Her dark eyes watch me calmly.

"Hello, Shyanne." I lift my hand, letting her take in my scent. Within moments, she accepts me.

She moves like smoke wrapped in velvet, utterly captivating as we ride along a thicket of young trees. When she finally breaks into a run through the undergrowth, it feels as though sea air fills me from the inside out.

I gather the reins loosely and rest them across Shyanne's neck, trusting her steady pace as I unroll the small map. My eyes find the circle Mamá marked—Snowflake Tea House.

The plan is for Myst to take on a personal handmaiden. Me.

I've never seen her before. I don't know how I'll react when I do. But whatever happens, I must hold myself together.

After dismounting, I promise Shyanne a treat before looping her reins through an iron ring fixed to a weathered post. The village hums around me, and suddenly I feel conspicuous in my clothes. I straighten the leather apron layered over my white shift, its hem stopping just shy of my knees. My boots cover most of my legs, but the braids and beads woven through my hair draw the most attention.

Grabbing the straps of my satchel, I pull it over my head and adjust it as the sea breeze slips through the harbor alleys.

"You must be Olyvia. Bienvenida!"

I turn toward the voice to find a striking woman whose smile lights her eyes. "Hola. I'm Liora. I've known your mother for a very long time. Come inside—let's have a warm cup of té de jamaica, hybiscus tea."

The tea shop charms me the moment I step through the door, reminding me of home in a way I hadn't expected. Liora's kindness settles over me like a soft feather brushing my cheek. We drink tea and speak quietly about the plan Mamá set in motion.

Before I leave, Liora presses a sachet of beads into my palm and gestures toward the small boutique along the harbor walk. "If you need anything, I'll be here." Then she pulls me into a hug, and for a moment, it feels as though I've known her my entire life.

Inside the boutique, the owner guides me to a mirror at the back. I remove the apron bearing the castle's monogram, sit on the stool, and begin doing what I love—braiding my hair, weaving in more beads.

Then the door opens.

An excited voice carries through the space. That must be Beatryx.

A softer voice follows.

I know exactly who that is.

My entire body breaks out in goosebumps.

Myst

The carriage ride from the castle to the fishing village is quiet until Beatryx, who has been staring intently out her window at the docked ships in the harbor, finally confesses what's bothering her.

"It's a shame there's no jasmine among those imports. I'd love to breathe in its scent fresh from the vine."

Ready to explore, I exit the carriage, pleasantly welcomed by a light sea breeze laced with ocean salt. Beatryx steps out next, and both guards watch her closely as she descends. The pebbled path catches my attention, and despite what's happening behind me, I move forward—straight toward the trail leading into the village. *Hopefully, I'll find a small treasure today.* The first thing I notice is the row of quaint boutiques, though I wonder which one we should enter.

Beatryx catches up and points toward a peculiar boutique, insisting, "That one."

On the way there, we pass a tea shop, and a pretty lady with dark, wavy hair smiles kindly while standing at the entrance, sipping from her teacup. She is intriguing, and I swear her dark eyes twinkle the moment I look at her. The breeze lightens. I feel magic—the way I do when I enter the Whispering Woods. Something pulls my attention back to the woman at the storefront of the tea shop. She's still there, lifting her cup again. Each quiet sip seems to intensify the magic I feel.

Beatryx takes my hand and leads me into the boutique, the door closing gently behind us. Sunlight filters in through the tall windows as my gaze lands on a single dress on a rack, its fabric catching the light in a way that makes it shimmer. Beatryx's face brightens.

"I knew it," she says with excitement. "Something told me we should come to this charming shop."

The boutique is modest, but every detail feels intentional. I pass shelves of hats and gloves while dresses sway gently in the open shutters. Toward the back, an older woman works at a table, pulling crimson thread through golden fabric with steady hands. The gowns are exquisite, but it's the tunics that catch my eye, their stitching delicate.

Beatryx calls out again. "Myst, come and look at these colorful accessories."

She's right, and my eyes instantly land on a brooch. I cannot believe what I'm looking at when she startles me once more.

Moving toward the back of the shop, I see a girl who looks a little younger than us. She's braiding her own hair, and the style is unlike anything I've ever seen. Jewels, beads, and flowers intertwine throughout the braids, and it's stunning.

Beatryx glances at me and winks. I step forward beside her. "Hello, my name is Myst, and this is Beatryx. May I ask your name?"

The girl looks away from the mirror, and when her eyes lock onto mine, a shiver runs through my entire body.

"I am Olyvia. It's very nice to meet you both." Her tone is soft.

At once, Beatryx begins the interview, clearly excited as she asks Olyvia, "Do you only create these braids and adornments for yourself as a hobby, or is this a service you provide to others?"

Olyvia explains that she has recently moved to this kingdom and is hoping to find a position.

Moments later, the bell above the entrance door chimes,

bringing in Shayn and Garrett. Shayn very loudly announces that he now has a few new daggers, and Garrett gives him a long, unimpressed stare before asking, "Princess, are you ready for lunch?"

Then he diverts his gaze to Beatryx, and the look he gives her is different. *I think he wants her for lunch.*

"Yes, but I need a word with someone we just met," I tell him.

But when I turn, the girl is gone.

Beatryx chimes in, "Olyvia said she had to go, but would see us soon. Don't worry—I told her what to say to the guards to gain castle entry."

Then she cocks her head and gives me a huge grin, and I laugh despite myself. "Thank you, Beatryx. I've got an item on hold with the shopkeeper that I want to purchase before I join you. What are we having for lunch?"

Shayn's voice cuts through the moment when he answers with a single word. "Fish."

I don't like fish.

Beatryx and my two guards leave the shop, and I return to the counter to retrieve the intriguing piece—a classy amethyst hybiscus brooch. I still have no idea why I keep seeing this bloom, but I feel a connection.

On the way back to the castle after lunch, Beatryx shows me a colorful shawl and a perfume sachet she selected. I keep my gem tucked inside my small satchel, thinking of Olyvia. Something about her feels familiar, yet I've never met or seen her before.

Sage

Liora steps out of the shop, arms open in greeting, a radiant smile breaking across her face as she comes toward me. "Hello," she says as she gathers me into her embrace.

She draws back just enough to study my face. "Your daughters are beautiful—externally, yes, but mostly within."

My eyes fill with tears, a secret affirmation, a truth I didn't know I needed. I hug my dear friend again—after more than eighteen years apart—and emotion floods us as she ushers me into her vintage tea shop, the moment surreal.

"The girls seemed to get along and made arrangements for Olyvia to visit the castle," Liora says, pouring hot water over dried rose petals. She takes a bottle from the shelf and adds a few drops of dark amethyst liquid before sliding the cup in my direction.

"This is exquisite, mingled with rose," I remark, handing her a bag full of hibiscus blooms.

She beams with excitement before she says serenely, "Thank the goddesses the curse did not touch the hibiscus harvest."

I nod, the thought unspoken. So much else has grown thin this season, as though the realm itself has chosen sleep.

Our conversations have always flowed, and this time is no different. Then the door opens, and Liora's wide eyes shift to the man who enters—his gaze locking onto hers. A smile rises before I can stop it, and I dip my chin, turning my head away.

"Andrés, mi amor. Tienes tantos peces," Liora says, as he steps forward with a net full of fish, her two young boys at his side.

"Mamá! Mamá!" her youngest calls out excitedly as he rushes to her, kissing her blushed cheeks. "My biggest catch was today!"

Liora smiles warmly as she hugs him in return. "Iriel! Good job, mijo. And what about you, Ayan?" she asks her oldest, who stands tall beside the group.

He grins mischievously. "I caught the smile of a pretty girl."
We all laugh.

The last to walk inside is a young girl who is anything but shy. She makes her way around the counter, plucks a strawberry from a plate, and pops the entire thing into her mouth just as her father reprimands her.

"Rosalie, where are your manners?"

Rosalie offers her manners through the half-eaten berry. "Gracias, Liora."

As I sit here, watching how much can change over time, I reflect on the moment I approached Liora and her husband. What I asked of them wasn't easy, yet they uprooted their lives and moved to this realm.

The curse prevented me from entering this realm until Myst reached her eighteenth year, so I planted others here to watch. Everyone agreed without hesitation. Their two boys were born here, and they made this kingdom their home. But her husband became ill. The guilt I carry never leaves me, even though she assures me it was no one's fault.

It has been some time since he departed this life, and seeing her happy and smiling fills my heart with joy.

Liora and I step out of the tea shop, leaving the fishing crew to it. I hug my friend tightly. "Thank you for everything. I have missed this."

Tears fill her eyes as she responds, "These tears stand for many things—family, friendship, loss, and newfound love. You will feel this very soon, amiga. But remember one thing. *Move in silence.*"

Back at the castle, I step into the kitchen to find everything prepared for the evening meal. Things have run more smoothly since I arrived, yet tonight's quiet feels off. The ache in my heart—for whatever stirred in Olyvia—runs deep. My youngest is strong.

Then I feel his presence drawing close.

Silently, I move.

10

Arkaik Alpynz

Myst

Today I discovered an intriguing hybiscus brooch, and due to my excitement, I simply cannot sleep. It is well past late, but I want to visit the castle's library in hopes of finding information about the bloom that has my full attention.

I slip into a dark gray fitted dress with a high neckline and second-skin sleeves, while my braid falls over my shoulder, unraveled. Midnight waits anxiously by the door, tail twitching.

Grabbing my satchel and pushing the large doors open, I assure her, "Let's go, Midnight. It's time—Krys is on her way to us."

Her ears perk up as she leads the way. Upon seeing Krys, Midnight rushes forward and sniffs her, tail swaying with approval. We both giggle before walking toward the back staircase that leads to the third floor.

"Yes, Midnight, I have something special for you, like always." Krys hands the silky beauty a slab of dried pork. Then she looks at me and asks, "Do you think your guards will catch us?"

The response is immediate. "No. Why do you think I dressed this way?"

We laugh low, but she isn't convinced. "I wondered why you looked like you were going to the temple. And how can you be so sure those two aren't lurking somewhere?"

"First, those two barely know their own names. Second, they have no idea how to watch me—or catch me."

"Tell me again what we're researching?" Krys asks while Midnight runs ahead of us as if she knows where we're going—and, fairly, I think maybe she does.

A quick reach into the satchel brings out the card revealing the amethyst hybiscus bloom, and I pass it to Krys as we turn a corner. We take a different flight of stairs up and finally reach a corridor that leads north.

Krys studies the card for a long moment before passing it back with a curious look.

"Is this a playing card from Tea and Cards?"

"Have you ever seen this bloom?"

"Never."

I slip the card into my dress pocket, and we both lift our heads together, our eyes pulled upward.

The library.

"It's magnificent."

An exhale leaves me as we step inside. Magic stirs at my fingertips—eager, restless.

"I haven't been here in years."

When I was five, my lessons were suddenly moved from this library to a cramped study near the queen's quarters. I never knew why. Those torturous evenings continued until I turned sixteen.

Krys looks at me, then downward, so many questions in her large, dark eyes. "Myst?"

I answer her silently, lowering my gaze to follow the trail her eyes have taken—and realize my mist is covering the floor.

I place my hands at my sides, palms facing inward, and the mist subsides instantly.

"Just excitement," I say. "Follow me."

The library is overwhelmingly large, with curiosities in every direction. The walls are nothing but bookshelves—an array of volumes in countless sizes and colors. Chandeliers hang at varying heights, casting a soft glow, and the scent is one I will never forget—ethereal.

The marble floor gleams so intensely I could likely see my own reflection in it, if I wished, creams and grays arranged in a checkerboard pattern.

I stop mid-step, gaze lifted. Before us rise three aged staircases, their intricate structure calling to me.

Only one piece of information brought me here, but my poise falters. Minerva, Goddess of Wisdom, guide me to the book—the one that will lead me to the truth of the hybiscus bloom.

Then, out of nowhere, gold-dusted pawprints appear on the gleaming marble floor, circling me and Krys before vanishing.

"This is strange," Krys says.

I nod, eyes lingering on the prints—two small figures chasing each other in playful arcs.

"Should we follow?" She hovers, anxious, like the answer matters more than the question, but I am already heading toward the prints. Krys catches up.

As a five-year-old, this library was enormous—and it remains nothing shy of that now.

"It seems like our tour guides are luring us upstairs," I say under my breath, and we ascend.

The two figures seem harmless as they play, leaving behind only one symbol—a single pawprint on the marble—before it fades. They want us to follow.

At the top of the stairs, I veer off, choosing my own path before these mysterious creatures lead us over the balcony. I am here for one reason.

Turning my head, I notice towering bookcases packed with catalogues behind a shiny wooden desk. A small candelabra burns peacefully in the corner, its flame steady and warm.

I move toward the desk to examine the collections that guide visitors through this maze of knowledge. The volumes are immense—too many to count. This is going to be more than challenging, but I am desperate for answers. A long sigh escapes me.

On the ornate desk, a plaque reads: Library in Antiquity. Well, okay. I am fine with that.

"Myst, look," Krys whispers, squeezing my hand.

What I see is astonishing. Hand in hand, we walk closer to a small group of hushed voices, drawn in by the quiet conversations.

"Why would scholars be copying texts and studying maps at this hour?" Krys asks, then continues with more questions as we listen. "Why are lectures being held, orators trying to impress, and intellectuals gathering to discuss matters with fellow visitors in the tranquility of the library?"

We move faster than falling snowflakes.

"Leaving so soon, ladies?"

Eyes caught off guard, I recognize the familiar voice as it rushes across the atrium—a whisper from long ago. Krys and I halt instantly.

Before us stands the most intriguing woman, perfected in every aspect. She holds two gorgeous kittens, one in each arm.

"You were a very young child the last time I saw you. My, it has been some time since I have placed my eyes on the future queen of this kingdom."

Swiftly, I loop my arm through Krys' as we stand there, staring. From my memory, she has not changed at all. Not a single detail. *How is that possible?*

The librarian is adorned in a fuchsia dress that fits closely to her voluptuous body. Her auburn hair is in a loose bun on the crown of her head, and she wears whimsical pink glasses low on her nose, revealing big eyes that reflect the color of the sea. A long gold chain hangs from her neck, holding a magnifying glass pendant embossed with delicate snowflakes. Counting, I see three earrings in her left ear and a tiny, sparkling silver stone in her nose. A black, floor-length mantle drapes over her dress, and a large brooch shaped like a golden book is pinned near her collar.

She is deeply fascinating—like a story you begin before sleep. One whose words linger as they continue to flow through your mind.

My hand slips toward my dress pocket, drawn to the now-sacred card. After a moment, I step closer to her and extend my hand, offering what I have come to cherish—

She halts me abruptly and says with a warm smile, "You may or may not remember me. I am Saffi, the librarian of this castle's very impressive world of knowledge. Please, join me at my desk, and I will explain the catalogue arrangement. Then, if you need further mentorship, I am happy to guide you in the right direction."

Well—just as I remembered.

No hand-holding. Here to teach, not enable.

The tension I'd been holding releases the instant Saffi lets her playful magical kittens loose on the marble floor, and they dart across it with Krys chasing behind them.

Saffi pulls one of the larger volumes from the shelf and sets it on the desk. She opens it with care, then looks up to brief me.

"To find the book you are looking for," she says, "you must consider four things: author, title, subject, and time era. Never neglect the fourth—it is more important than you might think."

I ask, "What if I only know one of those four?"

She smiles, already prepared. "Excellent observation."

Saffi offers a surprisingly easy explanation of how to use the cross-reference system, and I cannot help but feel impressed by the incredible organization. I would have been lost without the guidance.

Saffi is brilliant, and she leaves me to it.

Skimming through the third of several "H" volumes, my head begins to bob from exhaustion. Krys left a while ago, and I should do the same.

A soft tickle grazes my cheek, enough to make me stir. I open my eyes, heavy with fatigue, and find two sets of wide, curious gazes fixed on me. Sleep must have taken me for a moment.

"Hello, darlings," I murmur. "Do either of you know where I can find a book about this bloom?"

They purr loudly in response, and I melt at the sweetness of it. Midnight is going to be so jealous when she catches their scent on me.

The library is calm and quiet as I retrace my steps—down the staircase, through the atrium, and out the main entrance. But as I leave, my breath catches. It feels as if every secret I have learned here is drawn from me, left behind in the pages I hunted so fiercely.

I know where to find you. And I will be back.

I turn and whisper into the thick air, "Thank you, Saffi."

Then I begin the walk back to my chambers, alone—until something shifts behind me. A presence presses close, unseen but undeniable. My mist coils tight around my shoulders. I quicken my pace.

When I reach the staircase to descend, I stop and plant my feet. Nothing.

And nothing means something. And something means someone is playing games with me.

Who are you?

11

Arkaik Alpynz

The Arrow Flies

Shayn

"En garde!"

With swift precision, I reach behind me, wrists grazing as they cross, and draw two gladius swords from the holsters on my back.

I charge Garrett.

He reacts instantly, freeing his heavy sword of war from its leather sheath at his waist. His large hands grip the intricate work of art at both ends as he blocks my strikes with ease.

Iron clashes between us, echoes carrying through the alpynz that ring the training yard.

With full force, I hurl both short swords into the cold sky, then catch them in a perfect crouch. We train hard—discipline never faltering.

A war cry bursts from me as I rush Garrett again. This time, he is ready. He knocks the sword from my right hand.

Bastard.

Panting, we strut to the edge of the training yard while younger soldiers watch, their eyes sharp with envy. We guzzle water, breath steaming in the frigid air, as Garrett—ever the spectacle—tilts his head back and lets the water cascade over his face, ice beginning to form in his perfectly trimmed beard.

Damn winter kingdom.

Garrett and I arrived in Arkaik Alpynz within two moon

phases of each other and were trained according to the kingdom's procedures before being assigned to Myst. Then, without warning, he looks at me and says, "About the other night in the tavern—what was that about?"

Caught off guard, I answer evenly. "I cannot explain what came over me. Apologies."

He glances away, confused. I do not mention Beatryx. Women come and women go; I leave it at having a bad day, and it is not a lie.

Women look at him and me differently. We are both handsome, each in our own way. Garrett wants practically every woman he sees, while I've always been more reserved, only recently beginning to experience sex—and he pursues it endlessly. No wonder he is so accommodating, with all the practice he gets.

I clear my throat. "Speaking of the tavern… did you spend time with Myah the other evening?"

Garrett shoots me a wicked grin and winks. "I never kiss and tell."

Then, out of the corner of my eye, I see my thoughts made flesh.

There she is—the culprit.

Beatryx walks along a path with the princess, but the moment our eyes lock, I am captivated until I force myself to look away.

She is a huge distraction.

Myst

Looking at Beatryx, I ask, "There are many gardens on the grounds. Why do you insist we walk this way?"

Her dreamy eyes guide us forward as she sashays down the path at an unhurried pace. "Look at them," she says.

My gaze follows hers, landing on Shayn and Garrett.

"I do look at them. Daily," I reply.

She mutters, "Pure longing. I want them."

The words slip out before I can stop them. "I have never experienced it. Enlighten me. Please."

Beatryx's playful eyes smile. "If you can relax and clear your mind, it is wonderful—allowing a man to explore your body while you discover yourself."

Is that what longing feels like?

Then I ask my next question. "Which one do you want?"

Beatryx struggles to keep her eyes from them, and her response shocks me. "Both."

Why it surprises me, I have no idea. This is Beatryx.

My curious mind begins to wander as we continue along the path that inevitably leads back to the castle. Along the way, I admire the small blooms pushing through ice and snow. Beatryx glances over her shoulder, and I ponder, *I am a princess, and that is not an option for me.*

A sensual kiss is something I have never experienced. Damn, I am quite boring. Beatryx is experiencing life—and sex. I know she has been with Garrett, but why in the realms is she interested in Shayn? Now that I think about it, Shayn may be interested in her too. He seemed irritated after seeing her with Garrett, though he did not say so outright.

Hmm. My thoughts are running wild.

And here comes the queen.

My mother's pace is deliberate, her gaze sharp. I know instantly she is displeased we passed the training yards. Beatryx curtsies low, her eyes never leaving the queen's. Innocently, I want to protect her decision to walk this course.

"Mother, the usual walking path is frozen over, so with extreme caution, we chose this alternative route."

The queen answers sternly, "That was a good judgment call, darling. I will accompany the two of you for the end of this walk."

Once inside the castle, the queen speaks again, directly to

Beatryx. "Dear girl, tea and cakes are being served in the grand hall. Please excuse us."

She turns to me and smiles through her next words. "Let us do something amusing."

My secretive mother leads us toward the stables.

Interesting.

"Myst, be careful around Beatryx," the queen says casually, though her tone is serious as we approach the girl who is always here, working.

Then my mother commands, "Marshal, ready two mares."

She turns back to me and speaks in a low voice that seems to flow into the wind—yet I hear clearly. "Currently, I am working on Beatryx's exit from court, but her father, Lord Blake, is a powerful and honorable man, which makes it complicated."

Sadness settles over me. Even though Krys has always been closest to me, we do not see each other often, and when we do, there is not much to say. That leaves Beatryx, who has been coming around more. Honestly, I love her company and attitude.

The marshal leads both sweet girls forward and lifts her gaze to me, sorrow lingering there. I do not know her name, yet she carries a gentle devotion to the animals. I return a small smile, hoping it eases the strain my mother leaves behind.

After the queen selects her horse, I approach Adiva and rub her shoulder, readying her for our ride. The marshal steps to my side. "I am Hayze. I will assist you up."

I still have no idea why we are taking horses or where we are going. Her plans rarely include me unless there is something to gain.

We ride out of the stables toward a bridge and move north, toward the Whispering Woods—a place I escape to. Woods I only visit alone, so going with my mother feels uneasy.

The queen is constantly aware of our surroundings, daring the forest to disrespect her presence, as if these tender woods would. Her arrogance demands reverence from every living thing here, and I cannot help but wonder if we are going to Grandpapá's cottage.

If we are, I wish I could warn him. Can I?

Magic runs through me, but I have little knowledge of how to harness it. Understanding it would certainly be to my advantage.

The horses neigh in warning as we move deeper into the woods. When I glance at the queen, searching for a sign, I find nothing. I carry no weapons and have never lifted a blade, arrow, or sword of any kind. Mist is all I can conjure—and with little control.

The queen carries an exquisite bow in her dominant left hand, reins in her right. A matching quiver is strapped over her shoulder, dark-feathered arrows shifting gently with each step of her horse.

Beautiful.

Deadly.

An owl shrieks.

I look at the queen.

She smiles at me, holding it as she reaches back and draws an arrow from her quiver. She positions it meticulously and brings the bowstring back as if it is an extension of her body—one that welcomes the tension, thankful for the stretch—her eyes never leaving mine.

Then she whispers, darkly, "Do not move."

Snap.

The arrow shoots straight up. In that instant, I wonder what life she is taking—and why.

Then I feel the breeze of the arrow graze my cheek with a stinging kiss, but I keep my focus on her.

Warm blood beads. Instinct brings my hand to my face. Red blooms on my white glove.

The queen rides to me and lightly blows frost, sealing my flesh as she says, "Your second scar. It will not be your last."

She turns her horse with perfect control and kicks the mare into a full gallop.

Adiva surges after her, and suddenly both mares are carrying us faster than I thought possible.

I want to run straight to Grandpapá instead, hide in his arms until this ache fades.

Was that intentional? An illusion? A punishment for walking past the soldiers?

So when she said, Let us do something amusing… she meant this.

Thoughts race as we return to the stables. I remain mounted while she dismounts, then walks away with the confidence of every goddess.

"Assist Myst back to the castle," I vaguely hear her say to Hayze as she exits.

Hayze approaches, sensing my awkwardness. Reins in hand, she leads the horse deeper into the stables, then offers her hand, which I take.

She is warm—not just her skin, but her presence. As if she sees me, even when I do not know what I am feeling.

Hayze rests my shaking hands on her shoulders, then places her own on my waist, lifting me easily from the horse before grounding me. We stand there, frozen, before slowly backing away.

She says dryly, "You look a bit different from when you left. It is cute, but—"

Reflex takes over. I slap her across the face, then spiral into a frenzy.

Hayze plays along without missing a beat. "Well, now we both have fucked up cheeks."

Laughter bursts from me as tears carve wild rivers down my face.

Hayze takes my hands and lowers us into the hay, then cups my face. "I have watched you for years now and have no idea how you keep from losing it daily."

And that is it—my madness tipping into hysteria. I weep as Hayze holds me, watching me unravel. No one—not even myself—has ever seen this part of me.

Calm eventually settles, and a pretty sapphire haze fills the space.

Hayze rises. "Do not move."

She returns with a damp linen scented with cloves and mint, cleaning my cheek and tear-filled eyes with delicate care.

"Let us get you back to your chambers."

We walk in silence. The release is worth it.

What just happened?

I think I needed it.

The castle is quiet this evening, with only a handful of guards at the back entrance. Hayze looks to me for instruction, and I gesture subtly north with a tilt of my head. We move through the halls and staircases, finally arriving at the tower I seclude myself in whenever possible.

My languid gaze is the key to Hayze's entrance into my chambers. Once inside, she closes the door and creates a barrier of intoxicating sapphire haze. Hayze studies me with stern focus and says, "Undress. I will start a bath for you."

I obey, because tonight I need someone else to guide me. My mind is lost in fog, yet something stirs beneath it. I feel altered—wanting something I do not yet understand.

After sinking into the warm water, I whisper my request. "Bathe with me. Please."

Hayze slides into the heated bath behind me. She plays with my hair, and I reach for her hands, placing them gently on my chest before leaning into her. She kisses my neck and shoulders tenderly, and something unfamiliar begins to bloom inside me—something that unravels me.

She reads my body language and lets her hands drift lower.

When her touch lands where it does, I unravel completely. A rush overtakes me, and the moans that escape are foreign, unrecognized.

As she bathes me, Hayze tells me her story—how she came to work in the stables and eventually became marshal. Her parents were killed in an attack on our kingdom when she was seven, and my father chose her, along with a few other children from the orphanage, to serve the crown.

Hayze is tall, her frame slender but strong. Her brown hair is cropped short, with just enough length for two braids on the right side. Two designs are etched into her skin in memory of her parents. She carries them with her. Always.

She asks about the snowflake art on my body, now clearly visible, and I answer, "One appears every year on my birthdate." She reaches beneath my knee and whispers, "I claim this one. It is adorable."

She holds my hands as she helps me from the water—water now exposed to our dark, forbidden secret—then dries me gently. She pulls back my bedding and surrenders me to the softness of my blankets. With her hands, Hayze shapes snowflakes from her sapphire haze, the faint scent of cloves lingering as they drift, and they mesmerize me.

Before she leaves, she gathers herself, comes to my side, and kisses my forehead. "Sleep, beautiful princess."

Then she is gone, and the snowflakes dissipate. I feel dirty— but more than that, I feel good. Alive. As though I have control, too.

I dress in black and slip from the castle, moving quietly through the back gardens, my thoughts tangled and restless. Why do snowflakes appear on my body year after year? Why have the snowflakes in the Whispering Woods never whispered to me? And why does the amethyst hybiscus continue to appear?

Thinking of Grandpapá brings a smile to my face. Then my thoughts drift elsewhere, and my cheeks burn as I continue my confused walk.

The memory of the bath and its lingering aftermath warms my skin even in the cool night air. As I walk, another craving stirs—something sweet, something familiar. I know exactly where to go.

Pulling the hood of my dark cloak over my head, I hurry back toward the castle. Once inside, I slip down a rarely used back staircase and head for the kitchen.

I hear Sage's voice—low—speaking to someone whose voice is familiar, though I cannot place it. The language itself is ancient, unintelligible.

I move carefully, hoping to hear more, but the conversation falls silent. At last, I step inside, feigning ease.

Sage greets me with a warm smile. "Hello, Myst. What are you doing up so late?"

The kitchen feels more welcoming since Sage took the steward position, and from what I can see, she's alone. I cross to the worktable, where she slices into a cherry pie with a knife warmed to glide cleanly through the filling. It looks divine. She cuts two generous pieces, places them neatly on plates, and pours us each a cup of fragrant tea.

Before serving me, she retrieves a small glass bottle from the cupboard, its liquid shimmering with the same hue as the bloom I seek. She lets a few drops fall into both teacups.

"You are old enough to indulge a little," she says. "This will relax you. And once your belly is filled with cherries, you will sleep like the true princess you are."

Back in my chambers, exhaustion claims me. She spoke true. Sleep takes me so swiftly that I do not even remember sinking into my pillow.

12

Arkaik Alpynz

Beatryx

The queen is a bitch, and bowing to her feels vile. There is something odd and unsettling about the woman. Myst may not see it, but I sense it. There will be no tea or cake for me—yet the trip I plan to take into town feels promising.

When I step from my father's carriage, I place my gloved hand into the coachman's warm grasp as he guides me down the steps. He is an older man, very handsome, and would likely make an interesting lover. But I never entertain those within my own household, so I gift him a playful smile that must suffice—and he returns one. *Instant butterflies.*

Emporium Charms glows in large letters above the door, and even from outside, I am eager to see what intriguing pleasures await within. The windows emit a soft radiance, daring me to enter. I push the heavy wooden door open, and a rush of mysterious scents washes over me.

The first thing I notice is the wooden shelving—lined with colorful glass bottles holding potions and elixirs. A thrill rushes through me as I take it all in, momentarily dazed, intoxicated by the magically infused air. When I emerge from that small trance, an alcove catches my eye, and I wonder what mysteries it might hold—but my attention is stolen by a rustic table covered in spellbooks and other enticing reads. I open one, and the erotic artwork inside leaves me flushed and heated.

"Are you looking for something special?" a voice asks. "Perhaps something for a trio?"

The sensual, raspy tone pulls me from my thoughts. Behind the counter stands a middle-aged woman, her glimmering eyes and eager posture ready to assist.

That quaint little shop does not disappoint. The leather pouch slung over my shoulder is now full of interesting purchases, and the handsome coachman—Calvin—carries several indiscreet parcels. He steadies me as I climb back into the carriage, and as the road winds toward the castle, I savor the promise of the evening to come.

I ascend one of the main staircases, then turn down the hall leading to the room I occupy during my visits to this court. A rascal of a maid catches my attention.

"Fetch Lucinda," I say. "Please—hurry."

Inside my chamber, the memory of my first encounter with Shayn lingers, and my body tingles. Moments later, Lucinda enters.

"Bath," I say simply.

She moves at once, and so do I. I sit at the writing desk, dip my swan quill into my favorite ink, and begin to scheme—then slip into the bath.

"This fragrance is bliss, Lucinda," I say softly. "Please deliver these missives to their intended chambers. Nothing further will be needed this evening."

Once the door closes, I stretch my shapely legs before me and sink into the bubbling jasmine soak. The warmth unfurls like silk, pulling me deeper. A slow ache builds in my chest, and I bite my lower lip.

Water droplets trace my curves as I reach for the linen, pressing it lightly to my skin before stepping out—already preparing for the night ahead. The satin robe feels exquisite as I move to the dressing area and consider the powders, ultimately choosing a shimmering pink to dust across my body.

A soft crystal shade outlines my hazel eyes; my cheeks and lips match. Rose-petal combs secure my hair. After all my careful work, I am flawless.

My thoughts drift as I push open the balcony doors and step into the night. Roses perfume the air below, sweet and heavy. On a high table rests a silver tray holding three flutes, each bubbling with a pale blue drink. I open the bottle from the emporium and mix each glass with a magical lust potion.

Outwardly, I am dressed in soft pink satin and lace. Beneath, sheer undergarments are secured with silk ribbons, keeping my secrets hidden. A long strip of satin wraps my waist and ties at the center.

Tonight, I am the present to be unwrapped.

All that remains is to wait.

Garrett

The hot water from the newly installed shower—reserved for only a few elite guards—feels incredible as it runs over my aching muscles. Where has this been all my life?

I partially dry off and toss the linen over a hook. After shaking excess water from my short hair, I step into my chamber and notice a shy knock has come and gone. A slip of parchment rests beneath the door, and a familiar, sweet scent lingers.

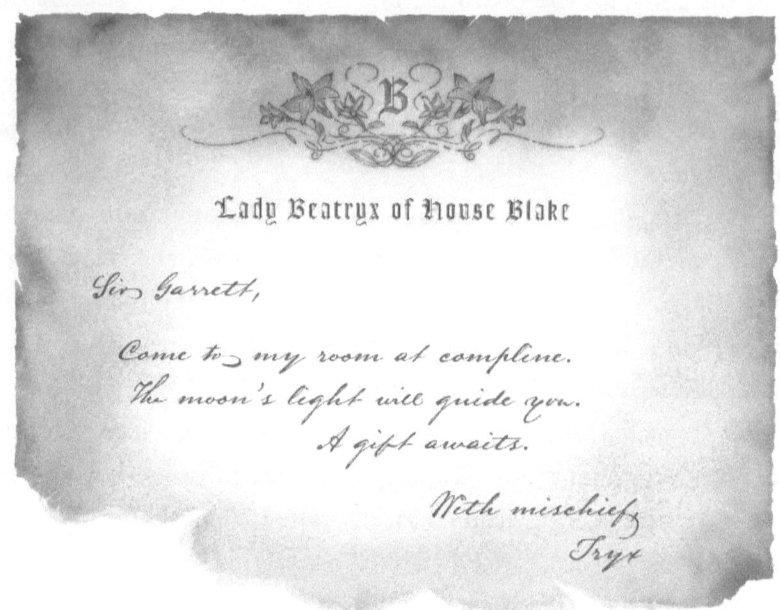

Compline—the final hour of night—and that hour is now.

Before my thoughts make it impossible to lace my breeches, I pull on a soft brown cotton pair and fasten them loosely. A casual white tunic follows. Boots on, I secure two daggers—one high on my left arm, the other at my right thigh.

Hopefully, I will not need them.

As I round the corner near Beatryx's chamber, I see Shayn ascending the staircase. My gaze locks on the folded parchment in his hand—identical to mine.

"Where are you going, Shayn?"

He looks puzzled but answers. "Beatryx's room."

He lifts the parchment and waves it. "I was invited."

I glance around, then lean in. "So was I."

We stand there, irritated, until Shayn finally says something sensible. "Protocol. Assuring the princess's safety."

Threats arise daily within the castle. None can be ignored.

I knock three times, turn the unlocked latch, and step inside.

Jasmine engulfs me. Shayn follows close behind as candlelight flickers and a sultry melody drifts from a music box. He locks the door behind us, and we move deeper into the room.

I see her before I feel anything.

One arm drapes over the balcony railing, the other cradles her face, as if posing for a portrait no one is allowed to paint. Beatryx looks through us—not at us. Her lazy gaze beckons before she turns and glides inward, casual as breath. We follow, puppets on strings she never has to pull.

At the tall, round table, something bubbly waits. She smiles— not at us, but at our obedience.

With delicate hands, she lifts two glasses and offers them forward, each one begging to be taken.

"Gentlemen," she says, "this toast holds gratitude, friendship, and pleasure. May we harmonize all three this evening. This beverage offers a single promise of seductive enticement."

Under her spell, I take the glass. Our fingers brush— intentional. She raises her own flute, its liquid glowing, alive.

We toast. We drink.

The taste is sharp, cold, and far too easy to swallow.

Beatryx

"Let's play a dangerous game."

Both men follow as I move to the dressing table and lift the golden hand mirror, its warm frame steady in my grip.

"When I look into this mirror, my deepest desire will be revealed."

Heat rises as I loosen the sash of my robe, letting it fall open to expose more of my body beneath sheer satin and lace.

I gaze into the mirror and see myself—relaxed, ready. Using my latent gift of mind reading, one I have never fully mastered, I reach inward and read my own desire.

The image shifts. My reflection fades, replaced by something stirring—something real. Anticipation swells. My fingers tremble.

The mirror slips.

It shatters.

And then—we all do.

Reality answers the vision.

I turn to Garrett and let the robe slide from my shoulders. His eyes roam—neck first, then lower. When his lips find the hollow of my throat, a sharp, aching rush surges through me. This man's touch is smooth as silk, and he knows it.

Garrett teases with a sensual confidence, his gaze locking mine as he traces slow patterns along my skin. Want floods me. He knows exactly what he does to me.

Then Shayn is behind me—his hands firm at my hips. I am held between them, suspended in desire and danger.

Both men are hard. Garrett unties the ribbons securing my bodice; Shayn frees the silk at my hips. Everything falls away at once. Shayn's hand finds me, teasing until the tension inside deepens, while Garrett claims my mouth and chest with reverent hunger.

Shayn lifts me, guiding me onto Garrett's warmth. *Death may take me tonight,* I think, wrapping my arms around Garrett's neck as Shayn kisses my back, lifting and lowering me with perfect control. Garrett's attention never wavers—his mouth, his hands, his focus utterly consuming.

This is pleasure unlike anything I have known. I float— unmade.

The night stretches on in indulgence: more games, more bodies, shared water, shared breath.

Later, as we bathe together, I watch the water ripple and think, *Perhaps I will become a novelist.* I will write about the way two men moved in perfect harmony with my body, as though the stars aligned solely for us.

A night I will never forget.
Neither will they.

13

Arkaik Alpynz

Treasure Chest

Garrett

Damn it—I must get up. My limbs feel leaden, my head pounding so hard that thinking clearly is impossible. The room tilts as I fight to focus, spinning with the remnants of drink and chaos. Shayn and I are scheduled to escort Myst to the seamstress this morning, yet memories of last night flood in, jagged and unrelenting. How or when I returned to my room, I do not know.

I jolt upright, heart hammering, and glance over my shoulder, scanning the shadows for another presence. Finding only emptiness, I steady myself. Calm settles—uneasy but necessary.

In the bathing area, I stand at the wash basin and splash cold water over my face and neck, then slap my cheeks with both hands, trying to snap free of this lingering, glossy haze.

Finally dressed and as prepared as physically possible, I open the door to find Shayn leaning against the wall.

"Good morning, beautiful."

Lacking both the energy to throttle him and the patience to engage, I walk past, wondering what Beatryx put in our drinks. Thinking hurts. *She magic-fucked us.*

"Walk in formation with me, Shayn," I say. "I do not want to discuss last night—ever."

Ignoring me, he glances over.

"Did we… you and me…?"

I stop abruptly, inhale slowly, then turn toward him. "I do not want to discuss it."

Then I continue down the hall toward the wide staircase leading to the north tower—to Myst.

Myst

A consultation with the seamstress, Estelle, has been arranged for today. After a refreshing bath, I reach for a warm linen, wrap it around myself against the chill, and slip into my dressing room. A light linen dress will be best, as Estelle will be taking measurements.

Once the fitting is complete, I hope to return and spend the remainder of the day reading.

A light knock startles me.

"Guards."

With Midnight at my side, I open the heavy door and step out. Garrett and Shayn escort me to Estelle's enchanted workroom on the main floor, just beyond the kitchen.

For several moon phases, I have considered the ideal gown design and gathered thoughts to share, but they tangle as we pass through the busy corridor. I steady myself and follow Garrett down the wide stairway while Shayn walks behind me.

Garrett knocks on the heavy wooden door before pushing it open.

The chamber lies low within the castle, its windows tucked beneath the courtyard stones. Magic hums here—enchanting and subtle—while cool, timeless air rebounds off the stone walls to brush my face. Narrow windows stand cracked open, letting in a faint breeze and the soft cooing of pigeons settling above.

When I look up, gold-and-silver bobbins brimming with colorful thread spin in perfect enchanted circles. When Estelle reaches for one, the others shift, realigning the sphere.

Fascinating.

Rustic wooden tables are piled with fabrics of every texture, as wall sconces pour out light touched by magic across the riot of color. This hidden sewing room feels less like a workspace and more like the castle's true treasure chest.

"Viola, fetch the silver taffeta that recently arrived—quickly, girl."

Viola must be new; I have never seen her before. With the summer solstice approaching, Estelle likely needs extra hands. The poor girl looks frail—pastel skin, tired eyes—but she moves swiftly.

Estelle rises from her spinning wheel, the soft hum of thread fading as she pushes back her stool. A length of silken yarn trails from the spindle, gleaming—perhaps destined for my gown's embroidery. Her hair is swept into an intricate bun, loose strands framing her face as she steps forward, eyes bright with inspiration.

"Princess, please sit."

The plush velvet lounge is wonderfully comfortable as she begins outlining her dramatic vision. I stand.

"Thank you," I say gently, "but I also have ideas regarding the gown."

The room stills.

"First, I want the gown to symbolize the occasion. Second, it must represent me—which makes this more complicated. Please allow me to see the fabric swatches you've collected, and then I would like to review the sketches."

Estelle gathers the materials with easy grace. A long worktable is covered in fabrics of every hue; scissors gleam in the light, needles scattered among half-finished patterns. She lays the swatches before me, and together we sit, shaping the design with care.

As I lean forward, imagining possibilities, a flicker of movement catches my eye.

I glance over my shoulder.

Shayn and Garrett are no longer standing.

They sleep, leaning against one another on the lounge.

I turn to Viola, irritation sharpening—her eyes glow amethyst until she notices my gaze. She blinks, and they return to brown. Her pointed ears shift.

She is fae.

"How long before my first fitting?"

"Ahem." I clear my throat loudly enough to wake the guards.

Estelle's brows knit as she casts them a displeased glance before answering me. "Three days."

The walk back to my quarters is heavy with frustration. When we arrive, I turn on them, unable to restrain myself.

"Shall I report the two of you to Captain Edwin?"

Garrett looks mortified. Shayn stares into nothingness.

Garrett opens the door. I step inside, then motion for them to follow. They hesitate but obey. I press both palms to the door, easing it shut.

"You both look like a disaster," I say, "and I want answers."

Silence.

After dismissing my guards, my thoughts drift to Beatryx, whom I have not seen today. It feels strange—especially since I have spent more time with her than with Krys of late.

I leave my chambers and head toward the main staircase. As I begin to descend, familiar laughter reaches me.

"Myst! Look who I found."

Beatryx waits below, refreshed and radiant. She turns to the woman beside her, smiling brightly. "Olyvia, your timing couldn't be better."

"Let's walk," I say, then pause at the kitchen doorway. "Let me grab one thing."

Inside, warmth from the hearth brushes my cheeks. The kitchen is quiet, filled with the soft crackle of embers and the lingering scent of butter and sugar. A tray of shortbread cools beneath a linen cloth. I lift the edge and take three—still warm. Sage's treats never disappoint.

I wrap the cookies in a few folded cloths and return to the girls. I hand one to each of them. Their faces brighten.

"Treats?" Beatryx teases.

I raise mine. Olyvia mirrors the gesture. We tap cookies together in a soft, playful toast before walking on, crumbs sweet on our tongues, the moment lightening the day.

Beatryx and Olyvia follow me up the narrow spiral staircase, our steps echoing on worn stone that remembers every footfall. As the light thins, Olyvia reaches for a wall torch and lifts it, flame casting warmth across the walls.

"Heat steadies me," she says.

At the top, I press my hip to the heavy oak door until it groans open. The circular chamber beyond is bathed in soft afternoon light. Dust hangs suspended until Beatryx bursts in, sending it swirling. She sneezes, and we laugh.

A tarnished brass telescope stands at the center, fixed eastward like a sentinel.

I step toward the arched windows where ivy clings to stone. Below, the training yards hum with motion—soldiers sparring and shouting.

Two are missing.

"I'm clearly not the only one who thinks Iyce is handsome," Beatryx remarks.

I sigh and cross toward her. She steps aside and gestures to the telescope.

At the forest's edge stands a girl, gazing up at Iyce with unmistakable intent. They speak quietly, alone.

She has always been quiet—unassuming. But now, from this height, she is transformed. Hair swept back, gown tailored, cheeks flushed.

She wants to be seen.

I see you.

Olyvia peers through the lens. "Who are they?"

My gaze drifts east, toward the Forest of Shadows. Toward Mairi. Toward the bargain I made at thirteen.

When will she come to collect?

"My future husband," I say quietly. "And Krystelle."

Silence follows—heavy, unanswered.

"Another?" I ask.

Olyvia laughs. We return to the kitchen for one last piece of shortbread before stepping into the courtyard. Pigeons crowd the stone path, pecking and cooing.

"Well," Beatryx says, stopping short, "they're enjoying themselves."

Olyvia lifts her cookie like an offering. "Should we be worried?"

I laugh softly, the sound easing my anger and confusion alike.

We walk on, pigeons parting around us, and finish our cookies beneath the open sky.

14

Arkaik Alpynz

Blooms of Frost Survive Monsters

Myst

Where has the day gone? Twilight gathers, and the stars will be twinkling before long.

I sink onto my lounge, gathering my robe around me as agitation stirs in my chest—until loud cheers and war cries shatter the quiet, pulling me toward the southern window. Frantically, I scan the horizon, where soldiers and guards swarm in every direction, too many to discern the cause.

Then I see him—right in the middle of it.

Iyce.

My gaze catches on large carts, each holding covered cages. Glaycyr Falz and Crescere Moonz work with my father to go beyond our borders, to preserve a balance, as they call it. But I have never seen anything like this before.

What has he done?

I must get down there.

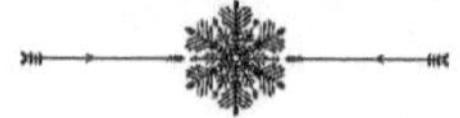

Slipping from my chambers unnoticed, I thread through the castle's quiet hollows and descend to the ground floor. Corridors stretch long and empty, shadows clinging to the walls. The castle is ghostly still—everyone must be outside. I pass the kitchens, their fires reduced to embers, then skirt the servants' quarters, doors ajar but silent.

At last, I slip into the laundry, passing laundresses unseen—their faces pressed to the windows as they watch the chaos beyond. The scent of lavender and wildflowers guides me toward the rear, where large cauldrons hang over wood fires. Hot water boils over their rims, sending thick steam into the air.

Hastily, I rummage through garments. There must be a guard close to my size. *Please.* Finally, I choose the smallest uniform I can find and pull it on, discarding my dress behind a mound of soiled linens. Hopefully, I will remember to retrieve it. It would be odd for someone to find it here—especially with my initials, **KMS**, embroidered into every piece I wear.

Stories would be forged. *What does the K even stand for?*

A black raven perches rudely on the windowsill, interrupting my imagined downfall. It croaks loudly, its shrill cry racing across the nearby river.

Is it warning me—or someone else?

"You're so loud," I whisper. "Shh."

The obnoxious messenger only deepens my unease.

Unrecognizable even to myself, I head east toward the queen's wing. In the main hall, I stop before the cherished painting of my grandparents. Grandpapá stands tall, wearing the crown my father now bears.

He was never unfit to rule.

They fabricated that.

Softly, I recite the spell and step straight through the wall into the queen's hidden staircase—a secret I discovered at thirteen, the night I followed my mother to the Forest of Shadows. I still wonder how often she used it, and why.

Darkness swallows me whole. I feel for each step with my foot while my hands trace the cold stone walls. I am in too much of a rush to fetch a torch.

Next time.

Emerging from the passage, I kneel and slam my palms into the earth, smearing mud down both sides of my face—sealing a new, unknown identity. I drift toward the noise, allowing the crowd to absorb me.

Iyce's voice carries like frozen flurries. "We have claimed a rare prize from the Vanishing Isles."

Cheers erupt—unbearable.

I need to get closer.

Three wagons come into view. I work my way toward one and pause, fear tightening my chest as I reach for the canvas. The rustling beneath does not help. I close my eyes, steady myself, and slip beneath the heavy cloth.

When I open them, the sight silences everything inside me.

The younglings are feathered, their bodies covered in soft down. Some appear older, their plumage deepening to ash gray and golden amber. Their wings—broad but untested—twitch with instinctive urges to fly. They move with feline grace, long tails flicking in precise, playful motions.

Nearby, someone hums—a captivating melody that nearly lulls me into a trance. It soothes the animals. I edge around the wagon and peer past its corner.

My breath catches.

"Sage."

The word escapes before I can stop it. Even in my disguise, she recognizes me instantly. My own mother might pass me by unknowing, but Sage does not.

She is pouring magic into the cages—gentle, sustaining. No wonder Iyce wants them. Beyond his obsession with claiming what is not his, this will make him appear a hero.

Sage steadies herself. "Myst, do you know where the castle's war room is?"

I see her differently now. Magic flows through her effortlessly. Curiosity outweighs caution. I nod.

She pulls up her hood and follows.

Her presence there would raise questions I cannot answer. To bring her unseen, I must move with precision. The queen's hidden staircase is our only option. Hesitantly, I guide her to it. Once inside, she flicks her wrist, and tiny flowers bloom, glowing low to guide our ascent.

That is handy.

Before I speak the word to pass through, I take her hand. A spark passes between us—noticed, unspoken. We step through the stone.

"The war room isn't far," I whisper. "With most outside, we should enter without trouble."

She nods, and we move.

Sage

How did Iyce reach the younglings? How did he bypass the curse shielding the realm?

Myst moves quickly for her size, and I match her pace, driven toward the heartbeat of the kingdom—the war room. It has been too long since I walked these halls. I need to see their strategies, their symbols, their favored paths.

The thought of destroying Iyce brings fierce satisfaction—but reason tempers it.

Another time, Iyce.

Myst guides us through wooden doors, and I am grateful passage offers no resistance.

Inside, brass sconces flicker over the maps. Myst watches me carefully.

We approach the central table. The map shows **SNEEUWVLOK**. I memorize it, then move to a second table of smaller charts. Myst lingers behind.

My fingers linger on **HEILALA**, pain tightening through my chest, before I let my hand fall to the southern isles.

"This is where they took the younglings from," I say. "A land untouched by snow or ice. They will not survive here."

Grief floods her. Hatred rises in me—ancient and sharp.

Unable to stop myself, I hover my palms above the map and whisper in my tongue. The spell pours forth. Borders pulse. Terrain thrums. The map lives.

A tear slips free.

Myst takes my hand. "Why does this make you cry?"

Unbidden emotion surges. *What else will this kingdom take from me?*

I smile and offer a half-truth. "This new position has been intense. Some days I am more sensitive than others."

I lie. The curse holds.

Myst's gaze drifts to the weapon racks—blades, axes, spears. Her posture tightens.

"Have you been trained to use any of these?"

She hesitates, shame flickering. It wounds me more than her lack of skill.

"We should leave," I murmur. "I hear voices."

Myst

Before I am discovered and questioned, I must return to the north tower. Sage remained behind to care for the younglings, using her magic to keep them warm. Flustered, I begin the long trek down the final corridor—until my arm isn't my own.

He wrenches me back, revealing himself with a sneer.

"Do not think for a moment I failed to notice you—barely more than a wisp in that crowd. The ungrateful look on your face made certain of it."

"Let go of me," I hiss, my voice laced with venom. "You're a monster."

In one brutal motion, Iyce slams me against the wall. His arms become chains, his grip locking around my wrists with merciless precision. His knee shifts between my legs, using his weight to lift and pin me, raising me off the floor as if I weigh nothing at all. I hang suspended, breath knocked out of me, strung up like some obscene piece of dungeon art as the corridor darkens and he closes in.

He leans in, voice low and vile. "The monster is in my breeches. And very soon, you'll meet him. Then this nonsense will end."

Nausea surges through me. Spittle bursts from my lips before thought can form, striking true.

He recoils, dropping me without mercy as his palm rushes to his eye. The back of his hand clips my cheek before he reaches for my hair, pulling the pins free. It tumbles down, and he runs his fingers through the strands as if claiming them. "Your long hair turns me on wildly," he says, almost singing as he walks away.

"Lovely days are ahead for you and me, Myst."

The bath was meant to wash away the mud I smeared across my face—but now it is to wash away Iyce. I scrub until my skin stings.

In bed, I lie still beneath the weight of silence. My thoughts drift to Heilala, the realm Sage could not look away from. Its shape lingers, oddly familiar—like the hybiscus bloom, its delicate petals curling outward.

15

Arkaik Alpynz

Deep Roots

Myst

At the stables, Hayze has the horses ready. Today, Beatryx, Olyvia, and I will ride to the alpyne meadows—Olyvia's idea. Just us girls. She wants to gather blossoms from the fields to weave into our hair for the upcoming ball.

Olyvia and I are already astride, while Beatryx stands beside her mare, hands firm on her hips as she waits impatiently for a mounting block. As we linger, my thoughts drift to the sudden bond with Olyvia—a friendship that bloomed overnight. When she arrived at the castle, Beatryx was the one who found her, and together they found me. Somewhere between our talk of hair arrangements and the quiet moments spent stringing blooms through it, I realized I genuinely enjoy her company.

The young stablehand's face is generously dusted with dirt from a long day's work. His linen tunic carries more dust than the terrain, and his boots look as if they've survived a dozen storms. Whistling a carefree tune, he positions the block and does his best not to stare at Beatryx's unforgettable curves.

"This should do nicely, Miss."

Hayze steps forward, takes Beatryx's hand gently, and helps her up.

Something shifts in me. *A strange feeling I can't quite name. Jealousy, perhaps.*

Beatryx settles onto her horse, and Hayze hands her the reins.

"Let's go!" The outburst slips free with the impulsiveness of a petulant child, prompting Olyvia to glance at me with intrigue. Beatryx quickly finds her seat, and the three horses walk out of the stables, hooves clinking softly against stone before shifting into a light trot.

We canter through the fishing village, past nets drying on posts and the scent of brine and smoke, until we reach the edge of the alpynz, where the scenery changes.

Olyvia leans forward, challenges Shyanne with a sharp whisper, and before time can catch up, they're gone—galloping full tilt into the wind. One kick, and Aspen knows he's expected to follow.

We do.

Olyvia and I ride wildly, the wind hitting us so hard I wonder how our skin stays intact. *This feels savage. I love it. I needed it.*

The flowers seem bashful at our arrival, nodding gently in the crisp, refreshing breeze. It's been some time since I last rode this way, yet the meadows still stretch wide—lush with wildflowers, resilient grasses, and low-growing shrubs that thrive in the harsh mountain conditions. Silver streams wind through the open fields, their waters glistening as they tumble over stone and root, carrying the memory of snowmelt down from the peaks.

Our horses lower their heads to drink, muzzles breaking the surface with quiet ripples.

When I look back, Beatryx holds a basket Sage prepared for us. We savor the delicious things she packed as hawks circle overhead across the meadow.

With a mouth full, Olyvia says, "I love the blooms I'm finding here."

Beatryx and I begin sorting through her gathered treasures—petals in every hue, stems still damp with morning dew. I spot a primrose nestled among them, its yellow soft as sunlight, and ease it free.

"Here," I say, offering it to Olyvia. "Take in its scent."

She leans in without hesitation. As she brushes the petals, a dusting of yellow pollen settles across her nose.

Beatryx snorts first. Then I can't help myself—the laughter spills out, bright and unrestrained.

Olyvia blinks, confused, until she touches her nose and sees the smear on her fingertips.

"Oh." She laughs with us, cheeks warming as she wipes at the golden streak.

The sound of it—our laughter mingling in the open air—feels like something I haven't had in a long time.

Something I didn't realize I missed.

The ride back is calm. We soak in the beauty of the alpyne aster and let the quiet settle between us.

By the time we return to the stables, Hayze is already waiting.

I don't need her help. I swing down from the saddle and step away, following the path toward the keep. Gravel crunches beneath my boots, the air pressing heavier with each step.

Olyvia catches up. "Are you okay?"

No, I'm not okay.

But I give her a faint smile and keep walking. "A wave of fatigue hit me, and I need rest," I say, unable to keep the irritation from my voice.

Exhaustion finally wins the war with my mind—but as my eyes begin to flutter, an essence makes itself known. Mystical vapors slip beneath my chamber doors, sapphire light sparkling within the fog, entrancing and beckoning, a faint scent of cloves lingering in the air.

The snowflake pendant at my chest warms. My body tingles.

A gentle knock sounds.

I grab the silk scarf from my dressing table, pushing a loose strand of hair back as I wrap the fabric around my midsection. It settles low on my hips, sheer and suggestive. I open the door.

Hayze enters.

"Hello, Hayze."

Two glasses of wine in hand—pulled from the cellar. We've seen each other only a handful of times since that first contact—when my mother tried to take my face off.

But her timing couldn't be more perfect.

I need this.

I drain my glass in two slow swallows, warmth blooming in my chest. Wine clings to my lips, and I let my tongue soak up the last of it. The empty glass settles on the bedside table as silence thickens between us.

Sometimes, I ache for her touch.

A step closer—and the air shifts. My pendant stirs with heat. Fingers brush my cheek, light as breath, and my body responds—nipples tightening—because she knows exactly how to touch me.

When I meet those golden-brown eyes, my voice drops, certain.

"Ask your questions later. Right now, I need you."

Hayze loves women—only women—and offers gentle pleasure without breaking rules. She finishes her wine, then removes her tunic and the thin strip of cloth around her small breasts, which I admire.

Guided backward, I feel the edge of the bed press against my legs before I sink onto it. Her palms rest on my knees—then widen them.

The silk lifts.

A slow kiss through the fabric. Teeth catch, teasing, dragging it down—

My breath catches.

Hands find me, and I gasp.

Her mouth follows—one hardened peak, then the other. Cool

breath, teasing, deliberate. I shiver. Hayze is tender—but sometimes rough.

I crave that.

My hand is pressed beside my hip.

What I need is release.

Lower now—lingering, precise—kissing where it matters most. Where everything wakes. Where everything rests.

These perfect lips…

She rises again, frees the scarf, folds it, and places it gently between my teeth.

I surrender.

Hayze returns to my flame, devouring me as I arch beneath her, silk muffling my whimpers until bliss overtakes me. She doesn't stop until I'm trembling and undone—until my body yields, blossoming beneath her kiss.

A whisper—she misses me.

Sapphire haze curls around us like a spell.

Then she's above me.

I reach upward, claiming her breasts. A low, rough moan answers. The ribbon is freed, my wrists bound.

I'm pushed down.

One leg lifted over her shoulder.

Unveiled.

Slow at first—then firm—until I lose myself again.

A hand covers my mouth as she leans close. When her fingers are offered, I take them, tasting the truth.

Hayze disappears into the bathing chamber.

When she returns, a warm linen rests in her hands, scented with cloves and mint. She tends to me with a tenderness so deep I nearly crave her again—though weariness pulls me under.

The teacup of chamomile is placed in my hands. She watches me sip. Then—softly—my cheek is kissed.

"Sleep, beautiful princess."

In three heavy-lidded blinks, the sapphire haze dissolves like a dream.

She is gone.

Morning comes.

Estelle promised three days, so tomorrow my drowsy guards will escort me to her enchanted chamber for the fitting. I should feel joyful—but unease rises instead.

Seeking comfort, I head to the kitchen for a buttered biscuit. Sage balances on a stepstool, reaching for a basket overhead.

When she descends, a sigh slips free.

"Sage."

She turns, smiling. "Hi, Myst. I'm about to harvest cherries. Would you like to join me?"

Before I answer, she presses the basket handle into my palm. "Wonderful. Follow me."

I trail after her, confused, as we step out toward the orchards.

The cherry trees are ancient, their branches heavy with fruit and memory. It feels shameful—like I've ignored something sacred.

Rows stretch endlessly, branches laden with bright red and deep purple fruit. The soil beneath is soft and tended. Some trees are draped in netting to protect the harvest.

It's more sacred than I imagined.

Silence settles.

Sage plucks cherries carefully. "I know where the younglings are. And I've visited them without being seen."

Unease prickles my skin. "Show me."

She sets the basket down. "Follow me."

Although I've lived here all my life, she knows this kingdom's hidden places better than I do.

"Do we need a horse?"

She shakes her head.

At the edge of the Whispering Woods stands a newly erected tent. Before parting the canvas, Sage mutters a word I don't understand.

"We're no longer visible."

Inside, boys tend the pens—but within moments, they're gone. The younglings flock to Sage as she speaks in the ancient language, her voice low and melodic.

She turns to me. "Myst, can you release a small amount of your mist so I can assess an idea?"

Excitement stirs. I do as she asks.

She runs her hand through it. A spark ignites.

"With them enclosed, my heat is too warm. But mixed with your mist, we could create balance. Will you try—with guidance?"

I smile.

Sage steps before me, palms up, inviting. I lift mine to meet hers.

She hums, heat rising, drawing mist from me until a pale steam curls up between us.

The younglings stir, moving with ease.

They were waiting.

For comfort. For breath.

We smile.

"Thank you, Myst," Sage says, hugging me tightly. "This will last one day."

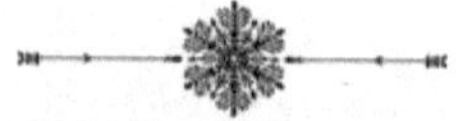

We make our way back in silence, the warmth between us slow to fade.

In the kitchen, Sage wipes each cherry with care. She removes the pits slowly—mostly because she eats every other one, and I do the same.

Our laughter is quiet.

"Let's make a pie."

She prepares the filling, then gestures to the dough. "Would you like to knead? It helps release frustration."

She's right. The rhythm grounds me.

Midnight lies nearby. I slip my foot free to rub her neck. Sage kneels, letting my sweet girl lick sugar from her fingers.

This moment feels like a secret.

Like something I'll carry long after the cherries are gone.

16

Arkaik Alpynz

BLUSHED PARCHMENT

Olyvia

Shimmering pawprints bounce across the marble floor as I step into the castle's library.

"I see you both," I say, my voice echoing softly.

Golden eyes kindle, and in a shimmer the kittens take form, darting forward and circling my steps. One is solid black, her long tail swaying like she knows it's something special. The other is black with white markings. They are clearly sisters.

Again, I remember why I'm here.

Shayn.

The spell my mother will shape will make Shayn forget. But it asks for my kiss, and I refuse. I do not want to kiss that man. He watches Beatryx like his life depends on her existence. And even if he didn't, he is not my type. I like tall boys, and while I wouldn't call him short, he's not tall enough for me.

Looking back at the kittens, I ask, "Can either one of you direct me to a book of spells?"

Their ears perk. Golden eyes shimmer with unguarded curiosity. But the moment the words leave my mouth, the kittens vanish, replaced by a soothing voice.

"They cannot, but I certainly can."

Mesmerized, I halt mid-spin, captivated by the woman standing before me. She holds both kittens—one in each arm—and continues, "Coco and Lexi seem quite intrigued by you."

Startled, I stand my ground, unsure whether to speak or retreat. *Who is she?* Her presence is calm but commanding.

"What type of spell are you looking to research?" she asks, her tone shifting to something formal. "I'm Saffi, the librarian. My schedule is tight, but I can point you to the correct shelf."

My mind hits a barricade. I don't know how to respond. The words I need feel too raw, too exposed.

But desperation pushes through.

I clasp my hands and shift my weight. "I am Olyvia, and I need someone to forget the first time we met. When he sees me again, I want him to see me with new eyes."

"Ahh." Saffi cocks her head, studying me more closely now. Her gaze lingers—not only on my face, but on my hair.

I ignore her curiosity and wait. *Please just help me.*

She finally sets the kittens onto their cushions, giving each a gentle pat before crossing to her desk. She gathers a small stack of books, their spines worn from years of use, then motions for me to follow.

With the kittens padding behind us, she leads me to a higher level of the library and points out several volumes on spellwork before guiding me to a quiet nook.

The kittens curl in my lap, purring loudly as I flip through the fourth section of the book Saffi selected. The spells I've read thus far are precise about timing, and each repeats the same rule: you must be in the same location as the first interaction with the individual whose memory you wish to alter.

There is no way I can wait for Shayn to return to that tavern.

As it is, I'm already avoiding him several times a day—making excuses to Myst about why only us girls should go places without her guards.

Strange noises pull my attention from the page.

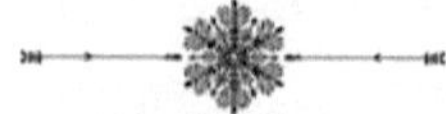

Beatryx

"Shayn, why did you bring me to this level of the library? What is so important?"

This handsome man takes both my hands and places them on his chest, then slides his arms around my waist, drawing me firmly into him. He knows exactly what he's doing—how to get to me—because I can feel how excited he is and there isn't enough space in his breeches for his goods, even when he's not stiff. A flush warms my cheeks at the thought.

Shayn brushes my lips with a light kiss, then murmurs, "I want you. Right now. In this library."

Heat floods my body. I know I won't resist him. Returning the favor, I kiss his soft lips and begin unlacing what keeps pleasure hidden.

The last time an encounter occurred, I was with him and Garrett. Garrett and I had sex, but Shayn and I did other things. Still, I must admit—I'm a little excited about these library books watching me in pure bliss. *A free tale for their parchment.*

Shayn works quickly at the corset cinched tight around my waist, his fingers swift and confident. His mouth never leaves mine, kisses growing rougher, charged with anticipation. My hands fall to caress him, and he is more than ready.

With my bodice loosened, his mouth traces the valley of my chest, my breasts behaving like twin sisters competing for attention. When he bites my nipple—sharp, possessive—a jolt tears through me. *I want this man.*

Shayn kisses me once more, then turns me around and bends me forward. My face dips toward the rug, close enough to see the coarse twine woven through its fibers, and everything else blurs the moment I feel him press close.

"Shh," he murmurs. "Be very quiet, my little damsel."

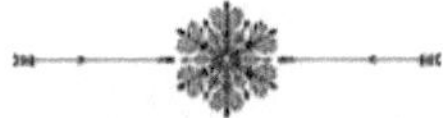

Olyvia

I breathe, "Too late for your shh, idiot."

I set the book on a nearby table and move toward the sound, peeking around the corner— only to bolt backward and hit my head on the table's edge.

"Damn…"

Shayn and Beatryx are having sex in the middle of the library— in front of the books, the sconces, two kittens, and me. A girl cannot even do honest research anymore. Research—because of him.

After composing myself, I walk calmly down the stairs, one hand casually pressed to my head as if smoothing my hair. I stop at Saffi's desk and thank her, angling my body to hide the tender spot.

She studies me curiously. "Looks like you found what you needed. You're leaving sooner than I expected."

Her shock is immediate when I reply, "I didn't find exact answers, but some useful material. Staying longer isn't a possibility—I'm fairly certain I saw a mouse near where I was sitting."

"Oh no. That won't stand," she says briskly. "I'll investigate at once."

Exactly the reaction I wanted.

Take that, Shayn.

Saffi

I climb the stairs toward the quiet corner Olyvia occupied. I've never seen a mouse in this library.

Whatever she encountered unsettled her. The book lies open on the table, and the air itself feels… wrong.

Then I hear voices, and heat rolls through the air.

"Gods, you feel so good," a man mutters, voice rough and muffled.

There's a small alcove for private reading just beyond the shelves. I move quietly, slide two books aside, adjust my glasses—and then freeze. Oh.

A handsome soldier holds a disheveled woman against him, one hand firm at her waist, the other possessive at her throat as he fills her with desire. Her head rests back on his shoulder, sounds escaping her lips until he covers her mouth.

He barely gets the words out through tight breaths and clenched teeth. "I'm right there, Beatryx," he grits out. "Own it."

He pulls her close and whispers vulgarities into her ear—and she comes undone.

Heat rushes through me, uninvited and overwhelming.

Thank you very much, soldier.

Something other than shock settles in my expression now. That was… stimulating. Sensations I haven't felt in eons stir awake.

I need to find my husband.

17

Arkaik Alpynz

Strawberry Moon

Olyvia

A discussion with Mamá leads to the original plan I dread. After I tell her about the spellbooks I found in the library, she praises my effort but informs me they may work—just not precisely. Meaning, every time I see Shayn, he'll think he's meeting me for the first time. And that would become strange.

The next time I see him—and his dick isn't rammed inside Beatryx—I'll kiss him.

The Summer Solstice Ball is this evening, and I set out with my basket and shears toward the kingdom's articulated gardens. A wide array of delicate blooms awaits, each one a potential match for the hair art I've envisioned for the princess. Kneeling, I match petals to fabric, noting which ones blend best.

This must be flawless.

Gently, I place each clipping into my basket, pleased with my final assortment of primrose, camellia, winterberry, snowdrops, and so many more, including the little ladybug that slips in as well.

Just as I begin to stand, a large hand appears.

"Allow me."

When I look up at the outstretched hand, I know exactly whose voice matches it. He offers to help me from the ground. First, I don't need his help, nor did I ask for it. And second, I'm not looking forward to what's about to happen.

What if the spell isn't a success?

Of course it will be. My mother conjured it.

As I allow him to help me up, the flowers slip from my lap to the ground. With my feet beneath me, I turn toward him, and our eyes lock, but his eyes widen with confusion.

I pounce.

The kiss I hit Shayn with is savage, and it gives me the strength to pour a little of my own magic into it—magic that ensures he'll never see me as anything more than a girl he isn't interested in. When I tear my lips from his, I shove him as hard as I can. The force of it throws me off balance, and I land on my backside, flower petals scattering around me.

Shayn looks disoriented and out of sorts. Thank you, goddesses.

Frozen on the ground, I wait to see what his next move will be. Because if this doesn't work, I'll be forced to tangle him.

"Are you hurt, my lady?" Shayn asks.

Taking my turn in the game, I reply, "The wind is relentless today. It seems I've lost my balance."

He scrambles to his feet and dusts himself off, then comes over to lend me a hand, but I'm already up.

"The name is Shayn. Who do I have the pleasure of meeting today?"

I practically leap for joy. He doesn't remember me. "Olyvia. I've only recently begun my service as a handmaiden."

"Have a good day then, Olyvia."

Those are Shayn's last words before he turns and walks away.

Perfect. Both spells hold.

Lightly, I knock on the heavy door, then enter Myst's chambers, and the entire room sparkles. Beatryx and Krystelle are spinning, their dresses incredible, and the glow even better. Silver-blue, light pink, and lavender intertwine into one spellbinding flow of color and gleam.

Myst sees me and calls out, "Olyvia, hello! We're so excited for you to style our hair."

Beatryx and Krystelle step away from Myst, then watch her spin. Her full skirts float like a light breeze, and it's simply the most beautiful gown this kingdom has yet to see.

This is precision at its finest, I think, watching as she slows down. The thread, ornate snowflakes, and silver dust on the dress slow too.

Perfection.

Moving toward Myst, I ask, "May I?"

Once she nods, I lift her thick hair to get a better look at the back of the dress. As I lean in, her gaze flicks upward, sharp with concern.

"Olyvia… what happened to your head?"

My hand drifts instinctively toward the tender spot before I force it down. "Oh—nothing. I bumped into a shelf earlier. Clumsy of me."

She doesn't look convinced, but she lets me continue.

Next, I study Beatryx and Krystelle's dresses, ensuring their hair adornments will complement the gowns rather than compete with them.

"Viola, please help these ladies remove their dresses. Then we can begin to work on their hair."

Estelle allows the tiny faerie to help me today, and she eagerly responds with a big smile before she blinks—her large eyes turning amethyst, then quickly back to brown.

We begin with Myst, because she turned eighteen this season and a painter waits nearby to create a masterpiece once she's ready. Her hair is braided, then pulled into a high bun atop her head. A section along the bottom of her hairline is left out of the bun, and I braid it into several tiny sections, designing each one to weave into the hair that leads to the bun.

Stunning.

Blue primrose and white snowdrops are shy secrets along the right side of the bun. Strictly, these blooms should be on the left, considering she's betrothed—but I refuse. On this evening, she's an elegant girl belonging only to herself.

Shadow walks in, and my reaction shows that I'm thankful. "Hi, Shadow. Do you have time to help Myst into her gown?"

She lowers her chalice to the table, the scent of wine lingering in the air, and crosses to the gown that hangs as if held by invisible hands. After examining it, she sternly speaks to the faerie. "Viola, I know you've got a cute little pair of wings under that jacket. Can you fetch Estelle quickly and request she bring a mending kit?"

Viola blinks, her eyes once again turning amethyst before nodding. And sure enough, those wings emerge, and Viola flies right off the balcony, excited to have an assignment.

Shadow turns back to Myst. "Sit. Let's touch up your powder and lips."

When I watch the interaction between them, it feels more like mother and daughter than personal maid and princess.

Beatryx wears a sad look, so I motion her over. "I have an idea for your hair that I think you'll love."

Her eyes light up. "I'm ready."

Using tongs, I strategically place curlers in her hair that have been sitting over a hot flame. Between each curler is a small piece of fabric to prevent burns.

"Would you like help with your face powder while we wait?"

Beatryx gladly accepts, and I match the powder a shade lighter than her creamy skin. She's wild, enjoys life, and never hesitates to say whatever comes to mind—and I respect her for it. The dress she wears this evening is soft pink, so we use eye powders to accentuate the gown. Her hazel eyes are stunning.

Back to her hair—I remove the now-warm curlers, then lightly twist sections from the front to the back, connecting the sides. It leaves a chunk of curls flowing like a waterfall down the middle of her back. The camellia and winterberry are stunning in her hair.

The door flies open, and a flustered Estelle enters with Viola on her heels. She walks straight to the dress and recites one word. Her work of art lowers to the perfect position. Then she gets busy unstitching, thread snapping between her teeth, before she finally says, "I do believe we have a wide enough space for Myst to get through without disrupting her lovely hair." But this is going to take all of us. Shadow, Beatryx, Krystelle, and I will hold the skirts out. Olyvia, you go under the dress with Myst and keep any loose fabric away from her hair and face. Viola, you have the most important job of all. Fly to the top and shift any fabric that nears her as she comes through the opening. Are we ready?"

Everyone gets into position, and Estelle counts to three in her own tongue:

"Ūnus, -a, -um… duo, duae, duo… trēs, tria."

We all move in unison, and when Myst and I go under the dress, we begin to giggle so intensely we nearly ruin the entire plan. Finally, we pull ourselves together, and up she goes. Viola moves the fabric aside, and Myst slips out, hair in place, and we all take a moment to sigh.

"Excellent, everyone." Shadow smooths her hair away from her face while Estelle sews the dress back in place.

Myst is a sight to take in and never forget. She's unforgettable.

"Krystelle, I'm ready for you—if you're ready."

Krystelle has a fragile look, and I want her hair to reflect that softness. But then my mind snaps back to the moment Myst saw her and Iyce speaking in private—how unsettled she was. Who is Krystelle, really?

I style a subtle wave, then part her hair across the middle. With the remaining sections, I weave four braids, blending them into her dark hair before finishing with a relaxed bun at the nape of her neck. Finally, I add purple crocus blooms.

Krystelle walks to the floor-length mirror and takes in her own reflection, and I see a small smile on her pretty lips. Myst mentioned weeks ago that this is the first solstice ball she'll attend, so I'm glad I can make it a little more special for her, even if she is being mysterious about something.

As I begin to pick up the supplies I used on everyone's hair, Shadow stops me. "We have assistants to help with this. You must be exhausted."

The response comes with ease. "I'm happy to do it."

Then I continue gathering the scattered pieces and putting them away. Her chambers resemble chaos spun from silk and mischief.

Shadow speaks again. "You did an amazing job on the girls' hair. Thank you."

The busier I am, the better. Because the moment I stop, I begin to think too much.

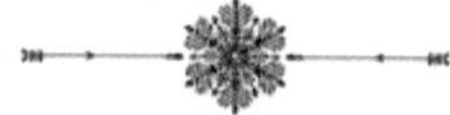

Beatryx

The throne room in this kingdom, like others, is designed to flaunt power and wealth. Even the massive stone columns demand respect.

The entire ceiling is glass, allowing all to marvel at the moon, which rests low in the sky with an amber hue. This solstice coincides with the Strawberry Moon, named for the ripening of strawberries during this season. Of course, strawberries have found their way into nearly every dish tonight.

Myst leaves for her session with the artist, and a handsome man walks by with a tray full of cocktails, the glasses chiming softly as he passes. I take two flutes and head toward a duke I've had my eyes on for a while now.

"Lady Beatryx."

The way he purrs my name sends my bottom lip between my teeth, stopping the idiotic things I might say, like Do you want to go somewhere a little less… And he'd probably finish with, Crowded?

I place a glass in his hand, and he lifts his arm, allowing me to slide my hand around it, steadying myself against the quiet strength beneath my palm.

Garrett and Shayn stand like the dutiful guards they are as I walk past and wink. They both look furious, which only means one thing.

Sex with them will be even better.

Myst

Back in the ballroom, I find Krystelle and ask, "Have you had a moment to meet anyone interesting this evening?"

She shrugs her shoulders and lightly says, "I have had my eye on someone."

I purse my lips, still thinking about the way she had her eyes on Iyce only days ago. I'm on the verge of forming the question when light fingers brush my bare shoulder. Beatryx stands beside me, her voice quiet. "Is my hair messy?"

The hand she touches me with is close, so I grab it and turn, leading us to an alcove, then a small sitting room. "Beatryx, what in the goddesses? Yes, your hair is a mess—what happened?"

For the first time since I've met her, she looks sad.

"I had a random encounter, and it felt good. And stop judging me. I felt loved the entire time. It makes me feel alive."

I don't judge her. I feel empathy.

Her hair is worse than I realized, but I do my best to set it right. Olyvia pinned it in a very specific way, and I'm incapable of doing my own hair. Honestly, I'm making it worse.

We pull every pin from her hair and let her curls fall, framing her face. She is striking.

It's not well received for a girl—or a woman—to go without a formal hair arrangement, but this will simply be Beatryx for the rest of the evening.

Music begins to play, and my companions dance with young lords from other kingdoms. I rest my hands, lightly clasped, in serene composure before my bodice, close my eyes, and sway to the music. A slight dizziness sets in. When I open them, I see Iyce surrounded by several young ladies-in-waiting. The look on his handsome face is disgusting.

Immediately, I think of the younglings that Sage and I watch over every night, with her flames and my mist combining to create an ideal shield of elements around them. How dare he take those babes from their homeland, from their mothers? Hatred fills me.

In need of a distraction, I turn my head before my face betrays me, then walk toward the edge of the ballroom, but I trip on my own hem. What is happening? Arms out, about to fall, strong hands catch me.

We rise together, hand in hand.

"I've got you," he says.

A nervous laugh escapes me as I grab his hands a little tighter and walk us to the center of the dance floor. The current tune subsides, but we quickly draw the attention of everyone.

I whisper, "What is your name?"

"Noa."

"All right. Do you know this next one?"

His eyes find mine, piercing straight into my soul. That answer suffices; I set my hands for the dance as the music swells, and Noa gathers me in his embrace. Together, we weave an invisible web of silk across the floor, never missing a beat. We glide over marble like butter, and he spins and twirls me with effortless beauty.

A soldier?

When the timeless piece ends and I return him to his post, he holds my right glove a little too tightly—and it becomes his. A shiver runs down my back as I walk away.

Before I can look back at Noa, a large hand wraps around my waist, pulling me into him. He lowers his mouth to my ear, quietly barking madness. "If you wanted to dance, my pet, you should have come to me."

Mist unfurls from my fingertips. He flinches, and I vanish into the crowd.

Combined with Krystelle and Beatryx, we share a strawberry beverage that Beatryx insists we toast.

"To this majestic summer solstice evening," Krys says cheerfully.

"To all the charming men in attendance," Beatryx adds.

And I finish it with, "To us."

Clank.

Everyone is a little more intoxicated now, and the music surges, shimmering through the ballroom like a spell. We step off the dance floor, and Beatryx goes straight to Shayn and Garrett, her laughter trailing behind her like a wild fragrance. Krystelle drifts shyly toward a high table, finally speaking to a man she has been exchanging glances with all evening.

Letting my head fall back, I glance up through the glass. The summer solstice moon is luminous and full, casting silver light across the marble floor. It's incredible.

On the dais, Queen Frost sits like a statue carved from ice, her gaze holding every breath in the room captive. The king laughs with high lords near the kitchen, where Sage slips in and out unseen, like petals opening at dawn.

Thirst prickles at me, so I start across the dance area toward a tall man holding a tray of flutes, until...

A woman I do not recognize steps into the ballroom. She is

dressed in a black gown that clings like smoke, the fabric catching the torchlight in sharp, silver edges. No one at this ball wears anything like that. It is bold, even defiant, and far too dark for a winter celebration.

Her beauty is striking, but something about it feels… arranged. Her cheekbones too sharp, her smile too smooth, her eyes too bright. As if she has been polished into this shape rather than born to it.

She glides toward the refreshment table, her fingers trailing along the crystal as if testing it. She plucks a flute of sparkling wine without looking, lifting it with unhurried ease. The musicians shift into a softer melody, and she tilts her head as if listening for something beneath the notes.

Guests lift their eyes toward her, unsure whether to stare or to look elsewhere. I am staring, and she moves as if she belongs here more than any of us. A prickle moves along my skin as I watch her sip from the flute, her eyes scanning the room with a veiled hunger.

Who is she?

Voices.

we see you we see you
we tattle when we see…

The air shifts. Winds begin to swirl around me, whispering dark secrets. Evil secrets. My vision blurs. The room spins slowly, and when I look upward again, the solstice moon is vanishing into the night sky.

we see you we see you
we tattle when we see…

I press my hands over my ears, but wooziness overtakes me. Fog thickens around my feet, yet the ballroom continues untouched. Beatryx charms both guards, and they're falling for it, toasting something unseen.

Then I place my eyes upon the king.

His voice booms through the hall, laughter echoing off the crystal chandeliers. But then I can't hear him anymore. The mist inside me is fighting something horrifying and wrong.

A sudden gust of wind tunnels through the center of the ballroom, and the candles flare, shudder, then vanish into darkness all at once. Gasps ripple through the crowd as the woman stands in the middle of the ballroom. Her eyes find mine instantly.

She lifts her hands high above her head and whispers something to the moon, and at once she is Mairi, the witch from the Forest of Shadows. Power ripples through the air as she sweeps one hand outward, and dark magic encases us, suspending the two of us in a tunnel of wind and silence. "Girl," she says, voice low and sharp, "you remember our deal."

Queen Frost rises from her throne and hurries down the steps from the dais and begins walking toward us. "What is the meaning of this?"

The witch flicks her wrist, and the queen is held back by an invisible force.

Garrett and Shayn break into a run, pushing through startled guests. But they can't reach me. No one can.

Inside the tunnel, the wind howls. My heart pounds as the witch leans close, her presence cold as winter. "Who is your mother?"

Why is she asking me this?

"Answer me, girl. Now!" the witch demands.

"Queen Frost is my mother!"

The moon disappears entirely, and the ballroom falls into pure darkness. A heavy tension settles through me as the candles and sconces flare back to life, and the musicians play as if they never stopped. Only Queen Frost stands frozen in place, her gaze fixed on me. A faint shimmer fades from her fingertips—the last trace of the spell she cast to halt the darkness at the very moment the witch vanished.

No one remembers what just happened.

Olyvia

As I stand alone on a high balcony above the ballroom, invisible to all, I watch the end of the solstice ball. This evening, my emotions are heavy because I miss my home. I miss Mykah. Tears slip from my eyes before I can stop them, and then I see the strangest thing. Myst stands in the middle of the ballroom, and she seems disoriented. Her mist flickers around her, as if it is unsure of itself. Then Mamá is at my side.

"We must get away from this castle. Now," she says, grabbing my hand.

We rush through the shadowed halls, the whole place tense with expectation. We slip through the servants' corridor and into the frost garden, where the roses have closed in the rising wind. When we reach the temple, we stop. My mother gives a small nod, and we step inside.

Candles are lit one by one, their steady flames casting long shadows across carved pillars and painted icons. The scent of beeswax mingles with a faint trace of old incense. Acolytes move silently, their robes sweeping the stone floor, tending the altars and refilling the shallow bowls of oil. In the center of the temple, a single brazier glows with low embers, offerings resting at its base. A priestess kneels before the main altar, whispering an invocation that seems to fill the chamber.

"Are we under their protection here?" I ask Mamá, who looks disheveled, her braid half undone, her eyes fixed on the candle flames as if they might speak.

"What is it, Mamá? Tell me. What is happening?"

I stare at her, waiting.

"We are safe here," she says at last. "The gods of this temple will not allow her sight to reach us." She touches my arm. "Come.

There is a place where we can speak without fear."

She leads me past the main altar and through a narrow side passage, the air cooling as the light fades behind us. At the end of the corridor, she opens a small wooden door, revealing a quiet chamber meant for private prayer. Only a single candle burns inside.

"This will do," she whispers. "No one will hear us here."

She starts pacing, her hand pressed to the back of her neck. Finally, she speaks. "Mairi, the witch who conspired with Queen Frost, is with Myst."

I lose it.

"What? We must get back. Myst needs us."

My mother shakes her head. "The witch will bring no harm to her. She is only trying to gather information." She pauses, her voice low. "I had pondered the thought before, but now I am certain Mairi senses my presence in Sneeuwvlok."

18

Arkaik Alpynz

A King Beckons

Myst

Standing at the wide balcony doors of my chamber, I stare out at the Whispering Woods, but all I can think about is Mairi and the chaos she left behind. The witch is gone, yet I've been confined to my chambers "for my safety," with no answers and no word from anyone. The silence gnaws at me as I cross to my dressing table, frustration rising while I pinch color into my cheeks.

I decide I will ride to Grandpapá's cottage today—if this strange confinement is lifted. Or if I can find a way to slip out on my own. He was not at the ball last night, and I have much to discuss with him.

A sharp knock echoes through my chamber, startling me.

Captain Edwin of the Royal Guard stands outside the door, posture crisp, voice low. "The King has requested your presence. I will escort you."

He walks a pace behind and to my left—close enough to protect, far enough to respect. His boots are all I hear against the stone as we wind through the palace's quiet wing toward the King's private library. Beneath my composed exterior, something tightens under the weight of being summoned.

The first thing I see in the library is my mother at the window. The queen stands perfectly still, her posture pristine, head held high, hands folded neatly before her. I dread the moment she turns.

The king speaks.

"Arrangements have been made. You will travel throughout the realm in preparation for your upcoming wedding. Glaycyr Falz, then Crescere Moonz."

He steps out from behind his desk, crossing to the far side of the room—deliberately distancing himself from where the queen stands—before continuing his one-sided commands.

"You will be accompanied by Lady Beatryx and one other of your choosing. You may ponder that."

At his words, the queen turns sharply, her face taut, eyes narrowed to slits. "Lady Beatryx has no business going. She—"

The king raises a hand, silencing her instantly, his gaze never leaving mine.

"Iyce departs for Glaycyr Falz this evening. Once you arrive, you must make things right between the two of you." He pauses, then adds, "Crescere Moonz is a gift, my daughter. You've never seen the crescents collide—but now you will. It is part of this realm's historia, and you must understand it."

"Saddle my palfrey," I command, authority ringing clear.

"Which one? And how about 'please' and 'thank you?'" Hayze asks, rolling her shoulders sharply.

"It's been a bad day, and I need a release. Ready Aspen," I retort.

"You are a princess from one of the three most powerful kingdoms, wearing the finest clothes, having just attended a ball—probably in your honor—and you're knotted up and needing release?" Hayze all but screams as she struts over to the powerful horse, rubbing his cheek. He neighs, signaling the bond they share.

"You will never understand. Ever," I snap, walking to my magnificent stallion—Aspen—snow white, with silver undertones fading to black. I pull an apple from my satchel, sling it over my shoulder with a huff, and rub his muzzle as he snorts and accepts the offering.

"Where are you going, anyway?" Hayze asks, grabbing the bridle and reins.

Unable to stop myself, I hiss, "Don't worry about it. But please—deliver this list to Jessye."

Once Aspen is ready, I mount him. With a soft kick, he trots obediently through the wide open stable doors. We move quietly around the back of the castle and down the frosty path lined with berries and thyme, finally reaching the forest's edge, where snow falls lightly.

I shouldn't be so rude to Hayze. Nor should I allow jealousy to take hold. We have an understanding, and despite the handful of times we've shared, I know I'll marry Iyce. I also know I'm attracted to men—but I've never been with one, so I have no idea what to expect. Is a man gentle? Will he be so focused on himself that I'm left frustrated?

Hayze makes my head spin. She's careful not to push me too far, but I ache to know what it would be like to feel a man's touch—and she cannot give me that. Still, I must see her again soon.

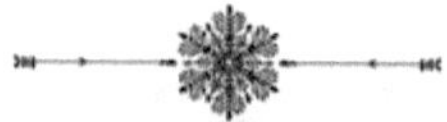

Hayze

I will do just that, I think as I hastily straighten the stables and stride out, my mood sharp. She needs release—and so do I.

The path stretches longer than it should as I walk it, agitation rising, fingers dragging through my short hair. I saunter into the servants' quarters and head straight for the tiny room that conceals the maid with jet-black hair.

I lift the iron latch, wondering if she barred the door. She did not. Who else comes here unbidden? I close it behind me and secure the latch, sealing us in secrecy.

"Hello," she whispers.

I don't hesitate before my mouth is on her full, arresting lips—my tongue sliding delicately over them, biting gently as she unbuttons my tunic. I shrug it off while she unties the fabric of her dressing gown and lets it fall away.

Her body hinges on my breath in a way that's different from Myst. Her bosom is small, her nipples begging to be taken. Myst's breasts are full and heavy, and I love them—but this is a welcome change.

Jessye loosens the laces of my breeches, her eyes lingering as if she can feel the storm inside me. She parts the flaps with restrained care and finds me, her fingers coaxing pleasure gently, aware I am tightly wound and cannot surrender easily.

Myst does not give me pleasure because I will not allow it. Enough of Myst. I have to get her out of my head.

I grab two handfuls of Jessye's hair, moaning softly. She senses the sound rising in me and slips two fingers into my mouth, silencing it before it escapes. I taste her skin as ecstasy overtakes me, the haze thickening around us.

I guide her to the small bed. A little too roughly, I bend her over and give her two hard slaps to her bare ass.

Then I spread her legs and drop to my knees behind her, shoving my tongue into her warmth—hard, exactly how she likes it. I move with relentless force, hands gripping her thighs as I hold her open, licking without pause until her sweetness coats my tongue.

I love to please. Tonight is no exception.

"This was unexpected," Jessye murmurs drowsily once we're spent. "Is something troubling you?"

I lift the pitcher and pour water into her basin, then dip a cloth infused with thyme and sage and move slowly over the most intimate places I've undone. Then I rinse the cloth and take care of myself.

"I missed you," I say quietly.

I leave Myst's list of chores on the side table and fill the space with a sparkling haze. Carefully, I pull the door closed and latch it, leaving Jessye suspended in her trancelike sleep.

As I step from the dim servants' quarters, Iyce enters, his shoulder brushing mine as if I am nothing at all. I pause in the shadows and watch him stride down the hall.

He stops at Jessye's door, fingers testing the latch. It yields—I could not lock it back. He pushes inside without hesitation.

Damn Jessye. She opens herself to anyone, and I let her touch me as if it meant something. But she has flings, just as I do. And Iyce—he has one thing I don't. A cock. Perhaps that was the hunger she craved tonight.

My thoughts burn, then circle back to Myst.

The stables are quiet. Aspen is gone—meaning she's still out there. I hope she's safe. The woods are vast, the snow magical, but unpredictable.

The small room tucked within the stables welcomes me back. I shed my garments and sink into bed. Thinking of her, I touch myself while listening to the soft whinnying of the horses.

19

Arkaik Alpynz

Myst

Beatryx is thrilled to join me on the journey across the realm. I've now decided on my second traveling companion. There's only one other person I trust, and I hope she will accept.

Please say yes.

"Have your attendants pack your warmest clothing. The first kingdom we'll visit is much colder than this one, being farther north," Beatryx says matter-of-factly while Olyvia braids our hair for dinner.

"I'm not doing well with the cool weather lately, and I'm not sure why. It's like my body is turning against me." I find comfort in Midnight, my fingers tracing the softness of her ears. *What is wrong with me?*

The mirror reveals the elegant fishtail braid—yet another lovely braid—before I move to the lounge with my best girl, Midnight. She follows close behind and hops up beside me, her presence a comfort. Leaving her is upsetting, but Sage promised to keep an eye on her. She'll be fine.

Olyvia breaks her silence while drawing an ornate comb through Beatryx's hair, a delicate piece carved from polished bone, its teeth smooth and spine etched with curling floral motifs. "You have several lovely wool scarves that will keep you warm on the journey and once you arrive."

Beatryx can't help herself. "Wool undergarments, hmm. That could be interesting."

With a final twist of ribbon, Olyvia secures Beatryx's braid before I speak. "Beatryx, tell us about Glaycyr Falz, since you've been there."

Beatryx crosses the room and drops into a chair across from Midnight and me. "Where do I begin?" she asks lightly. "Steam rises constantly from the ice, veiling everything in motion, while pine and evergreen follow you wherever you go, cleansing you to your soul. The castle holds its warmth thanks to the many hearths—each built to welcome you back from the cold and the outside activities."

Olyvia raises an eyebrow. "Such as?"

"Archery," Beatryx says, gaze shifting to the windows as if the scene unfolds before her. "You know this, Myst—because that's how your Grandmamá met your Grandpapá."

Eager, Olyvia breaks in with a smile. "How did they meet? Please elaborate."

Beatryx clearly enjoys *historia*, and as she does, I wrap my fingers around the snowflake necklace and continue the tale she loves. "Grandmamá was the daughter of a prosperous farmer in Glaycyr Falz. Grandpapá swore to marry the woman who won first prize in the ladies' archery competition and make her Queen of Arkaik Alpynz. He assumed it would be the princess. Guess who won?"

Olyvia throws her hands up in shock.

"Yes—Grandmamá. That's why my mother's skill with the bow is unmatched."

Olyvia's eyes shine as she reaches for my hair, loosening the fishtail braid and pulling it gently apart. "That is an incredible story."

It weighs on me that my mother took every one of Grandmamá's bow-and-quiver sets, leaving me with only faint memories. "She used one of Grandmamá's favored sets when she miscalculated and carved this lovely mark across my cheek."

"Miscalculated?" Beatryx blurts. "That explains the scar. You never told me—and I didn't ask."

I turn to her with a sigh. "Now you know."

And I know I'm not the only one who sees the scar as a rare mis-strike. She always strikes true. This time, my face was chosen. Punishment—nothing more. I will never tell Beatryx it happened because we passed the training yard. Maybe one day, I'll learn archery.

In need of a change, I announce, "Ribbon time."

Olyvia looks puzzled, so I explain. "We mark garments for packing by tying a ribbon to the hanger. The attendants handle the rest."

She nods. "How can I assist with your hair accessories?"

I meet her gaze. "Will you come with us? Bring what you need. Let your hands weave our hair with your gift—most of all, the flowers."

Her expression answers before her voice. "We shall show the ladies of Glaycyr Falz a new art of the hair," she says, smiling.

The three of us stand in my dressing closet, tying linen ribbons to my warmest garments while I finish the story of my grandparents' love.

"Grandpapá gifted me the snowflake necklace after my eighteenth birthdate. It was the one he placed around Grandmamá's neck when she won the contest. I never remove it."

Beatryx and Olyvia savor the sweetness of the story as we continue tying ribbons onto the hangers that hold the wool-lined garments.

A knock rattles the chamber door. Beatryx opens it. Jessye stands there, cheeks flushed, clutching something awkward.

"Myst requested these," she says, holding out a bundle of mismatched socks tied with twine. "They've been counted and arranged by shade."

Beatryx blinks before taking the bundle. Olyvia's expression softens, her gaze lingering on Jessye with quiet pity. Heat coils inside me.

So Hayze did give her the list.

Jessye waits, uncertain, until Beatryx sets the socks aside with forced composure. "You've done well. Go on now."

Back in the closet, the tension returns. The sweetness of my necklace story twists into guilt. I've dragged Jessye into my jealous whims. I should never have done that.

Another knock—heavier. We glance at one another and say in unison, "Shayn."

He enters, finding us among ribbons and wool. His gaze locks on Beatryx, and something unspoken passes between them before he clears his throat.

"Allow me to guide you to the dining hall. That's why I'm here."

"Of course you are," I reply. "Let's go."

Garrett waits in the corridor, a blade tracing lightly over his nails in idle habit. He laughs softly and holds up a folded parchment.

"I found this on the stone floor."

It's the list I gave Jessye. Heat floods my face. I snatch it, crumple it, and toss it onto the dressing table as if it never mattered. *I should burn it.*

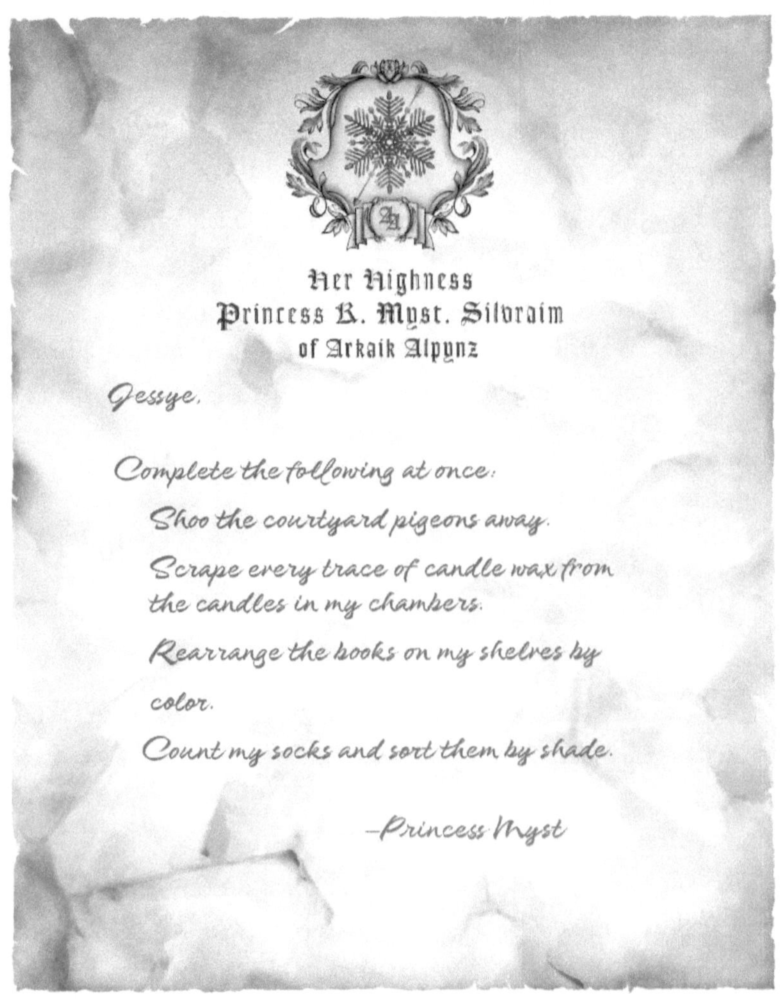

"I'm starving," I say, stepping past him.

My guards—and now companions—fall in behind us.

Inside the dining hall, I see Iyce speaking to Jessye, smiling with triumphant satisfaction. My skin crawls. No one is untouchable to him. Even though I do not want the man, I am exhausted by the humiliation.

Not again. Not in front of everyone.

Mist must be flooding the floor, because Shayn and Garrett grip my arms as Beatryx murmurs, "Myst, breathe."

My mother meets my gaze. I direct her gaze to Iyce.

Then I turn and leave.

"I will console Myst," Olyvia says, and Beatryx agrees.

When Olyvia catches up, I stop and wipe the angry tears from my cheeks. "I don't care what he eats, licks, or fucks—just don't do it in front of me."

Behind me, Olyvia says quietly, "He's a husband only briefly."

Back in my chambers, I bathe. Olyvia brushes my hair, and our words circle the magic I cannot master.

Why can't I control it the way they expect me to?

Shadow enters, ready to assist. Olyvia withdraws.

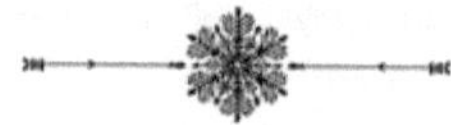

Beatryx

Shayn and Garrett remain where the queen gestures, halting them from following Myst. Her gaze flickers to Iyce—then freezes on me.

She's firing arrows, but I don't care.

My anger settled deep when Myst told me the truth about her scar. I feel no guilt—but I do feel blame. Perhaps that's why Myst and I connect.

"There's no need for customs this evening," I say. "Dine with me so I'm not alone."

We sit. Wine flows. The raven-haired girl approaches, eyes lowered—the same one who brought the matching socks to Myst's chambers.

Damn, her ass is lush.

Does it look better than mine?

Why do I think like this?

Iyce approaches. I whisper, "I'll handle this."

Once he's gone, I murmur to my boys, "Bathhouse?"

Sage

"Olyvia, this is a nice chess move. When does the group leave for Glaycyr Falz? How much time do I have to prepare potions you may need?"

My brave daughter answers, "I think within three days' time. Iyce will leave this evening, and the king and queen are striving to steady the kingdom's image by putting Myst back in his presence because of how heated the two of them are anytime they are near each other."

Before my next words, I roll my eyes. "That brute is something else. Tomorrow morning, I'll make a list of the herbs and petals I'll need, then I'll get busy—because you'll want them for what I have planned. For the known and unknown. Once everyone is asleep, I'll ward the carriages with a protection spell to the best of my ability. This realm unsettles my magic, and I suppress it still further to conceal myself from the witch."

Silently, I step from my small room, dagger at my thigh, cloak drawn dark around me, and move toward the royal stables. The air is unusually thick with mist and haze this evening, and I'm not sure whether that helps or hinders me.

Once I see my opening, I sprint toward the sight my eyes are set on. Now I need to determine which carriages will be used for their journey. The king and queen both wield powerful magic, and if I ward the wrong ones, they will most likely trace it back to me. Hopefully Hayze is busy fucking the new maid, since the area I need is connected to the horse stables.

Inside, I glance over my shoulder to ensure I'm alone before moving closer to the first carriage. This one clearly belongs to the king, and I doubt they would travel in his private means of transportation.

As I continue toward the next carriage, I hear, "We meet

again."

His silky voice sends shivers down my back, and I halt as he moves closer. I close my eyes tightly to compose myself, then turn to the handsome man and bow. "Sire."

He corrects me gently. "I thought we had already established that bowing to me was not necessary."

With blushed cheeks, I rise to stand before him. An innocent smile forms on my lips as I reply, "I will agree to that—if you could do me a favor?"

He steps closer. "Name it."

This man is weak, practically melting like butter as I make my request. "I am in the process of preparing a list of necessities for the princess' travels, but I'm uncertain which carriages will be used."

The lie drips from my lips too easily, and he accommodates without hesitation. "Ahh, let's see. It appears equipment has been pulled for these two."

We walk toward a pair of grand carriages—far more than simple transportation. They are small palaces on wheels, designed to exude regal splendor.

Concern shows plainly on my face because this is pure ignorance. *Why flaunt who's inside a carriage on a journey? Goddesses.*

"Thank you, Sir—"

He interrupts abruptly, placing a finger against my lips. "Shh. Sleet. Please call me Sleet. Allow me to walk you back to the castle. Besides, if these responsibilities press upon you late into the night, an assistant can be offered."

No one rattles me, but this man puts me on edge. I hold his gaze with effort as I respond, "The fault lies with me. I neglected to send someone earlier, and when remembrance stirred, the hour was late—so I resolved to see it through myself."

Sleet offers his arm, insistent. I relent, threading mine through his. The strength feels good—too good. Dangerous.

"Where is your room?" he asks. "I will escort you."

I shut that down immediately. He feels too good. Too many things about him stir something empty inside me—but I am here for one reason, and a fling with a king is not it.

Once inside the castle, I thank him for his kindness and head straight to the kitchen.

That was intense.

Queen Frost

Heavy panting. My voice, raw and demanding.

"Harder."

He obeys—gripping my hips, driving into me until I shatter. My hands clutch the footboard, my body arches, and when it is over, I scream, "Get out!"

He scrambles to pull his breeches over the very thing that wrecked me, tosses his tunic around those sculpted shoulders, and leaves without a word.

From the moment I saw him guarding the back entrance to the castle—my secret entrance—I wanted him. The night was predictable.

Now, wrapped in a warm robe that feels nearly as good as he did, I sip wine and step onto the balcony, letting my thoughts consume me. From the east side of the castle, I often watch the courtyard below.

The air is heavy with haze tonight, but movement in the stables catches my eye.

Well, what do we have here?

The king—my husband—and the new steward.

Anger coils in my chest. *What is he up to? And why does she fall into it?* The woman appears sharp, grounded. But Sleet is painfully beautiful, and even the strongest minds bend toward beauty.

I must keep myself in check. A crazed woman is not attractive, and I refuse to be seen as anything less than sovereign.

There is only one thing that will distract me before I do something reckless.

My long legs carry me to the wooden doors of my chambers. I throw them open, step into the corridor, and speak the word that binds frost to my will. It races ahead—searching, sensing—then finds him and brings him back to me.

"Hello," I purr. "Ready for round two?"

His tunic already lies on the floor. I kneel before him, making quick work of the laces at his breeches, drawing them down— because I need the weight of him in my hands. His fingers tighten in my hair. In this moment, he is the king I bow to tonight.

"Lay on my bed," I order.

I mount him with intent, moving slowly at first, savoring the stretch as he fills me. Then I drive myself against him—harder, faster—until Sleet and Sage blur and vanish from my mind.

Fuck the king, I think as I let this handsome man ruin me again.

20

Arkaik Alpynz

Myst

Beatryx and Olyvia walk directly behind me as we exit the castle's main entrance. The inner court is alive with a controlled flurry of preparation while the final arrangements for our concealed journey take shape. Two carriages ease into position, their lanterns casting unsteady light across the stone pathways. As the handlers ready the horses, I learn that forty guards will ride with us.

We are expected to travel for three days with only brief halts— just enough to give the men and horses minimal rest. Stopping is always a risk—one never knows what or who is lurking in the shadows, wide-eyed and hungry. The thought sends a shiver down my nape.

Beatryx looks like a snow maiden in her taupe dress and matching cape, and as usual, she is stunning. Olyvia wears a simple traveling dress, her cloak drawn close against the cold. Her golden-streaked hair is woven into several braids, each strand catching the light. There is an effortless strength to her beauty, something steady and sure beneath the surface. A steel-gray wool dress was chosen for me—the royal colors of Glaycyr Falz, Iyce's kingdom.

Shadow's voice finds me, then her loving arms come around my shoulders as she pulls me close. "Safe travels, my sweet child. Before long, you will be right back here, giving me all the particulars—good, bad, and ugly.”

We laugh as I say, “Most likely ugly.” Then we both smile sadly, because of the nostalgic truth.

No formal goodbyes are exchanged between my parents and me, unsurprising given everything. The queen is disappointed because I left the dining hall early last night. Regardless, I have decided to experience something positive from this trip. *One thing is certain—it will not be Iyce. Never Iyce.*

The last trunk is loaded, and the horses seem anxious.

“Step inside, damsels,” Shayn instructs, motioning Beatryx and Olyvia toward the first carriage.

Beatryx giggles softly while Olyvia slips her satchel from across her body and holds it at her side before stepping forward.

Wind stings my cheeks, mist drifting from my fingers in thin ribbons. I’m tense. Then Garrett appears from the far side of the second carriage—the one I will ride in.

We exchange a committed look before I turn toward my home, telling myself to detach. Still, before stepping inside, I glance back once more, guilt settling in my chest at the sight of who watches from a window high above.

I once thought of her as my closest ally, someone I trusted beyond doubt. But after seeing her in hushed words with Iyce, every trace of that closeness is deadened.

A flash of noir hair, and the curtains sway back into place.

Garrett’s outstretched hand moves me forward.

Once inside the royal carriage, I am swathed in luxury. Plush ice-blue velvet seating, thick tapestries lining the walls, silver sconces holding tiny candles that cast a warm glow. In the corner, drinking water, tea, and freshly baked pastries await—though they won’t last long.

Beneath the seat is a concealed compartment for blankets and pillows, and below that, a small arsenal of weapons that will do me no good. *I wouldn’t know what to do with any of them.* Still, I commit the sight to memory—four daggers and two short swords, gleaming with promise not meant for me.

"Walk," the coachman calls, and we move.

I pull the drapery aside to watch the drawbridge lower. It feels as if I'm being torn from my warmest blankets as Arkaik Alpynz fades. I've left the castle many times—into the Whispering Woods, to the fishing village—but this is different.

With my palms pressed to the window, my face between them, I watch as we enter a western forest I've never seen before, then finally turn northeast—toward Iyce.

I don't want refreshments yet, but boredom draws my attention to the basket. Inside, I find a folded parchment tied with ribbon. My hand goes straight to it.

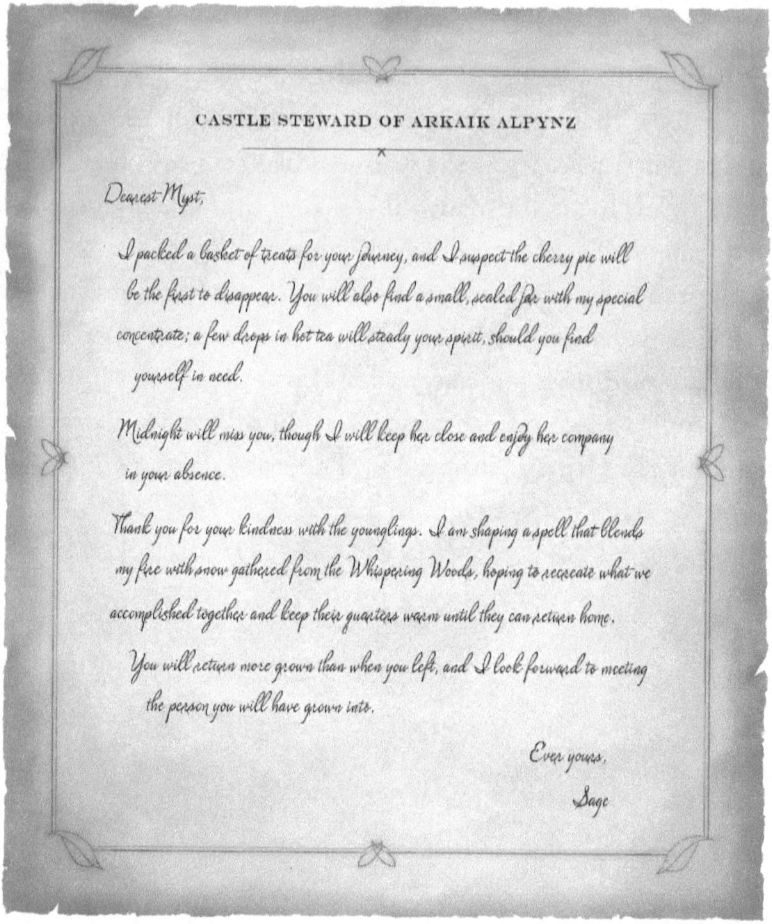

> CASTLE STEWARD OF ARKAIK ALPYNZ
>
> Dearest Myst,
>
> I packed a basket of treats for your journey, and I suspect the cherry pie will be the first to disappear. You will also find a small, sealed jar with my special concentrate; a few drops in hot tea will steady your spirit, should you find yourself in need.
>
> Midnight will miss you, though I will keep her close and enjoy her company in your absence.
>
> Thank you for your kindness with the younglings. I am shaping a spell that blends my fire with snow gathered from the Whispering Woods, hoping to recreate what we accomplished together and keep their quarters warm until they can return home.
>
> You will return more grown than when you left, and I look forward to meeting the person you will have grown into.
>
> Ever yours,
>
> Sage

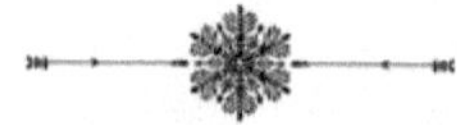

Olyvia

Beatryx describes in detail every dress, cloak, pair of slippers, and piece of jewelry packed in her trunk—and we haven't even taken our first break yet. I now know the full historia of each gown she owns and what realm it came from, as she continues to enlighten me with more specifics. I must pay attention; somewhere in all this chatter, there will be something worth remembering.

A faint hum brushes my ears—soft, almost imagined. It lingers at the edge of hearing, then dwindles as Beatryx opens a book, the pages worn and smudged from use. A glimpse of its illustrations sends my eyes wide as I turn away—figures entwined in ways that spark a startled thought. *Oh my, goddesses.*

Beatryx is likable, and I believe she genuinely cares for Myst, but I cannot let her near my satchel. She must never see what I carry. If she sees my potions, she'll start asking questions. I slide the satchel closer to my side, tucking it beneath the fold of my cloak.

The hum swells without warning, encasing me in a resonance that apparently only I can hear. I know what this is.

A female spirit. A banshee. Loud screams that depict death.

As the carriage winds its way higher among the mountains, I watch for danger through the window while Beatryx sleeps through the clip-clop of the horses' hooves. Panic grips me, for I seem to be the only one who hears the distant screams. *Can Myst hear them?*

Before something terrible happens, I need a reason to step from this carriage and face the creature. *Think, Olyvia.*

I bang three times on the roof of the carriage, as instructed should dire need arise, then slip one of the elixirs from my satchel into the front pocket of this constricting dress.

The coachman pulls the reins tighter—leather gloves straining against leather, then releases three or four times, each with a steady, "Whoa now, easy girls," and we slow to a stop.

"What seems to be the problem, Miss?" asks the coachman.

"She requires a private moment," I say, gesturing toward Beatryx as she begins to move and mutters, "Yes, truly—it will be a relief to stand. Where are we?"

"We're coming upon the Streams of Dreams Lake," the coachman says, resting his boots against the wheel and watching the road ahead in silence.

I take Beatryx's hand, fully aware that if everything goes according to plan, she will serve as my bait. Myst is asleep and is not to be awoken, which explains why she hasn't heard the spirit's screams. We begin making our way into the thick forest when the three unique streams appear. They wind mazelike around snow-covered trees, each one a distinct, sparkling shade of blue. Beatryx heads straight for them.

"Be careful," I say, but it's too late.

The banshee steps from behind the tree. She is ethereal. Her red hair spills past her waist like blood in water, and her eyes are the color of the streams, glassy and ancient. Her face is flawless, lips full and cheekbones sharp as moonlight. Though the air is freezing, she wears only a white flowing dress, its crimson ribbons cinched at her waist like a binding spell. Then she sings—a lullaby so haunting it seems to rise from the soil itself—and Beatryx drifts closer, helpless beneath its pull.

> *come take my hand young maiden*
> *and I will take yours . . .*
> *we will run through the meadows*
> *and swim in the streams . . .*

Beatryx is in a full-on trancelike state, and I fight hard not to be. *This damn hymn.* I pray to Athena, Goddess of Protection. I must move quick when the banshee reaches for Beatryx.

To protect my mind, I pull a strand of my hair and let it sear between my fingertips until it becomes my ward. *And here we go.* With my hands thrown up and my fingers splayed like webs, tiny sparks begin to fall, severing the chance of a connection. I place myself between the chameleon and Beatryx and shove her into the snow, out of reach. The angry witch's identity pushes through the camouflage of a young maiden—and it is truly horrifying.

"Close your eyes, Beatryx!"

Pure horror is what I see. Long, black, knotted hair flows around the creature as the wind picks up. Unable to look away, I see a large black hole where a mouth should be and empty sockets that shine red where eyes once appeared. Its limbs dangle loosely from its body, and the banshee is coming straight for me—because I prevented it from taking its maiden.

Ready to end this, I cry out, "Kavra!" Fire releases from my palms and crucifies the banshee, leaving only a bookmark carved in the ghostly outline of the creature in the snow. If more are close by, we're in trouble. I hope that one was a stray.

When I look back, Beatryx is gone. *No, no, no.*

I run after her and grab both arms, which causes me to trip, pulling us down while she claws at me. Damn, this girl is stronger than I thought. And I know I deserve this—she was my bait, but someone had to be.

The potion is in my pocket. I wrench it free, bite the cork loose, and spit it out.

Beatryx cries intensely and this must stop. I need to get this elixir down her throat. I grab her hair, pull her head back, and put the bottle to her mouth, reciting the spell that will erase her memory.

Her throat opens—something she's had plenty of practice doing, I'm sure. The bubbling draught fills her mouth, and I force it closed with my hands until she swallows. She has no choice.

It's done.

I release her, and she collapses into the snow, breath coming in sharp, startled bursts. A moment later, I hear boots crunching fast across the ice—Shayn and Noa must have heard her scream. They're already closing the distance.

Please. This had to have worked.

Time for the act. I stand up, panting, then force tears as I relay my half made-up version of the story. "I thought I heard a banshee, and my fear scared Beatryx. She ran and fell—possibly hit her head!"

That's enough for Shayn, who's instantly on his knees at Beatryx's side. If I didn't know better, I'd think this boy cared for her. He pulls his water canteen from his side and gently sits her up, talking sweetly. "Tryx, I'm here. It's going to be okay. Drink this water for me, please."

Her eyes flutter open. When she sees Shayn, she seems relieved. He insists she drink, and she finally does.

Her next words could end me. "Where is Olyvia?"

Cautiously, I go to where she and Shayn are and kneel. "I'm here."

Her pretty eyes lazily find me. "Those were the most intriguing streams I've ever seen."

Whew. I silently thank Mamá for her potions.

Shayn walks Beatryx back to the carriage, and Myst stands outside her own and asks, "What happened?"

I give her the short half-truth, and she hugs me and says she's glad we're okay.

We're only halfway through the day, and if this is a sign of what the rest of the trip will be like, I'm not sure I'm up for it. Noa and I need to have a conversation as soon as possible. He is another person my mother has planted in the kingdom to watch on her behalf.

Beatryx has pulled Shayn into the carriage with her. I grab my cloak from the seat and approach Shayn's horse, already familiar from that night at a tavern.

While I stand there contemplating how I'm going to get in the saddle without pulling this long dress over my head, I hear a familiar voice.

"Do what you need to do, Olyvia." The shadow I was looking at is Garrett, holding the handle to a blade out to me.

"Thank you."

I drag its sharp edge up the side of the dress, splitting the fabric clean through. Then I make a matching cut on the other side. With the blade held between my teeth, I tear the loosened edges higher until the skirt finally gives me room to move. I hand the knife back to him exactly as he offered it.

Garrett looks at me a little differently now. Respectfully.

The ruined fabric hangs in wild strips around my legs, but at least I can swing onto a horse without tripping over myself. Garrett steps aside and welcomes me into the lineup.

In my fantasy world, I am a soldier now—while Shayn sits pretty in a carriage, I move up in rank.

Beatryx

"What happened back there?" Shayn asks.

I feel like part of my memory has been extracted, because what I do remember makes little sense. After a sultry little huff escapes me, I answer, "Streams. Beautiful streams in colors I've never seen before."

Shayn gently sweeps back the loose strands of hair from my face while I give him a vivid description of the colorful streams. Then I pull his face to mine, and we kiss.

"Thank you for staying with me."

Shayn is so handsome it hurts. He goes on about how the two of us need to find some quiet places to be alone in Glaycyr Falz, and I couldn't agree more. The thought causes a wild look to escape, and then he deepens our next kiss. I feel him hardening before he asks, "Do you want my cock now, Tryx? Tell me what you want."

My head falls back as the words break free. "Yes, I want it."

Shayn reaches over and latches the lock, which makes me tingle all over in anticipation. He moves to the seat across from me and punctures my eyes with his own as he unties the laces on his breeches, then grabs his sensual weapon of lust and begins to stroke himself in front of me.

Eyes still on mine, he demands, "Pull your skirts up, my lady."

And I obey—because I want his cock in me, not his hand.

Skirts up, I push them aside. Once he sees the lace, he pulls me over to him and slides one finger underneath the sheer silk, teasing me even more. Then he rips them right down the middle, grabs my ass, and gently lifts me onto him.

"You might want to find something to hold onto," he whispers.

And I do, two hooks.

Shayn slowly lowers me further onto him, and before the moan escapes, he presses his mouth to mine again. We move together to the rhythm of the horses pulling the carriage, until we both find pleasure. My fingers slip from the hooks, leaving passion imprinted on the metal.

Once again, after being with Shayn, I'm sore. *Damn, I may need to sit in the snow.*

Shayn finds the linen cloths and water and gently cleanses me, which feels nice. Then he takes care of himself. Aside from the smiles on our faces and the ripped undergarments I still wear, we hold the exact same shameless expression.

Garrett

Ever since our group stopped for the night, I've had odd thoughts jogging through my mind. Normally, I'm not an overthinker—I live in the moment, carried by the wind's course. But that's no longer the case.

Right now, I'm trying to understand why in the darkest hell one of Myst's main guards is in a royal carriage with Beatryx.

Her powerful influence, I understand. Hell, I've done things lately I never thought I'd do. But this is becoming fucking odd.

Then the door flies open, and Shayn carries Beatryx out.

Did they get married in the damn thing?

Shaking my head, I look away, then turn and walk toward the rest of the men.

"How's everything going over here, soldier? Your name

escapes me."

The young man looks over his shoulder, extends his right hand, and our hands clasp. "Noa, sir."

He seems confident—which I like. We need more like him. He wears half his hair in a high bun, with the rest cut short. A symbol I don't recognize is etched into the top of his right hand. When he sees my eyes follow it, he responds, "My family crest."

Noa goes back to setting up a tent with another guard, and I make my way over to the fire. The moment I sit, someone hands me a tankard of ale and settles beside me, holding one of her own.

"You drink ale now, Princess?"

Myst takes a long draw, then wipes the excess with the back of her dainty hand. She's so very beautiful—spectacular, really—and sometimes it's impossible to look away. But from the moment I was first introduced to her, I resolved to never look at her in any way except as her protector.

"That gentleman over there said it would warm me up, so I guess I do—for that reason alone."

I turn my head in the direction she's looking. Sure enough, one of our newest guards, Nicolas, is passing out ale.

"You've been sleeping a lot. Are you okay?"

She drinks again, draws a steady breath, and speaks solemnly. "I'll be fine. Are we making good progress?"

I pull the map from my satchel, unroll it, and mark where we started and where we are now. She listens closely, intrigued by the plan.

"After we rest here, we'll enter the Granite Mountains. Once through that narrow passageway, we hit the halfway mark."

Shayn and Beatryx—the newlyweds—come to the fire and settle beside us. Nicolas passes them each a cup of ale. Shayn drinks his quickly, eager for the warmth. Beatryx declines, her gaze fixed on the flames.

I excuse myself. "Keep to the fire, Princess. I must see to the others."

At the back of camp, I spot Olyvia working alongside the guards to raise a tent and step closer. She is striking—and from what I saw earlier, she clearly knows how to wield a dagger.

"Do you need some help, Olyvia?"

She looks at me strangely but continues pulling ropes, each one running perfectly through stakes in the ground. "I've got it, thank you," she responds, mallet in hand.

Craving solitude, I walk down a snow-covered hill toward a small stream. To relieve myself, I loosen my breeches and let a stream of piss cut into the snow—when footsteps sound behind me.

The moment I smell jasmine, I start hardening. *Damn.*

"I could help you with that," she purrs. Her hand slips around me and takes hold, her touch soft against my cock.

"Where is Shayn, Beatryx?"

Anger is what I want to feel, but her hand is teasing me, running her finger around the tip, then stroking me before she moves around and puts her lips on mine.

"Who cares," she whispers.

"You're hard to resist, Beatryx." The words leave me on a tight breath as she uses the beads with a steady stroke that forces a sound from me, leaving me no choice as she wets my length.

"Then don't resist what we both want." The selfish side of me surges—I seize the front of her skirt and lift it. *Oh, goddesses…* she wears no undergarments. Even better.

We fall hard into the snow. I part her legs and push deep. Lovemaking has no place here; there isn't time for it. We're going to fuck.

After she accepts it, I slam into her over and over, hard, until she finds release. Then I pull out and find mine all over her sweetness.

We walk to the stream and clean up. The water is cold but

refreshing.

Maybe it is wrong of me, but I will allow our group to sleep through the entirety of the night. Before my assignment at Arkaik Alpynz, I traveled on this route; it is no easy path. We'll need our strength.

Beatryx left me softened, and drowsiness settles over me after our escapade.

Olyvia

Dawn breaks, and before we take down the camp, I catch Noa alone. "We need to talk. What power do you wield?"

Noa's eyes hold mine. "Wind. Nothing like your brother's gift. Why do you ask?"

I glance from side to side, ensuring no one is near enough to listen, then lower my voice. "In what little time I've had, I have studied the Granite Mountains. Strange occurrences are recorded, though not one says what they are. Stay vigilant—always."

It has taken our group some time to make our way to the mountain's crest, and I cannot shake the strangest feeling. Something does not feel right.

When nothing looks unusual from my window, I lean over Beatryx to check the view from hers. She notices my tension. "Relax, Olyvia. There is nothing to worry about. The soldiers are rested, and our pace is steady. We're nearing the crest now."

Beatryx lifts a small stack of books from beside her. "Would you like something to read?"

I scrunch up my face. Hell no, I have no interest in her books. The thought settles in as I turn back to the window.

And... *Oh, my goddesses—there it is.*

I watch Beatryx's eyes go wide. She has seen it too, and her skin begins to pale as she looks at me.

"Beatryx, listen to me carefully. We are carrying precious cargo, something far more important—Myst. Anything can happen, and if it does, I need you to remain in this carriage. Do you understand?"

Beatryx nods. I continue to watch through the window—until a scream rises from one of the guards.

"Stay in the carriage, Beatryx!"

Her scream reaches me through the chaos. "Why aren't you staying in the carriage?"

Turmoil encases me, and I beg Nafanua, the Goddess of War, to give me strength right as I hear Garrett holler, "Man down! Fight!"

What is this? Rock soldiers tear free from the mountain's side, and I watch them closely. The sound comes first—not a roar, but the grinding shriek of stone dragged against stone, vibrating through my teeth and into my bones. How do they attack? They are strong yet slow, and the fire magic I carry within is useless against stone. In power, I am no help. I can fight, I can take up any weapon, yet what stops them?

I run toward the carriage that holds Myst, but another soldier rips himself free from the mountain, granite cracking under the strain. They are dark gray, identical in form—massive creatures of living stone, towering so high my breath stutters.

The mountain shudders, and a massive hand reaches for me. I'm about to be crushed. Then Noa bursts into view, wind roaring at his command. The force slams into the creature, driving it from the cliffside until it shatters, raining stone across the slope.

Okay, they must be dislodged.

"Noa, we need to tell the others how to stop them, but I must get to Myst and make sure she is safe. Keep using your wind!"

Two more are coming straight for us. Frantic, I grab the rope that hangs from the carriage, then quickly tie a lasso, hoping this will work. Methodically, I begin to swing my loop over my head, and Noa looks at me with huge eyes. As soon as I let go of the rope, I know my mark is true. It coils around the rock soldier's neck, and

I pull tight, snapping it sideways, dislocating his head. *Yes!*

I need a horse. The thought is heavy as I run through madness until I spot one. But before I can get to the animal, I am confronted by another rock soldier. He takes two heavy steps, and the mountain shakes violently and I back up. He is too close for me to use my lasso ploy.

Oh, my goddesses, I cannot believe what I am seeing. Beatryx is running straight for Shayn. Has she lost her senses?

I seize the moment and slip beneath the rock giant's outstretched arm, sprinting straight for Beatryx—but I'm too late. Two of them have boxed her in, and she's screaming like the banshee that nearly claimed her.

I loosen the knot on my lasso and send it circling above my head, watching for my opening. The moment the first one lifts its foot, I let the rope fly and hook its ankle, yanking the creature down. Its rock body shatters across the ground.

Once I find Beatryx again, I grab her and pull her with me, away from the second one Noa took down with that deceptive strike.

This is not ending. Shayn is fighting his ass off, and he somehow dislodges one of the rock soldier's arms free—but it keeps moving, and we're all wearing down. We have lost two men already.

What happens next is beyond reason, and I glimpse it before I glimpse her.

Mist begins to rise around our feet and legs and grows thick. My fire magic begs for release, but I hold it down with everything I have. Still, it beckons to connect with the mist, and rightfully so.

Garrett's voice booms above the madness. "Retreat now!" Men run in all directions.

I feel three sparks at my fingertips, and my fire connects to the mist, creating a force of activity that is unbelievable. Small water droplets hang in the air and fill the entire space around us, causing confusion. Once the space becomes saturated with these fire-dew droplets, they dissolve into mist, ending the rock soldiers who can no longer keep their balance. They begin to slip and become dismembered, leaving large and small pieces of rock all around us.

The last one collapses, and the world stills.

I brush dust from myself as I stand in the middle of the battlefield on this mountain. Broken stone litters the ground, sharp edges catching the weak morning light. Heat lingers at my fingertips, fading slowly, as if reluctant to leave me. I make my way toward the carriage, and Myst stands by the wheel, her eyes wide, her face pale.

I swallow hard. "It's over," I say, though my voice barely carries.

Garrett strides through the wreckage, his boots grinding over shattered pieces. His gaze sweeps the mountains, then snaps back to us. "Women in the carriages. Now." Garrett shoots Shayn a look of pure disgust before turning back to the group. "We move before anything else comes out of these peaks."

Myst slips into her own carriage without a word. Beatryx climbs into the one we share, and I stand there, my breath still unsteady. Garrett approaches and looks directly at me. "I saw you."

I climb into the carriage with Beatryx, and the door closes behind us. The wheels jolt forward, and the battlefield fades into the distance.

Women won that battle.

21

Glaycyr Falz

Myst

The gate begins to lower, chains groaning under its weight, rattling through the cold air. From the window, I watch the heavy slats grind downward, then slam into place, sealing us in—cutting me off from the world beyond.

Why do I feel trapped?

Behind the castle, glaycyrs rise as the sun casts a blush across the icy ridges, turning them into rivers of rose and gold.

A man approaches, his gaze lingering on the guards, one hand resting on the pommel of his sword as he studies them before speaking.

"Welcome to Glaycyr Falz. I am Millard, Captain of the Royal Guard. Exhaustion must weigh you down. It seems you are missing two guards—did you encounter trouble along the way?"

Garrett and Shayn dismount at the same time, lowering their heads in a respectful dip before Shayn speaks—for once. "Thank you in advance for the hospitality that will be bestowed. We are delighted to be your guests and welcome the generosity that will be shown to our princess."

I almost choke. The irony is sharp—Shayn ignores the indirect question about the missing guards entirely.

The door to my carriage opens, and I step out. The air feels cold, as though the kingdom itself breathes through stone. Garrett waits, and I rest my hand atop his as I descend, stopping before Captain Millard, who offers a respectful bow.

"Your beauty surpasses every account that reached us. In the name of this realm, I receive you with honor."

Olyvia and Beatryx exit their carriage and take their places at my sides. Our attention shifts to a tall, slender woman emerging from the shadows. Captain Millard gestures toward her. "This is Auxilia, steward of the castle. She will see to your comfort and guide you to your rooms."

He turns to Shayn. "Your horses and carriages will be tended at once. Come out of this freezing wind—we'll see you settled. A hot meal awaits."

Several young boys hurry forward, taking the reins and checking each horse's legs and tack. One offers water while another brushes frost from their coats. Once the animals are calm, the boys lead them toward the stables.

Auxilia regards me with composed seriousness. "I trust your journey was pleasant."

Beatryx and Olyvia glance at me, and we share a quiet, knowing look before I answer—something in her tone tells me she already knows the truth. "The journey was long, and we are in need of baths, refreshment, and sleep, please."

We follow Auxilia into the castle, which reminds me of my own home—yet different. The air carries a chill, sharpened by stone walls that rise high and echo with every step. Deep blue tapestries hang over the windows, their threads glinting faintly in the torchlight. The vaulted ceiling arches above us, carved with patterns that resemble the glaycyrs surrounding the fortress.

At the top of the staircase, she turns with eerie grace. "All has been prepared. You, Princess, will dwell in the royal quarters of the south wing. Your ladies will be accommodated in the guest chambers."

A rebuttal rises to my tongue, but Olyvia speaks first, clearly trying to keep things calm. "Thank you, Auxilia."

A young woman about Olyvia's age approaches, introducing herself as Clarina, the steward's attendant. Her voice bubbles with excitement—she has been expecting us. "Beatryx, Olyvia, come with me. I will guide you to your room. The east wing opens to wondrous views. It brings me joy to see you settled. Your things will follow swiftly."

They follow Clarina, leaving me with sullen Auxilia. At least I know they will be in the east wing.

"This way, Princess," she says, her voice low and thin, edged with something almost cruel. Exhaustion consumes me, so tonight I will follow this irritated woman nearly anywhere—and I do.

Auxilia moves about the chamber, her long, crooked fingers shaking faintly as she draws the drapes closed and folds back the bed. "Supper has passed, but I will have something light brought up. A hot bath has already been prepared."

The room is arranged nearly identical to mine in Arkaik Alpynz, aside from the fabric colors and portraits, and I'm mesmerized by it all. I feel grown—apart from my kingdom and my parents. *Perhaps this change will be kind,* I hope, before answering. "That would be most welcome. Thank you, Auxilia."

She disappears without a word, likely weighing which poison to slip into my meal.

The bathing chamber is divine. A sunken tub swirls with herbs that smell of crisp winter evergreen.

"I cannot believe I've endured this gown and its damn colors for three days. For what—a man who could not be bothered to greet me upon arrival?" I mutter as I strip off the clothes, never wanting to see them again.

Once deep in the tub, I sink into the water's lucidity, letting it hold me.

I miss Hayze.

The only passion I have ever felt has come from her.

I tilt my head back. Above me, the ceiling gleams with solid panes of glass, some cracked open to let cold air spill through like secrets from the glaycyrs. It threads across my face—a startling kiss of frost that deepens the bliss of the bath's heat.

I press crisp linen to my damp skin, letting it comfort me before wrapping myself in a warm robe. I dry my hair as best I can. Olyvia would usually braid it each evening, but tonight she is housed in another wing.

When I return to the main chamber, a rich aroma greets me— hearty stew, thick bread, and tea steeped hot and sweetened with honey. I savor the simple meal, and at last my exhausted body melts into soft blankets.

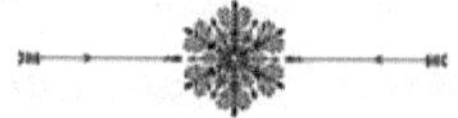

Olyvia

"The view is amazing!" Beatryx says as she steps into the chamber we will occupy, drifting toward the balcony to stare at the night sky.

I follow, and the sight explains everything. Incredible. The skyline glows in shifting shades of turquoise, ribbons of light threading through the dark.

A shiver runs through me as Clarina approaches from behind, speaking as if reciting from an ancient tome. "When two strangers meet without cause, it is the goddesses who wish it so. They whisper secrets, and light reveals the weight of their quiet plea."

"Who are the strangers?" Beatryx asks, her eyes never leaving the lights.

"It has not been revealed for centuries," Clarina replies. "But when their plea is fulfilled and their hearts turn toward one another, the colors will shift from turquoise to gold."

"Fascinating," I say.

"It is," Clarina adds. "Hungry?"

On the way to the kitchen—through dark corridors—we catch hushed voices from a side hall. Clarina slows, signaling for silence. We slip into the shadows just in time to see Iyce speaking privately to Auxilia. With a glance over his shoulder, he presses something into her palm. She closes her fingers around it.

We stay quiet as Clarina leads us down a different corridor.

"Follow me—I have the perfect idea." Her voice is light again, as if nothing happened. She sweeps ahead toward a staircase at the end of the hall, and after four flights down, we step into a magnificent, rustic kitchen—the only place in this cold kingdom that seems to hold any warmth.

The entire back wall is glass, and our eyes are struck by pure white snow and towering evergreens. Beyond them, an army of glaycyrs. If only I were an artist—I'd place the scene before me on a canvas in need, to be looked upon forever. Never have I seen anything like it.

A fire crackles in the stone hearth, drawing us in. The space hums with old charm—timber beams, dried herbs like gossiping old friends. The floorboards creak beneath our feet, proud of their years. A cast-iron stove and waiting cauldron sit ready for whatever tomorrow might bring.

Clarina walks to a wooden door past the glass wall, then turns back with a mischievous look. "Ever had snow cream?"

Beatryx utterly loses her composure, trying to speak through bites of it. "Thank you, all goddesses, in every realm! This is the best thing I have ever had in my mouth."

I tilt my head, unable to hide the look I give her.

She grins. "Well, almost."

She bursts into laughter, snow cream dripping down her chin. Clarina meets my eyes, and I shake my head. That's all it takes for the three of us to break into loud, helpless laughter.

22

Glaycyr Falz

A Ghost of Mist

Myst

"Myst. Myst…" Her voice presses against me, but my body does not respond. Sleep has wrapped me in something heavier than rest.

My eyes ease open to Olyvia's face, troubled and pale with worry.

"You had me terrified for a moment. Are you alright?"

It has never taken me so deeply. I consider her question.

With a soft touch, Olyvia lifts me into a seated posture. Her calm voice follows, unraveling the day's plans. A late luncheon with the ladies of the court is being held in my honor, only three hours away. The words land like a weight I am not ready to carry.

"Three hours!" My cry shatters the calm as I spring from the bed, my steps quick and uneven. "Oh, divine goddesses, how can I possibly choose a dress with barely any time at all?"

Olyvia closes the space between us and takes my shaking hands. Her tone is serene and unwavering. "You will be perfect. Nothing less."

The door swings open and Beatryx steps in, a basket overflowing with blooms in her arms.

"I ran into the gardener—he is gorgeous—and he insisted I take these lavish flowers for our hair." We will grace their kingdom with its own treasures."

Her hair seems to have grown overnight, cascading down her back in glossy waves. Holding a white petal to her head, she twirls with a teasing smile. "He swore he would show me the Glaycyr Gardens," she adds, eyes bright with mischief.

Olyvia guides me to the dressing table and begins tending to my hair as Beatryx pours a delicate porcelain cup of strong coffee, adding two neat lumps of sugar and a ribbon of cream.

Olyvia is amazing, and I do not know how I ever managed without her. She is so delicate, her touch guided by softness. She has made my hair look remarkable—and now we need to find a gown.

We walk to my trunk, and Olyvia lifts the lid. Her face tightens as she searches through the gowns, pulling at fabric as though something essential has gone missing. The silence between us grows heavier with each movement until I finally ask, "What is it?"

She meets my eyes, her expression carved with worry. "Nothing we chose is in this trunk."

"How?" I do not understand. I walk to the large windows, push the heavy drapes aside, and stare blankly at the view from the south wing.

After we fret, Beatryx seizes the moment. "We are strong and know how to improvise in any situation. And if we do not, we must learn. We need a plan—now."

Not a single dress I marked to be packed is here. Instead, the trunk is filled with unfamiliar gowns.

"How did this happen?" I whisper aloud. "I do not even have a seamstress here."

Olyvia gathers two of the gowns I had not planned to bring and inspects them with careful hands, muttering to herself. "I am no seamstress, but Beatryx is right—and I have an idea. We will use two gowns and create something new. Something warm. Something with style." She turns to Beatryx. "Can you find Clarina? Tell her we need a sewing basket at once."

Beatryx strides toward the door, pausing at the full-length mirror to perfect her look. She slips out, then leans back in with a grin. "I will find her and be back before you even notice I am gone." A quick wink, and she vanishes.

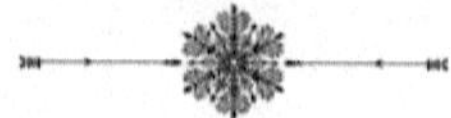

Beatryx

I need to find Clarina, but I do not know where to begin. The back stairway? No—I am unfamiliar with this castle. The main staircase? Even that feels daunting. I do not know the customs here. Myst believes I have been here before. I have not.

A deep sorrow settles over me. During a tender part of my life, while my father traveled to distant kingdoms, I remained behind, wrapped in the comfort of our estate, where familiarity was the only place I could breathe.

The choice is instant. I turn toward the room Olyvia and I share, trusting the current of other guests to carry me where I need to go.

As I round the first corner, I glimpse a woman standing in a doorway, speaking in a low, sultry voice. I step back, then lean forward cautiously, listening. I need to know everything.

"You have been nothing short of a gentleman. Thank you. Last night was pure bliss. So—will I see you again?"

Damn. I cannot see who stands on the other side of the door—only his large hand closing around hers, drawing her back inside before the door shuts.

Again is now.

I continue along the stone corridor in silence, deciding I do enjoy being noticed, and head toward the castle's main staircase. Arkaik Alpynz is cold—yet this feels colder in a different way.

The regal staircase welcomes me. I descend, my palm gliding along the banister as I absorb the castle's secrets. When I reach the landing, I stop.

What rises before me is nothing short of magnificence.

Hundreds of shimmering icicles hang from a great iron chandelier, glowing softly and chiming in the cool breeze drifting through the castle.

The moment feels pure—until a voice startles me.

"Splendid, is it not?"

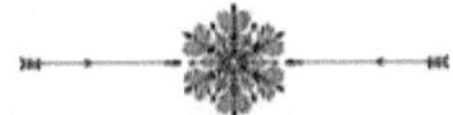

Olyvia

Myst is in pieces, and I am trying to hold us together. I hope Beatryx returns with a mending kit. *Please—let her hurry.*

What did Iyce give Auxilia last night? Was it a sleeping potion? Is that why Myst fell into such a deep sleep?

Not a single dress marked with a ribbon was in her trunk. Who would mix them up? There are too many questions.

From her trunk, I draw her warmest garments and hang them, intent on recreating what we can—at least until I speak with the castle's seamstress and have new gowns made. I have not seen a single royal here, nor any lord or lady of the court. I have no sense of their style.

"Princess, do you trust me?" Please say yes.

"Yes."

Myst needs security—then strength. I choose her kingdom's colors. A form-fitting ice-blue bodice, a single defining split climbing along her thigh, revealing the intricate snowflake art on her leg.

Tiny pins I use to thread flowers into hair line the table before me. Now I will use them to cut thread and dismantle one of the gowns.

Myst offers a sweet smile. "Thank you for all that you do for me, Olyvia. What can I do to help?"

The desperation in her eyes tells me she needs to be busy.

"Can you turn the second gown inside out? We can begin

pulling thread. And once Beatryx returns, we will have extra hands."

The first piece is already separated. I turn to the ivory velvet—it will keep her warm. I strip the wool blanket from her bed, tearing it as I begin cuffing her arms.

Too bad I cannot use my fire magic. Frayed edges would be remarkable. One day.

With a smaller needle meant for beads, I tear seams and pull thread until the fabric unravels, the edges ragged and organic.

A sheer chiffon will layer over the wool—loose and flowing, pinned tightly in precise places, mostly along her upper arms.

Arms that tell a fragile story. A girl guarded, yet longing for freedom.

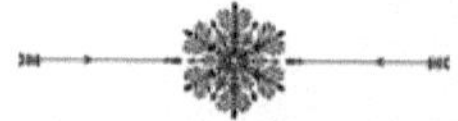

Beatryx

"Mother?"

I never knew emotion could strike so fiercely. Confusion, sadness, anger, happiness—yet loneliness weighs the heaviest.

I step back slowly, before I say something I might regret. Would it even matter?

She walked away from my father and me years ago, all because of the gods. I suppose belief fractures people in ways nothing else can.

I tried. Goddesses, I tried.

Research consumed me until my mind protested. She refused to hear any of it, rejected even speaking of it, scorching my thoughts into flame. That is reasonable... or is it?

I buried it as deeply as I could, but no veil is thick enough to hide the pain I carry each day. I loved her so much that I hope the pain she caused me never reaches her.

I dash.

Myst

The chamber door bursts open, and Beatryx stumbles through it, distraught.

I have never seen her like this.

"I take it you did not find Clarina," Olyvia says, words slipping around the needles clenched between her teeth as she pins torn bedding fabric around my arms.

Goddesses of every realm, please help us.

Beatryx begins to shake. My eyes meet Olyvia's, and we move at once.

She drops to her knees. We follow, collapsing into a tangle of limbs and tears.

In this moment, I realize this may be the greatest comfort a girl can feel—the strength of friends in crisis. The only thing that could surpass it is facing whatever, or whoever, has done this to her.

Through trembling breaths, Beatryx describes the sudden appearance of her mother. I brush her hair gently from her face. "You have never spoken of her before. I only know your father, Lord Blake."

She shares her historia, explaining that her mother left because of the gods, her beliefs never aligning with those of Beatryx or her father.

We stand and regain our composure, then Olyvia focuses on the final touches of my hair while Beatryx uses the powders we brought to give my cheeks and lips a splash of color.

"I do not understand why she is here. What is she doing—and with whom?" Beatryx frowns, then describes her mother so we will know who to watch for. Something about this woman feels wrong. We must be ready.

A knock interrupts us. I recognize it as Shayn. He and Garrett have come to escort me to the luncheon.

"Olyvia, will you be all right? Do you have plans?"

She stands amid fabric and thread, hair falling loose across her face. "I will begin a scavenger hunt to find Clarina—starting in the kitchen. And I hope to explore the castle."

Beatryx opens the door. Shayn whispers something that makes her giggle. Garrett remains in the corridor, ever watchful.

With them here, I feel a little less strained.

"Hello, damsels. Is everyone doing well on this fine afternoon?" Shayn asks, and the three of us snicker.

I rise slowly and turn. They all gasp. Even Garrett leans in, releasing a low whistle.

Olyvia and Beatryx circle me, delight bright in their eyes.

Their expressions unsettle me. "What is it? Is something wrong?"

They guide me to the mirror, and I gasp.

Mist curls around the entire skirt—*my* mist—and the effect is extraordinary. The gown feels untouchable.

An ice-blue, strapless bodice shapes my figure. Ivory chiffon drifts over the skirt. My arms are wrapped in warm fabric stripped from the bed, bound with the same chiffon. Every snowflake etched into my skin glows.

It is so different—so remarkable—that tears threaten, but I stop them at once.

"No, Myst—your face," Beatryx says, then spins Olyvia into a playful song and dance that draws laughter from me.

Shayn steps behind me and settles the tiara upon my head. Braids gather into a bun, strands left loose. Olyvia weaves flowers into it—an elegant touch.

Shadow would be proud.

Beatryx and I promise to return soon, then step into the hall, mist still unfurls around me.

"Breathe, Myst," Garrett says.

Olyvia

I hang the remaining dresses in the closet. Staying busy is the only way I will survive this, though hunger presses.

"Olyvia."

Clarina approaches, flustered. "How is everything going? I have not seen you or Beatryx since you arrived."

"Hello, Clarina. I am ready for lunch. We have had quite the morning." As we descend the narrow staircase, I explain the dress situation. "Let me know when we can visit the castle's seamstress."

The kitchen hums with activity. I follow closely as Clarina weaves between chefs and servers preparing extravagant platters—finger bites, baskets of bread, bowls of berries and cream.

So much food.

"Coming through," someone calls.

A tall, slender young man carrying two trays passes. One holds fragrant tea, the other steaming coffee.

"Hello, Clarina," he says with a wink. Her cheeks bloom pink.

Is everyone so taken with boys? I am sixteen—she cannot be much older.

Curiosity presses at my lips. "Who is he?"

Her eyes soften. "Come. Asher set lunch aside for us in my special place."

Hunger twists inside me. "Lead the way."

Fire burns between massive sheets of ice encasing the library's outer walls.

This is of particular interest—because I may be powerless here.

I follow Clarina up the spiral staircase to a high balcony where a table awaits. A window overlooks the winter gardens.

She points out sights, giving me a tour. We have a clear view of the Polar Gardens, where the luncheon is underway.

"That fountain is said to be cursed," she says.

She explains when I question her. "The whispers say its water froze the moment Iyce's mother—the queen—left the king. She cursed it, preventing anyone from finding her. Every stream froze mid-flow, never to fall again."

Indeed, the water is frozen. "Who is the woman meant to be?"

"The Lost Queen." Her eyes brighten. "There is Princess Myst. She moves with such elegance—and I love the flowers in her hair."

I watch Myst among the nobles. She looks composed.

And from here, I can study the gown styles.

Clarina is shorter, brown hair falling to mid-back, bright eyes always lit with joy.

"I could do your hair sometime."

She blinks. "You did that? Remarkable. Though I would look out of place."

We laugh. "We could find something simple."

Lunch eases my hunger, though my curiosity remains. I ask if she'll show me the library another day, and she agrees.

We leave her favorite place and head for the seamstress.

Myst

"They need more ice sculptures of Iyce. How many have we seen now?" Shayn gestures as we drift between warming tents—another introduction, another reminder that I am Iyce's future bride.

A pit forms in my stomach. Leaving my kingdom to live here...

I feel profoundly alone in this crowd. Hope tries to rise. I shape a smile across my face—a lie of happiness.

This kingdom is colder than Arkaik Alpynz. We gather in the Polar Gardens near the sea. Glaycyrs loom in the distance as flurries sweep past. I am grateful for the muff sewn into my cloak, warming my hands.

Faintly, I begin to hear lovely music and turn toward the direction it's coming from, noticing a trio of musicians—two women and one man. The women play harps, their fingers gliding so gracefully that the notes seem to shimmer in the cold air. I change course and follow the melody, lifting a warm cider from a passing tray as we walk.

Beatryx shivers beside me, so I link my arm with hers. Shayne and Garrett follow close behind, and the negative comments Shayne keeps muttering to Garrett about this kingdom don't escape my hearing. If I'm honest, I agree with him.

We stop, peacefully mesmerized by the harpists playing in perfect sync, their soft harmonies drifting beneath the strings. I could stand here all day listening to this soothing music and be perfectly happy.

Garrett catches the server before she moves on, plucks a cider from her tray, and presses it into Beatryx's hand, knowing she's cold.

Before the thought settles, a large hand closes around my hip, possessive enough to startle me; he looks at Beatryx, Shayne, and Garrett and says, "Excuse us," then leans close, the chill of his voice brushing my ear as he murmurs, "How did you sleep?"—and before I can answer, he takes my cider, places it into Shayn's hand, and steers me away.

Iyce guides me into the tent and draws me to his side, one hand settling at my waist in a gesture that feels less like comfort and more like claim.

"Father," he says, "it is time to introduce you to my future bride."

Bride.

The King looks exactly as I suspected he would—cold, cruel, and unmistakably Iyce's blood. He carries a more mature, handsome sigma to him, an unforgiving smile carved into his face. He steps away from the cluster of lords and ladies he'd been speaking with and turns toward us. Now I understand where the beast beside me gets his class. His father looks me up and down as he approaches, and mist slips from the tips of my fingers before I can stop it. I try to steady my breath, to hide the nerves—but it's too late.

"And she has magic!"

The King blurts it loud enough for everyone in the tent to turn. Damn. I have got to learn to control this, I think, smiling through the growing awkwardness. Annoyance sparks, and I let my own retort fly.

"I could fill this entire tent with it, causing vast confusion, Sire."

A wicked tilt of my mouth slips free before I can stop it—and he is suddenly lost.

23

Glaycyr Falz

EMERALDS OF TEMPTATION

Beatryx

I glance at Garrett, then Shayn, letting a sultry edge slip into my gaze.

"Before we go anywhere… are you two dismissed while Myst is with Iyce?"

Garrett straightens a little, as if reciting from memory. "If she is with her betrothed, yes. The contract states we step back unless summoned."

Shayn nods, already drifting closer to me.

"Perfect." I sweep my arms in a dramatic arc. "We need to explore. Myst will be occupied for a while."

Garrett speaks first. "I would like to see the training yards."

I answer before Shayn can steal the moment. "Absolutely. More warriors."

Shayn drifts even closer, a slow grin forming. "All warriors are not men, you know."

Garrett laughs and shrugs. "It is settled. Let us go, then."

The training yard is unlike anything I have seen before, and I know Garrett and Shayn must be thinking the same. *So many women.* Shayn called it—and he had no idea. The women spin swords through the air and around their bodies with the grace of an art form, standing in magnificent formations that shift as blades fly between them. These women likely make up a third of the army.

We close the distance as the general approaches. He fires one sharp question at Garrett and Shayn. "Care to join in?"

In an instant, they strip out of their tunics and seize weapons offered by the waiting attendants.

Standing at the border of the yard beside the general, I watch the mesmerizing skill unfold—men and women telling an untold story through their blades. The ringing strike of iron against iron will haunt my future dreams.

Both guards intrigue me in different ways, and I cannot fully separate the two. These stolen hours will not last forever, but I intend to savor them while I can—they pleasure me generously, and I enjoy it.

Lingering has its charms, but curiosity wins. I slip through the gates and into the town beyond, intent on discovering what lies outside the castle's hold.

My gown is modest enough that I might as well belong in a sanctuary—Myst insisted on something reasonable for afternoon tea. I only hope she's all right after Iyce drew her away from us and vanished beyond the tents. Today's dress is solid black, trimmed with green embroidery of foliage along the hem and down the long sleeves that nearly cover my hands. The material is thick and warm, wrapping close at the neck in a way I don't mind. Emerald clasps and cuffs adorn me, a trend I've grown fond of. My hair is bound in a low bun, softened by a few drifting wisps; Olyvia had no time for anything elaborate amid the chaos of the surprise wardrobe, though I did manage to secure a lovely comb near the bun.

"Miss. Miss!"

The child cannot be older than five or six.

"Yes?"

"I am not sure where you are headed, ma'am, but that way is not fun."

Well, this is interesting. "And why is that direction not fun, young darling?"

He points, and the moment I understand, I can't disagree. "Follow me, pretty lady, quick." I follow without hesitation.

For the second time, she appears: the woman who shattered me beyond repair—*my mother.* I cannot explain why the child recoils; my own reason is carved in stone. We move forward as the town moves at its slow winter pace—crooked signs dusted in snow, the air heavy with bread and smoke.

"Do you like snow cream, my lady?" the boy asks, rolling a smooth river stone between his fingers.

I stop to adjust the hair comb in my hair, letting the moment hang; "I sure do." He gestures for me to follow.

The child leads us past boutiques, bakeries, and flower shops—an odd little parade—and I cannot help questioning myself. *Why am I following him. Oh yes—snow cream.* We pass an old beggar woman, and the boy flicks a coin into her cup and blows her a kiss. She rewards him with a sweet wink.

"Julian!"

A deep voice cuts through the crowd. When I follow the sound, my eyes betray me, fixing on him before I can look away.

"Uncle!"

Julian's uncle sweeps the boy into his arms, pressing kisses on both cheeks until he is breathless with laughter, then sets him back on his feet. Julian glances at me, and the man's curious eyes follow—exactly as they should, since I am staring back. *Awkward.*

The weight of the quiet presses on me, and I speak. "I am Lady Beatryx Blake of the noble House of Blake. My father is the Duke of Blake, and I travel as a companion to Princess Myst on her journey to Glaycyr Falz."

His gaze does not waver, unsettling me. He looks at me as though my title means nothing, and I narrow my eyes, *as if he is a riddle meant to be solved.* Then he laughs, a rough, low chuckle, and *irritation flares hot within me.*

"Hello, Beatryx." His voice drips over me like thick honey, warm until the bee stings. "I am Ambrose. It seems you and Julian have met. I did not realize he had a taste for older women." Another low laugh escapes him.

Heat rises in my chest, and I turn, moving without purpose—anywhere but here. His footsteps fall in behind mine, silent, and suddenly the balance shifts. *Control slides back into my grasp like a familiar weapon.*

"You must learn to laugh, Beatryx." My name rolls off his tongue with a richness that steals my breath.

I find my voice as I keep moving. "Julian found me, saved me. Then asked if I liked snow cream."

He steps in front of me, walking backward, matching my pace. "Well—do you like snow cream?"

For only a whisper of time have I known this man, and *I would follow him to my death,* I think, as my smile betrays me. "Yes. As of late last night, I love it."

Ambrose holds his hand out, and I take it without hesitation.

Something in me eases. *I do not want his hand to leave mine. Ever.*

Keeping our eyes locked, he says, "Lead the way, Julian. The woman has confirmed her love of snow cream. She must not be held back another moment."

We follow Julian to a quaint creamery.

I choose fresh berries and thick cream stirred with honey, and the first bite feels enchanted. Julian's dessert is drowning in chocolate, enough that I have to wipe his face with my napkin, while Ambrose sips herbal tea, utterly unbothered.

No wonder he is perfect.

There I go, internalizing again. How does he sit in such stillness while my spirit claws to be free. He straightens and turns to his nephew.

"Julian, off to your games. I will see you come supper."

The boy is on his feet in an instant, waving—until Ambrose clears his throat. Julian runs back and stands before me, offering his sticky hand, which I accept. He kisses the back of my hand with such sweetness. "The pleasure was all mine, my lady."

And then he is gone, slipping back into the cluster of boys nearby.

The next thing I notice is Ambrose's outstretched hand, and my body reacts before I can argue with myself.

He is impossible to look away from. Dark hair pulled back at the nape, green eyes unwavering as moss in a haunted forest. A dusk-dark beard frames his face. Full, perfectly shaped lips, dimples hiding beneath—his eyes give that secret away when he smiles.

Stop noticing everything about him.

Stricken, I need to walk away.

He wears heavy fur, so I cannot see what lies beneath it. But my imagination has already sculpted him.

"It is getting late," I say, "and I am not sure where I am in relation to the castle. And I am freezing."

At that single word—freezing—he sheds his furs and wraps me in them.

Warmth encases me. The weight, the scent, the closeness—too much, too sudden. Something inside me reaches for him, instinctive and untrained, a pull behind my eyes I do not understand. A thread of thought stretches toward his mind—

—and snaps.

Euphoria surges, sharp and blinding. The world tilts.

Lashes fall. Darkness takes me.

Myst

"I've had enough of your little games. Why did you release your mist in that tent, before my father? Answer me."

I keep walking, ignoring him, until his hand seizes my arm and hauls me into an empty tent. I try to stand firm, but he drags me to a chair and forces me into it. Shame burns through me—I feel like a child, not a future wife.

He leans down until we are eye level. "Have you not been taught how this works, my love? You are here to make me look good. You will obey me. Simple."

Iyce is confirming what I already knew. I refuse to accept it.

He circles behind me, silent, then takes my arms and stretches them out, inspecting the dress as though it betrayed him.

"What are you wearing?" he says. "You look like a shattered piece of ice struck by a snowstorm."

My thoughts tumble. I have watched my mother bend to my father yet still find quiet ways to keep herself content without his knowledge—but that is not what I want either.

I feel like a caged animal.

"You have nothing to say, for once?"

He does not wait for an answer. He walks out.

As composed as I can manage, I leave the tent and head for the castle. It has been a draining day. I need a moment to myself.

"Princess," Shayn calls.

I offer him the only smile I have left. "Please escort me to my chambers."

In the corridor to my sanctuary, a voice interrupts.

"Myst, I met the seamstress," Olyvia says, a quiet thread of eagerness in her voice. "Her name is Lia. She is kind and ready to help. She said to bring you tomorrow morning for a casual visit and fitting, and she will get everything sorted."

Inside my quarters, Clarina slips in behind us, quiet as snowfall.

That should make Iyce happy. New gowns.

Once inside my quarters, my fingers go straight to the pins in my hair. I pull them out one by one, tossing them onto the dressing table. I am unraveling. Olyvia gently stops me before I tear half my hair out and finishes the task herself.

Clarina excuses herself for refreshments. I think she senses how frayed I am.

A light knock brings Garrett in and he goes straight to the balcony doors and opens them. A sharp gust sweeps a few loose strands of my hair across my cheek. He stares into the distance. Shayn sinks into a chair, exhaustion etched deep.

"Why are you so tired, Shayn?" Olyvia asks, brushing my hair smooth.

"We trained with the army," Garrett answers.

I incline my head. Strategic.

"Shayn had himself a fine time with the female warriors," Garrett adds.

"And you did not?" Shayn fires back.

Garrett smirks. "I did not say that."

A knock interrupts us. Clarina returns with bread, cheese, olives, grapes, and wine. She pours, then slips away.

Over a second glass, I speak of Iyce.

"There has to be a way to stop this marriage," Shayn says.

"I pray daily."

Olyvia pulls me into her arms. "It will work out. You are too good for him."

I tell them about the king, about my magic spiraling, about Iyce reprimanding me like a child.

"I may be speaking out of ignorance," Olyvia says gently, "but have you ever researched your magic—your specific kind?"

Her question stirs something old.

I tell them about Mairi, the witch in the Forest of Shadows—how she promised guidance, and the price she set: three questions, asked whenever she chooses, each one answered in truth. Her first came at the solstice ball.

Olyvia stiffens. Shayn asks, "There is a witch in that forest?"

I take Olyvia's hand. "Stay away from her. She is vicious and powerful. Promise me."

As I wait, memory flickers—Queen Frost's spell at the ball, the darkness no one remembers.

No one but me.

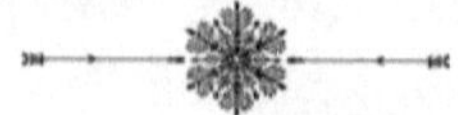

Beatryx

The bed is warm. Too warm. Heavy with sleep that does not feel earned.

When my eyes open, Ambrose is there—seated not far from me, one ankle crossed over his knee, a glass of amber in hand, a book resting loosely against his palm. Firelight breathes across the room.

Who is this man, truly?

Julian's voice slips in before the thought can settle. "Is she okay, Uncle?"

"She will be perfectly fine," Ambrose replies easily, without looking up.

I draw the blankets down—and freeze.

A slip. Nothing else.

"Where in the fucking hells are my clothes?"

Julian vanishes like a startled bird. Ambrose sets his book aside, then his drink, and leans forward, interest sharpening his gaze.

"Do you always speak that way in front of children?"

My eyes trace his mouth before meeting his stare—dark green, unsettling, weapons. I haul the blankets up instinctively. "Do you always undress women and put them in your bed?"

A corner of his mouth lifts. "Not necessarily in that order."

"Oh, my goddesses." I attempt to cocoon myself in the blankets and fail, spectacularly, as I stand.

He lifts his glass again, unbothered, watching me over the rim. "We are in my sister's home. That is not my bed. She removed your dress so you could breathe. I may have assisted with the corset— because that *is* my specialty."

The pillow strikes true.

I throw him a look that could wound, then turn to the mirror—and gasp.

"I look like hell. Where are my clothes? I need to return to the castle."

Ambrose rises at last. "Yes. And a carriage is already arranged."

I stalk toward him, snatch his glass, and swallow the remaining drops. Immediate regret tightens my face. "How do you drink that?"

He studies me with unsettling calm. "Your dress is in the armoire. And because I like it. Though I hope the three drops you consumed might steady you—if such a thing is possible."

He leaves without another word, closing the door softly behind him.

Once dressed, I attempt to tame my hair, pinning it up with more hope than skill. I turn to the bed—and immediately regret the decision. Making it is an exercise in humiliation; my inexperience announces itself loudly.

My boots wait neatly in the corner. My cloak hangs beside the small window overlooking a modest vegetable and herb garden. I smooth stray strands behind my ears and open the door, newly aware of how small the house is—orderly, intentional.

The scent of food curls through the space, something rich simmering above the hearth.

Julian finds me with strawberries cupped in his hands. "Are you hungry? Mamá always has enough for guests."

He has claimed a piece of me already. I bend to him, promise supper another day—just not today. "Please thank your mamá for me. I hope to see you soon."

I kiss his forehead and steady myself before stepping outside.

From the porch, I see Ambrose speaking quietly with the coachman. I step toward them. "I'm ready."

He opens the carriage door and places a hand at the center of my back as I climb in. Once seated, he leans close—close enough to be heard.

"Safe travels."

The door shuts before I can answer.

I have no idea what I will tell anyone about this afternoon. I know only that I will not tell the truth.

This is mine.

He read while I slept.

Cool glass presses against my cheek as the countryside darkens. My thoughts return to the moment I reached for his mind— without intent, without warning—and met resistance sharp enough to drop me.

That should not be possible.

When the town lights fall away, the sky opens, and the turquoise lights bloom overhead. Clarina's words return unbidden.

When two strangers meet without cause…

Does this have anything to do with Ambrose?

No. I am not important. Neither is he.

What could we possibly do together that would matter?

Maybe sex, I think, a quiet laugh escaping—followed immediately by exhaustion so deep it aches.

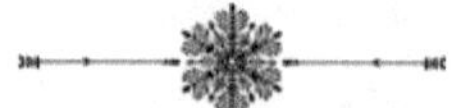

Ambrose

"Uncle! Beatryx left her hair comb!"

Julian runs out the front door and heads straight for me, shouting as he holds out the delicate piece. Emerald stones are set into each prong.

"Thank you, Julian. I will make sure it is returned to her."

I kiss my sister and nephew, then tell them I will be back tomorrow. I do everything in my power to keep them safe. No one else gives a damn, but I do.

Family is first. Always.

I refocus my thoughts on the feisty Beatryx as I ready my horse, preparing to follow the carriage that carries something precious—her. I need to make sure she reaches the castle safely.

What in the realm came over me today?

Why do I feel this strong pull to protect her?

Maybe I just need a good fuck. I will go with that theory.

Halting at the edge of the Forest of Frozen Dreams, I start thinking again, beginning with how much I hate staring at this damn castle and nearly everything in it.

The coachman opens the carriage door and helps her out, just as I instructed. She is a beautiful hot mess. Then I see two guards from the princess's kingdom take her by the arms and guide her toward the keep.

One of them clearly unsettles her, but in a moment, they are gone.

Tension coils through me, sharp and restless, and I need to get it out.

Home.

I ride deep into the darkest part of the forest, where the trees are thick with green foliage covering the ground in shadow, surrounded by frozen streams with fish drifting beneath a thin layer of ice. The air is extra crisp tonight, which is good. My head needs to clear after the afternoon's strange encounter and everything that followed.

I finally arrive in the heart of the snow-covered forest, where a haven of silence awaits—a place of warmth and luxury amid the icy wilderness. No one comes into this forest except me, the outcast. Julian and my sister are the only ones who have ever been here.

The cabin itself is a marvel, its strong timber walls crafted from live wood taken from the surrounding trees. When I look upward, snowdrifts cling to the roof, sparkling in the moonlight, while icicles hang from the eaves.

This retreat gives me the freedom to think whatever my mind conjures—along with the space to feel any emotion that surfaces—followed by a full-throated roar into the wind without it mattering to a single soul.

After tending to my stallion, I climb the never-ending steps toward my awaiting tranquility. I let out a dry laugh, more breath than sound, when I see the wrought-iron knocker on my front door—proudly displayed, yet never used. I give it three firm knocks before stepping inside, greeted by a fine atmosphere.

I do what I always do—bring fire to the waiting hearths throughout the place with a few snaps of my fingers, then watch as their warm glow deepens the softness of the fur rugs scattered across the stone floors. Plush loungers and sofas fill the space, each offering comfortable seating, warm blankets woven from the finest wool resting along their edges.

Nothing needs to be inviting, really. No one visits.

To be fair, I do not invite anyone here.

I remove my thick fur and let it fall across the back of the largest lounge before heading to the kitchen, where polished copper pots and pans hang from racks above a massive wooden table I built out of pure boredom. Julian was my assistant. The time we spent working on that project was unforgettable.

The shelves are stocked with jars of preserves and other necessities—enough to last through many moon phases. At my bar, I pour myself a fine amber into a thick crystal glass and move.

Upstairs, I pass two guest bedrooms I would describe as the perfect accommodation of pure comfort—lavish beds with plush quilts and fur throws. Each room has huge windows that look out onto snow-covered evergreens.

I keep walking until I reach my quarters.

Once in the lounging area, I begin removing my weapons, then the straps that hold them. This is not normal for me. Typical me puts everything in its proper place. But I am not in my ordinary headspace, so I do not give a single fuck.

I top off my beverage at the upstairs bar, then head to my bathing chamber.

This is phenomenal. My entire place here is impressive.

I pull the lavish hair comb from my pocket. It is ornate and stunning—like her—and it smells incredible. Jasmine. A scent I have not known in a long time.

I imagine my hands tangled in her hair, pulling her head back and kissing that pretty neck.

I pull my tunic over my head and toss it on the floor, then untie my breeches, releasing my cock, swollen with want. I step into the cascade of water and work the coarse ash soap into a gritty, warming foam.

Goddesses, this feels good—and the drink is quieting every twisted thought clawing at my mind.

I made my life choice years ago, so come what may, or may not. I have met women from many realms. They come, and they go. But never have I met one like Beatryx.

Wrapping a long wool linen around my waist, drink in hand, I walk straight out to my large balcony. When I look into the sky, I am mesmerized—instantly battling distorted thoughts.

I refuse to pull my eyes from what captures my attention—the dancing colors of lights painting the night with ribbons of turquoise. The air remains crisp and clear, filled with the magical silence of frozen dreams.

What are the goddesses begging for?

Now I am questioning everything that happened today, because I had no intention of meeting anyone.

Only time will provide answers.

In this perfect moment of need and comfort, I hear her welcoming screech and instantly turn toward the sound. Her keen eyes scan the landscape below as she navigates effortlessly through the twilight sky.

I stretch my arm out and whistle into the frozen air, giving her the perfect navigation point of my whereabouts—welcoming her home.

I narrow my eyes, peering into the darkness, and shapes take form—wings unfurling wide, beating in a steady, powerful rhythm. She brings them forward and begins a full backtrack, using the wind as an ally. Even from here, I recognize the proud silhouette that marks her as part of the Glaycyr Falz crest. Now she is in a graceful glide before extending her talons for an easy grasp onto a suitable perch—which, in this case, is my bare arm.

What a gorgeous sight.

"Hello, lovely."

She coos sweetly as we walk inside. I hold my outstretched arm to the wooden perch, and she settles in, patient enough to endure my rant.

Beatryx

"Where have you been? Once Garrett and I started training, you were gone. You could have said something to someone. People worry, Tryx."

Tryx. That name again.

I exhale, keeping my tone even. "I'm sorry. I didn't mean to disappear. I needed a moment to myself, so I went to town and did some shopping."

He does not let it go. "Shopping? You vanished. No word. No sign."

I blink at him. "I'm not a soldier under command, Shayn."

He steps closer. "You could have told me. Or Garrett. Or anyone."

"I explored," I say, sharper now. "Had snow cream. Saw my mother—again. Anything else you would like to log?"

I turn on my heel and storm off, hips swinging sharp enough

to rival the snowstorm brewing around us.

Once upstairs, I go straight to my room, shutting out the world.

Goddesses above, why am I so irritated.

Normally, I would be flirting with Shayn and Garrett at the same time, but now they are only managing to vex me.

Olyvia is not here, so I will have some time to myself. We share the suite but have our own private bedroom and bathing chamber. I have never been placed in this type of accommodation before, but I like the arrangement.

I remove my dress and lay it in the basket for cleaning. That dress will forever remind me of him—Ambrose. He is painfully handsome and carries himself like a man, not a boy. His eyes pierce straight through me every time he speaks.

My thoughts linger as I walk into the bathing area and realize something.

Damn. I left my hair comb at his sister's humble home, and my father just gifted that to me.

Well. I guess I will be hunting Ambrose down sooner than later. How sad.

Painfully, I remove the slip that still carries his scent. Snow and pine fill my senses as I drag it over my head. Then I draw my own bath.

I decant a few drops of my favorite oil into the steaming water and pour myself a glass of lemon-and-blackberry infused tea. Then I sink into the tub, still thinking of the man who captured my full attention this afternoon.

Hair piled atop my head and wrapped in my favorite thick wool robe, slippers on my feet, I walk toward the door that leads to the hall and notice a slip of parchment on the small table. *Oh, finally,* I think, picking up the quill beside it. I dip it into the ink, fill out my dinner choices, then place the parchment in the designated area in the hall.

In that moment, I hear laughter and retreat into my room. With the door cracked, I listen.

Oh my. It seems Garrett has found himself a warrior woman for the evening. She will enjoy him. He is a beautiful lover.

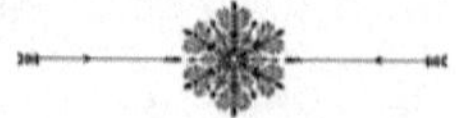

Ambrose

The outer walls of my bedroom are solid glass, and mornings arrive too soon. I stretch my body, then rise before walking to the falling water. It feels refreshing, and I cup my hands, catching it before tossing it onto my weary face.

Dressed, I take my thoughts to the writing desk and begin the first words of a new era, chuckling low as I dip my goose quill into a jar of indigo ink.

I will have to speak with the stationer soon.

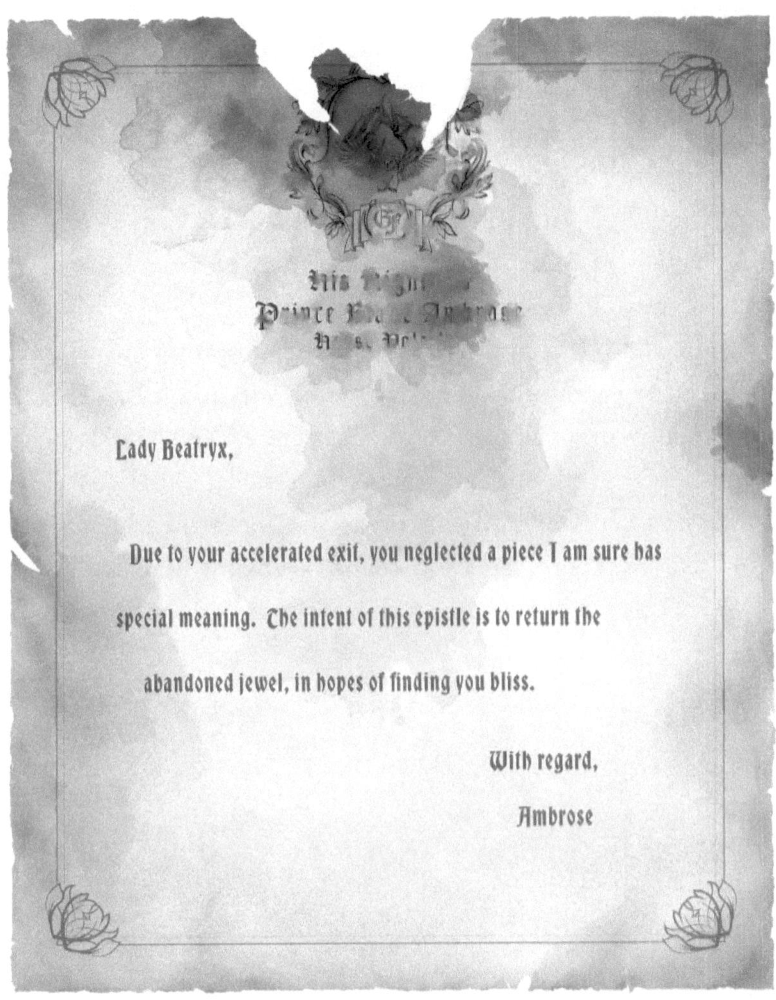

His Majesty
Prince Eric Ambrose

Lady Beatryx,

Due to your accelerated exit, you neglected a piece I am sure has

special meaning. The intent of this epistle is to return the

abandoned jewel, in hopes of finding you bliss.

With regard,

Ambrose

For the last time, I hold the hairpiece close, catching the faint trace of her scent before carefully wrapping it in cloth and placing it inside a trinket box. I set the folded parchment atop the bundle, its seal pressed firm.

This is the end of my pitiful state.

With my home straightened—because I cannot handle a mess—I strap weapons onto almost every part of my body, tie my hair back, grab a piece of fruit, and leave.

In town, I see Julian and my sister waiting on the porch as I approach.

"Morning, Julian. Can you take this package to Brantley and request a messenger for delivery service to the castle?"

Julian hops up from the bench, brimming with excitement, and reaches for the box. He agrees to handle the task—and just like that, he's moving. So is the little piece of her I still held.

"Thank you, Julian. Hurry. A storm is brewing," I call after him, though he's already too far to hear.

Refocusing, I sit and wrap an arm around my sister while she rests her head on my shoulder. "Iz, won't you and Julian move out of this small home and into the forest where I am? We can have a cottage built near me for the two of you."

She lifts her head and pats the top of my hand where it wraps around her shoulder. "You know what keeps me here."

"Yes, I do," I reply, "but it doesn't mean I have to agree—or like it."

24

Glaycyr Falz

Myst

Our morning's purpose is set. Olyvia, Clarina, and I move toward the infamous library she has whispered about for days.

The moment we step inside, one question rises to the surface.

"How is the ice not melting?"

Olyvia glances at me. "That is the burning question."

Shayn holds his post at the entrance as we venture deeper, utterly unfazed by the ice that should be melting but isn't. Garrett is elsewhere with the royal guard, studying patrol routes and terrain maps—learning the twists of the castle's catacombs, his quiet show of respect for the kingdom's defenses.

Clarina runs her fingers along the spines as we walk, pausing to point out titles with delight. "This is my favorite place in the entire kingdom. Follow me—I know where every section lies. Come, let us learn about your magic, Myst."

We reach the third level of the library, where the outer wall curves in a wide half-moon of glass. Beyond it, two massive slabs of glaycyr ice hug the arc of the structure like a frozen embrace. Between them, fire burns—contained, suspended—its glow flickering against the frozen walls. It shouldn't be possible, yet there it is: flames caged by ice so ancient and cold they don't waver.

Olyvia tenses each time her gaze drifts toward them.

Clarina pulls a large tome from an ice shelf and carries it to the table where we wait. "What exactly is your power, Myst?"

Olyvia answers for me. "Show her."

On-cue magic isn't my specialty, but I close my eyes and think of the Whispering Woods and Grandpapá. I lift my arms and let my fingers dance, moving with what little skill remains as snowflakes of every silhouette and proportion form and drift around the three of us.

They clap, and Clarina blurts, "Absolutely stunning, Myst!"

She opens the ancient tome to a section on controlling magic. The words blur together, so I take out the card with the amethyst bloom, set it on the table, and ask, "Have either of you ever seen this before?"

Clarina picks it up and studies it for a moment. "I have heard of this game."

A flicker of frustration rises. "Have you heard of that bloom?"

Olyvia pales, as if she's seen a spirit. Clarina finally answers.

"The Hidden Kingdom. This bloom is part of their crest. I've seen it—but the book is no longer available in this library."

Olyvia presses a hand to her stomach as she rises. "I'm going to get some fresh air—the spices at dinner last night might've been a bit much." She starts toward the far archway.

Before she gets far, I stand. "Olyvia, wait. I'll walk back with you."

Already halfway gone, she calls over her shoulder, "It's okay. Keep doing your research. I just need a moment. I'll be fine." Then she slips out of sight.

From my place at the table, my sharpened hearing picks up Shayn's voice at the library's entrance—steady toward Olyvia, unmistakable to me with my heightened senses. "Do you need a glass of water, Olyvia?"

"Feel better!" Clarina calls after her.

I stand there for a moment, wondering what could have come over Olyvia so quickly. Turning back to Clarina, I ask, "Where is the book now?"

She assures me she'll inquire and let me know, then slips easily back into talking about the game—Tea and Cards.

Beatryx

Whatever today has planned, I'll let it unfold. But one thing is certain—I must find Ambrose and retrieve my hair comb. *And, quite possibly, see his deep forest-green eyes.*

The thick white robe feels wonderful against my skin as I step into the sitting area, where elderberry tea steeped with wildflower sweetness fills my senses. Warm toast with blackberry jam accompanies the tea—a good start.

I don't care for these non-revealing, heavy gowns, but they're necessary here; the chill is brutal.

Today's dress mirrors yesterday's—high neck, fitted long sleeves. Ivory. I pair it with gold jewels and two gold hair clips aligned with my brows, the rest of my hair falling freely. Olyvia is with Myst, so I arrange my own hair.

Placing the folded parchment on Olyvia's night table is best. The less they worry, the better. I still feel terrible for snapping at Shayn—he was only trying to help. No one knew where I was, and I hate that I made him feel small for caring.

This way, at least they'll know I'm safe.

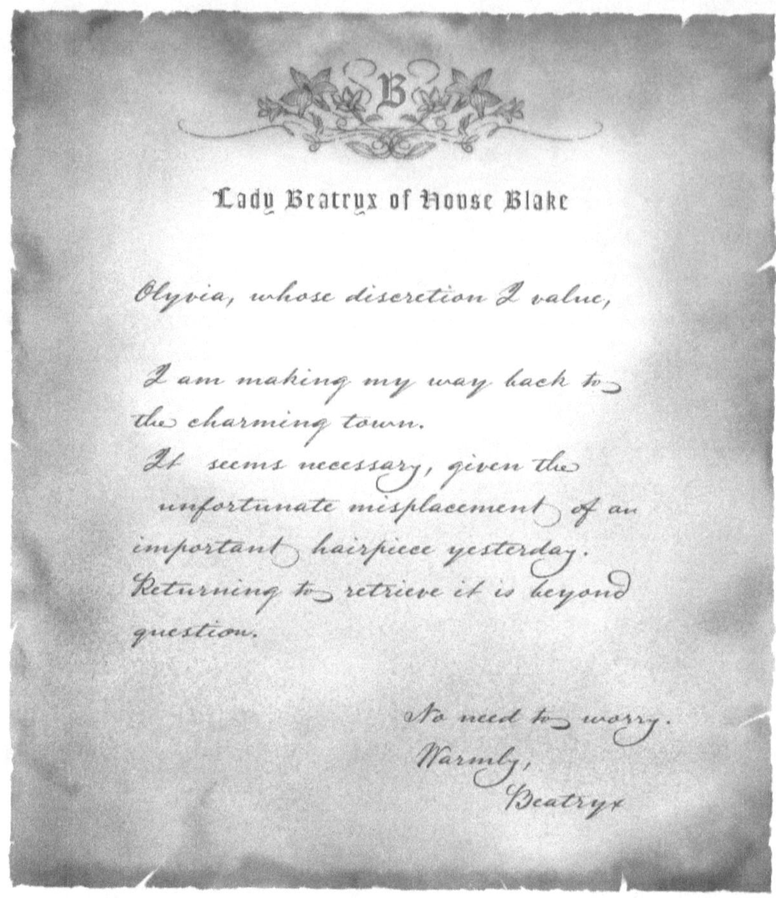

I tug on thick boots, lace them, grab the gloves I forgot yesterday, and head out—hopeful I won't see Shayn or Garrett. I'm glad my accommodation isn't near Myst's quarters, sparing me an awkward encounter.

Passing through the halls, I faintly hear a haunting melody. I follow its pull until the corridor opens into a vaulted chamber washed in pale light. Near the far end, a cello breathes slow, aching notes. I see only the player's back—a ghostly outline, glowing like moonlight caught in glass. The bow glides with restraint and urgency, the music carving through the silence.

I stand suspended, unsure if I've stumbled into memory—or something older.

I wrap my arms around myself and sway. *I could listen forever.* The music feels like a plea echoing through the bones of the castle.

Then it ends.

The figure flickers. Light fractures across the floor. And between one breath and the next, he's gone.

"Wait... Please come back and play again. Please..."

Nothing remains but the cello.

The echo of the melody clings to me as I venture deeper. I pass through wide open rustic doors that lead to a spiral staircase ascending to the uppermost part of the castle—the tower chamber. The view stops me cold. So many glaycyrs, yet a select few are invaded by volcanoes. Looking away is impossible. It's simply the most vivid scenery I've ever laid eyes on.

When I finally pull away and move into the opposite hallway, I find grand paintings of royals who once inhabited this fortress. They're stunning—until I reach Iyce. His hair is white as glaycyrs, his eyes a piercing ice blue, his face all hard, chiseled lines. He's massive, striking, impossible to overlook. But the man is such a prick that ugliness eclipses every part of him.

Time is slipping, and I need to find Ambrose and retrieve my hair comb.

The back of the castle is busy with servants and handmaidens buzzing in and out of guest rooms and along long hallways. Once I reach the main floor, not far from the kitchen, I hear a man say, "I have a small parcel for Lady Beatryx."

Stopping in my tracks, I slip around a corner and watch the two men go back and forth until one finally barks out the foulest language.

"Find the guest list, you witless lout."

The slap he receives from the other man cracks through the hall.

"You arse—how many times did your ma drop you on your foul fucking head?"

This is absurd. "Excuse me, I believe I heard my name."

The man who slapped first strikes him again. "Guest list, you fucking axe wound."

Eyes wide, I step in. "Please. Allow me to have a look."

They're in a full-on argument at this point, so I take the package and walk away. The stupid men never even notice.

Hurried steps and a fast heartbeat full of anticipation carry me back to my room—because his scent is all over this package. Once inside, I break the wax seal on the envelope—deep blue, the letter **B** pressed into the wax.

I trace my fingers over the **B**, wondering what it stands for—his surname, perhaps? Wonder swells before I unfold the slip of vellum and read four words: neglected, intent, abandoned, blissful.

What does this mean?

I tear into the box and find my hair comb.

Is he avoiding me?

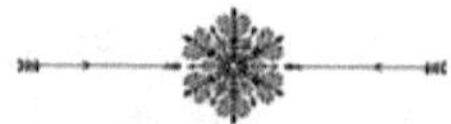

Ambrose

"You have plenty of firewood and enough provisions, and I've secured all windows and both doors. Are you sure you and Julian won't come with me to my home to weather the storm?"

I know the answer before my sister responds with a firm no—for the third time. Why are women so damn stubborn. "I love you, and I'll see you both in a few days. Take care of your Mamá, Julian."

The boy smiles. He loves having a task.

The town is shutting down early, preparing for the storm. Most shops are already closed. A few remain open, boarding up windows and securing anything left outside. These storms don't come often—but when they do, you take shelter.

The air has dropped sharply, colder than usual, and the wind has picked up—fast and heavy. I need to get home.

That's when I hear the chaos.

Beatryx is banging on the shop's door, demanding entry like the world owes her silk and emeralds.

"Madam, please, you can't be closed, I just got here!" she calls, her voice edged with desperation.

I watch from a distance, unseen. She's flustered, pacing, breath fogging the air. When she turns to face the cold, frustration sharpens her expression—fierce, unyielding. That's when she sees me.

She stops, her body going still.

And for a moment, the storm rolling in isn't nearly as strong as the one brewing between us.

Beatryx is worldly, with an accent I rather like—but beyond that, I only know she has hot blood that stirs easily. In boyhood, playing with fire was a thrill. When you become a man, that same thrill turns into a woman's temper. All the better. We get a rise out of it.

In this rare moment, as the snow begins to fall more intensely, she looks stunning and helpless in her ivory gown. Ornamental snowflakes drift around her face, a few settling in her dark hair.

The moment ends with a voice.

"Beatryx, what are you doing? A snowstorm is fast approaching. We must get you to safety, now!"

The guards appear to be the same two knights in shining armor I saw irritating her yesterday evening when she returned to the castle.

"Olyvia found your parchment," the second one hollers over the gusting wind as he dismounts, the folded sheet slipping from his hand.

This is somewhat entertaining. I lean casually against a post in front of the bakery. Those two blokes haven't even noticed me—they only see her. Idiots. And gods, how many men does it take to get this petite woman on the back of a horse.

A low chuckle escapes me.

"Do you want her in front of you or behind you, Shayn?"

Ah—one name.

"I don't bloody know, Garrett. What do you think?"

And there's the second.

Beatryx looks at me one last time, and if I'm being honest, I feel sorry for her. Watching this unfold with those two isn't the best feeling.

Garrett says something to her, and then—this woman gathers her dress, pulling it up to her thighs, and he lifts her, settling her behind Shayn.

"Hang on, damsel!" Shayn hollers back, and they ride toward the castle.

When I look down, the parchment lies at my feet, carried there by the wind.

After reading it, it's clear she hasn't received the package I sent. Goddesses, please help them get her back safely. I should make sure of that myself—but if I do, I'll never get home.

Very frustrating.

As snowfall increases, visibility drops, making it harder to judge what the distance hides while the storm intensifies.

At home, thick snow has gathered on every surface. I secure my deep-auburn horse in the stables, then move inside my own haven and begin the same routine.

After retreating from my steaming hot waterfall, I pull on lightweight breeches and a tunic, then step out onto a higher balcony I only visit when I'm in a particular mood.

Raising my arms, I speak a single word.

Flames surge to life, blazing high around the entire space, warming the air as snow continues to fall.

Behind my cello, I draw out the same haunting melody I played earlier today.

25

Glaycyr Falz

His Cello Weeps

Beatryx

I don't want to be on this horse with Shayn a moment longer. Nothing is going according to plan, thanks to Olyvia for sharing my sealed parchment with everyone. She doesn't understand, and it isn't her fault, but damn. I feel so pulled to Ambrose, and now this storm is upon us, and only the goddesses know how long it will last—or what the outcome will be when it's over.

A beverage awaits.

Once we're back in the castle's keep, Shayn helps me dismount. Pain screams up my chapped legs, and the frustration finally breaks loose. Damn everything. I wrench free, turn on both guards, and demand, "Why did you come after me?"

Shayn looks at Garrett, who answers for them both.

"Everyone was worried, Beatryx. Look, I don't give a varmint's dick what you do, who you do it with, or where you go. It's everyone else that seems overly concerned—while I get dragged along for the ride."

What an ass. I turn toward the kitchen and keep moving.

I want a beverage. Something strong, like that amber drink Ambrose had at his sister's home.

Clarina is filling oil lamps, trimming wicks, and arranging the candles upright in a wooden crate. She looks up when she sees me, surprise flickering across her face.

"Beatryx."

I greet her softly. "Hello, Clarina."

She nods, relieved I'm back at the castle where it's safe and warm. Then she begins recounting the historia of these storms, but my attention drifts—because only one thought consumes me.

A very tall, formidable, beautiful man.

"Clarina, I'm hoping for a drink—something rich, amber in hue."

She pauses, thinking, then moves to a tall cupboard and steps onto a wooden stool. When she returns, she carries a slender bottle and a delicate flute. As she sets them before me, I notice a faint symbol pressed into the glass, worn but still visible.

"I'm not sure I know what you mean, but this is mead—made from honey and spiced in the fashion of our kingdom. I've never tasted it myself—I'm too young—but all the ladies adore it. They say it's neither too sweet nor too dry, balanced in between. And it doesn't sparkle—it's still."

"Thank you, Clarina. With the storm approaching, I feel unsettled and could use something warm."

She gives me a knowing look, assures me she understands, then gathers the cloaks, mitts, and hoods into a basket for the storm and heads out—leaving me to the quiet and the drink.

With the bottle in my hand and the glass tucked beneath my arm, I walk toward the one place I cannot banish from my thoughts.

As I step into the gallery, snow falls in sweeping sheets beyond the floor-to-ceiling windows. The sconces along the walls flicker as I set the bottle and glass upon a high table and pour the honey-wine.

I drink deeply.

By the goddesses, it is exquisite.

I fill the glass to its brim and cross to the cello near the windows, brushing my fingertips lightly across the strings without drawing a sound. The melody I heard here earlier was haunting, and I wish—truly wish—the one who played it would return.

I lift my face toward the falling snow and whisper into the silence.

"I wish you were here."

I sip the mead again.

This drink is dangerously delightful.

Beyond the tall windows, the world is a blur of white and shadow—glaycyrs rising like pale spires, huge evergreens bowed beneath the weight of fresh snow. To stand here, watching it while I drink this honeyed draught, feels utterly perfect.

I laugh—

then powerful arms close around me.

His palms press to the freezing window, his warmth wrapping around my body.

His lips brush my ear as he whispers, low and rough.

"You wished for me?"

The glass slips from my hand.

He catches it.

And the moment shatters into darkness.

Ambrose

This woman is going to bring me to my end. Twice now, she's tried to use her mind-control enchantment to push into my thoughts—and both times, she's slipped into unconsciousness.

I replay it again, beginning with the instant her voice slipped into my mind.

She turned to face me the same moment my gaze found her— eyes widening, body going still, breath caught on an inhale. I don't know her well enough to name the expression.

But I knew what I saw.

She was frozen in my presence.

In that moment, though, all control was lost. I can't seem to justify a single decision I've made these past two days. I felt her soft fingertips the instant they touched the strings of my cello, and everything that followed unfolded without restraint.

Ancient magic guided me here—to her—once again.

Her half-full glass of what I believe is mead rests in my right hand, and she is in my left arm. No need for this to go to waste, so I drain the rest of the golden liquid—too sweet for my liking—set the glass aside, and lift her easily into my arms.

I have a couple of guesses as to which wing she's staying in.

We pass a few of the castle's guests, none of whom notice us— thanks to the spell I've cast around us, cloaking our presence from everyone.

Her scent leads me straight to the chamber she's been given while here at court. I push the door open, and within a few steps, we're inside.

It may upset her—but I'm not hesitating.

I'll remove most of her clothing before resting her pretty head on the soft pillow.

Pure, agonizing torture—that's what this is—as I unfasten the last of forty-five tiny gold buttons on the front of her dress, beginning at her neck and ending at her waist. I slip her arms from the sleeves and ease the dress from her body.

A laced corset, the same ivory as her gown, threatens my sanity.

Beatryx's small boots come off last, leaving her in the slip and whatever lies beneath it.

She rests peacefully in bed. Water waits at her bedside.

"Goodnight, rare gem."

Before leaving, I notice the hearth fading to ash. I set fresh wood upon the embers, nudging them until a low flame rises. It will burn for a few hours, no more. By morning, someone will need to rekindle it.

Beatryx

Again, I've woken with fewer clothes after being with him.

Where is he?

Where did he go?

Was that real?

Sitting up is easy—until the chill hits me. The fireplace crackles only faintly.

A robe lies at the edge of the bed. I pull it around myself and walk to the tall window, pushing the heavy drapes apart.

The storm has passed. Outside, the world lies hushed beneath a fresh blanket of snow—everything winter white, gleaming in the morning light.

A hot bath sounds nice.

I walk to the bathing chamber. The dress I wore yesterday hangs neatly, every button undone. Heat rises in my cheeks.

He is, without question, a patient man.

The ivory corset lies beside it, unlaced. My fingers graze the fabric, trembling at the sight.

Today's dress is soft gray, with long tulle bishop sleeves and a sweetheart neckline. The lingerie and corset beneath it match, of course.

"Wow. You look stunning, Beatryx," Olyvia says.

I turn to face her. She steps closer, her long fingers moving instinctively through my hair. Her soft touch makes my eyelids flutter.

"Would you like me to braid your hair for the day?"

Excitement stirs in my chest. "Yes, that would be marvelous. And you can tell me what you've been up to since we arrived."

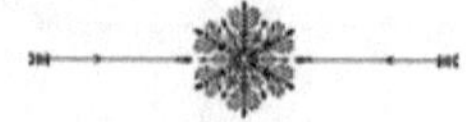

Olyvia

Something new always happens with Beatryx's hair—because she's relaxed about it, and she trusts me completely.

I take a long pin and draw a deep part from her left ear up to the crown of her head, then braid that entire section back and tie it off. On the opposite side, I work slowly, guiding the loose strands into smaller braids and weaving them together. Half her hair falls loose, the other half cascades in a waterfall of braids.

Stunning.

Together, we sift through her jewels and settle on a black pearl choker and matching ear cuffs—gorgeous and daring.

Beatryx vents about the day's planned activities. Anyone of importance will be learning the kingdom's dances for the upcoming ball. She rolls her eyes and says, "I know every dance already. This will be so monotonous for me, and I'm sure I could spend my time doing something more meaningful."

We leave our chamber and make our way toward the grand staircase. At the landing, Myst appears—perfect as always—with Shayn and Garrett close behind. Beatryx joins her at once, speaking without pause, while I trail after them.

Clarina emerges from a side corridor as we descend, and without missing a beat, she falls into step with us, as though she's always belonged.

Arriving at the grand ballroom is intense. I feel completely out of place. Clarina and I are only here to act as placeholders for those who couldn't attend. Sensing my tension, she smiles and says, "We could be in the library. This is a nice change."

"Ladies on one side and gents on the other," the dance tutor calls out, his voice slow and clear as it carries across the ballroom, echoing from marble to glass. I tilt my head, eyes narrowing with amusement. Myst shoots me the behave look, and the man continues.

"We'll learn two prominent dances today. The first is the

Paval—a formal procession where men and women share the faintest touch of fingertips. The second is the Gavotte, a popular medium-tempo dance that includes a kiss in one of the steps. You may do what you wish with that."

I glance around the room, my eyes darting from one man to the next, wondering all at once who might try to kiss me during the Gavotte. The thought makes my chest tighten.

Clarina leans closer, her quiet smile steadying me, and the tension eases.

My first kiss was a couple of years ago. The necklace I wear is from him—but it wasn't love. Not for me.

Beatryx drifts through the lesson as if half-asleep, her movements dull, her gaze distant. Without a word, she excuses herself and slips from the ballroom.

It surprises me. This is her prime chance to meet a prospective husband, yet she shows no interest at all.

Her rendezvous with Shayn continues, but he is hardly marriage material for someone of her standing. Strangely, he seems to know it too. I catch him watching her vanish into the grand gallery, his expression unreadable.

Beatryx

The gallery stretches before me, its tall glass doors gleaming with the reflection of snow. I push them open and step onto the castle's stone terrace. The cold air settles around me as I pause to take in the winter-white grounds.

There isn't a single man in that ballroom who stirs me. *Not one.*

I feel his presence before my eyes find him—unexpected, yet undeniable.

At the bottom of the terrace steps, half-hidden in shadow, he stands. His gaze holds mine, unwavering, before he turns and walks away—as if asking me to follow.

I slip down the stone steps, drawn toward him until the distance is gone.

My fingers rest against the chilled stone rail. "What are you doing near the castle today?"

"Looking for you. I have a surprise."

His smile could move glaycyrs.

"Oh? You have my full attention."

Just past the steps, a sleigh waits—an ornately carved masterpiece, drawn by six reindeer and poised to carry us into the kingdom's snow-laced wilds.

At the landing, Ambrose offers his hand and helps me in. Then a warm blanket comes across my lap, shielding me from the chill, and he gathers the reins before turning to me. "Are you ready?"

One deep nod is all he needs.

The sleigh glides forward, gently swaying. The only sound is the soft crunch of snow beneath the reindeer's hooves, their breath rising in delicate puffs of steam against the cold air. Behind us, the castle fades into the distance.

Around us, the world transforms—trees dressed in white, the open land glittering like a meadow of diamonds.

"This is the best time to sleigh," Ambrose says quietly. "After an ambush of snow, sleet, and ice."

And I believe him.

It's magical.

We stop not far from a lake, and what I see is the most enchanting beauty I've ever laid eyes on. This kingdom never ceases to surprise me. The wonder here feels endless.

Whatever lingers in my expression is enough; Ambrose steps from the sleigh and extends his hand, and I place mine in his once more.

"Welcome to Glass Lake."

White and black swans drift across the surface, so still and clear it looks like polished crystal. They move with such quiet grace, it's hard to pull my eyes away—from them… or from him.

Ambrose gestures toward the lake where a lone black swan drifts across the silver water.

"She's the friendliest of them all," he says softly. "Her name is Ophelia."

Another swan glides closer to our sleigh, its feathers a deep, glossy black. I lean forward, watching the way it studies us with calm curiosity.

"And who's this one?" I ask.

Ambrose follows my gaze, a faint smile touching his lips. "That is Oscar. He keeps his distance from most people, but he seems to like you."

We linger there for a quiet moment, the sleigh still, the world hushed around us. Ophelia circles lazily across the lake while Oscar drifts nearer, the water rippling in soft rings around him. The air feels suspended, as though the lake itself is holding its breath.

At last, Ambrose exhales and gathers the reins.

"There's one more surprise."

The sleigh glides over the snow toward the town. Above us, the sky spreads in strokes of blue and deep pink, the sun lingering at the horizon's edge.

That's when I hear it.

"Uncle!"

A soft glow fills my heart.

Ambrose calls back, his voice full of happiness.

"Julian!"

The boy climbs in, shivering, until we nestle him between us. Then we're off again—ready for more adventures.

This moment will stay with me forever.

A sleigh ride through a winter fairyland, reindeer gliding over snow, the man of my dreams beside me, and a boy who dreams wildly.

Happiness. Enchantment. Everything I didn't know I wanted.

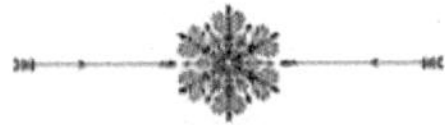

Olyvia

They say you learn something new every day—and today, I've learned two: the Paval and the Gavotte.

And I'd like to forget them both.

The castle gardens sleep beneath the storm's weight, but in the stone conservatory near the forest's edge, where the leaded windows glow faintly, the blooms endure. I want to gather a handful of ornate flowers from there—a place I was warned not to linger near.

Today, I will ignore that warning.

I need a dark, quiet place deep in the forest—where I can unleash my power before I shatter.

I wear the most comfortable clothing I can find as I head straight for the forbidden forest.

The Forest of Frozen Dreams.

What could possibly be so frightening out there?

A tingle spreads across my skin, and I shiver—not from cold, but from anticipation. Power stirs in my blood, rising with each step into the thick snow, eager for the fire dance I've been holding back.

The trees press closer, the path narrowing, the silence absolute. At last, deep within the forest, I let my arms fall to my sides. Sparks trail behind me, a breadcrumb path glowing in the frozen snow.

I can't hold it in any longer.

I dance—freely, wildly—for the trees, the snow, the sky. Fire blazes from my soul, spilling through my fingertips. Perfect circles of lassoed anger swirl above me, bright and alive.

I glide across the ice, fire burning all around, spinning faster, releasing every emotion I've kept locked away.

With one final leap, I land on my knees, spinning out of control until I press my palms into the snow, a burst of fire stopping my slide. The flames flicker, then fade, sinking deep into the ice.

I need to get back.

Once inside the chamber, I place my hand to my wrist—and my eyes instantly drop.

Where is my bracelet?

It must have gotten caught on something in my thrilled moment of releasing magic.

And now it could be anywhere.

Hopefully anywhere means buried deep in the snow.

Damn.

26

Glaycyr Falz

A Name Waits in Silence

Beatryx

This day has long been expected—yet now, as the departure from Glaycyr Falz draws near, I find myself dreading it.

The ache in my chest at the thought of saying goodbye to Ambrose is heavier than I expected.

Don't cry, B.

Tears slip through the cracks of walls that have already begun to crumble, defying the promises I keep making to myself. I tell myself I'm strong, that I've survived worse, but my reflection gives me away—showing just how deeply this goodbye has carved into me, reopening wounds I thought I'd sealed.

Today, I choose the color of Ambrose's wax seal for the fabric of my dress. Lia, the kingdom's seamstress, has outdone herself—her embroidery alone belongs to another realm, silver-threaded stars shimmering like captured constellations. The deep V-neckline could bring any man to his knees, the storm-lit blue fabric—nearly silver—drawn together with fire-red stitching. Long, fingerless gloves complete the ensemble, elegant and restrained, a whisper of danger wrapped in beauty.

Ambrose won't be there. He isn't royal. He isn't noble.

But we'll find each other afterward.

The instant my fingers touch the doorknob, a sudden knock breaks the silence.

When I open the door, two young pages stand outside, their arms trembling under the weight of roses.

"Delivery for Lady Beatryx," one says.

I step aside, and they hurry in, wobbling under the weight. I lead them to my bedroom, where they set four enormous vases—each brimming with nearly fifty red roses—on the dresser and side tables.

Ambrose.

Of course he sent them.

I pluck a single rose from one vase and lift it to my cheek, its petals cool against my skin and its fragrance trailing through the room as I step out.

I head to Myst's chamber, where Olyvia is already waiting to help with my hair—her designs are prodigious. I'm ecstatic to see what she's done for Myst, and even more eager to discover what she'll create for me.

Shayn and Garrett stand guard outside Myst's chamber. Their eyes flick over me as they open the doors in perfect sync, letting me pass without a word. I keep the rose low and close, its stem hidden against my gown—a quiet secret.

"Oh, my goddesses, Myst!"

She stands on a pedestal, framed by a snow-kissed window. Evergreens stretch toward the glass behind her, tiny flakes falling like rain—soft, endless, impossibly beautiful.

"Hello, Lady Beatryx. Please, help yourself to a glass of bubbly—and bring me one too," she says with a mischievous grin.

I don't hesitate. I take two flutes from the silver tray and hand her one. "It is no trouble at all."

"A toast," she declares. "Someone fetch a glass for Olyvia as well."

The room stills.

I lift the tray, ensuring each person has a glass—Lia and her assistants included.

Myst raises hers, her gaze sweeping the room.

"To women," she declares. "Intelligent, strong women."

We lift our flutes, the rims meeting with a delicate clink—and just like that, the room dissolves into laughter. Glass taps glass, and joyful sips follow, bright and unguarded.

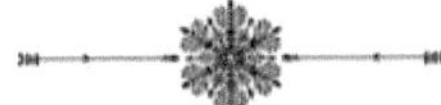

Olyvia

Well… I suppose I indulge now. The champagne slides down like silk—and I can't deny I like it.

Since arriving, I've taken up a quiet pastime—collecting the unique flowers that grow in the gardens and along the forest's edge. Clarina suggested drying them in a cool corner of the kitchen, and just as she promised, it worked. Now I can weave them into Myst and Beatryx's hair, the colors holding fast through every dance.

Myst sips her drink, and I turn to Beatryx. The plunge of her dress demands her hair be worn up; anything else would distract from the skin she has chosen to reveal. A low side bun—braided and swirling, finished with embossed dried periwinkle and miniature red roses—completes her look.

Now Myst. Her look must be elegant, crowned in the chill of regal ice.

I pull all her thick waves into a high bun at the crown of her head and pin three white roses into it.

Her dress is silver, layered with a delicate blue lace overlay that rests just off her shoulders, revealing a tiny silver snowflake just above her shoulder—and the newest one, slightly larger, nestled beneath her jaw.

I haven't seen them all. But the ones I have?

Exquisite.

Mystical.

Everyone is ready—and a little tipsy. Beatryx excitedly links her arm through Myst's, and the corridor swallows them as they head for the ballroom.

Beatryx

Myst's trembling hand finds mine, and she halts us mid-step as we near the towering iron doors that open to the ballroom, already filled with guests.

"What is it, Myst? Take my hands."

She listens and inhales deeply.

Myst gives a single nod to Shayn and Garrett. Without a word, they each take hold of the large iron doors and pull them open in perfect unison.

The trumpet sounds.

Then the Herald's voice rings out:

"Lady Beatryx Blake of the noble House of Blake, daughter of His Grace Aldric Blake, Duke of Blake. May her grace and beauty light this hall."

A ripple of polite applause follows as I step forward, passing beneath the open doors into the ballroom. I roll the rose between my fingers and lift it to my face, breathing in its scent.

Shayn leans in beside me and asks quietly, "Did you enjoy the gift?"

My fingers tighten around the stem until a thorn pricks me. The rose slips from my hand and falls at Shayn's feet, its petals scattering across the stone.

I should have known the roses weren't from Ambrose.

I take my place at the end of the assembly line, where each guest waits for the royal announcement of their future queen.

Just once, I would love to be in her shoes—shoes she would gladly give away.

The thought vanishes with the blare of trumpets.

The Herald speaks again.

"All rise and give way! By command of His Majesty, please welcome Her Royal Highness, Princess K. Myst Silvraim, daughter of Their Majesties, King Sleet and Queen Frost Silvraim of Arkaik Alpynz. May her grace and splendor illuminate this ballroom this evening."

The guests tremble in want—want of a queen who will love, perhaps even replace. Their bodies fold in half, yet their watchful eyes stay upright, silently judging the one who may or may not leave, as the last did.

When she passes, we rise slowly. Myst looks as though she's stepped out of another realm—exquisite and radiant, a true royal.

Fit to be queen.

Deep in my own thoughts, I'm swept up by the aromas—first the perfumes and oils clinging to the noblewomen like a veil, then the warm, lavish scents rising from the feast, layered with spice and sweetness. Only then do I realize I'm famished.

But what I'm truly hungry for is the one man who isn't here. The feast must suffice.

I retrieve my matchmaking token—one of many handed out for the evening—and lift a flute of something shimmering from a passing tray, lingering at the edge of the crowd instead of heading to my assigned table.

"Lady Beatryx," a voice calls, smooth and expectant. "I do believe you are assigned to our table."

Reluctantly, I turn.

As I sit, two older men lock their eyes on my chest. Heat crawls up my neck, but I force myself to breathe and lift my chin. I tilt my head and meet their gaze, letting the power stir the way it does when I focus on a single point. It gathers behind my eyes—a pressure I push outward, testing whether intention alone can shape it.

Their attention jerks upward. Not because they choose to, but because I tug at that pressure and direct it—a clumsy attempt at control that still lands. I hold them there just long enough to make them squirm.

Then I release them, lifting us all back to eye level as the invisible tether dissolves as quickly as it formed. I must learn to wield this.

Assholes.

The parts I have weaponized are entertaining. Except with Ambrose. With him, it always betrays me—I lose consciousness.

But was it him last night?

The thought feels far-fetched, almost impossible. Who would slip past guards, patiently undo the buttons on my dress, and simply put me to bed? It makes no sense.

And yet.

I feel it as surely as breath in my body, even if I cannot prove it.

"Lady Beatryx, do tell us—where does the inspiration for your gown come from?" one of the older nobles asks, his voice brittle as bone, the question delivered with all the subtlety he can muster.

For a heartbeat, I remember who these men are. Landed. Loaded. The kind whose signatures shift borders, whose coin could buy me a place among the highest ranks—if I ever cared to play that game.

The thought of using my mouth for the only act these men could still fumble their way through turns my stomach.

Absolutely not.

I raise my flute and drain it in one go. Perhaps that will silence him.

It doesn't.

Until I see Myst approaching—her timing precise. She offers a gracious excuse on my behalf and steers me away from the bleating old goats toward a table pulsing with youth and mead.

A gentle melody hums through the air, the same musicians from the garden weaving their notes once more. Their sound is serene, occasionally lifting into playful rhythms that stir anticipation for the dances soon to unfold.

I still cannot get the cello out of my mind—nor its musician. I tried to enter his thoughts. The effort overwhelmed me, pulling me into darkness. It was the same when I met Ambrose.

And yet…

The resemblance in spirit feels undeniable. Perhaps I only want it to be so.

My heart insists, even as reason falters.

I claim two glasses of honey mead from a passing attendant, their golden scent rising warmly as I hand one to Myst and sip from the other.

"Beatryx," she says, her voice edged in something softer now, "what has kept you so busy since we arrived? I've seen so little of you."

The question lands with weight. I have been distant—in presence and in thought.

I lean back, tracing the rim of my glass in slow, absent circles. With Myst—who hears me fully, without assumption—I find I'm ready to speak.

"Well," I say, a smile tugging despite myself, "I've met someone."

Myst laughs, light and teasing, perhaps coaxed by the mead. She leans into me, her shoulder brushing mine. "Beatryx, that is nothing new. You meet someone quite often. No judgment."

A flush warms my cheeks. I wish she could feel what I feel— just for a moment. Maybe then she would understand that this is different.

I glance down, something quieter settling in my chest. I take another sip before continuing.

"I met him in the small town beyond the kingdom—the day they prepared the luncheon in your honor. After Iyce drew you away, Shayn, Garrett, and I went to the training yard. Once those two decided to spar with the women's army, I wandered off. One thing led to another."

Myst's expression sharpens.

"No, Myst. We haven't."

A breath of laughter slips out—light, but threaded with something heavier beneath. "Oh, I want the man, believe you me—but it's more than that. I can't find the words. His name is—"

"Blayze, my son!"

The king's voice cuts through the room like a blade—cold, sudden, absolute.

Silence falls. Every head turns, including mine.

The only sound that follows is the shattering of my glass against marble.

Before I can react, Myst's hand slips into mine, steadying me—replacing the broken weight with something solid.

The world beneath me shifts.

When I lift my gaze, the composure he wore before the king is gone. He is already turned toward me—as if the sound tore straight through him.

And I know those eyes.

Only by a different name.

Ambrose's gaze locks with mine, and mine with his, until the room begins to notice. One by one, heads turn. The air thickens—curiosity, suspicion, something sharper.

At last, his father intervenes, cutting through the moment and silencing the spectacle we never meant to create.

The king resumes, though not without casting me a look steeped in confusion. Ambrose catches it too. His jaw tightens.

Myst's grip on my hands sharpens.

"Beatryx, look at me. Stay with me. Do you understand?"

Before I can answer, she exhales a stream of cold mist into my face. Calm settles over me instantly.

We leave the ballroom, turning sharply onto a glass-lined balcony. A few windows stand cracked open, letting in a cool breeze that steadies my breath.

She guides me to a bench, and we sit. Two attendants arrive with water. She presses a glass into my hand.

Then, softly—

"Okay... what in all goddesses is going on?"

I tell her everything.

Myst

"Iyce has never mentioned having a brother or a sister, so this is certainly interesting—and we need to understand what is unfolding here. But I need you to pull yourself together and hold steady until I can."

Then again, Iyce and I don't exactly spend our days sharing tender conversations over tea.

Beatryx promises she will. Goddesses, I hope she does. Her track record isn't exactly reassuring when it comes to restraint. Still, I believe she's truly falling—relentlessly—for this man. So we shape a plan between us.

On the way back to the ballroom, we stop by a perfumed retreat tucked behind the grand hall, where a sweet fae girl with enormous lilac eyes helps restore us to something resembling composure. She reminds me of Viola, Estelle's assistant back home.

Beatryx and I reenter the ballroom, each of us veiled in attitude. Almost instantly, I catch Blayze shifting his attention toward her. I do believe he cares for her—just as much as she does for him—because he makes a direct line for the woman now fanning herself with something she grabbed from a table, her wrist fluttering faster than a hummingbird's wings.

I brace myself and plant my feet—then large hands wrap around my waist, and I stiffen.

"Myst, dear, dance with me," he says.

Iyce sweeps me up like a winter gust, and before I can blink twice, we're on the ballroom floor, lined up with the others for the Gavotte.

Lovely.

Well, I'm not sure what Blayze said to Beatryx, but they've now joined the group—Beatryx taking her place beside me, and Blayze next to Iyce, who honestly couldn't be less interested in him if he tried.

The music begins, and we move. Each time Blayze and Beatryx pass one another, the air thickens, charged with something unspoken.

Beatryx

I'm in his arms—I hate that I want to be.

Blayze pulls me into the infamous spin, and I let him, though my body is taut with restraint. His whisper grazes my ear, low and cautious. "I can explain."

I keep my voice sharp, edging into mocking. "I'm sorry, have we met before? Do I know you from somewhere? Hmm… you do look familiar."

He doesn't react. Just spins me, hard. With one flick of his wrist, I'm pulled flush against his chest, my hands gripping his arms as I brace against his strength.

The dance ends, and I catch Myst recoiling as Blayze's arrogant brother kisses her cheek. Then the king—who insisted Blayze attend this ball for some grand announcement—bangs a fork against his overflowing goblet, demanding attention for the Monarch's Toast as he climbs the dais stairs.

I stand as still as porcelain, staring at the king. Attendants sweep through the ballroom, offering flutes of Blanquette de Limoux to every guest.

"Royals… no, no—Your Majesties and Highnesses… all you noble folk—Lords… Ladies… those envoy chaps from over the sea… and the rest of you poor souls down here… raise your glasses!" he slurs.

I glance at Blayze. His expression is unreadable, but something wild flickers behind his eyes.

Then the king continues, "We have a verrry special guest in attend'nce this evenin'. C'mon, my darlin'."

He motions to a shy girl, who approaches slowly, and draws her forward before the crowd.

"From the fair and gracious Kingdom of Kastanjebrun, I present to you Her Royal Highness, Princess Anabelle—hic!—who, by joinin' her hand to that of my eldest son, Prince Blayze Volcelyn, will bind our two realms in lastin' alliance. Raise your goblets high— hic!—and drink to friendship, prosperity, and love everlasting! We celebrate!"

I'm not breathing.

Dropping my glass a second time is not an option—my fingers are clenched around it so tightly, it might burst. But faster than shooting stars, I turn to Myst, lean in close, and whisper, "I've completely lost it now. Please, do not follow me."

Myst spins, her eyes pleading. "Beatryx, please."

I give her a solemn look, then soften it with feathered words. "I'll be fine. I need air."

I slip out of the ballroom as discreetly as possible, praying no one notices.

But someone does.

"Tryx, where are you going?"

Shayn is trailing me now.

Goddesses above. Why did I ever think signing those invitations as "Tryx" was a good idea—for him and for Garrett?

Walking—just walking—is all I do, knowing neither he nor Garrett can abandon their post outside the ballroom to follow me.

Blayze

Battling my own thoughts, I wonder what in all realms is going on. Has my father lost his damn mind? He banished me—and now he plans to use me as a pawn. He'll have to be dealt with later… after I talk this through with—

Damn. She's gone.

Frustrated, I shift my gaze to Myst—a woman I've never formally met. But her confused shrug speaks volumes. The goddesses know she's endured her own struggles with my brother. I respect her deeply, this future queen.

And yet I allow myself to be carried by the moment.

"Hello, Princess. I'm Blayze. We'll pick this up again soon. And remember this—you're lovely, and my brother is the most doomed man alive for not deserving you."

Her smile grows, just enough to tell me she heard me. Felt it. She tips her chin toward the door, a silent command to go after Beatryx.

I don't hesitate.

Until I feel a massive hand close around my arm.

"Brother. Leaving so soon?" Iyce questions.

I pull my arm from his grip, step closer, and speak low. "Think carefully before you ever do that again." Then I take my leave.

What would a woman do in a moment like this? No one knows.

It feels wrong to reach for the power that lives in me, the trickle that answers without question. But I do—just enough to stir the thread that binds me to her. I close my eyes and know exactly where she is.

I step onto the balcony, my breath frosting in the dark.

"Don't bother. Now, if you'll excuse me, Blayze."

Beatryx stands at the balcony's rail, staring out into the night. "Are you the cello player, too? How many selves do you wear beneath that name?"

She's wearing a stunning gown—no coat. She must be half-frozen.

She stays there, one hand lightly resting on the rail, in the same spot she must have found while exploring the castle the day she discovered the cello. My mother's cello.

She's captivated by the view. And in that moment, I take my chances, like the ignorant man I am—yet instead of stepping closer, I lean against the cold stone, watching her from where I stand.

"The burning glaycyrs. Ancient and full of meaning. Would you like to see them up close—something few ever experience?"

She breaks her gaze, turns fully toward me, and says, "Do you have more secrets to show me?"

She casts the bait. And I take the hook.

I step closer, voice low. "You asked if I was the cello player." I lower my chin in quiet confirmation. "I am."

Then I extend my hand, hoping she'll trust me again. "You asked about my secrets. Come—I'll show you."

She hesitates. I see it—the war behind her eyes. She's trying to make sense of everything: the masks I've worn, the truth I've withheld. Then my father's announcement—the sting still lingering in the air. I don't blame her for questioning it all.

But she doesn't walk away.

She accepts, and her hand in mine feels like everything.

For this moment, she trusts me.

And that is enough.

I wrap my coat around her shoulders, shielding her from the cold. Then I lift her into my arms and carry her to the edge of the balcony.

Held against me, she breathes steadily, and I whisper the words I've been holding back—words that invite her to wrap her arms around my neck and close her eyes, if she wishes.

She slips into stillness.

I summon the whistle from deep within, the one that calls the ice vixen only I command. In an instant we're airborne, landing on something solid, swift as lightning. She keeps her eyes closed for a moment longer, but when she finally opens them, I feel the shiver move through her.

She's never seen a beast like this. Few have.

Behind her, reins firm in one hand and the other encircling her waist, I feel the guarded tension she carries in her heart.

The creature slows as we enter the frozen forest. Snow and ice hush the world—the mystical glaycyrs unfolding before us in solemn stillness.

She lifts her head, looking around as if she can't take it all in. "This is unbelievable."

My hand leaves her waist and settles at her neck's hollow, steady and tender. I draw her back until my mouth is at her ear and whisper, "So are you, my star. Welcome to the conflicted Glaycyr Forest."

The vixen glides between two towering glaycyrs, their frozen spires reaching into the highest stretch of the evening sky. Pools of molten lava shimmer below and stir at my presence, as they always do. But this time, she notices.

She tilts her head back, eyes wide, taking in the unreachable crowns. I place both hands around her upper arms, steadying her as she stares at something that resists reason, tightening my hold on the vixen with my thighs to keep us balanced.

She's quiet. But I feel the shift in her. She doesn't want to feel pain again.

I dismount the ice creature, who purrs beneath me—a sound that thrills and unsettles even me. I take a few steps, then turn back and close the space between us.

"Ready to explore?"

She smiles. That's all I need.

I place my hands on her hips and lift her down. The beast lets out a restless cry and launches into the starry sky, as if glad to be rid of us.

There is so much to show Beatryx and even more to tell. Where do I begin? I've spent years keeping my life and my feelings under iron control, yet I want to share this moment with her.

I've been offering my hand to her often lately, though I always want her to choose it freely. When she does, our fingers link without hesitation, and we begin the historic walk of the burning glaycyrs.

"Here, one is neither cold nor hot; the clash between ice and fire never slows."

"Has this always been here?" Beatryx asks.

I take a breath before answering.

She's curious.

Open.

27

Glaycyr Falz

Olyvia

With everyone fussing over the ball and the castle hands occupied with their duties, I finally have the perfect chance to slip away into the castle's vault of secrets.

If I don't start finding answers soon, the fire inside me will keep asking questions I can't silence.

The moment I step inside the library, the feeling returns—fire imprisoned by ice. It's not metaphorical. It's intentional. The contrast settles over me the way cold does when you cross a threshold too quickly.

The sconces along the walls and the candles on the tables burn low. I pause, tempted to summon more light, then decide against it. A brightly lit library would draw attention—and tonight, discretion matters.

I climb the stairs to the highest level, passing Clarina's favorite alcove along the way. Near the back, several rolled maps rest against the wall. One lies spread across a table, weighted at the corners. I glance at it, curious, but the terrain is unfamiliar.

Don't get sidetracked.

I slip my bag over the back of a chair, free my hands, and step onto the ladder propped against the towering shelves. Only then do I begin my search—books on the historia of Glaycyr Falz. A few titles immediately stand out. I pull three volumes, gathering them into a neat stack against my chest before climbing down to the table.

I study the titles carefully: *The Royal Story of Glaycyr Falz. The Lost Queen. The Feud Between Brothers.*

Just as I settle in, voices drift through the space.

I'm no longer alone in the library.

Clarina

"We cannot get caught, Asher," I whisper as he leads us deeper into the upper alcoves and up the stairs to a quiet lounge overlooking the burning glaycyrs. He kisses me as he loosens the front of my corset, then presses me sweetly against the wall.

About six months ago, Asher was brought into service here from Crescere Moonz—one of the three kingdoms in this realm. Not long after, Auxilia punished me for breaking a teacup at a royal dinner. She dragged me to the barn and beat my bare backside with a leather strap. Neither of us knew we weren't alone.

Asher was there. He heard everything. Later, he told me he hadn't seen it—which I don't believe. He's too kind for that, too careful with my pride. He came to me afterward, comforted me, and one thing led to another. He swore he'd hold her head beneath freezing water if she ever touched me again, though doing so would mean exile.

That night, after he kissed away my tears, he carried me to the edge of the forbidden Forest of Frozen Dreams and settled me onto an iced-over pond. The cold numbed the pain—and the memory of who caused it. Then he kissed me until a pleasure I had never known surged through me.

Now, with the final string released, Asher pulls the corset apart and slides my dress down just enough to bare my aching breasts. He cups them immediately, still kissing me, murmuring about his day and asking about mine between each touch.

"What do you want, Clarina, my little fox?" he murmurs. "Do

you want me buried deep inside you, or…?"

His mouth closes around my nipple, a soft bite, while his hands roam my body as though learning it without sight. He's ravenous— and I let him be.

I reach for his breeches and begin unlacing them, intent on rescuing the part of him I need most. With the flaps parted, I draw him close and lead him into my chamber of treasures. He lifts my leg and drives into me, sending me headlong into ecstasy.

Don't stop.

Don't ever stop.

Olyvia

Since arriving in this realm, I've learned quite a bit. The most important lesson? Never expect a library to behave like a library. At any moment, it might become the setting for a live sex act right before your eyes.

Get out of here, I think, snatching all three books and shoving them into my bag. I swing the strap over my shoulder and hurry toward the back staircase, magic humming uneasily as I pass the towering glaycyrs on my way down.

Hunger rises as I move through the halls, music and laughter spilling from the ballroom. Everyone is busy tonight, celebrating Myst.

Well—almost everyone.

I know for a fact two individuals are not doing their jobs. They're in the library.

The large kitchen greets me with warmth, familiar in a way that almost feels like home. Maybe it's because I've claimed an entire corner—dried flowers hanging where pots once did, the space unmistakably mine. The worktable is piled high with food for those not attending the ball.

As I turn toward the doorway, movement catches my eye.

Iyce strides past with three jeweled women clinging to his arms, their laughter echoing as they follow him up the staircase toward torchlit chambers.

So that's where his loyalty lies.

Not with the kingdom.

Not with Myst.

With himself.

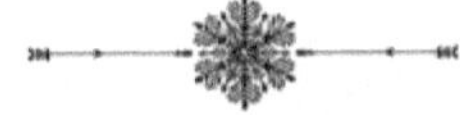

Myst

My parents sent me here to make things right with Iyce? *How?* That man leaves the worst taste in my mouth. Something is off with him. I feel it deep in my bones.

The ballroom watches the back of my head as I walk away. But I feel them—two shadows falling into step behind me—when all I want is to be alone.

The guards outside the ballroom glance up as I turn, my expression cold.

"Stand down."

Shayn and Garrett halt mid-step, stunned. I don't stop there.

"Leave me at once."

They hesitate, blinking like confused children.

"Yes, I know what you're thinking—the king has the final word. But hear me. We're not in his kingdom. And he's not in this one. You yield to none but me."

I leave them behind and step into the narrow cloakroom. My coat hangs alone on its hook, the one thing in this castle that still feels like mine. I take it, wrapping the familiar weight around my shoulders before pushing through the doors and into the cold.

I do not even know where I am going—I just keep walking.

Grandpapá made everything better. I miss him. And I miss Midnight.

So many thoughts swirl through my mind as I tromp through

the snow toward a barn I spot in the distance. I need a horse, because riding is exactly what I do when nothing else makes sense. I reach into my coat pocket, pull out my gloves, and tug them on as I walk.

The snowflake necklace I've never removed begins to glow faintly as I approach the dark structure, and a strange, mysterious feeling hits me. The barn looks as if it was built from stone quarried in the mountains of this province—solid, heavy, and likely warm enough to shelter animals in a kingdom this cold.

With a push, the door creaks open—reluctant—revealing a dark interior, save for soft moonlight sifting in through narrow windows high above. Slowly, I walk inside and look past the gleam. Thick beams rise overhead, with stalls tucked along the edges.

"Well, hello, beauties," I say, greeting the various horses as I walk past the only other live companions in sight. My scent reaches them instantly, stirring a chorus of whinnies before I choose the perfect ride.

"Which one of you would like to go on an adventure with me?"

My eyes drift to a large basket full of apples. I grab one and continue to persuade them. "My beauties in my kingdom love apples. I bet you do too."

And there it is—I feel it. I know which one.

I walk to the stall and begin to unlatch the clip when I hear, "I wouldn't do that if I were you."

The deep male voice, laced with an accent I don't recognize, startles me.

"Show yourself, at once!"

The only thing I hear next is dark, mesmerizing laughter. The nerve. I repeat myself. "I demand it. Reveal who you are this instant."

Then, in a low and serious tone, he retorts, "Aggressive, are you? Use your magic to reveal me."

My curiosity sparks. He clearly knows I have no idea how to

do that.

He continues, "What flows through your blood is power like no other. Learn how to use what you have."

Silence.

I contemplate his words and decide he's not revealing himself for a reason.

I carry on with my plan, but when I turn back to the stall, the latch is back in place—and the horse is gone.

Turning in all directions, I search for the horse or the man. Then something catches my attention—a spiral staircase. Where does that lead? Once I reach the top, there's nothing of interest—just sacks of grain and bales of hay.

The wooden floorboards moan softly beneath me as I walk to the window overlooking the castle. Guests are beginning to drift onto balconies. Then I notice one specific balcony, and the man who isn't alone on it.

Iyce.

My heightened eyesight is not disappointing, and what I see feels vile. This entire kingdom is a joke as far as I'm concerned. I hope Beatryx can get answers from Blayze, because the king and Iyce have no interest in anything worthy.

I take the steps back down, and the sleek mare I originally selected is waiting, as if she chose me too. I don't think twice. We gallop toward the nearest forest I see.

I don't care if it's full of witches, warlocks, trolls, or fae.

I need an escape. Now.

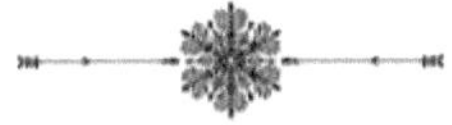

Anabelle

Respectfully, I watch the midnight-blue ink swirl inside the crystal jar each time the king dips his ornate quill into it. Power radiates from him, threading through the air of his private library.

But mine pushes back.

"Is that a letter to my father?" I ask.

He lifts his ice-blue eyes, and I know he will lie before the reply falls from his lips. "No, dear. This is of no concern to you."

Then why does it reek of secrecy? Why am I betrothed to a banished prince?

He looks up at me, his expression unreadable, but I'm reading everything else. I nearly turn to leave when a vision strikes—brief but clear. His intentions are certain before the final stroke of his quill.

Yes, he's writing to my father.

Anger surges through me. "Do you know how many long days and nights it took for me to travel here? What happened in that ballroom was humiliating, all because you and my father conspired for something that will never take place. Blayze doesn't want it, and neither do I."

Now I have his full attention. He stands, turns his back to me, and walks toward the window overlooking the majestic glaycyrs.

Still, I press on. "You may rule this kingdom, but you do not rule the entire realm—and you certainly do not govern mine. I also know my family was allied with—"

He cuts me off, faster than a blade to the throat. His voice booms, "Do not say her name. It's forbidden! The planned union between you and Blayze will be made official," he declares again, cold and final.

A rush of relief washes over me as I walk out, finally escaping his suffocating aura. But the tears come anyway. This kingdom feels wrong—its people, its pulse—and I have no idea where I'm headed.

The hallway to the left feels right, so I follow it. When I look up, I see a mural of wild horses—so vivid it looks alive. Then a second vision takes hold.

Wild horses. Running free.

Garrett

"Why is Myst so upset? She seemed fine—tense, sure—but fine when we arrived at the ball," I say to Shayn as we walk away from the furious princess.

He doesn't answer, just simmers beside me. I press on. "Should we follow her in secret? We did take an oath to protect her."

Finally, he snaps. "I'm tired of being treated like shit every time her moods shift. I'm going to find something to drink—and then someone to fuck." He veers down another corridor without a backward glance.

I'm left standing there, frustration settling heavy in my chest. Before I can sort it out, soft giggling pulls my attention. Two maids scurry away, cheeks flushed, eyes wide. Little eavesdroppers. They heard everything.

Enough. I'm done with tonight. A hot soak and a strong drink sound like the only cure. I head through the grand gallery toward my room.

But something stops me.

A mural—wild horses painted in deep, rich tones. They charge forward, dust swirling around their hooves, as if they might burst from the wall. I'm caught, mesmerized.

And then I collide with something solid.

Someone.

We drop to our knees. Instinctively, I reach for her arms, steadying her.

Sapphire-blue eyes meet mine and hold. Time stretches. Long black hair frames her face like ink over porcelain. She's unlike anyone I've ever seen.

"Are you hurt?" I ask, voice low.

"My day has been a whirlwind," she murmurs. "I only need some peace. Would you walk me to the garden? If you have time."

I have time for her.

"Yes."

Our eyes stay locked as I take her gloved hands and help her to her feet. My gaze flicks back to the mural—the horses look different now. Wilder. Alive.

Side by side, we follow the narrow path toward the Polar Gardens. She's petite and graceful, her gown catching the light with every step, her eyes capable of undoing a man.

She pauses at the fountain, studying its design. "I completely empathize with this queen," she says softly.

Then she straightens. "I apologize for my rudeness. My name is Anabelle."

She slips off her left glove and extends her hand. I take it without hesitation, meet her gaze, and lift her delicate wrist to my lips.

"The pleasure is all mine. I'm Garrett."

Olyvia

A spacious sitting area lies between Beatryx's bedroom and mine, a quiet lounge with two chairs and a small table set for tea near the outer wall. Behind it, a tall counter holds the essentials: dishes, flatware, and a generous bowl of fruit, bread, and cheese. At the far end, a crystal decanter rests, its water infused with berries.

The fires in this suite—and throughout the castle—never burn hot enough to offer true warmth. I call on my magic, weakened as it feels, coaxing the main hearth into a full, satisfying roar.

As the flames settle, I pour myself a glass of water and sit at the table with the food I brought from the kitchen. Then I turn to the books I gathered from the library.

Each title is intriguing. Which one holds the key to understanding why ice overpowers fire? It could be any of them.

I reach for *The Lost Queen.*

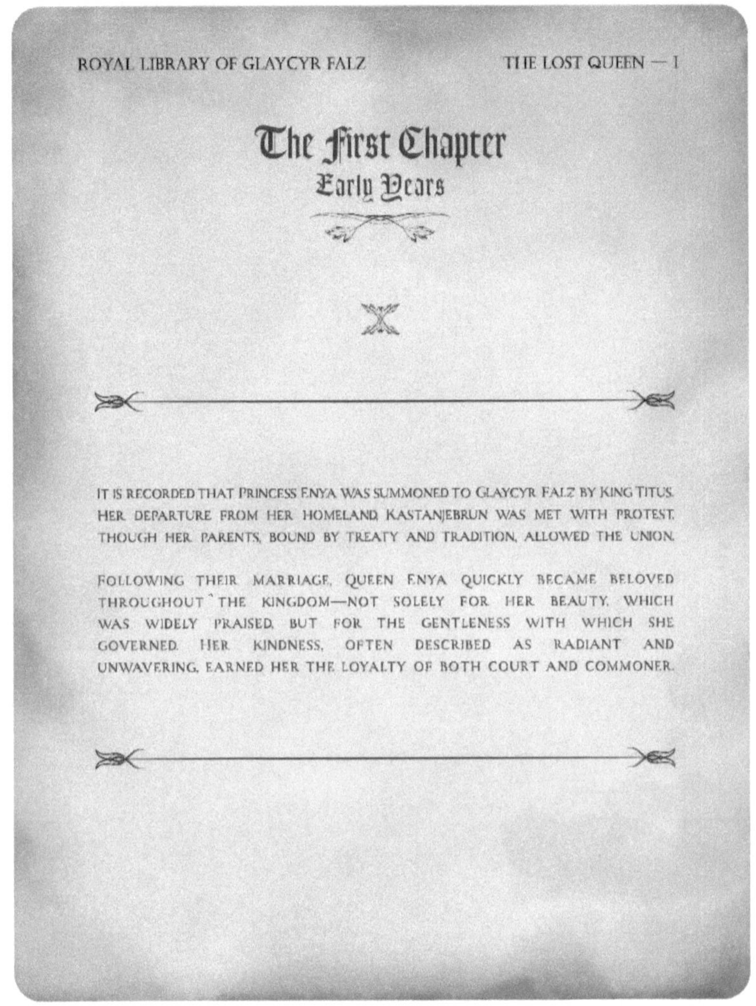

The First Chapter
Early Years

IT IS RECORDED THAT PRINCESS ENYA WAS SUMMONED TO GLAYCYR FALZ BY KING TITUS. HER DEPARTURE FROM HER HOMELAND, KASTANJEBRUN, WAS MET WITH PROTEST, THOUGH HER PARENTS, BOUND BY TREATY AND TRADITION, ALLOWED THE UNION.

FOLLOWING THEIR MARRIAGE, QUEEN ENYA QUICKLY BECAME BELOVED THROUGHOUT THE KINGDOM—NOT SOLELY FOR HER BEAUTY, WHICH WAS WIDELY PRAISED, BUT FOR THE GENTLENESS WITH WHICH SHE GOVERNED. HER KINDNESS, OFTEN DESCRIBED AS RADIANT AND UNWAVERING, EARNED HER THE LOYALTY OF BOTH COURT AND COMMONER.

The rest of this chapter is rich with detail, but none of it helps me right now.

The Second Chapter
The Queen's Magic

HISTORICAL ACCOUNTS SUGGEST QUEEN ENYA POSSESSED ELEMENTAL FIRE MAGIC, A GIFT INHERITED FROM HER MOTHER'S LINEAGE. HER USE OF THIS POWER WAS MEASURED AND DISCREET, LARGELY DUE TO KING TITUS'S GROWING ENVY. HIS OWN MAGIC—ICE—WAS FORMIDABLE, YET IT PALED BESIDE HERS IN BOTH POTENCY AND REVERENCE.

IT IS SAID THAT TENSIONS BETWEEN THEIR POWERS SHAPED THE EARLY YEARS OF THEIR RULE, THOUGH FEW DARED SPEAK OF IT OPENLY.

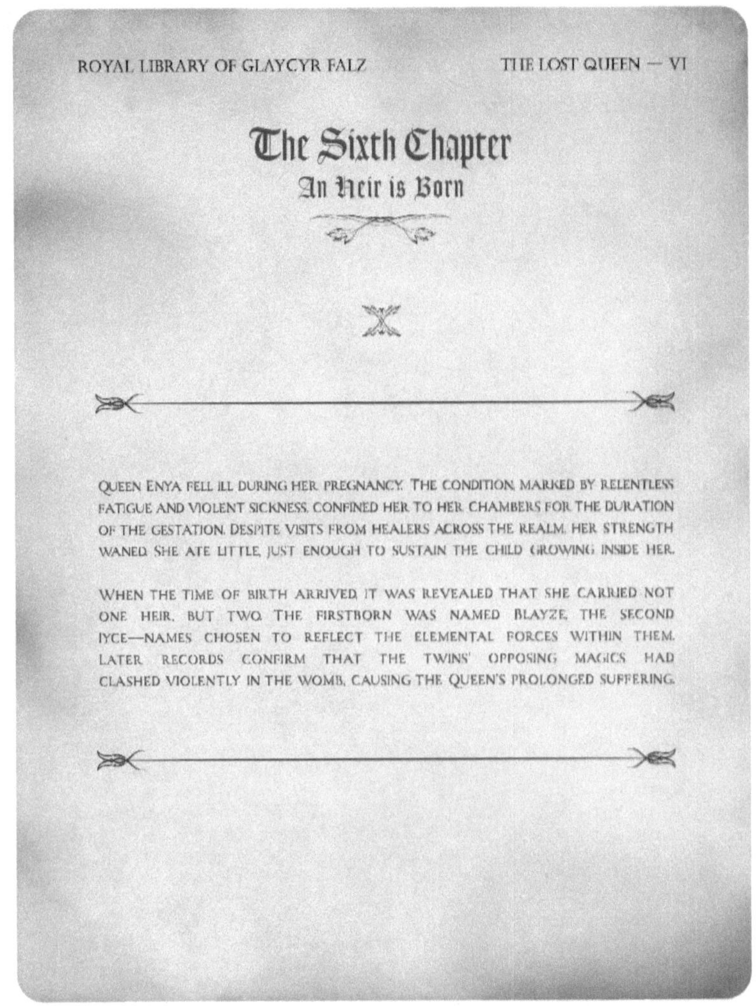

ROYAL LIBRARY OF GLAYCYR FALZ   THE LOST QUEEN — VI

The Sixth Chapter
An Heir is Born

QUEEN ENYA FELL ILL DURING HER PREGNANCY. THE CONDITION, MARKED BY RELENTLESS FATIGUE AND VIOLENT SICKNESS, CONFINED HER TO HER CHAMBERS FOR THE DURATION OF THE GESTATION. DESPITE VISITS FROM HEALERS ACROSS THE REALM, HER STRENGTH WANED. SHE ATE LITTLE, JUST ENOUGH TO SUSTAIN THE CHILD GROWING INSIDE HER.

WHEN THE TIME OF BIRTH ARRIVED, IT WAS REVEALED THAT SHE CARRIED NOT ONE HEIR, BUT TWO. THE FIRSTBORN WAS NAMED BLAYZE, THE SECOND IYCE—NAMES CHOSEN TO REFLECT THE ELEMENTAL FORCES WITHIN THEM. LATER RECORDS CONFIRM THAT THE TWINS' OPPOSING MAGICS HAD CLASHED VIOLENTLY IN THE WOMB, CAUSING THE QUEEN'S PROLONGED SUFFERING.

Ah, I understand, now we're getting somewhere. Fire magic confirmed. And the king—jealous, of course.

The book is becoming intense, pulling me deeper with every page. I gather my things, pluck a lovely pear from the bowl, and head to my bedroom to continue reading.

Before settling in, I draw back the heavy tapestries from the window. The stars tonight are radiant. I pause for a moment, letting their quiet power wash over me.

Then I lay the books across the bed, sink into the covers, and pick up where I left off, skimming past the less important chapters in search of what truly matters.

ROYAL LIBRARY OF GLAYCYR FALZ   THE LOST QUEEN — XII

The Twelfth Chapter
Queen Enya Becomes a Grandmother

THE BIRTH OF A GRANDCHILD IS TRADITIONALLY MARKED AS A TIME OF JOY AND LEGACY. YET FOR QUEEN ENYA, IT IS REMEMBERED AS A TIME OF SORROW AND DIVISION.

FIVE YEARS AFTER THE BIRTH OF HER TWIN SONS, ENYA BORE HER THIRD CHILD— A DAUGHTER NAMED PRINCESS ISABELLA. HISTORICAL RECORDS DESCRIBE ISABELLA AS BEING TOUCHED BY THE RARE GIFT OF HEALING, A MAGIC SHE USED GENEROUSLY TO AID THE SICK AND IMPOVERISHED. HER ACTS OF COMPASSION EARNED HER QUIET REVERENCE AMONG THE OUTER PROVINCES, THOUGH THEY PROVOKED IRE WITHIN THE PALACE WALLS. UPON LEARNING OF ISABELLA'S NIGHTLY EXCURSIONS BEYOND THE CASTLE—OFTEN DISGUISED AS A CHANDLER, WITH THE SICK BEING BROUGHT TO THE CHANDLERY, KING TITUS ISSUED A ROYAL EDICT FORBIDDING HER FROM HEALING ANYONE OUTSIDE THE COURT. HE CLAIMED SUCH ACTS WEAKENED THE KINGDOM'S STRENGTH AND COMPROMISED ITS SOVEREIGNTY. DESPITE THIS DECREE, ISABELLA CONTINUED HER WORK IN SECRET, SLIPPING PAST GUARDS AND INTO THE SURROUNDING TOWNS TO OFFER AID.

DURING THIS PERIOD, ISABELLA MET A COMMON MAN—NOT WHILE TENDING TO THE ILL, BUT THROUGH HIS REGULAR DELIVERIES OF PRODUCE TO THE CASTLE FROM HIS FAMILY'S FARM. THEIR ENCOUNTERS, THOUGH BRIEF AT FIRST, GREW INTO QUIET FAMILIARITY. OVER TIME, AFFECTION BLOSSOMED BETWEEN THEM. HE WAS SAID TO HAVE TREATED HER NOT AS ROYALTY, BUT AS A WOMAN OF HEART AND CONVICTION.

EVENTUALLY, ISABELLA CONCEIVED A CHILD. WHEN KING TITUS DISCOVERED THE PREGNANCY, HE BANISHED HER FROM THE CASTLE AND EXILED THE MAN FROM THE KINGDOM. A SECOND DECREE FOLLOWED: SHOULD THE MAN RETURN, HE WOULD BE SENTENCED TO DEATH.

IN THE MONTHS THAT FOLLOWED, QUEEN ENYA WAS INFORMED BY DIRECT COMMAND THAT SHE WAS PROHIBITED FROM ANY FORM OF RELATIONSHIP WITH ISABELLA OR THE UNBORN CHILD. THERE WAS TO BE NO CORRESPONDENCE, NO VISITS, NO ACKNOWLEDGMENT. QUEEN ENYA'S GRIEF IS SAID TO HAVE BEEN PROFOUND, THOUGH NO OFFICIAL RECORD DOCUMENTS HER RESPONSE.

Finally, I've reached the last chapter, and still I have found nothing to explain why ice is overtaking fire in Glaycyr Falz.

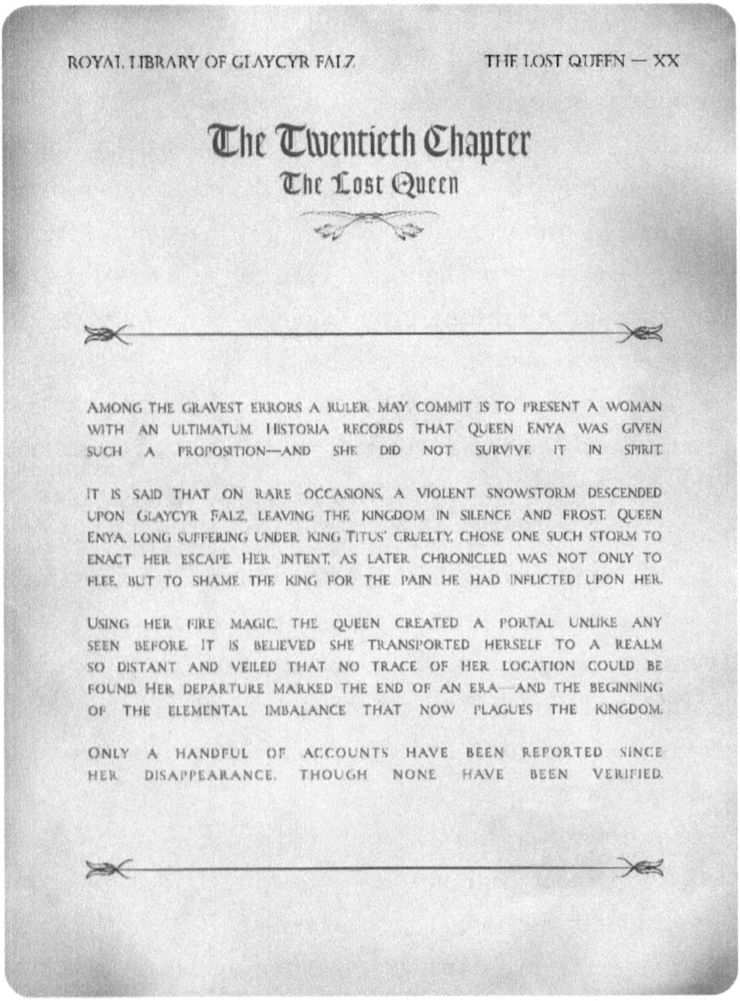

The Twentieth Chapter
The Lost Queen

AMONG THE GRAVEST ERRORS A RULER MAY COMMIT IS TO PRESENT A WOMAN WITH AN ULTIMATUM. HISTORIA RECORDS THAT QUEEN ENYA WAS GIVEN SUCH A PROPOSITION—AND SHE DID NOT SURVIVE IT IN SPIRIT.

IT IS SAID THAT ON RARE OCCASIONS, A VIOLENT SNOWSTORM DESCENDED UPON GLAYCYR FALZ, LEAVING THE KINGDOM IN SILENCE AND FROST. QUEEN ENYA, LONG SUFFERING UNDER KING TITUS' CRUELTY, CHOSE ONE SUCH STORM TO ENACT HER ESCAPE. HER INTENT, AS LATER CHRONICLED, WAS NOT ONLY TO FLEE, BUT TO SHAME THE KING FOR THE PAIN HE HAD INFLICTED UPON HER.

USING HER FIRE MAGIC, THE QUEEN CREATED A PORTAL UNLIKE ANY SEEN BEFORE. IT IS BELIEVED SHE TRANSPORTED HERSELF TO A REALM SO DISTANT AND VEILED THAT NO TRACE OF HER LOCATION COULD BE FOUND. HER DEPARTURE MARKED THE END OF AN ERA—AND THE BEGINNING OF THE ELEMENTAL IMBALANCE THAT NOW PLAGUES THE KINGDOM.

ONLY A HANDFUL OF ACCOUNTS HAVE BEEN REPORTED SINCE HER DISAPPEARANCE, THOUGH NONE HAVE BEEN VERIFIED.

She left through fire. He stayed in ice. And now everything burns cold. But why? Why does his power still reign when hers was stronger?

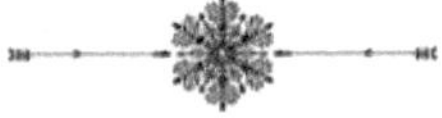

Myst

The horse is pure power beneath me as we ride deep into the

forest. The mare seems to need the run as much as I need the cool night air and the steady rhythm of her stride. We've been in this kingdom for two moon phases, and no one has bothered to give me a proper tour, so I'm learning on my own.

Gradually, I keep my posture tall but sink deeper into the saddle, signaling her to slow. I close my gloved fingers around the reins, applying gentle pressure. "Whoa, girl… whoa." After a few half-halts, she eases into a light trot, then settles into a soft walk.

She chooses the resting place herself—a quiet stream cutting through the snow—and lowers her head to drink.

"I'm sorry I don't know your name, but I bet you love having your ears rubbed." She answers with a soft neigh. She's solid white with dark brown eyes, her mane and tail a striking fire-red. Swift as lightning.

This forest is nothing like the ones in my kingdom. Snow lies thick, and the stars feel lower, as if they're watching me.

A distant melody drifts through the trees. I dismount while the mare drinks from the stream and move toward a light—toward the music. Fireflies drift like tiny lanterns, and blossoms glow softly in the undergrowth along the path.

The notes ripple through the cold air, and my mist reacts, engaging with every life in the forest, each breath of magic harmonizing with the song.

The music stops, startling me. Then a voice: "There is my beautiful girl, Priya. I have missed you."

A woman separates herself from the snow-laden trees, and the horse goes straight to her. Their bond is unspoken and undeniable. Instinctively, I back away.

"Do not be afraid. I'm here to warn you and to offer guidance."

She looks around my mother's age—an elegant figure with olive skin and long auburn hair streaked with crimson. But it's her eyes that strike me. Forest green, framed by dark lashes. I've seen eyes like these before.

She remains still, then says, "Hello, Myst. I am Enya. I see you've found my mare, Priya."

Enya... the Lost Queen. She's real.

"How do you know my name?"

Queen Enya explains that this moment was woven into fate before I was born. She speaks of the king—what she despises about him—and of her two sons.

"Iyce is my son, and I will always love him. How could I not? But he is much like his father. Your destiny is something far larger than Glaycyr Falz or Iyce."

The question slips out before I can stop it. "Why did you disappear from the kingdom? You're the queen."

Sadness softens her features. "That will be answered in time."

"How do I learn to control my magic?"

She laughs softly, almost to herself. "You will be taught—sooner rather than later—many things. That includes how to control the magic within you, which matters more than using it. Crossing paths with you here... it's a moment I've been waiting for."

Queen Enya promises we will meet again—when the time is right. She lifts her arms and whispers into the anxious wind, releasing a slow ribbon of fire that carves a path of ash before us. Then she looks at me and says her final words—for now. "This is a protection passage that leads to the barn. Please take care of Priya. I miss her so."

And then she's gone, leaving only burning embers in the shape of an **E** on the ground.

I mount the mare and click my tongue, easing her into a cautious walk toward the path. "Don't be sad, pretty girl. Your queen will be back for you."

Priya steps onto the trail, embers glistening beneath her hooves. An owl shrieks in the distance—a sharp, lonely sound that cuts through the cold. I glance back, heart tight, but the snow keeps its secrets.

Priya shifts into a full gallop, her mane and tail blazing like fire as they stream behind her, embers sparking beneath her hooves all the way back to the barn.

She's gone—but not forever. I'll see her again.

28

Glaycyr Falz

GODDESSES BEG

Olyvia

The next book, *The Feud Between Brothers*, cracks open as though it hasn't been touched in years.

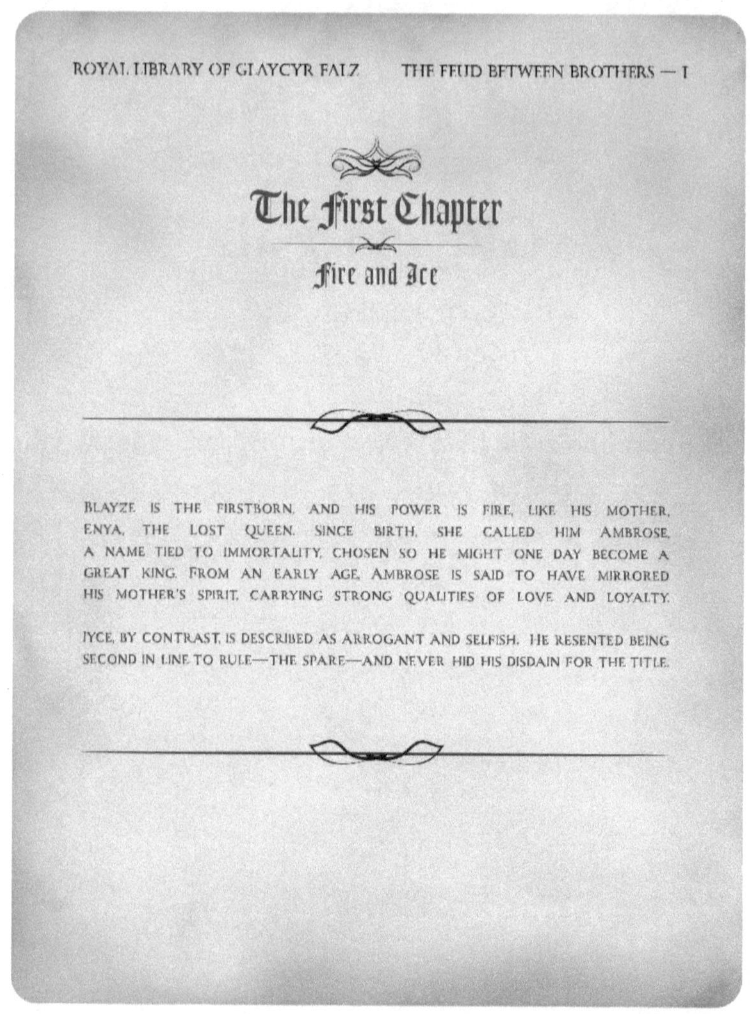

So, they were born into conflict. Fire and ice—love and resentment.

My teeth sink into the glossy pear as I continue skimming through chapters, reading only the sections that feel important.

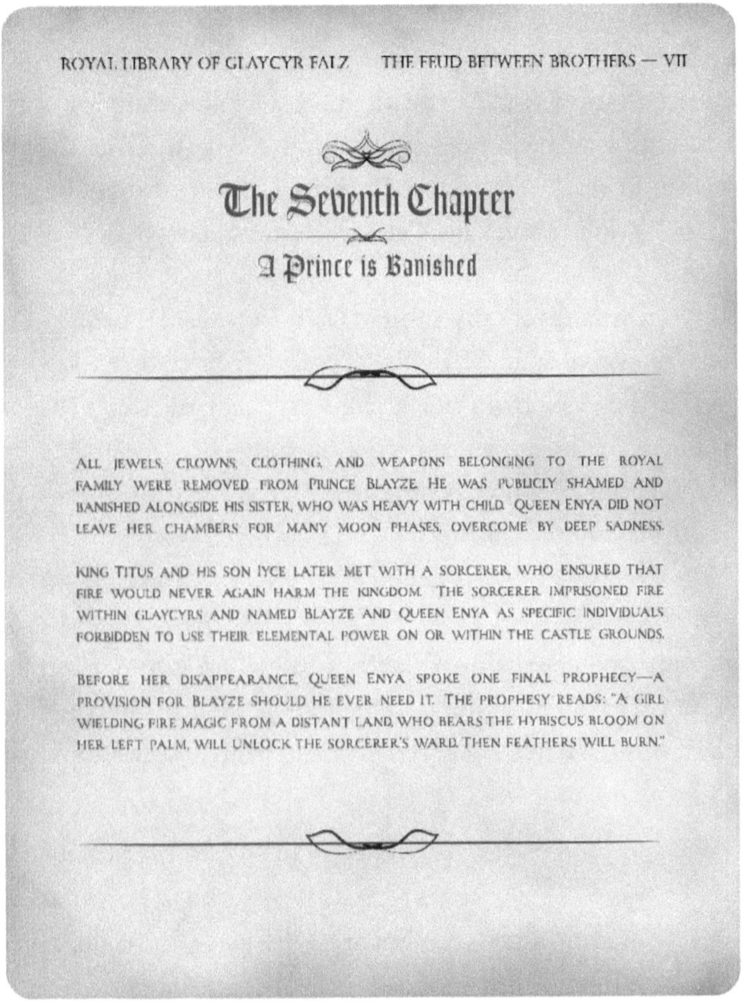

ROYAL LIBRARY OF GLAYCYR FALZ   THE FEUD BETWEEN BROTHERS — VII

The Seventh Chapter

A Prince is Banished

ALL JEWELS, CROWNS, CLOTHING, AND WEAPONS BELONGING TO THE ROYAL FAMILY WERE REMOVED FROM PRINCE BLAYZE. HE WAS PUBLICLY SHAMED AND BANISHED ALONGSIDE HIS SISTER, WHO WAS HEAVY WITH CHILD. QUEEN ENYA DID NOT LEAVE HER CHAMBERS FOR MANY MOON PHASES, OVERCOME BY DEEP SADNESS.

KING TITUS AND HIS SON IYCE LATER MET WITH A SORCERER, WHO ENSURED THAT FIRE WOULD NEVER AGAIN HARM THE KINGDOM. THE SORCERER IMPRISONED FIRE WITHIN GLAYCYRS AND NAMED BLAYZE AND QUEEN ENYA AS SPECIFIC INDIVIDUALS FORBIDDEN TO USE THEIR ELEMENTAL POWER ON OR WITHIN THE CASTLE GROUNDS.

BEFORE HER DISAPPEARANCE, QUEEN ENYA SPOKE ONE FINAL PROPHECY—A PROVISION FOR BLAYZE SHOULD HE EVER NEED IT. THE PROPHESY READS: "A GIRL WIELDING FIRE MAGIC FROM A DISTANT LAND, WHO BEARS THE HYBISCUS BLOOM ON HER LEFT PALM, WILL UNLOCK THE SORCERER'S WARD. THEN FEATHERS WILL BURN."

I look down at my left hand, then slowly flip it over. The hybiscus marking I've always had fades in and out, pulsing with what I now understand—begging to be unhidden.

This is talking about me! Oh goddesses!

Blayze

"I'll take you to the one place that knows me best—between fire and ice."

Beatryx and I walk beneath the glaycyrs, through a wooded stretch, until a stone cottage comes into view—a retreat I built far from the Forest of Frozen Dreams, meant for solitude, not dwelling. "You're shivering. Let's warm up while you ask whatever you wish."

The hearth reacts the moment we step inside, heat sweeping through the small space. Bringing Beatryx feels right.

I slip the coat from her shoulders, set it over a high-backed chair, and guide her toward the fire burning soft.

"I don't have your favorite mead, but I can offer my special brew. Or blackberry tea."

"I'll have what you're having," she says, a mischievous smile tugging at her lips.

I pour two glasses of my amber brew and return, placing one in her hand before motioning to the lounge. She sits first, and I take my place opposite her, prepared to speak truths buried so deep they sting to touch.

Maybe mentioning Isabella's pregnancy was too much. Beatryx must see the pain on my face as I struggle to respond, because her eyes—so open, so pretty—fill with tears. Quietly, she answers her own question.

"Julian."

I lower my gaze, slow and heavy. "Yes. Julian is Queen Enya's grandchild. A child she has never met."

Beatryx finishes her drink in one swallow and sets the glass on the table. She rises and walks to the window, standing so long that worry begins to press.

At last, she speaks. "So, when do I find out your true name?"

There it is. I promised—and now I must deliver.

"Ambrose Blayze Volcelyn," I say, voice low. "Former Prince of Glaycyr Falz."

She studies me like a rare piece of art. "Which name do you prefer?"

I step to her side, my voice soft but unmistakably firm. "Call me Blayze, Lady Beatryx Blake, of the noble House of Blake."

A faint huff of laughter ripples through her.

Her expression shifts, steady and serious. "You're the rightful heir to this kingdom, aren't you?"

The truth in her argument slips out before she can stop it.

"Yes... no. I was next in line. But when my father banished my sister, Isabella, I lost control. I went berserk. I used my fire to destroy—gardens, mountains... whatever I could reach. I lit it up. Iyce and I fought our final battle at the place that had always been our mother's refuge—and we destroyed it, leaving a ruin."

I sigh.

"I was banished. Deemed unfit to rule. Isabella was forced to watch. And my mother, whom I love dearly... she disappeared."

Beatryx stands in stunned silence.

"I was summoned back only because my father has an ulterior motive."

Beatryx kisses my cheek, then gathers our glasses and rinses them at the basin. When she returns, her voice is steady. "I feel something deeply for you, and I know this will all be made right."

I hold myself still.

"You have two options. I can take you back to the castle, or you can come to my cabin in the Forest of Frozen Dreams for a delicious meal."

Sharply, I whistle for the ice vixen.

Once we enter the Forest of Frozen Dreams, the cold deepens. I summon fire in each hand, casting warmth on either side of us as my thighs hold her close. We ride in silence, the night pressing in, until the sky opens above us.

Turquoise ribbons shimmer overhead, threading through the stars. We've never spoken of them, but the way Beatryx leans into me tells me she wonders too.

Are the goddesses begging for something of us?

29

Glaycyr Falz

FIERCE TALONS

Beatryx

I wake peacefully. My arms stretch overhead, unhurried, and I ease into a sitting position.

There's only one problem.

I'm in bed alone.

But when I turn to the small bedside table, I find a teacup beside a folded piece of parchment. His crest sits at the top—untouched this time, clear and deliberate. The sight lingers with me as I read.

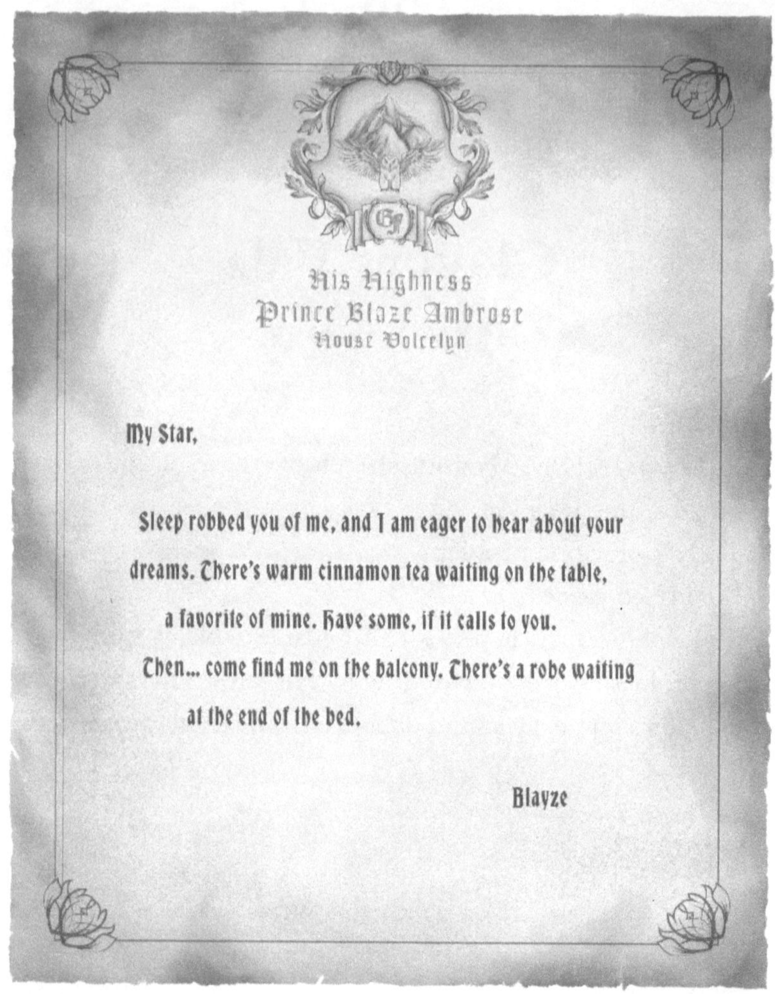

He thinks of everything.

The tea is delicious, and I sip it slowly as my senses begin to stir. The last thing I remember is his strong hands on my body, making me feel like royalty.

Gently, I set the teacup down, noticing the kingdom's crest etched into it—an owl guarding the majestic Glaycyrs. I reach for the robe, wrap myself in its warmth, and stand. As I step onto the balcony, I tie a neat bow with the sash.

Blayze sits in a chair, sipping his tea, and speaks before I reach him. "How did you sleep?"

The balcony railing draws me in, and I drift toward it, resting my teacup on the ledge as I take in the snow-covered stillness. Birds sing their morning plans into the crisp air, and for a moment, I allow myself this small solitude of happiness.

The chill finds me, and I walk to him, settling into his lap without hesitation. "I slept beautifully. Thank you."

Blayze kisses me softly. "There's someone you need to meet."

A flutter ripples through me. *So—he does have more secrets.* Something tells me there will always be surprises.

He rises with me still in his arms, carrying me to the edge of the balcony. Below us, the evergreen forest stretches wide and hushed, morning dew glistening on tiny blooms that brave the snow.

He lowers me slowly, my feet hovering for a breath—bare toes swaying over open air—before the cold stone meets me and I take my weight.

Blayze releases me only then, mimicking a low, rhythmic hoot as he lifts his arm in quiet invitation.

Moments later, a rush of air sweeps past—heavy wings slicing through the morning calm. A sharp screech follows, and I instinctively draw closer as powerful talons settle gently on his arm.

Awe strikes me. The beauty of the owl takes me by surprise— this is what's etched across his back, the one I saw for the first time last night.

"This is Sasha," he says. "She lives in the forest. Don't be jealous now."

A light laugh escapes me as I shrug. Blayze massages the hidden indentation between her eyes, and she leans into him, content. I can't help but smile.

We walk back inside, and Sasha glides from his arm to a large perch. Blayze takes my hand and leads us toward the stairs. "Let's have something to eat."

It sounds perfect; I'm hungry. But a quiet sadness settles in. In two days, our little entourage leaves for Crescere Moonz.

Downstairs, a simple table setting greets me—poached eggs, warm oats, rustic bread with jam and honey. A bowl of berries and juice sits beside each plate.

After we finish eating, Blayze carries the dishes to the kitchen. I sip my tea, watching him rinse them for a moment, then stand and bring over the water glasses.

"Thank you," he says. "There are linens on the worktable. Would you mind drying these?"

A laugh slips out. He thinks I'm helpless—and honestly, I am. But for him, I'd blow them dry.

Walking to the worktable, I pass the window, and something in a crystal bowl catches the light. When I step closer, confusion hits.

"Why do you have Olyvia's bracelet?"

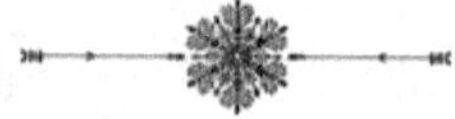

Blayze

And there it is—the information I needed.
Perfect.
But I have no idea who Olyvia is.

I look at Beatryx and answer truthfully. "I found the bracelet in the forest and wondered where such a unique piece came from. Do you know her? You could return it and let her know I found it. I'm sure she's missing it."

Letting Beatryx take it eases any doubt Olyvia might have had about why it was here.

"Yes, I can certainly do that," she says. "She always wears it, so I know she's missing it—and she'll be happy to have it back."

After a beat, I ask, "Who is Olyvia?"

Beatryx considers. "I'm not sure where she's from, honestly. She's genuine, though. A handmaiden to Myst—and to a few others, myself included. She helps with our attire, especially our hair." A faint smile curves her mouth. "She loves flowers, weaving them into intricate braids unlike any others in the realm. Myst has taken to her."

Myst

I slept—but not well. Last night's events still churn through me.

Queen Enya gave me information that was thrilling and confusing, but one thing is clear: I can hate Iyce freely. According to her, he is not my destiny—and thank all the goddesses for that.

It's not like I ever truly wanted him. But after he paraded his royal body across that balcony with three women who should be ashamed of themselves, I'll do everything in my power to keep him from ever touching me.

Biscuits. That's what I need.

I haven't seen Beatryx or Olyvia since yesterday evening, so I'll manage on my own this morning. The seamstress's work is remarkable, and I have so many elaborate gowns to choose from.

Today, I wear a soft yellow dress with long sleeves and a square neckline. Red birds are embroidered across the bodice and hem—work that must have taken days. My thick hair is tied back low, and I slip into yellow shoes tipped in red. A touch of powder, gloss to my lips, and I'm ready.

I leave the chamber composed.

Shayn and Garrett are nowhere in sight. Good. I need a long break from those two.

The stone corridors are always breezy, and being completely alone feels strange… until a drunken voice calls my name.

Not just any drunk.

"Where do you think you're going, bride-to-be?" he slurs.

I ignore him and keep walking. Mist coils inside me, pressing for release. Before I can blink, he's on my heels, shouting for me to stop.

He's not in a normal state.

Iyce circles ahead and blocks my path, towering over me. "We're betrothed," he growls. "That means you're mine— whenever I want you."

My breath quickens. Chest pounding.

His meaning lands with cold clarity.

He's twisting the truth to suit his own power.

"Iyce," I say evenly, "you caught me on my way to the dining hall for the day's first meal. Would you be so kind as to join me?"

He steps closer, eyes narrowed. "Who do you think you are, leaving the ballroom early last night? A ball in your royal highness's honor."

Before I can answer, he seizes my arm and forces me into an empty guest room.

The room tilts around me.

Iyce's strength overwhelms any attempt to steady the moment. He fists the front of my dress, and the stitched birds are ripped from their flight, thread snapping as the work gives way. My undergarments are left exposed.

A shocked breath escapes me. I try to move away, but my footing falters. He catches a handful of my hair and drags me toward him.

My reaction is immediate. I strike his face with everything in me.

It may not have been wise—but I've had enough.

His grip tightens, dragging me toward the bed. I scream and claw at him, refusing to go still.

My body feels powerless. My mist stays dormant.

Something inside me sharpens. I feel savage.

He shoves me onto the bed and slaps me across the face.

A burst of light erupts around me.

Then darkness.

Iyce

I will not take her today. When I do, I want her to remember every moment—every stroke. And right now, she won't remember anything. *Poor, helpless little princess.* She's blacked out.

I could place myself between those stunning, full breasts, barely held by the corset, and leave a little gift upon her face. But she's not even worth that.

Instead, I walk to the table, lift the pitcher of water, and toss its contents onto her beautiful face. Then I hurl the vessel through the window—glass shattering, fragments flying—and let out a low roar that cools the air around me.

I leave.

And they say she's powerful. I've yet to see it.

I use the back of my hand to wipe blood from my cheek.

The feral kitten left her mark.

By right of our betrothal, her virginity was owed to me many moon phases ago. But she isn't ready. What a child.

Myst

Slowly, I open my eyes and take in my surroundings. I'm still in the same guest room, lying on my back atop the bed, shivering.

Cold clings to my skin.

I sit up, sluggish and aching, and realize the dress is ruined—and I'm soaked.

Tears slip down my cheeks, born of anger, pain, and humiliation.

How dare he do this.

Queen Enya's words return to me. She said he wasn't part of

my destiny. I cling to that, because I cannot live under the shadow of that monster.

Another fear rises—darker than the rest.

With trembling hands, I slip my fingers beneath my undergarment.

No blood.

I would have thrown myself from the window otherwise—or found a way to kill him.

My body feels battered, as if I've been through a war.

This room isn't far from the one I'm staying in. Maybe—hopefully—I can reach it without being seen.

Dimly, I crack the door open and glance both ways.

No one.

This wing is reserved for high royalty, so it's mostly unoccupied.

Silently, I slip out and walk fast, clutching the torn dress together as best I can—when I hear—

"Myst! There you are."

No.

The word screams inside me. But I can't stop the tears streaming down my face.

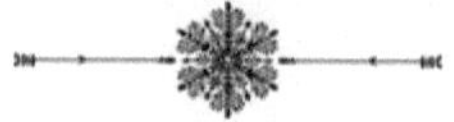

Olyvia

"I've been looking for you," I say urgently, following Myst into her chambers. She doesn't respond. I trail her to the bathing area, where she finally stops.

In the mirror ahead, her reflection stops me cold.

Her hair, once tied neatly at her nape, hangs loose and tangled around her face. Her cheek is red and swollen, the discoloration spreading toward her eye and lip. Her dress is torn from neckline to waist, the corset beneath exposed.

My hands lift on their own, shaking with fury.

Myst stands there, silent, and the sight of her takes the breath from my chest.

Heat flares across my palm—the hybiscus bloom glowing bright. I curl my fingers around it until I can mask it with a potion.

I need answers. Now.

"Myst…" Her name leaves me in a thin whisper before she turns and collapses into me. We both go down, and she cries against my shoulder. I soothe her, running my hand through her hair as she weeps.

When her breathing steadies, I dampen a linen and gently clean her face.

"This is going to bruise. And your eye… it's not right. You need a healer?"

"Isabella is a healer," Beatryx says as she steps into the bathing chamber. She drops to the floor beside us without hesitation, eyes sharp with concern.

"You know Isabella?" The words slip out before I can stop them. I've been reading and learning things I shouldn't know.

Myst looks between us, confusion clouding her expression. "Who is Isabella?"

After Myst recounts what she remembers before blacking out, heat surges through me. I want to burn Iyce to ash.

Beatryx shares what she's uncovered about Blayze—most of it I already knew. Then she adds, "I know where Isabella resides. We need to get you changed and leave this castle quietly, without being seen."

Myst nods. She says Iyce is passed out—drunk and apathetic, likely from a night spent on the balcony with castle whores.

The three of us form a plan, and hope stirs in my chest.

She must reach Isabella.

Myst slips into the closet to change, leaving Beatryx and me alone.

Beatryx's voice pulls me from my thoughts. "Are you missing

anything important? Blayze found this in the forest near his home."

She hands me my bracelet—the one my mother gave me—and relief crashes through me so fast I nearly forget to breathe.

"Oh goddesses, yes. Thank you."

There's no time for questions. And I'm grateful she doesn't mention it in front of Myst, who has grown fiercely protective.

I watch Beatryx as she shifts her weight, her mind already elsewhere.

She's made a decision.

Confirming that Iyce is truly passed out will fall to her—and if he isn't, she'll handle it. Myst can't do it. And I am too young.

That leaves Beatryx.

She begins to prepare without saying another word.

Layer by layer, she turns herself into temptation—corset fitted tight, neckline low. The skirt splits high in the front, revealing flashes of leg as she moves. The dress is entirely black, save for a fuchsia lining that flickers with motion.

It's far too beautiful for him.

But she isn't dressing for beauty.

She's going into attack mode.

Her hair falls over her shoulders, three braids on each side meeting in a high bun. The look is deliberate—dangerous, inviting.

I let out a low whistle before I can stop myself.

Myst, still pressing a wet linen to her cheek, looks up. "Please be careful, Beatryx. He is dangerous and powerful."

Beatryx nods once.

The sight of Myst's bruised face hardens her expression, sharpening her resolve.

"We meet at the stables within the half hour," she says lightly. "I'll be fine."

Then she's gone—leaving us with a wink, as though this is nothing more than an errand.

But I know better.

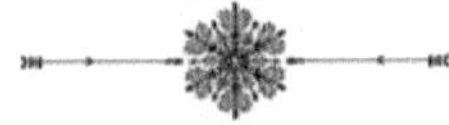

Myst

"Myst, we must get to the stables."

Olyvia's voice cuts through my thoughts. I was there last night, yet I still don't know who spoke to me. The question follows as we slip from the castle in silence.

Once we're off the path, we run.

The moment we step inside, the scent presses in—horses, hay… and something else. Old wood and leather, stone soaked with years. Beneath it all lingers a presence that doesn't belong to this age. Something ancient.

Him.

It lingers as I guide Olyvia up a winding staircase to a small loft cluttered with supplies and cobwebs. Below, the horses stir at our arrival, restless neighs rippling through the stable.

"There they are. She made it in—damn, she's good."

Olyvia follows my gaze through the loft window, her sight just as sharp—sharper, even, catching details I missed.

"What is that mark on his face? Did you get one in on him this morning?"

I glance at her, annoyed. She doesn't look away.

"Well?"

I roll my eyes. "Obviously."

Damn, she knows how to turn a man on quick.

The thought slips in as we watch Beatryx work—drawing Iyce in without so much as a touch. And yet, he's already lost, eyes fixed, breath held.

Then, suddenly, his hands are at her throat, pulling her close. Not hurting—but holding. Claiming. His mouth hovers near her ear.

Olyvia speaks before I can.

"Get the horse you rode last night. We must find Blayze."

30

Glaycyr Falz

Myst

Priya finds us as soon as we reach the bottom of the spiral staircase. The fiery beauty is out of her stall, prancing through the barn, ready to move—as if she can feel our uneasiness.

"How did you get out, pretty girl?" Priya snorts with excitement, and I turn to Olyvia. "Are you ready? We need to move fast."

Priya nudges me with urgency. She trusts me—but she's also warning me. It's time to go.

"Sweet Priya, can you lead us to Blayze?"

She whinnies in response, a restless force rippling through her.

I mount the powerful mare and extend a hand to Olyvia. She grips it, swings up behind me, and settles in just as Priya surges forward. Without hesitation, she carries us straight into the Forest of Frozen Dreams, as if instinct alone guides her.

"It's so serene," I murmur, and I feel Olyvia smile against my back.

She's a little mysterious—this girl. There's a thread between us. Distant, but real.

Snow spreads beneath Priya's hooves, pristine and untouched. The ash path that led me back to the barn last night is gone, buried beneath white, as if it never existed at all.

Olyvia suddenly grips my waist.

Before I can ask why, we see Blayze ahead of us, riding hard in our direction, forcing his horse through the snow. Worry is etched across his face. The moment he sees us, confirmation flickers in his eyes—as if he sensed something was wrong.

Priya reacts before we do, breaking stride to rub against him and neigh softly.

"What's going on?" Blayze asks, catching Priya's reins to keep us close.

We give him the condensed version of everything—what happened between me and Iyce, the plan we crafted, and what Beatryx is doing now: slipping Iyce into a blissful haze long enough for us to reach Isabella.

Blayze looks like he might come undone, though he holds himself together.

"This is Olyvia, by the way."

It's the shortest introduction I've ever given.

Blayze nods once, then looks at her. "I know who you are. Let's ride. Hold on to Priya—she'll stay close to Lakshay."

And we're off.

The Whispering Woods and the Forest of Shadows are the only forests I know. But this one is something else—frightening and enchanting, with weather that demands control from both rider and horse.

We push through the frozen air until we reach the tree line. Beyond it, the forest lies breathtaking and still, blanketed in snow and ice.

Incredibly, all three of us can see what's happening on the balcony. We stand at the edge of the clearing, stunned, while the two horses mingle below like old friends reunited.

Side by side, Blayze, Olyvia, and I wait—staring, watching, assessing.

"Wait here. I'll get her," Blayze says.

He doesn't hesitate. He's back on Lakshay in a heartbeat, riding hard until he reaches the castle wall. We watch as he leaps from the saddle, grabs the iron trellis, and climbs straight up toward Iyce's balcony.

I hold my breath, heart pounding, praying he reaches her in time.

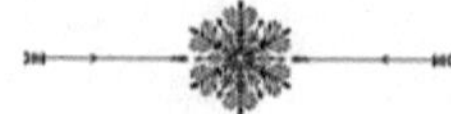

Beatryx

"My pathetic brother's scent is all over you. Don't you even bathe after he's been inside your body?"

He did not just say that. Blayze and I haven't even—

He's trying—and succeeding—at getting into my head. *I have to shut him down. Now.* Think. Stroke his ego.

"You're the one I'm interested in," I say, voice low. "You're strong. Assertive. A true king."

I wet my lips, letting my dreamy gaze linger.

Finally, he begins to soften. His grip loosens. He releases my neck.

I breathe out through parted lips and deliver the lie. "I think you'd make him look like child's play, Iyce."

He gives me his glass, claiming mine in exchange. Our eyes linger, daring each other—then we drink.

Fight the potion, B.

He hits the ground, and I spit what I managed not to swallow onto his chiseled face. "Both drinks were laced, you stupid fool."

Just flash a nice set of boobs and you win the game—every time.

But the potion takes hold. I stumble, the ground swaying—until—until two warm hands close around my waist.

"Blayze…"

Lady down.

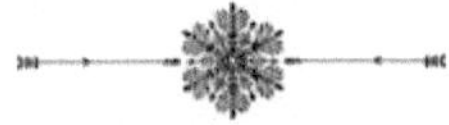

Olyvia

Myst and I wait.

My thoughts drift back to the books I've read as my gaze lifts to the castle. "He is powerless here—his fire magic holds no sway within the walls or on the grounds. So whatever's happening up there... I hope he planned for it."

Myst tilts her head, her gaze sharp. "He said he knew who you were—what did he mean? And how do you know all this about him?"

I hesitate, still weighing my answer, when Blayze appears—galloping hard, Beatryx slumped before him, limp and silent, her hair tangled in the wind.

He doesn't slow. His horse is restless beneath him, anxious, and he seizes Priya's reins again. Myst and I mount her quickly as he urges us forward.

"Stay close," he says, voice clipped.

Time stretches. Snow thickens. Blayze slows, and Myst instinctively tugs Priya's reins, though the mare already matches his pace. The forest deepens around us—ice-laced branches, a heavy silence, something primeval.

Out of that frozen stillness, it appears.

A structure rises from the snow, half-hidden by trees. Wooden beams first, then glass—so much glass. Blayze leads us down a narrow path, hoofprints the only markers. Priya follows to the rear, toward a small barn.

I dismount quickly, taking charge of the horses while Blayze carries Beatryx and guides Myst inside.

Priya tosses her head, a faint mist rising in the cold, and Lakshay paws at the snow. I lead them to the trough, only to find a thin sheet of ice sealing the surface. I press my hand against it until the brittle layer yields, splintering into shards.

I linger, watching their throats work as they drink—the rhythm oddly soothing. Then I set the bucket upside down and sit, letting the barn's warmth settle over me.

"I wish you two could talk," I whisper. "I bet you've seen more than you'll ever get credit for."

A brief laugh escapes me, and I blink back tears. I miss Mamá. But being here with Myst feels right. *It's where I'm meant to be.*

One more kingdom.

Then we return—and everything will fall into place.

Several steps rise before me. I climb them and draw open the heavy wooden door. Warmth greets me instantly. Inside lies a space both cozy and vast—rustic floors, rugs alive with horses and snow foxes, furniture elegant and inviting.

Three fireplaces hum with soft crackling. Relief floods through me. Here, fire endures. Ice doesn't win.

Beatryx lies on a lounge, a blanket draped over her. Blayze glances at Myst. "Do you mind loosening her corset?" Then he disappears into the kitchen, lighting a flame beneath an iron kettle.

I step farther in. Beatryx looks peaceful—too peaceful.

"What did she lace their drinks with?" I ask.

Blayze returns with a tray of teacups. "I have my own speculations. But once Isabella arrives, she'll know for sure."

He turns to Myst, hands her a cloth, and gestures to the side of her face—the side Iyce tried to ruin.

"Thank you, Blayze," Myst says softly. "This is truly soothing."

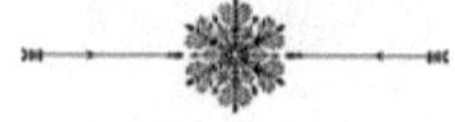

Myst

"I never knew Iyce had a twin brother, let alone a sister. Do my parents know this?"

Blayze clears his throat, a quiet reprimand. "Myst, I believe you've been… overly protected. Your potential marriage to Iyce plays a vital role in Glaycyr Falz's future."

Of course it does.

Before I can respond, the door clicks open. A striking woman enters, followed by a young child who immediately cries out, "Beatryx!"

The boy runs to her, then looks at Blayze. "What happened? Will she be all right, Uncle?"

My eyes sting. The love this child has for her is pure.

Blayze moves quickly, scooping the child into his arms. "Beatryx will be fine. She's in a deep sleep, but your mamá will make everything better."

The boy continues. "Do you promise, Uncle? Do you swear it?"

Blayze tries to redirect him. "Julian, I need your help in the barn."

"I don't want to go to the barn," Julian protests. "I want to stay with her. I want to help Mamá."

Isabella bends to meet her son's eyes, her hands closing sweetly around his. "Julian, darling… you trust me, yes?"

He nods.

"Beatryx is only sleeping. And we need your help too. Uncle Blayze needs help with the horses. They need tending. That takes strong men and strong boys. And I have two ladies here to help me with Beatryx. Can you be strong, trust me, and do what I'm asking?"

She kisses his cheeks. Julian sniffles, then nods.

Are these people even kin to Iyce? They're nothing like him. They're loving. Caring.

Isabella is striking. Her features echo both brothers. Forest-green eyes. Snow-white hair.

She bows before me as she introduces herself, then lowers her head to Olyvia, who is still staring into her tea, lost in memories. This has been too much for her.

Isabella kneels beside Beatryx, places a hand on her forehead, and closes her eyes. She sinks into a quiet focus.

Isabella opens her eyes. "There are a few things I must gather from the garden."

She walks to me and asks, "May I?"

I lower the cloth from my face. Isabella shakes her head, stunned. "I will heal what I can on the outside. But only you can heal what's within. And however you choose to do that, I will stand with you."

I've just met this woman, and already she has my full respect. A sister. A mother. A friend.

"Thank you, Isabella. Please… let me help with the herbs. I cannot sit here and do nothing."

Olyvia offers gently, "I can sit with Beatryx. Is there anything specific I need to do?"

Isabella responds without hesitation. "Yes. Watch her facial expressions for any signs of struggle and keep a close eye on her breathing. Her patterns will tell us what's happening within. If the body begins to struggle, the breath will quicken. And honestly, as strange as it sounds, talking to her is the best medicine, at least until I can finish the potion."

"What should I talk to her about?" Olyvia asks. Her gaze lingers on Isabella, as if she's met her in another lifetime, still trying to understand this woman who radiates both calm and command.

Isabella smiles. "Anything you like. She's sleeping deeply, but her mind is intact. What you say might come to her later as a dream or a distant, uncertain memory. Thank you again, Olyvia. We won't be long."

Isabella

"Myst, you cannot marry my brother. Please. He's horrible. Selfish." I pause; the words catch in my throat. "I don't even know what to call him. He has no concern for anyone."

Myst stops mid-step. Her shoulders stiffen, and when she turns to face me, her expression is pure heartbreak. Her eyes fill with tears that speak of grief. "Being royal is complicated," she says softly. "Thank you for saying out loud what so many others ignore."

The weight of her words settles between us. I lower my head, unable to meet her gaze. She has a beautiful heart, yet the confusion in her eyes sends an ache through my chest. Like me, she was raised to marry a prince. But I chose another path. One that cost me.

But I would never change the decision I made.

Back inside, we head for the kitchen. For the first time in a long while, I feel a flicker of hope. Not by marriage, but by choice, I claim her as my sister—and the thought steadies me.

We begin chopping what we gathered, the rhythm of our hands smoothing the air between us. As the brew starts to simmer, I reach for the top shelf and pull down a set of slender blue-glass beakers. Blayze's beverage stash is exactly where I remember it. I pour generously into two glasses, filling them to the brim before glancing at Myst.

"This is going to be a long afternoon." I press a glass into her hand, and she takes it without hesitation. "While the herbal brew simmers, I want to begin preparation for the salve for your cheek."

Myst offers to help, and I'm grateful.

Blayze has a habit of throwing things out or hiding them. He likes his home to look untouched, as if no one lives here.

"Blayze, where's the herbal book I left in the kitchen?"

He steps in, disappears into a back pantry, and returns with the book.

I flip through the pages, scanning quickly until I find what I need. "Ah. Here's the recipe."

The Fifth Chapter
SALVES

SNOWROOT BALM

Ingredients:

ONE HANDFUL DRIED ARNICA BLOSSOMS

TWO SCOOPS OF COMFREY ROOT SHAVINGS

A PINCH LAVENDER DUST

ONE LADLE OF SUN-INFUSED OLIVE OIL

A LUMP OF BEESWAX FROM GOLDEN COMB

THREE DROPS OF MISTBERRY EXTRACT

Preparation:

WARM THE OIL OVER A LOW FLAME UNTIL IT GLOWS. STIR IN THE
ARNICA AND COMFREY, LETTING THEIR STRENGTH SEEP INTO THE
OIL. ADD LAVENDER DUST AND BEESWAX, BLEND UNTIL SMOOTH.
DROP IN THE MISTBERRY EXTRACT, BINDING THE BALM WITH
WINTER'S BREATH.

Use:

LAY UPON BRUISES AND HURTS OF THE FLESH, FOR TWISTED SINEWS
AND WEARY HINGES OF BONE.

APPLY TO BRUISES. REST UNTIL THE SNOWROOT'S CALM TAKES HOLD.

Once the ingredients are mixed, I lean over the bowl and inhale the scent. "The combination is flawless. Floral, with the faint sweetness of mistberry extract. It's the secret ingredient found only in the Forest of Frozen Dreams, said to carry the memory of warmth and awaken the body's hidden healing. We'll need to chill this for the time it takes to milk a cow," I say, glancing toward the window. "We'll nestle it into the snow."

Myst laughs, and I join her. It feels good to be around another female.

Once back inside, I dampen a linen and pack it with the snow I gathered. "Here." I hand it to Myst. "Sit back and hold this to your cheek while we wait for the salve to thicken."

She settles in, and I turn to Olyvia. "Olyvia, would you mind going out to the barn and letting Blayze know I need ginger root and fresh peppermint? I'd be grateful."

"Of course," she replies without hesitation.

She sets her teacup down with care, wraps herself in a thick cloak, and slips out the door.

She's so cute, I think as I watch her go.

31

Glaycyr Falz

Awoken Memories

Olyvia

At this point, doing something—anything—helps.

I descend the steps and follow the path to the barn, greeted by clusters of tiny red berries glowing in the underbrush. They're quietly pretty. The color settles something inside me.

Julian is perched on Blayze's broad shoulders, brushing Priya's mane with careful strokes.

"Aw, Priya, how pretty you are," I say warmly. "Julian's doing a great job."

Blayze glances my way, and I relay Isabella's message. He lifts Julian from his shoulders and steadies him on the ground. The two of them step outside briefly to the herb racks, then return with a small bundle.

"Julian, would you take these herbs to your Mamá?" Blayze asks. "We'll be in soon."

The boy darts off, and I wander to Priya, gently rubbing her ears. Out of habit, I reach for a strand of her fire-red mane and begin to braid it.

Blayze speaks before I do. "Do you want to talk about that power you keep bottled up?"

I pause, tie off the braid in a special knot, then turn to face him, my hand still on the horse. "Myst doesn't know about it. No one does, so—"

Blayze cuts in. "I will not speak of it."

I look away, letting out a heavy sigh I didn't realize I was holding. "I know a lot about you, too. I found books in this kingdom's library. Like you, I'm a fire bringer. And what I've seen in this kingdom is disturbing—ice overtaking fire."

Blayze clicks his tongue. "Damn books."

What I do next, I can't explain. But for some reason, I trust this man. And I have more than power bottled up right now.

I flip my left hand over and recite a spell to reveal the marking. Then I hold it up. "What does this mean for me?"

Blayze's eyes go to my palm, then to the bracelet, then back again.

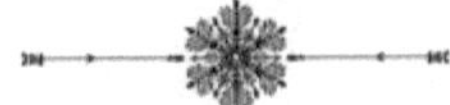

Isabella

"Myst, I think we should get Beatryx into something less constricting," I say.

I head upstairs, and when I return, I've found what she needs.

Myst and I work together to ease the soft garment over Beatryx's head, then slide the revealing dress down without exposing her. We arrange pillows behind her to ease her into an upright position.

"Once I get the last two herbs, it won't be long," I say, stirring the brew. "The vapors will be ready. We need to figure out how to keep it confined to her."

I walk back to Beatryx and place my hand gently on her forehead, reaching inward to sense her mind—but I'm met with a wall. Solid. I've never felt anything like it.

"Mamá, I have the plants you asked for!" Julian bursts into the room, proudly presenting the herbs.

"Thank you, darling," I say, taking them with a smile.

I rinse them carefully, then pat them dry on a clean linen before adding them to the simmering brew.

Blayze and Olyvia return moments later. Without a word, Blayze crosses the room and sits beside Beatryx. He brushes her cheek with the back of his hand, then leans in to press a soft kiss there.

Never have I seen my brother like this with anyone, and it warms my heart to see it now.

He forfeited his right to the throne for my honor—and to be part of Julian's life. He deserves happiness.

The group gathers in the main room around Blayze. I offer my plan.

"The brew will be placed on the table next to her. But if anyone can come up with a way to keep the vapors around her, please let me know."

Olyvia speaks up. "Myst could use her power. She could use her mist to encase the vapors around Beatryx."

Myst hesitates. "I'm not in full control. What if I do something wrong?"

"That's a wonderful idea," I say. "Myst, will you try? I'll guide you through it."

Myst stands and nods. "For Beatryx, yes."

Blayze lifts the steaming bowl, unfazed, and places it near Beatryx. "Myst, are you sure?"

"I'm sure."

Myst steps closer to Beatryx, using her hands to guide her mist and keep the vapors close.

"Everyone, follow my lead," I say. "Close your eyes. Now breathe in and out. Deep breaths. Think of happy memories— moments you shared with Beatryx."

When I close my eyes, their memories begin to surface like soft lanterns drifting through fog.

Myst remembers a moment of laughter between them; dresses scattered across the floor like fallen petals.

"This is good," I whisper. "Keep going. Push those thoughts

toward Beatryx."

Another memory rises. Myst again, standing at the iron doors that lead to the ballroom I once danced in. Her hands tremble. Beatryx reaches for her, calming her with a gentle touch.

Now, Olyvia's thoughts begin to swirl...

Olyvia remembers a young girl offering snow cream to her and Beatryx when they first arrived at Glaycyr Falz. The cold sweetness melted on their tongues, and Beatryx, instantly captivated, began talking with a mouthful, unable to contain her delight. It was one of those rare moments when joy overruled etiquette and laughter came easily.

Julian's thoughts drift gently into the shared space, and what I glimpse brings soft tears. He looks up at Beatryx with his usual warmth, offering her a place at our table with the innocent generosity only a child can give. Beatryx's tender voice promises to join him and me for supper soon.

Lastly, I'm inside Blayze's mind—and it's intense.

Goddesses, help me.

I see him extend a hand to Beatryx. She takes it, and he leads her to Glass Lake. He speaks of our mother, and the sorrow in his heart pulses through me. It aches. The moment he shares with Beatryx is quiet and tender.

"We can open our eyes now," I say softly. "Myst, I need you to focus on the vapors. Picture them circling Beatryx like a gentle breeze against her cheek. Guide them with your hands. Keep them close."

Myst steadies herself and follows my lead. What unfolds is nothing short of magic.

The vapors respond to her mist like an old friend, swirling toward Beatryx in playful, protective arcs.

No one looks away. We wait for the brew to do its work.

Then Beatryx's chest begins to rise and fall. A cough escapes her lips.

Blayze kneels beside her, takes her petite hands in his, and holds them.

"Keep going, Myst," I urge. "It's working."

Myst stays calm and focused, holding the steam close to Beatryx, pushing through her own pain to keep it steady.

At last, Beatryx's eyes flutter open. She looks dazed, as if her spirit still lingers elsewhere.

Myst's arms drop to her sides, and I gently guide her into a chair.

Before I can speak, Olyvia moves quietly. She slips into the kitchen, pours a glass of water, and returns to place it in Myst's hands. Myst drinks every drop.

"You did amazing," Olyvia says softly.

Myst

Steam carries the fragrance to me.

"What type of tea is this?" I ask, unable to hide my curiosity.

"Hybiscus," Isabella says. "But I'm afraid this is the last of it. Would you like a cup?"

"Yes, please."

Too much has happened today to question her about the bloom—though when the moment comes, I will.

Blayze insists we all stay with him tonight, and I agree. No one truly knows what Iyce is capable of when rage takes hold. At least here, in this forest, we are safe.

Olyvia and I will share one of the guest rooms, while Isabella and Julian stay in the other. As we begin to settle in for the night, Olyvia sits behind me, her fingers working gently through my hair. The quiet rhythm of her braiding steadies my thoughts.

Just as the braid nears its end, a soft knock sounds at the door.

Beatryx steps inside, her eyes already glistening. She crosses the room without hesitation and sits on the bed beside us, then begins to cry—gentle, grateful tears. Her hands clutch ours like links, her silence heavy with emotion.

We embrace as one, and I whisper, "You were so brave. What you did with Iyce… it took everything."

For a moment we linger, three souls bound by pain, magic, and fierce love, until Beatryx gently pulls away. At the door she pauses, blowing a soft kiss before leaving us to rest.

Olyvia and I nestle under the warm blankets.

"Does it hurt?" she asks tenderly. "Your cheek?"

The room falls still until I answer, "I suppose I'll always carry the scar my mother left from her arrow. But this is different. Bruises on the heart cannot be seen."

Her question doesn't bother me. She genuinely cares. It's clear in everything she does. The creativity she brings to our hair alone feels like a soft kind of magic.

I glance over and find her already asleep, her face serene in the stillness.

Sweet Olyvia—she never realized how much this path would ask of her.

As my thoughts fade and sleep takes hold, I'm haunted softly, secretly.

His whispers drift through my dreams, sending tremors through every part of me. There is beauty in his presence, a blend of seasons—warmth and frost, bloom and dusk.

Who are you.

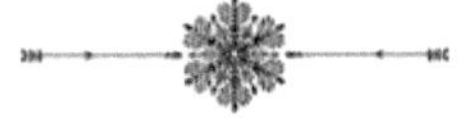

Olyvia

Breath quickening, I wake abruptly. Myst lies beside me, her skin pale, a sheen of moisture shining on her forehead. Then she murmurs, the faintest sound escaping her…

"Who are you?"

She's dreaming. And I know I shouldn't intrude, but I want to anyway. Mamá can walk in others' dreams, and at last she entrusted me with the spell as well. With my eyes closed once more, I focus.

What unfolds is surreal.

A land of lush green grass stretches endlessly, split by frozen snow lakes that shimmer like glass. Ice-blue butterflies drift through the air; their wings catch light like scattered gems.

This is the place Mother and Mykah spoke of, the land I've only heard about, never seen. A realm where seasons collide in harmony. It's mesmerizing.

Then I see Myst.

Not as she is now, but different. Her hair is shorter, tousled by the wind, snowflakes swirling around her like a crown. She stands in the heart of the scene, radiant.

And then I see him.

A man watching her with reverence, as if she's the center of his existence. And she's looking back at him the same way.

Wait. *Is that—*

Oh my goddesses.

I jolt awake, breath shallow, chest tight.

Was that her future?

Moonlight spills through the window, casting a soft glow across Myst's face. She looks peaceful. Serene.

And me?

My smile is huge. If dreams come true, she will not marry Iyce.

32

Glaycyr Falz

Beatryx

Waking in Blayze's vast bed feels comforting. Warm blankets cradle me as I press my palms into them and lift myself upright. The first thing I see is Sasha, perched nearby.

"Hello, mysterious one," I whisper. "Please watch over him for me."

She turns her head with ease, meeting my gaze as if she understands.

I slip into the soft robe and step onto the open balcony, drawn to the gentle glow of firelit torches at each corner. Their warmth holds back the frozen air.

A deep breath clears my thoughts.

Sasha glides from her perch to the balcony's edge. I step closer, tracing the back of my finger along her neck. She coos, low and soft.

"Soon, I must leave," I murmur. "And I will miss him so much."

Sasha tilts her head in that haunting way, her silence full of knowing.

"I will miss you too, mystic one."

Then she takes flight, her wings carving elegance across the sky.

The scent of warm bread and butter meets me as I head

downstairs. Isabella and Julian are in the kitchen, busy as bees.

"How can I help?"

Julian hears my voice and runs to me, wrapping his arms around my waist. "You're awake! Mamá and I are making morning bread."

This little boy makes me smile. He simply does. A happy child is always precious.

Julian leads me to the counter, proudly showing me the berries he picked this morning.

"You did an excellent job," I say. "I'm looking forward to having one."

Isabella unties her apron and sets it aside, gathering the bowl of berries and placing them on the table.

"Blayze has gone to the kingdom," she says gently, "to quietly set your passage to Crescere Moonz in motion. He doesn't want any of you returning to the castle after what happened—with Iyce and Myst, and with you and Iyce. This evening, Myst's guards will arrive at the border with their carriages. They'll escort you, Myst, and Olyvia safely toward the next passage."

My bleeding heart.

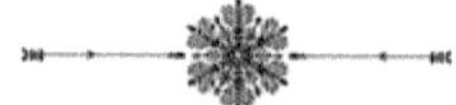

I look up as Myst descends the stairs.

"Myst! Your face—it's healed!" I rise and rush to her, hands outstretched. She takes them, and together we smile, relief easing between us. Isabella steps closer, and Myst embraces her warmly.

"Thank you, Isabella."

As they part, I catch the quiet moment when Myst lifts a finger to her cheek, tracing the scar her mother's arrow left—a mark that still whispers of the past.

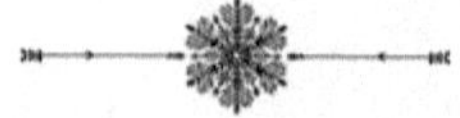

Myst

Blayze's voice breaks the silence.

"All has been arranged. Shayn has been informed and will discreetly see to your belongings being packed. The carriages will arrive at dusk."

He turns toward the hearth, running both hands through his hair before facing us again.

"Iyce… he's working with a witch. Probably more than one."

Isabella rises, her expression tight. "I'm furious. I use my gift to help people, and my own brother is trying to shut that down. Whatever he's doing, I'll uncover it. But damn… we need our mother."

I step forward, the words pressing against my lips. "I have spoken to your mother."

Isabella's eyes widen, wonder stirring as I take her hands.

"Maybe I shouldn't have said anything," I admit. "Sometimes, in sleep, I dream—windows opening, showing me what's to come. But this… this wasn't a dream."

Isabella exhales, steady despite the shock. "No. It comforts me to hear this. To know she still comes around, that she's watching. I only wish I knew her plan. And I miss her terribly."

As I watch this unfold, my heart aches—for Isabella, for Blayze, for all of us. Blayze steps outside, drawn toward Beatryx and Julian beyond the door.

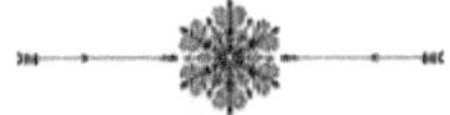

Beatryx

Julian crouches near the winterthorn berries, plucking the dark fruit and stuffing them into his pockets. Blayze draws me into his warm arms, his scent of snow and evergreen wrapping around me.

Blayze.

Just thinking about leaving him aches.

As if sensing it, he turns me to face him, warm hands cupping my cheeks, tilting my head until our eyes meet.

"We're good, my star."

I let my smile reach him before my uncertainty can. He leans in, brushing his lips against mine, feather-light.

It feels as though we've survived a war together—and we've only just met.

He holds me there until Julian wraps his arms around both our legs, breaking the moment with a burst of laughter.

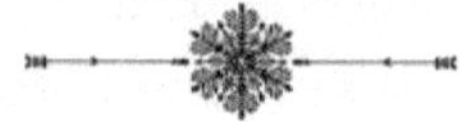

Garrett

Shayn notified me that we must leave this kingdom abruptly. Still, as I stand before the mural of wild horses, I cannot tear my gaze away. I yearn to run as freely as they do—to find Anabelle and say goodbye. But time presses hard.

I steady myself and turn from the mural. A glint on the marble floor catches my eye, not far from where she and I collided days before.

A ring.

It must be hers.

I've been ordered to leave. Now.

"I will find you again, Anabelle," I whisper.

I kiss the ring, tuck it into my satchel, and hurry to rejoin my guards.

Isabella

"Julian, please don't be upset," I say gently. "Blayze and I are taking you to Crescere Moonz in only a few days."

He frowns, unhappy that these new friends are leaving. "Go say goodbye to Olyvia."

Julian sighs, then runs to her. She scoops him up and spins him until they're both laughing, singing some silly little song as she twirls him through the air. After the day's first meal, she braided the sides of his hair into a style I'd never seen before. He loved it—called himself a warrior.

I step into Myst's carriage and settle beside her, taking her hand.

"Myst, these hands are powerful. What you did for Beatryx was extraordinary. Never forget your strength. Never let anyone question it. I don't know much about destiny, but something grand is waiting for you—and it is not Iyce. I feel that deep within myself."

Myst pulls me into an embrace.

"Thank you, Isabella. Hearing that was needed. Your mother said the same."

I fight back tears. I miss my mother terribly. But I choose to see this as a gift—that Myst crossed her path for a reason.

Brighter days must be ahead.

Blayze

Beatryx is not making this easy. We've grown close—cozy even—but I haven't taken her to the core. That must be her choice, in her time.

Still, our encounters have nearly undone me. When she leaves, I'll need to gather myself, clear my head, and focus. Too much waits before Isabella, Julian, and I depart for Crescere Moonz.

"I want you to enjoy yourself in this next kingdom," I tell her. "If you can let yourself relax, I know you'll love it."

She looks up at me with those enormous hazel eyes, and I'm lost all over again.

"What will I love about it?" she teases. "Tell me, Blayze."

I step back, steady myself. "I won't spoil the surprise. But two things: men serve women day and night, and the clothing is boldly different. Sultry."

She grins, sliding her arms around my neck, her voice brushing my ear. "There's only one man I want serving me all day and night."

She giggles and starts to pull away, but I catch her hand and draw her back. Our lips meet in a kiss that's fierce and tender all at once. When we part, our fingers linger—the last to let go—before she turns toward Olyvia and Julian.

Shayn and Garrett glance at me, puzzled. I ignore them.

Olyvia—ancient fire magic coiled beneath calm—is the true protector. We spoke earlier. If things go south, she won't hesitate.

Myst's magic gives me the same unease. Strange that none of us—not even her—knows the full extent of her power.

We say our goodbyes.

Then Isabella, Julian, and I stand together, watching the small entourage disappear into the distance. A hollow settles in my chest—*an emptiness I've never known.*

Isabella senses it, resting a hand on my back. "You'll see her again soon," she says. "Until then, stay busy."

We watch until the road swallows them whole.

33

Crescere Moonz

Myst

The six crescent moonz hold my full attention. Never have I seen such a sight.

As though she hears the whisper of my thoughts, Olyvia drifts to my side, her gaze lifted. "Fascinating."

Four women emerge from a wooded path and bow low. One glides forward, her voice steady. "Welcome to Crescere Moonz. Destiny awaits."

Two men step from behind them and move toward Shayn and Garrett. They begin gathering information, unpacking supplies, and tending to the horses.

"Please, follow us," the smallest girl says, drawing my attention back.

They wear sheer dusk-colored skirts that fall low at the waist, with simple cotton strips bound across their chests, leaving their stomachs bare. Flat slippers hug their feet, and delicate rings glint on their toes. Ankle bracelets with tiny bells chime as they walk, each pair of women hand in hand.

Olyvia offers her hand, and I accept it, gratitude settling softly in my chest.

The air hums with faint music—drums, tambourines, and unfamiliar instruments—guiding us toward the palace entrance.

In the center of the courtyard rests an enormous fountain

carved from smooth white marble. Water cascades over its broad, unbroken surface, catching torchlight until the whole basin seems to glow from within.

The four women pause, giving us space to take in the sight. Then the smallest girl steps forward again, her voice soft with reverence. "The fountain was carved to honor the crescents of Crescere Moonz. The great moonrise at its heart drinks in the night sky, reflecting its mysteries back to us. The gold tracing its edges is said to glisten with the blessings of those who came before. It reminds us that even in darkness, light endures."

Five women rise from the fountain's massive base, sculpted from onyx and opal. They stand at varying distances and angles around the central crescent, each one turned toward it as though drawn by devotion, grief, or longing. One lifts her arm high in praise. Another leans forward, her posture heavy with sorrow. A third sits with robes flowing like water. Each figure is lifelike, haunting, and tied not to a crescent of her own, but to the singular moon they all face.

I lift my gaze beyond it, back to the crescents floating in their eternal arc. As my eyes find the smallest one, it twinkles, a sharp glimmer against the velvet night.

What story do they tell?

I force my gaze from the sky as we begin to walk again. Two towering iron doors swing open.

Inside, more women, lightly draped, lounge within the grand gallery while men feed them grapes and caress their hands. Others dance in slow, hypnotic rhythms, bells chiming from their ankles and wrists. A few wear zills that cling softly as they move, adorning their fingers like jewels. Most wear their hair loose, their lips shimmering in every shade of red.

They do not so much as notice us.

We pass through the seductive gallery and move toward a quiet passageway, where streams run alongside the polished stone path.

The air is cooler here, touched with mist.

One of the women speaks. "You will be cleansed."

Olyvia

We are guided to the bathing area framed by open archways that encircle the space, offering views of a stream that winds toward the gardens beyond. Small lamps glow along the walls, their light catching on crescent patterns carved into the stone, which shimmer faintly in the breeze. The fragrance of sandalwood lingers in the air, mingling with the soft sound of running water.

An attendant in linen robes leads me to a secluded alcove and removes my garments with care. I feel exposed, yet *strangely unburdened,* as if shedding the fabric lifts a weight I did not realize I carried.

She dips her fingers into a bowl of fragrant oils—rose and saffron—and traces crescents upon my wrists. I shiver at the touch, sensing the devotion of the six moonz of Crescere, though I do not understand their meaning. *Glaycyr Falz claimed my attention, and the moonz never reached my research.*

A light robe is wrapped around me, and I am guided into a pool. Myst and Beatryx are already within, their forms half veiled as marigold petals drift by. Clay vessels shaped like crescents pour water over us, each stream representing one of the six moonz. The water is cool and cleansing, as if sorrow itself is being washed away.

We are wrapped in warm linens as we step out. I glance toward Myst and Beatryx. In the quiet exchange of our eyes, there is a shared understanding; no words are needed.

A jug of golden liquid is brought forth by a healer's aide, and we are each given a tonic to drink.

Our quarter in the palace is a secluded pavilion. Each bedroom is elaborate, with silk tapestries that ripple in the breeze from an open doorway that leads to gardens fragrant with flowers of every kind.

The stillness I have been craving finally settles around me, broken only by the calls of nesting birds and the soft rush of nearby streams that flow beneath tall flowering bushes.

Near the large bed covered in pillows and soft throws, a small table holds a lit candle and a teapot scented with vanilla and almond. I pour myself a serving, unable to resist. After the cleansing ritual and the hot tea, the bed looks more inviting than before.

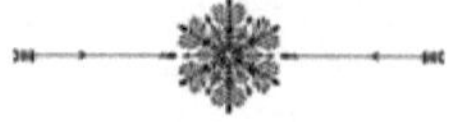

Myst

The moment I pull the bedroom doors open, a soft evening breeze kissed with magnolia filters in. There is a calm here I have never felt before. The chaos in Glaycyr Falz was overwhelming, and perhaps the worst of it was Iyce.

Outside, I wander through the small gardens, pausing to notice the unique blooms scattered along the paths. Their delicate shapes remind me of Olyvia, who is always searching for flowers wherever we go. The thought makes me smile, and I return inside to see what she and Beatryx are doing.

Beatryx lounges with a cup of tea, sipping softly. "Did you rest?" she asks.

I join her on the sofa. She lifts the small teapot and pours a cup for me.

"I enjoyed a quiet walk," I say, settling beside her as I rest my hand on her shoulder. "Thank you for being here."

Beatryx looks at me before her gaze drifts toward the terrace, where twilight dew clings to pale blossoms. "I am falling for him," she says quietly, her attention returning to me. "But being here with you matters to me. I was chosen to walk this path at your side, and I want to honor that." She pauses, fingers curling around her teacup. "Blayze will arrive in a few days. I miss him more than I expected. And Isabella and Julian—I feel their absence."

I lower my head, the warmth of my cup steady in my hands. We'll all be together soon.

A light knock draws us from our thoughts. The door pushes open gently, and two young women enter. They both have deep brown skin, long dark hair, and eyes black as midnight.

"Hello, I am Laila, and this is Veda." Her accent is rich, warm as melted chocolate.

Rising to my feet, I say, "Let me check on Olyvia. One moment, please."

I take a few steps down and notice the unfinished tea. I lift the cup and breathe in the scent—vanilla, and something else I cannot name. She is still asleep, deeply so. I touch her cheek and whisper, "Olyvia, hello."

She groans and rolls over.

"Olyvia, we have guests. Please wake up."

She stirs, and I return to the main chamber where Laila and Veda wait.

Veda looks at Beatryx and me. "Our queen has arranged an evening banquet to welcome you formally. We have come to dress you and assist with your hair and accessories."

"I will take care of their hair," Olyvia says from the archway, her voice rough with sleep as she stifles a yawn.

When I glance at Laila and Veda, they are giggling, and I cannot help but laugh too. Olyvia really should see her own hair.

"Your clothing was prepared in advance," Laila says with a smile. "You will be quite pleased. The fabrics, silks, and jewels await you."

She looks at all three of us, and when I see Olyvia's ecstatic expression, my heart fills with warmth. She has been more to me than a handmaiden.

As promised, Laila dresses me in the ceremonial attire of this kingdom, while Veda tends to Beatryx and Olyvia. When I stand in front of the full-length mirror, I am caught—mesmerized, a little unsettled. So much skin.

I glance at Laila. "Is this appropriate?"

Her smile is forgiving. "Bashful Myst, it is proper to absorb the customs of any kingdoms you visit. Wait until I add the jewels."

My eyes grow eager, then I glance at myself again. A rose-colored skirt patterned with green beetles and trimmed in gold wraps around my waist, leaving my midriff bare. The choli echoes the skirt's deep green accent, its fitted sleeves tapering tightly at my wrists. The back is striking, a square cut low at the center. My hair falls to my waist; its weight softens the curls into gentle waves.

As I take in my reflection, I feel a subtle shift—a sense of ownership. I recall a time not so long ago in my kingdom, when I was finally permitted to wear gowns that no longer made me feel like a child. Compared to those, this is scandalous. I embrace the sinful smile staring back at me, then shut the thought away.

Laila lifts a shawl. "Please, allow me to add the dupatta to complete the beauty you will carry." She drapes the sheer fabric over one shoulder and winds it around my waist, laying both ends in my hands.

"This is extraordinary, Laila."

"You are wearing a lehenga, and it is stunning on you." Her smile widens as she adjusts the dupatta.

I chuckle. "I suppose I could strangle a man with this dupatta if I had to."

Laila looks momentarily startled, then laughs. "Oh, Myst, do not worry. There are not many men here. It is mostly women."

Shock flickers across my face. Thinking about it, I have hardly seen any men.

Then my eyes drift to Olyvia as she enters the room, and for a heartbeat, my breath falters.

She wears a deep blue lehenga that mirrors her eyes. The skirt is full, dusted with tiny gold blossoms. Her choli gleams in solid gold, its sleeves ending just above her elbows. A gold dupatta drapes elegantly across her frame. Her golden hair, kissed by the sun, falls in soft waves, looser than mine. Her lips are the shade of a forbidden rose.

Laila lifts the gold choker that displays tiny crescent moonz nestled within the metal. "Myst, this was pulled from the queen's collection for you to wear this evening. I will keep your necklace in safekeeping."

My hand instantly clutches the snowflake pendant, and Grandpapá flashes before me. *How do I tell her that I cannot?*

Veda tilts her head, then hums in thought. "Well, who says a choker must stay at the neck? Tonight, it becomes a crown."

She settles the piece across my hair, improvising it into a tiara. Laila joins her, arranging the moonz so they arc like a constellation above my brow.

My slippers echo the rose color of my skirt, and an anklet with two delicate bells encircles my left ankle.

Olyvia's jewelry features other treasures. Ear cuffs hug her right ear, and bracelets chime softly at her wrist. She glows beneath the attention, and I love watching her bask in it. She deserves to be treated like a princess. All girls do.

Beatryx enters last, and she looks as though she belongs here. Her lehenga is soft ivory, adorned with red roses flanking a high split that reveals her thigh. Her choli is solid red, sleeveless and striking; silver jewelry gleams at her wrists, and a dove-shaped hairpiece tucks back a single strand of hair on her right side.

I feel beautiful. We all do.

A familiar knock sounds through the room. Olyvia opens the door to Shayn and Garrett, who wait to escort us.

"There is one final step to complete the beautifying ritual," Laila says, dipping her hand into a glass bowl filled with something fragrant. Veda mirrors her, and together they let the droplets fall around me. Veda repeats the gesture with Beatryx and Olyvia. The scent is rose.

We leave the chamber and drift through corridors that twist like silent serpents until we spill into a garden by the sea where most of the palace guests are gathered. Hesitation is not a possibility, as my hands find Olyvia's and Beatryx's.

Who is the Queen of Crescere Moonz?

The banquet tables overflow with trays of jeweled fruits and sugared almonds, and I lift a goblet of spiced wine, its warmth steadying me as sweetness dissolves on my tongue. Beatryx and Olyvia linger close, their laughter soft against the music.

Beyond the crowd, I catch sight of a small fountain set in the middle of the feast. We weave our way toward it, slipping past guests until the sound of the water is louder than the voices.

Beatryx slips her hand into the small embroidered bag dangling from her wrist, its tiny bell chiming softly as she moves, and draws out three coins. She presses one into my hand, another into Olyvia's, and with a quick wink says, "Wishes."

We toss them together, the coins flashing before they vanish beneath the ripples. I whisper a quiet plea to Tyche, Goddess of Wishes.

Our laughter rises—a brief joy before the queen's summon breaks the spell.

"Myst Silvraim, approach."

The Queen of Crescere Moonz worships Selene, Goddess of the Crescents, and wears a crown that shimmers with moonlight. She defies traditional customs when addressing or speaking to royals. I know without question that no argument, no excuse, no plea will ever sway this Queen of Moonz.

Beatryx and Olyvia squeeze my hands a little tighter, and I squeeze back before letting go and moving forward before the queen.

At last, she speaks. "There is unfinished business between your mother and me."

Again, I bow deeply and wait for her permission to speak.

When she finally inclines her head, I say, "I am here to honor and learn from your kingdom."

Her eyes narrow, and I pray to Athena, Goddess of Wisdom.

The queen shifts her gaze to Beatryx, standing slightly behind me to the left. "Dear, I also have unfinished business with your mother."

My confused glare moves to Beatryx, who looks bewildered.

Then the queen bursts into loud, unrestrained laughter. She lifts a glass, drinks deeply, then lets it shatter at her feet.

She stands and turns her attention to the crowd.

"Welcome to Crescere Moonz, where women rule all living things. We drink, we dance, we enjoy ourselves. The crescent moonz symbolize growth, change, the transition from one phase to another—but also death, rebirth, and the eternal cycle of life. The six crescents, unlike the sun, scatter across the night sky, yet once each year they reunite as one before splitting again. They remind us that nothing remains the same. Make wishes. Plant your seeds."

She turns and walks away, flanked by two women.

I lean into Beatryx and Olyvia and whisper, "I need something to drink. Come with me."

Laila and Veda hide in the shadows, watching, while Shayn and Garrett linger nearby—my ever-faithful guards.

A man approaches with a tray of colorful glasses, and I pluck two, handing them to my companions before claiming one for myself.

Beatryx drifts toward a musical group, distracted, while Olyvia and I wander to a balcony overlooking a tranquil lagoon, its surface kissed by moonlight. We clink our glasses gently and sip the clear, bubbling liquid, letting the beauty of the moment settle around us.

Then a voice startles us. "May I please take a memory of the two of you?"

We turn to find a striking woman standing at a respectful distance, her long dark hair framing enormous light-brown eyes that seem to enfold us in warmth.

"What exactly is a memory?"

She smiles. "It is my gift. My ability allows me to capture a moment in my mind and send it to the kingdom's artist, who paints it onto canvas."

Olyvia's eyes widen with excitement. I hesitate, then nod.

"You will not regret this," the woman says warmly. "Few are chosen, and I was drawn to you both. My name is Jen. Please, continue as you were. Pretend I am not here."

We make an effort to look composed, but the pretense lasts all of two breaths before we burst into laughter. The queen's lingering tension slips from our shoulders as we laugh beneath the glowing crescents.

When we look back, Jen is already walking away, our laughter carried with her—our memories now hers.

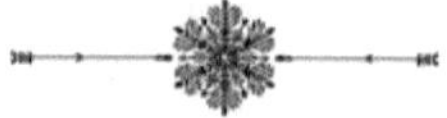

Olyvia

This kingdom is vastly different from Arkaik Alpynz and Glaycyr Falz.

At some point, Myst and I are separated, likely because guests are eager to meet her. It becomes the perfect opportunity to wander toward the gardens and glimpse their florals.

On the way, a tall man with dark eyes holds a tray of crystal flutes filled with something sparkling. His smile persuades me to accept one.

The path that leads me away from the palace feels steeped in a strange calm, and a rising push to explore stirs in me, guiding my steps toward the lagoon. The water seethes with a dark, living eldritch light, as though the crescents above are breathing their essence into it.

I pause at the edge of the path and slip my fingers beneath the beaded belt at my waist. A small linen pouch hangs from it, decorated with tiny opals that cast color faintly in the moonlight. Something brushes against my fingertips—a tiny sachet tied with silver string. I draw it out, remembering the queen's voice as she spoke of wishes and planting seeds.

I loosen the knot. A few pale seeds spill into my palm, smooth and weightless. I study them in the moonlight. *What are you meant to become.*

Kneeling, I press the seeds into the cool ground beside the path. The soil gives easily beneath my fingertips, and I smooth it over them with a gentle sweep, as though sealing a promise I do not yet understand.

When I rise, the aura of the lagoon catches the living surface of the water, and for a moment it feels as though the night itself is watching.

Rose-colored starfish glitter lazily at the water's edge, their glow wraithlike. It makes me ache for home, for Mykah, for Mamá. Being with Myst is a gift, but she doesn't know my secret. And each day, it grows harder to keep it hidden. Even if I wanted to tell her the truth, the curse would seal my lips.

I sigh, the quiet settling over me until a sudden startle breaks it. Two fairies with pointed ears and enormous eyes hold hands as their wings buzz with quickness.

I'm intrigued. "Hello."

"Did we frighten you?" the tiny girl asks in a voice no louder than a whisper.

They giggle. I extend my hand, and they step lightly onto it.

"Just a little. What are you two doing this evening?"

"Can you keep a secret?" she asks.

Obviously, and my smile assures her I can. She leans close and whispers the softest truth.

I smile.

They buzz away, hand in hand. A curious, fleeting distraction.

Tears fall without permission as I tilt my head toward the

intriguing crescents peeking through the clouds. *If only I could tell Myst everything.*

"You're too pretty to cry."

The voice startles me. When I turn, I see a boy who seems to be my age, standing back, watching me with more confidence than I'm ready for.

"From what land do you come?" he asks.

I bristle protectively. "What does that mean?"

"You don't appear to be from Crescere."

I drag my toes through the sand, eyes fixed on the twinkling starfish at the shoreline. He steps closer, and I snap, "Neither do you."

Just as the words leave me, the clouds drift apart, allowing the crescents to reveal themselves fully, casting silver light across the lagoon. Everything I had not noticed before begins to shimmer. The waves splash with an iridescent luminescence, and the starfish pulse with color. It is mesmerizing. The lagoon holds magic.

"Are you going to stand by this lagoon and cry until the water joins you," he asks, "or do you want to see something more interesting?"

He is tall, with silver hair and a crooked smile. Blunt words but not unkind. He watches me closely as I process his proposition, then extends both hands, and I take them without knowing why.

"What is your name?" I ask.

"Tell me yours first," he replies, voice low and controlled.

Something in his tone breaks through my defenses, and I smile. "Call me Lyv."

His grip firms, still gentle but more certain, and he meets my gaze. "And you can call me Karze, Pretty Tears."

Our walk turns into a light run. "Wrap your fingers around mine and don't let go," he says. "I know you bear fire, but have you ever flown?"

How does Karze know about my fire magic. But before I can

ask, we are no longer on the ground.

We soar through the night sky, and the kingdom below unfolds in silent beauty. As the lagoon fades, the palace remains, its lights twinkling in the distance.

When we land, I look up, my eyes locking onto his wings, shimmering in the light of the crescents. Karze wraps me in them, a quiet cocoon of warmth and wonder.

Then he begins to tell me stories of the crescents, his voice low. Before the tales drift too far, he glances toward the lagoon and says, "Did the fairies speak to you? Be careful there. It is enchanting, yes, but its magic is not always kind. It listens. It learns. And it uses your fears to frighten you."

What kind of magic listens. The thought settles uneasily as his wings fold back.

Karze

"Try not to fall asleep. This is interesting, and it took me years to piece together through reading and exploring."

Lyv looks intrigued as I begin the saga of the six hauntingly beautiful crescents.

"A powerful king and the queen who rules today once governed Crescere—not Crescere Moonz as we know it. The king longed for a son, but fate had other plans. Instead, five daughters were born, one every five years.

"Each time a daughter was born, the moon severed. A crescent broke away, removing itself completely from the full moon. The kingdom believed it to be a celestial omen, but the king took it as shame. With each birth, his disappointment grew. When the fifth daughter arrived, five crescents had broken from the moon—five pieces of light, five symbols of his scorn. Left behind was one small piece.

"With each passing year, the daughters grew bitter toward their father's absence of love. But, in the end, filled with rage, they ended his reign with blood, only to be undone by guilt, resulting in them taking their own lives.

"The crescents curve like the horns of a young moon deer," I explain. "The space around them is dark and empty, but there is hope. Light returns when each piece comes back, forming the full moon. It happens once a year."

I turn to Lyv, and she asks the question I have been waiting for.

You said five daughters were born, yet six crescents hang in the night sky.

"And the story continues," I say. "After the five daughters took their father's life, then took their own lives, no one knew the queen was pregnant with a sixth. A final daughter. The last piece of the moon—smaller than the rest—remained. But over time, it became the brightest and most powerful of them all, as if it carried the light and strength of the others within it. It represents the child born in silence, after sorrow. The one who was never named, never claimed, yet destined to rise."

I let the weight of it settle.

"The true mystery is not the tale itself," I continue softly, "but the girl. *Who is she? Where is she?* Many have guessed, yet most believe she moves unseen among us, waiting for the hour to reveal herself."

Myst

If I am presented to one more person…

Everyone has been lovely—truly—but I am exhausted.

When I glance across the sea-breezed pavilion, I see Beatryx laughing as she rolls her ivory dice with some of the ladies she met this evening. She looks at ease—too at ease to interrupt. I wonder if Olyvia is already in our quarters, wondering where we are. I should have checked on her sooner. I feel protective of her.

Laila finds me on the path and falls into step beside me as if we have walked together a hundred times.

"Did Jen find you?"

"Yes, she did. The painting should be… interesting."

Inside, Laila guides me to my appointed bedroom. Without a word, she begins removing my jewelry, her hands steady as they move from clasp to clasp.

I peel off what clothing I can, and she helps with the rest; the air here feels different, thicker somehow, and the fabric clings to my skin in a way it never does in Arkaik Alpynz. As soon as the last piece is gone, she wraps a large linen around me, and I clutch the ends to keep it in place while she lifts my hair and ties it loosely.

"I will draw a bath and bring you a cleansing drink."

The thought alone makes my shoulders loosen as she slips away.

The bathwater is laced with fragrant oils, the scent soft and soothing. I sink into the warmth, letting it rock me, and the tension in my body begins to melt.

And then, without warning, I miss Hayze. *If I am honest, I want to feel pleasure again.* She is the only one who has ever given that to me.

Laila returns with a glass of chilled water infused with clove and a single rose petal. I sip gratefully as she chats about Jen and the artist, her voice carrying lightly over the steam.

All the while, she tends to each small task—setting a fresh linen within reach, placing a bottle of aromatic oil beside the bath, draping a robe across the stool, and laying an antler-handled brush upon the vanity, its pale surface etched with delicate patterns.

"He is a gifted painter," she says, smoothing the linen with care. "Sight left him long ago, but his visions are clearer than most. He paints late into the night and says the crescents guide him."

I am drawn in, yet before I can ask another question, she smiles politely. "I have other duties to tend to. I will see you tomorrow."

Most of the infused water is gone when I let my hand trail across my skin, my body aching not from pain but from something deeper.

With closed eyes, I think of Hayze—of her touch, of the way she made me feel—and I follow the memory, letting it guide the very tips of my fingers.

The pleasure builds slowly, tender and aching, until it crests and breaks, leaving me undone in the water's embrace.

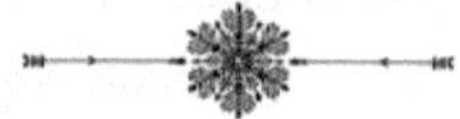

Queen Frost

Standing at the windows, looking toward the Forest of Shadows, I realize it has been a long day, and I hope this correspondence brings good news.

I watch the quill glide across the parchment, transcribing a message from my much older sister, the Queen of Crescere Moonz. We have communicated this way since I can remember. Once the letter is read, it vanishes—dust in the air.

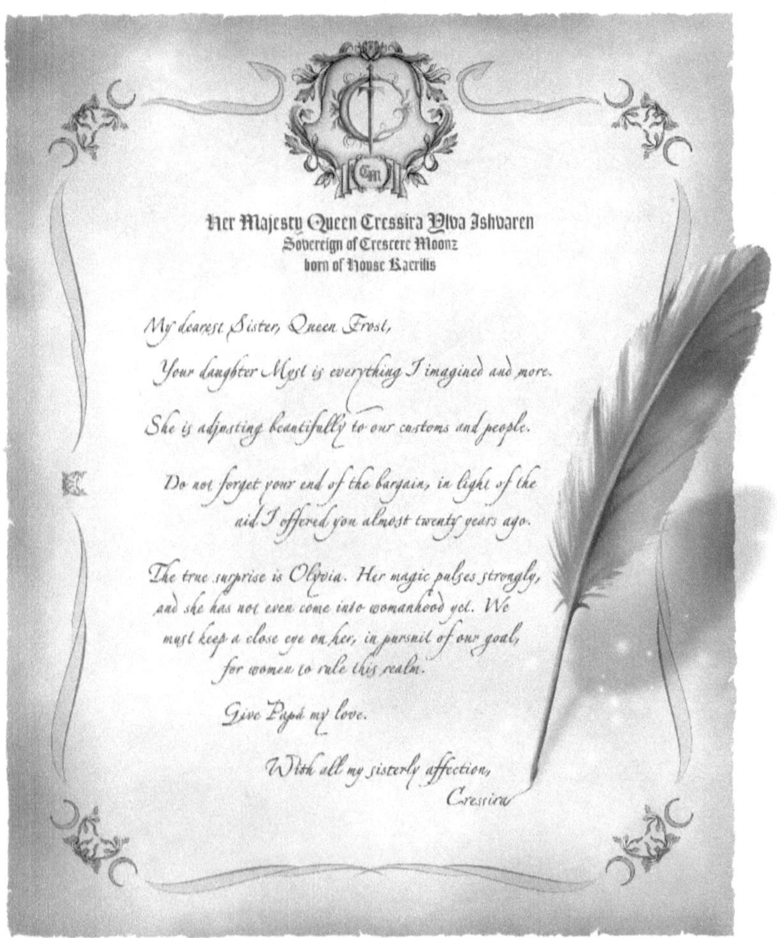

I blink at the words. What is she babbling about? Olyvia is a handmaiden. She braids hair.

My deranged sister needs to stop smoking herbs from dusk to dawn.

I turn toward the velvet chaise where Krystelle lounges, her long black braid spilling over the armrest.

"Krystelle, darling," I say smoothly. "Are you ready to take a trip to Crescere? We need to know exactly what Myst is doing—and who Olyvia is."

34

Glaycyr Falz

SHE RISES FROM SILENCE

Blayze

Isabella fixes her eyes on me, her teacup touching the saucer with a soft click. "Did you speak with Father about your engagement to Anabelle?"

"No, he was nowhere to be found. The truth is, neither Anabelle nor I have agreed to this betrothal. It is spoken of as a Binding Accord, yet in truth it is nothing more than a Silent Vow—an arrangement made in the name of kingdoms, not in the will of our hearts."

I pour myself an amber drink, the liquid catching the light, before telling her what I learned. The weight of it leaves her undone. "Iyce departed for Crescere Moonz. The guards who still keep faith with me reported that he left with a small entourage."

Her eyes blaze with anger. "Did he somehow discover that Myst's group was leaving the kingdom earlier than planned and not returning to the castle? How can you trust what those guards say?"

I hold her gaze and take a deep drink, letting the burn steady me. "They are my loyal men. Even banished, I am not forgotten, Iz. Their whispers are the only truth I have left, and I must cling to them. There have always been men loyal to Iyce and those loyal to me. It has been that way for a long time."

Isabella's control wavers, her hands trembling. "Loyal men? Whispers?" Her voice rises, breaking into a jagged laugh. "Do you not see? Iyce is weaving shadows, and you cling to scraps like a beggar."

I take the cup and saucer from her hands just as she pulls away from me, hair spun from ice wrapping around her delicate form, anger dripping from her soul. Her voice is laced with pure darkness. "Why does he always prevail? Why, Blayze!"

She is not done. The tears surge, a tide of rage and sorrow she cannot contain, her nails biting into her palms. Then her voice cracks, torn between wrath and grief. "What will it take… for him to recoil? All I see"—her breath splinters into sobs—"is the three of us playing in the castle as children. Why did he change? What was so terrible that it twisted him into this? That this is who he has become?"

She crumples to the floor, palms striking stone, pleading with the gods to take her.

I am there before the last syllable fades. I gather my sister—the strongest woman I know—into my arms and refuse to let go. I hold her through the trembling until her tears finally quiet.

We ride through long stretches of darkness between towns. I keep my eyes sharp, hoping nothing wild is out there waiting for the next best thing, but worry creeps in. I have a woman and a child with me, and every bit of road matters now—because Iyce has gone ahead to Crescere Moonz, and we must reach it before his shadow falls too deep.

A bang on the carriage roof pulls me from thought—Isabella's signal. They need a break.

It works out. We are about a third of the way through the trip. The town is small, but I guide the horses to a gentle halt and angle the carriage just inside the tree line of the woods nearby. I step out and wedge a block behind one of the wheels.

Isabella steps down and says, "Julian is asleep. I will make haste."

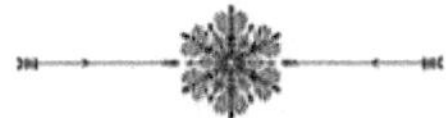

Isabella

This town makes my heart flutter, but I must make haste. I need to gather supplies and return to the carriage.

The old door creaks as I ease it open and step into the quiet shop. Behind the counter, the owner offers a languid welcome, barely looking up. I'm dressed in plain clothes, hood pulled low to hide my glaycyr-white hair. Recognition isn't an option—not tonight.

Swiftly, I add necessities to my basket.

Then two strong arms wrap around me—one low at my waist, the other across my arms—and I'm pulled backward into a narrow alcove between towering shelves, tucked far from the shop's entrance and the hush of passing footsteps. He kisses my neck with urgency, and I reciprocate.

"Stay. I need you. I miss you."

My tears fall as the painful truth follows. "You know I cannot."

He spins me around—our lips collide, our hands move with desperate familiarity, and the basket falls, apples scattering across the floor.

"I want to see him. I want to see my son. Please, I beg you, Isa," he pleads, and my heart folds in on itself. The pain was unbearable six years ago, but this is worse. My chest locks, refusing to draw in air. I break free, leaving him undone.

Evading his perfect embrace, I run toward the woods where the carriage waits. My body gives out before I reach it, and I fall, nails digging into the soil as if I can anchor myself to something real. But all I see is the day they took him—and the moment they placed our child in my arms. The memory crushes me. I can't breathe.

Then loving arms come around my upper body—arms that

pull me back to the present. Blayze holds me and gently rocks me until I sob the pain away.

"It hurts so much. The ache is too great, and I feel like I'm dying." A raw scream rips through me.

Then I hear my brother's voice—soft, steady. "Iz. Match your breathing to mine." He guides my head to his chest, the rise and fall slow and even, a steadying rhythm for me to follow.

And I do, until there is nothing left.

After some time, Blayze speaks again. "Listen to me, Iz. There's a little boy not far from us who needs his strong Mamá, so I need you to hold on. If you can't, tell me—and I'll handle whatever comes next. But if you can, then do it. Not for me. Not for you. Only for Julian."

I pull myself together, steadying my thoughts. "I'm okay. Thank you, Blayze." My voice is fragile, but it holds.

He pulls me into a warm embrace, holding me as if he can shield me from everything that hurts. We don't speak. We don't need to.

Together, we gather the pieces of my broken heart and walk back to the carriage.

Iyce

As my small entourage and I draw closer to Crescere Moonz, my thoughts spiral again—obsessive and relentless. No one disgraces me. Ever. I dissect every moment, replaying what Beatryx did to me, the way Myst rejected me, disrespected me. These thoughts consume me as we ride forward.

"This kingdom should be overthrown by a man," I say to Lars, my most trusted companion.

"Maybe we'll do that soon," he says.

I laugh—low and dark—as we enter the town that leads to the palace.

Women flood the streets—their laughter, their confidence, their power.

"There are women everywhere," I say, voice thick with contempt. "Perhaps we should entertain ourselves before continuing."

Lars snorts, dragging a hand down his jaw. "Moon pussy," he says, like it's a delicacy.

I give a dry huff. "On that note, indulge yourself. There's no rush. Choose a house."

His grin turns feral. "Shattered Moonlight."

"Excellent choice."

After surveying the area outside, this is the place we choose. Women in plain long skirts and narrow tops that offer little coverage across their chests hang garments and bed linens on a line to dry. They hum a hypnotic song, and the sound lingers in the air like incense.

In the background, I notice a cluster of children playing. How many unknown bastards are in that group? One of the younger women catches my stare and walks protectively toward the children, glancing back at me with unease.

What do I care? I think as we continue forward and step inside.

The music is enticing as darkness surrounds us, broken only by small lights shaped like stars. The air feels erotic and heavy with suggestion.

I throw my forearm in front of Lars, stopping him cold. His eyes are wide, already lost in the beauty of the women here. They are mesmerizing. But I need him focused.

"Calm yourself," I growl.

He blinks, regaining composure. "One woman. One night. Keep your senses."

A voice greets us. "Hello, I am Madam Ruhi. What are you interested in this evening?"

She's older but has aged well.

I step forward, place my hand firmly around her neck, and press her gently against the wall. My voice drops to a whisper. "Do you not know who I am?"

She coughs through her response. "Please forgive me. I do not—but I will never forget after this night."

Smart woman.

I release her and lean in. "Good. I am the future king of Glaycyr Falz. We expect your finest welcome."

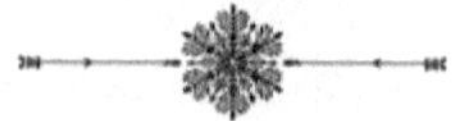

Isabella

Back inside the carriage, Julian rests his sleepy head on my lap while I look out the window, my deep stare pressing into the evening, past the thick trees, until I see him in my mind—the man I love, Julian's father—waiting for me. Once again, I feel him holding me, kissing me and saying my name.

Then the horses shift abruptly, disrupting my thoughts as we slow, the carriage wheels turning.

Instantly, I recognize our surroundings.

Neither of us has traveled through this land in a long time, and I'd forgotten how uneasy it makes me. The people who live around these waterfalls are angry—and they have every right to be. Forced to take refuge in the harsh center of the realm, they now slip away to the ocean to harvest their food, hoping not to be seen.

Many of their young daughters have been taken to Crescere Moonz to serve at the palace. From what I hear, they're treated well, but still—their choices were stolen. I know that loss. It's brutal.

"Blayze, what brings you here?" The man's voice is strong.

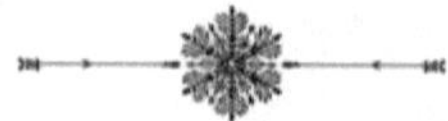

Blayze

I step down from the carriage and respond, "Cali, my old

friend. We are passing through peacefully."

Cali moves closer. "Who is with you?"

Truthfully, I answer, "My sister and her young son."

"Your hospitality and the nourishment are deeply appreciated. How can I repay the kindness you've shown us?" I ask Cali, leader of his people.

He looks solemn, but finally answers, "Bring my princess back to me from Crescere Moonz."

Isabella looks at him, confused. "They have your wife there?"

"No," Cali replies. "My oldest daughter. The future queen of my people. The one prophesied to return us to our homeland."

Before we resume our journey to the kingdom of many moonz, I ask one final question. "What is your daughter's name?"

"I am forbidden from saying her name," Cali says, drawing a whetstone along the arrowhead, the stone worn smooth from years of use. "But she carries a mark that distinguishes her from everyone else—vibrant green vines wrapped around a blue cosmos bloom, etched into her left shoulder and flowing down to encircle her waist."

I incline my head toward the flames. "If she's there, we'll find her. You have my word."

As I walk from the glowing fire fading behind me, Cali's warning stays with me. His people aren't the only ones suffering. Across this realm, families are fractured, choices stolen, futures rewritten by force. I think of Isabella, of Julian, of the promise I made. Change is overdue.

Iyce

That was the most unusual brothel experience I have ever had. Damn—

that was depraved. Morning light blinds us as we step outside.

Lars walks beside me, his left ear pierced twice and both hands covered in henna. I glance at him. "Did you indulge in flesh—or in lessons of craft and jewel-work?"

"Both."

I shake my head and keep walking.

Instead of mounting a horse or calling for a carriage, we take the streets on foot, letting the night air strip the brothel from us. I have never walked this kingdom before. It deserves to be seen.

Lars veers from tavern to tavern, returning each time with a different drink for us to taste, until something ahead arrests me completely.

A man sits on a wooden stool, painting, his eyes open but unseeing. Yet every brushstroke is precise—his fingers ghosting over the canvas between strokes. He sees the scene only in his mind, and still the canvas breathes beneath his hand. I step closer, drawn to the woman taking shape in oils and light.

Then I realize exactly who she is.

Myst.

The girl beside her burns with blue-fire eyes, but it is Myst who holds the center—rendered with reverence, as though sacred. She is everywhere I turn.

I will end this. I will end her. She will be mine, and the marriage will happen sooner than planned.

"Move to the gates," I command, and my soldiers surge forward.

Lars lingers, dulled by ale. I halt him with a look, then step in close. "Forget last night. Focus on now. Do you understand me?" A sharp slap snaps his posture straight.

By the time we reach the palace gates, rage coils tight in my chest. I seize the iron bars and rattle them, frost threatening at my fingertips.

"Open at once! I'm Iyce Volcelyn, and I will be King of

Glaycyr Falz. Open this gate!"

Queen Cressira

A frantic knock shakes the door, followed by two women bursting in, voices tumbling over each other about a wild man at the gates. I rise, cross to the window, and glance down.

Prince Iyce.

A grown man's tantrum.

He was insufferable as a child—but this is absurd.

"I will see to this," I say, and walk from the room without haste.

I stop short of the iron bars and declare, "A letter regarding your arrival was not received, Prince. Moreover, you have no right to stand here and make demands in my kingdom, presumptuous man. The rules here are made and broken by one person—me. Which means you will obey them while you are in this territory."

Iyce begins to look shaken. I restrain myself from laughing outright. *How pathetic he truly is.*

"Your betrothed is doing exactly what she was told—visiting the realm. You need to return to your kingdom and give her some time, arrogant boy. Before you know it, she will be in your bed, her belly heavy with child, all while you conquer. Have patience. Learn to compose yourself."

The barbaric prince roars—sending the air around us shuddering—then bows and leaves.

Back in my room, I settle into the chair at my writing desk and watch the enchanted quill scratch out the final words of my sister's message.

Iyce

"That queen will see me again," I murmur, leaning close to Lars's ear. "And it will not be pleasant for her."

We return to the road we arrived on, yet I stop near a timid stream. Its surface lies hushed, as though awaiting a sigh.

One final game before I go.

"Lars," I say, "I want Myst to know I traveled all this way to check on her welfare. So—I have an idea."

He looks confused as I whisper the foreign words that cause a bright, icy-blue smoke to rise from the stream, twisting upward before shooting toward the palace like a comet.

"I just cast a location spell," I say. "It will terrify her."

Lars still looks puzzled, so I clarify. "She and I had an encounter in one of the guest rooms in Glaycyr Falz. I left with a fistful of her hair, and I keep it in this pouch." I tap the small leather satchel at my side. "With it, I will always find her. She cannot hide from me—unless I am dead."

And that is not happening anytime soon.

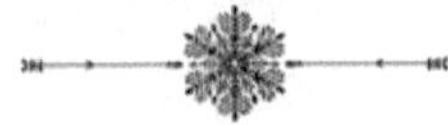

Myst

The bath was divine. I slip a silk robe over my still-warm skin and begin to consider an evening drink—until a light knock interrupts me. Mist escapes instinctively from my fingertips, and I know who is here. Iyce. I move.

I feel him the instant my mist senses him. Somehow, we flee together—I and the magic. Wherever Beatryx and Olyvia are must be safer than here.

Thank the goddesses for the warmer weather in this kingdom. There is nothing beneath the silk as I run through the gardens, the flowers whispering secrets to one another. I follow their gossip, letting it guide me through unfamiliar paths. But then my thoughts begin to press in. *Why is he even here?*

I keep moving until the path ends—at a beach of pink sand, laced with moonlight, cradling a magical lagoon. It is alluring in its calm. I move into the water, starfish scattering at my feet.

"You are safe. I will not hurt you. Please hide me." The whisper fades as it leaves my lips—perhaps inaudible, perhaps heard by the sparkling beauties.

I walk across sand beneath the water, soft as silk. Tiny crabs hurry past, brushing my toes. Then the bottom drops away. I tilt my head back, taking in the crescents above while the robe drifts from my body into the blue water. It takes me into a trance.

I float, weightless, while birds sing a sweet melody overhead. This is the best healing magic I have ever known.

Then I wonder, why are the sparkling water creatures gone? The winds shift. The birds fall silent. I am in the middle of the lagoon. *Oh, dear goddesses—I cannot swim.*

Panic overtakes me. I do not know what lurks beneath these waters. I am frantic as I try to swim, arms and legs flailing, but my body will not respond. My mist bleeds into the depths.

And then it happens. The current drags me under. The water turns dark around me, swallowing every trace of light. *I cannot move.*

But something shifts. A faint glow stirs below—soft, shimmering. Amethyst hybiscus flowers drift up from the darkness, their petals luminous beneath the surface, floating with me as if they have been waiting.

I reach for them, fingers drifting, the petals brushing my skin like a promise. And then I feel a presence. I feel him.

He whispers, "I will always protect you."

My eyes snap open. *Was it a dream?*

No—it was not. The damp weight of my hair clings to my neck, dripping into my eyes. The scent of salt still lingers on my skin.

"Myst, I am right here. I am here with you."

Beatryx sits at the edge of my bed, her hands enclosing mine. Her voice draws me back. I rise and fold myself into her embrace, weeping softly.

"What is it?" She tenderly strokes my hair.

I tell her everything—how I felt Iyce's presence, the pull of the lagoon, the trance, the fear.

Beatryx frowns. "How did you get back?"

I am close to admitting I do not know—that someone was there, that he helped me—when Olyvia's voice…

"Karze warned me," she says, her voice soft and edged with

caution as she steps closer. "He said the lagoon's magic is not always kind. That it listens, learns, and uses your fears to trap you."

I pull back, blinking. "Who is Karze?"

Olyvia's eyes widen. "I met a boy."

Beatryx and I lock eyes, then turn to her in unison. I narrow mine and say, "We want every detail, little miss."

35

Crescere Moonz

Dancing Rings

Myst

"We have dresses set out for dancing in the garden later," Veda says, her voice bright as she and Laila enter after the soft knock I now recognize as theirs. It is strange how everyone has a particular knock. I always know who is about to enter.

Veda motions for Beatryx and Olyvia, and the three of them slip into Olyvia's room. Goosebumps rise on my skin as I watch Olyvia's excitement.

Laila interrupts my thoughts. "I chose this one for you myself. I know you will love it."

I look up and smile at the lavender and silver garment she holds out. It is lighter than what I wore the night we met the queen, yet just as elegant. Its fabric promises easier movement. The jewelry is minimal—perfect for dancing. A slim silver circlet rests against my hair, marking me as royalty. *Some days, I wish no one knew who I was.*

"Veda, the costumes are gorgeous on Beatryx and Olyvia. Thank you for helping them."

Beatryx wears teal with tiny bells along the hem, while Olyvia's soft pink dress is accented with silver buttons. Like mine, their skirts are full. If we spin fast enough, they might actually fly.

"Wouldn't a piercing right here, where my belly dips, be pretty?" Olyvia asks.

"No."

Beatryx hides a mischievous smile but says nothing, already slipping her attention back to the book she's been devouring since we got here.

Olyvia ignores me and twirls before the mirror, as if the rest of the room has vanished.

Once we are dressed, the room glows with color and jewels.

A knock sounds at the door—one I do not recognize. Veda opens it.

A young girl with big, curious brown eyes stands beneath the open archway, holding a tray. On it rests a black envelope and a cream-colored box tied with a red ribbon.

Veda steps aside and motions her in, then glances at Olyvia. "Lyv?"

Olyvia looks puzzled. She kneels to the child's level. "What is your name?"

"Hana," the girl replies.

"That is a very pretty name, Hana. Thank you for bringing this." Olyvia's voice softens. "You remind me of someone special. Someone I miss. Her name is Nala Veya."

She opens the envelope, scans the note, and tucks it away. With care, she unties the ribbon and lifts the lid. A soft gasp escapes her as she draws out an ornate piece of jewelry.

I step closer. "Is this from the boy you told us about?"

Veda lifts Olyvia's hair, and I fasten the piece around her neck. The starfish pendant glows, casting a shimmer across her skin. Olyvia startles.

"It possesses magic," I whisper. "Do not be afraid."

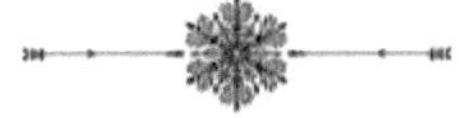

Olyvia

I'm sure it's warded with magic. But it's also reacting to my own power. I play it off in front of Myst.

Hana looks mesmerized. I kneel again and ask softly, "Can you keep something safe for me?”

She nods, eyes bright with excitement.

I reach behind my neck and unclasp a simple necklace—a tiny rope holding a seashell. It was given to me by someone I once held dear—someone who is still part of my life, just not in the same way. I place it gently around Hana's neck and let that chapter of my story fade as hers begins.

“Thank you. It's so pretty,” she says, beaming as she runs out, nearly forgetting the tray.

Veda takes the envelope and box from my hands, sets them in my room, and leads us along the open walkway.

Myst mutters, “I have no guards. Why are they even here, and what are they doing?”

The echoes of the fountains ripple around us as we walk through the palace, marble floors carrying us toward the sound of drums. They are not the rhythms I grew up dancing to. This beat is unfamiliar.

Outside, the air carries an ocean breeze and the scent of flowers. We follow Veda and Laila along a stone path where small groups of women practice dances. These are not the Paval or the Gavotte. My eyes fix on the vibrant colors wrapped around their graceful forms. Everything here is stunning—plants, flowers, clothing. It feels dreamlike.

Most of the women and girls watch Myst with quiet curiosity, wondering about her status.

The looks I receive are different.

Before we can react, our hands are seized. Myst, Beatryx, and I are pulled into a circle of women.

“Where are the men?” I whisper.

“Dungeon,” Beatryx replies quietly, a dark laugh escaping her afterward.

We hold hands and move in a circle, then two, then three. We learn quickly not to let go. The few times we do, we end up on our backsides, laughing as though tomorrow will never come.

It is wild, and I love it. Myst looks radiant. I feel free, shouting with joy at the end of each perfect dance.

We pause for a drink that tastes sweet and floral. It gives me enough energy to keep going as the dances grow more intense, the circles weaving together.

I have never seen Beatryx move this much or this fast, the tiny bells on her dress chiming in a constant, bright flurry, and she is enjoying herself, which is good to see.

After several dances and henna traced across my hands, my thoughts drift to the note Karze sent with the starfish necklace. He asked me to meet him at the lagoon when the crescents slip through the clouds. And I'm pretty sure he's using his magic to make that happen.

Myst is still dancing, lost in the moment. When she pauses for breath, I whisper my request. She gives me her blessing but reminds me that Karze's warning about the lagoon is real. I nod and slip away.

I move through the gardens, large bumblebees buzzing ahead like escorts. Then they vanish, leaving me in a daze as I reach the magical lagoon.

But the true mystery stands at its edge—black breeches, black tunic, hair the color of the crescents.

"You are too exciting to be standing there all alone, staring at glowing starfish," I say.

He turns slowly and walks toward me. "I felt your presence the moment you stepped onto the path that led you here."

My insides flutter, overtaken by butterflies. Karze lifts a finger to my chin, tilts my head back, and says, "Yes, you are still as pretty as I remember. Ready to have fun?"

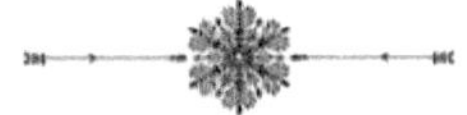

Karze

"I'm not comfortable doing this. Please."

Lyv's voice hardens. "Do it. Now."

Quickly, I drive the bone pin through the soft indent of her belly. She bites down on braided sea grass, its salt-damp strands pressed between her teeth. The starfish necklace flickers, reacting to her pain.

"Use your fire to stop the bleeding, Lyv!"

Thank the goddesses. One of us is thinking clearly.

For the first time, I witness her fire magic. It is beautiful. She runs her palm over her skin, and a small flame answers her, sealing the wound. Heat kisses the place where the piercing entered and left. Her porcelain skin returns as though untouched.

"That was… sexy." The words escape before I can stop them. The piercing. The fire. It was hot. I fight the craving. Her blood smells sweet. Delicious.

Lyv stands and begins to dance, hips moving, head tipped back. "Look at my belly gem. Gorgeous, huh?"

Her smile flashes white teeth as her blue eyes shine. She wraps her arms around my neck, and I bend to her as we kiss beneath the crescents.

The moment feels enchanted.

"The crescents will become one in two nights," she whispers. "I'll find you."

36

Crescere Moonz

Heat Beneath Rafters

Shayn

"Damn, I love this kingdom," I say to Garrett as we walk toward the stables. "I've never fucked this much in my life."

Garrett keeps walking, focused on finding two horses so we can explore the grounds. We are still on duty.

"What about you? Found a lover yet?" I press.

He walks faster, so I push harder. "Well, well, well—for once I'm getting more action than the ladies' man."

His long strides turn sharp until he finally snaps. "Shut the fuck up, Shayn. Sex isn't the only thing I think about. Some of us use this." He taps his head.

"I use mine too—when the other one isn't busy," I quip, my laughter intensifying. He doesn't find it funny. *He really needs a woman. Badly.*

"Come on, Garrett. What really bothers you? Tryx—I miss her too. But she's moved on. The best thing you can do is find someone. Or several. That's what I did. Look how happy I am."

Garrett shrugs. "This conversation is over."

We reach a wide, sun-washed barn, hay-scented air drifting out to meet us. We step through the open doorway and halt, exchanging a brief, confused glance.

"Is that a man… moaning?" Garrett asks in a low voice.

We edge closer, peering around the wooden partition of an

empty stall—and yes, one man is there, another kneeling at his waist. The one above threads his fingers through the other's hair, his grip tightening as his composure fractures.

"Is that the stableman?" Garrett whispers.

"Most likely," I say, unable to look away. "But I'm not breaking that up."

Garrett looks disgusted. I counter, "What's so bad about it? We were naked together with Tryx and we—"

"Stop," he snaps. "That was different. We weren't sucking each other off. The pleasure was for her—about her. It was her little game. Stop bringing that shit up, Shayn."

We step outside.

"I need a damn glass of anything," Garrett says under his breath. "Let's find a pub. And why do I only see women in this kingdom? Where the hell are the men?"

"In the barn," I say. He snickers, and we head off, stepping back into daylight as we keep walking.

The first tavern we find is small. We walk straight to the bar. A tiny woman with long black hair—like the night sky—wipes glasses and whistles low. Cute. Her light green eyes sparkle as she speaks in a raspy voice. "Welcome to the Full Moon. What can I get for you, men?"

Garrett slides four coins across the bar. "Surprise us."

She gathers the coins and walks away.

I turn to him. "Surprise us? Where do you come up with these lines?"

Garrett throws me his serious-not-serious face. "Are you jealous?"

Before I can answer, the barmaid returns with two small glasses of steaming liquid. Tiny stars float atop the drinks, then sink and twinkle at the bottom. It's iridescent, and it pulls me back to another night—another drink—and a mysterious woman who stole my horse, my weapons, and my keys. Her face is lost to me, no matter how hard I try to remember.

Garrett downs his drink and asks for another.

Please, goddesses, watch over us today. I whisper, "Fuck it," and throw mine back too.

Live music begins. The tavern fills.

"Look, Garrett—there are some men. Does that make your dick hard?"

He ignores me, but I'm genuinely surprised by how many walk in.

"What's your name?" Garrett asks the barmaid.

"Kalyani. 'Kaly' for short. And your name, soldier?"

Oh, he loves that. He leans over the bar—flexing, adjusting, getting close. "Garrett. Can I buy you a drink?"

As he finishes the question, a broad-shouldered man steps out from the back, eyes locked on us. "Is my attentive daughter taking good care of you?"

Kaly looks mortified. She gathers our empty glasses and slips away.

"Yes. Excellent drinks and service," Garrett says, far too matter-of-fact. *Shut up, Garrett. This man could crush me with one hand. His daughter has magic. I'm sure he does too.*

I cut in before he can continue. "We were just saying our goodbyes. Thank you."

Garrett

Anabelle's shadow clings to me still. I know so little about her, yet she lingers in every thought, every heartbeat.

Shayn's jests about finding another woman grate—he doesn't understand, because I haven't told him the truth. And when Kaly's gaze locked on mine, guilt twisted hard in my chest. I shouldn't want her. I shouldn't even try. But maybe if I let her close, I can ease Anabelle out of my mind.

"I don't understand you, Shayn. One minute you're telling me to find a woman, the next you're dragging me away when I do."

We head back toward the stables, hoping the stableman is done with whatever he was doing. I wish I could burn that scene from my mind.

Shayn opens his mouth to respond, but we're interrupted by Kaly and another beauty.

"You two clearly aren't familiar with this kingdom," Kaly says. "Would you like a private tour? My friend Shyla and I can show you the real sites."

She dismounts and walks toward us, eyes locked on mine. Shayn nods in his cocky way. "You can thank me later. The goddesses have answered my prayers—and you get to be part of it."

The black stallion paws the ground, snorting with excitement. I mount the beast and hold out my hand to Kaly. She swings up acrobatically, landing in front of me, giving me quite the view.

She wears sheer pants and riding boots. Her top is kept in place by little more than a few strings, sending my mind wandering.

Then she shouts, "Let's ride, Yeiri!" and we're off.

"Which direction are we headed?" Shayn yells.

Kaly points straight ahead.

"Can I guess?" I lean in.

"Sure. But if you're wrong, I'll throw you from my horse and leave you to figure it out."

Damn. Aggressive little woman.

Above us, the sky glows gold with streaks of lavender. Arkaik Alpynz is beautiful in a cold, distant way—but this… this is something else.

Kaly guides Yeiri toward the shoreline. The horse seems to enjoy the tide. She slows her beast and glances back.

"Welcome to Twilight Sands," she says, her voice easy. "I read shells. It's an ancient custom in this kingdom—the royals once believed the sea whispered truths if you knew how to listen. Help me down?"

I dismount and reach for her. Ignoring my offer, she swings her leg over the horse but uses my hands as footholds. Her hair glistens in the fading light as our eyes meet, but she turns away, adjusting the reins.

"Search for the perfect shells. I'll walk Yeiri," I say with a soft smile.

She's different. Wild—but there's a timidity in the way she carries herself. I take the reins in one hand, the other turning Anabelle's ring in my pocket.

Kaly has my attention. But Anabelle still holds my heart.

Shayn snaps me out of it. "Look—those are our ships, heading for the bay."

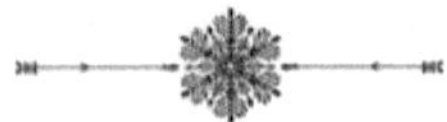

Shayn

"Shyla, dear. Can you get us out of plain view for a moment?"

She shoots me a sharp look. I don't care.

"Garrett, we move out. Now." No minced words. He understands.

I shift around the woman who thinks she's in control and take the reins. Something strange is happening, and we need to get back to the palace and speak to their guards—then report this to Myst.

We ride hard, cutting across the dunes and up the ridge, the wind biting at our backs.

"Whoa!"

The jump from the horse is fast. I reach for Shyla—she refuses.

"Thanks for the scenic beach outing, ladies."

Why have ships from Arkaik Alpynz arrived here? I run through every scenario. None makes sense.

Garrett is by my side as we move through the open archways toward the pavilion where Myst is staying.

Myst waves us off, her voice calm—too calm. "They'll anchor

at dawn. Check back tomorrow."

Garrett and I exchange a glance, breath still sharp from the rush, but there's nothing to do except obey. Frustration burns in my chest as we follow the stone path that curves beside the streams toward our rooms.

Shyla was pretty, but I have no patience for attitude. My first love is gone. Beatryx—gone too. All I want now is no-strings pleasure.

Liar, I think. But I let the thought fade.

My room is small yet surprisingly comfortable. The bathing area gleams, stocked with rich soap and oils, cleaned more often than necessary. I set aside my weapons and recall the stableman with his lover. Garrett was unsettled. I was not.

Damn, I bet I'd be good at that.

I laugh softly, tugging at the laces of my breeches.

The hot water feels incredible on my aching body. I close my eyes, letting it dance down my skin as I choose the perfect oil and run my hands through my hair and over myself.

I'm going to sleep well tonight.

I wipe my face, then my body, before wrapping a cool linen around my waist.

"Shayn, baby."

The voice is soft. Sultry. Two hands glide down my back, meet at my stomach, and undo the linen. It falls to the floor. Petite kisses trail along my skin, locking me in place—then I melt.

She moves around to face me, wicked and generous. I lift her easily, hands beneath her, bringing us eye to eye. She licks her finger, drags it across my lip, then presses her full pout to mine.

I met Kayin on the second night in Crescere Moonz, and the moment we noticed each other, something fierce sparked—*I need you; you need me.* No masks. No hesitation. Just heat.

"Did you have a good day?" she asks.

"I am now," I whisper between kisses.

The words I place at her ear are seductive as I slide the thin fabric from her chest. "How much time do you have?" I run my tongue across her skin, drawing a heavy exhale. I savor pleasure, but all I want is to make her happy. She spends her days serving others.

We wrestle for control—both of us pleasers—but my strength prevails. I have her on her back, thick thighs in my hands, knees bent and held firm. My mouth meets her heat, and I take her in like a wild animal. She tastes divine. I kiss her softly, delicately, while she begs.

At last, she's over me, straddling me. Her warm, honeyed thighs glow in the moonlight. She plants her palms on my knees and moves with a knowing roll of her hips. Watching her in pure ecstasy, her body wrapped around mine, is the best feeling imaginable. When we shatter together and collapse, it's bliss.

"Stay with me. Sleep all night with me, Kayin," I whisper before she drifts off.

I rise, soak a linen in warm water and herbal oils, and gently wipe her body, starting with the tight curls around her face, still damp from the exertion she's just endured. Each time I'm with her, I can't help but notice the sexy art etched into her skin. A vine wraps around a gorgeous blue bloom on her shoulder. I wonder what it means as I kiss it lightly.

I spread a soft blanket across us, holding her close.

By morning, she is gone.

"Farewell, my love."

I ache for her.

37

Crescere Moonz

THE EXODUS OF BATS

Olyvia

Spending time with Karze is nice because his vigor mirrors mine perfectly. We tease. We laugh. And most of all, his lips feel as though they were made for mine.

Today we will travel to the isle he calls home. Myst and I talked it through beforehand; she hasn't met Karze yet and was protective enough to ask if I needed someone with me, but I told her I didn't. She begged me to be careful and made me promise I'd return in time for the grand festival—just two evenings from now.

The weapons I borrowed from Shayn when I first arrived in Arkaik Alpynz—along with a few other provisions—are stuffed into my large satchel. Thankfully, after pleading with the seamstress for something practical and insisting it allow me to blend into the forest, she finally agreed and delivered.

I'm dressed in shadow-green breeches and a corset the color of bark, its sturdy straps holding me firmly in place. Over the breeches, a sheer moss-green skirt drapes around me, patterned with faint leaf shapes and tied with a dark sash. A high split runs straight up the middle.

What is it with this kingdom and exposed bellies?

Still, it works. My newest jewel gleams like a hidden treasure.

There's just one problem. The slippers on my feet won't do. I need boots, but I have no idea where the stables even are—and even if I did…

That's when I catch sight of Karze.

Draped over his shoulder is a pair of boots, laced together and swinging in time with his familiar, confident stride.

Problem solved.

While threading the second boot—long laces clenched between my teeth as I tug them tight—I smile. "Perfect fit. Thanks." I turn toward him with a quick wink. "What exactly are we doing today?"

Karze holds out his hand, and I take it, springing to my feet. The shift in what I'm wearing hits me all at once—light, easy to move in, familiar.

Goddesses, I've missed this.

He steadies the small rowboat and offers his hand, helping me step in before settling opposite me and taking the oars. The water is calm, dark, and endless as we glide forward. Slowly, the isle rises out of the horizon, its jagged cliffs sharpening into view—towering like dark sentinels, their stone faces climbing impossibly high before disappearing into a thick canopy. A low mist coils at their base, drifting over the water as if the isle itself is exhaling.

With the same effortless confidence, he rows us toward a narrow cove hidden between the rocks, navigating with the surety of someone who grew up knowing every secret this place keeps.

Once we reach the shore, he drags the rowboat onto the sand while I stand there staring upward, the cliffs towering until the sky all but disappears. He dusts off his hands, gives me a sharp chin-jerk—no hesitation, no fear. "Come on."

I follow as he leads us to the path, which climbs steadily beneath the trees, the air thinning with the faint scent of wild red roses drifting through the branches. Karze pauses long enough to pluck a rose from a trailing vine and press it into my hand before sweeping aside the low-hanging limbs. "There are three forests on this dreadful isle. Twilight Grove and the Masquerade Rainforest—

both breathtaking. And then the Timbers of Blood, which is where we're going for a little fun and excitement."

His gaze drops to my waist. "What weapons are on you?"

I show him the dagger strapped to my left thigh but say nothing about the smaller one tucked between my breasts.

You can't tell a boy all your secrets.

"Who'd you steal this from?" he asks, pulling the dagger from its sheath so fast I barely see him move.

I huff. "You scared?"

His low, haunting chuckle catches me off guard.

Then he asks, "Are you any good with a sword?"

"I can use anything you put in my hand."

My arrogant reply makes him laugh again—louder, the forest quietly soaking up the sound.

We pass through Twilight Grove, and it's magical. Massive trees reach toward the sky, their branches swaying while birds glide overhead, and shy streams weave through the underbrush, sharing secrets.

Karze glances back at me. "We'll visit this oasis again before you leave the kingdom. It's enchanting." I draw a slow breath, taking it in.

Then the forest darkens as we cross into the Timbers of Blood. The setting sun struggles to pierce the thick canopy as a breeze stirs the forest around me. A chill settles in my bones as I remember my promise to Myst—to be careful. A promise I've already broken.

The entire forest sings in delight at what it thinks will be my death, but whatever it is, I will defeat it. I'm not afraid of any of this.

He steps forward until he stands directly in front of me. One hand finds my cheek, and just like that, I'm calm. I hate that he can feel how fast my heart is racing.

I ground myself.

"I want to see how tough you really are, Fire Girl," he says as he draws a sword from the harness on his back and places it in my palm.

Karze towers over me, yet when he leans down and speaks softly, I don't feel small at all.

"Your only friends here are the bats—and me, of course. Nothing else."

Karze's eyes settle on mine, as if reading the story written there. I'm mesmerized by him. Then—his lips find me. I bite, anchoring us, as the forest waits.

Watches.

A metallic tang brushes my tongue. His lip, marked.

His voice is low, steadying me even more.

"You know my scent. And now you know my taste."

A breath passes between us.

"Close your eyes."

When I open them, I'm alone. Only the sword remains in my hand. Then his voice echoes through the forest.

"Find . . . me . . . Lyv . . ."

Oh, goddesses above—what do I do? Do I move?

I don't get the chance. Something coils around my ankles, then begins winding up my legs. I react instantly. Fire bursts from me, searing everything around my feet.

Karze's voice returns, sharp and commanding.

"Survive!"

Painting, I rake the forest with my gaze, unsure which direction to take—but honestly I doubt it matters. Evil waits on every path.

I sprint forward, dead leaves crunching beneath my feet as I leap over fallen branches—until the sky shifts.

Bats.

The air is thick with woodsy scents of damp soil, rich foliage, and faint sweetness from blooming flowers. As the light fades, the bats weave a choreography of dusk—a dance in the forest's heart, heralding the night's arrival.

Bats burst from ancient crevices, their tiny bodies slicing through the air like living spirits. Their high-pitched calls mingle with rustling leaves—leaves that still feel alive beneath me. They weave through the trees with supernatural precision. Haunting beauty.

They rise higher. Then they vanish.

A warning.

Something is coming.

Deep breaths, Lyv.

"I'm so sorry, seamstress," I mutter as I burn through the sash and rip the sheer skirt free. I need to move.

I close my eyes and let my senses stretch outward, absorbing everything around me. Then I call on my power.

When I open my eyes—I know I've changed.

The fire inside me feels sharper.

Ancient.

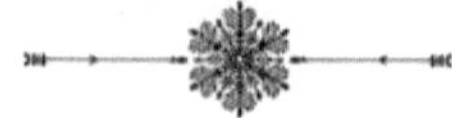

Karze

Damn, she's faster than I expected.

I stand near a towering tree as I watch her erupt. I will not let anything truly horrific happen—but she needs to burn through this rage. That much is undeniable.

The forest falls silent, thick with tension and the scent of dampness. Shadows stretch long across the ground, and something ancient stirs beneath the surface.

The fallen leaves begin to gather into disturbing shapes. They twitch and twist, rising as grotesque creatures—limbs of bark, eyes of glinting sap, mouths that shouldn't exist. They lurch toward her, as if summoned by the forest's own hunger.

She's holding her own. And damn, she's incredible with my short sword. She moves like a dancer, precise and fluid. The blade is her partner, answering every strike with grace. She is born for chaos—made of fire and fury, preparing for what's next.

"Lyv! Over here!" I shout.

She turns—and oh, my goddesses above. "Your eyes!" Her blue eyes ignite, burning gold.

She bolts past me so fast I'm forced to sprint just to keep up. She glances back, voice low and focused. "Did you see the bats? They flew from this way. Whatever we're after—it's that way." Then, from the tight corset held together by little more than tension and determination, she draws a dagger I didn't even know she had. "Let's go!"

She's in full battle mode—and I love it.

"I'm about it, girl. Lead the way."

And she does—straight into the nest of creatures.

They emerge from the underbrush, twisted and snarling, limbs tangled with bark and bone. Lyv doesn't hesitate. She rushes in, sword in hand, cutting through the first wave with sharp, practiced strikes. Golden fire surges from her—contained yet fierce—and the creatures recoil. She's focused, fully in her element.

Now we're in full hand-to-hand combat, blades slicing through beasts she's never faced before. Then she shifts—her fire becoming golden ropes, twin loops of flame spinning at her sides. She strides into the fray, daring them closer. And when they do, they fall—strangled by fire, consumed by her wrath.

She's hot. Literally. In the flesh. Just fucking hot.

My own war rages against beasts immune to fire. I tear through main arteries with my fangs—primal, yet precise. Together, Lyv and I are unstoppable—until…

The forest king awakens, roused by the screams of his dying servants.

Towering.

Ancient.

Furious.

Lyv's breath catches, her eyes going impossibly wide, and I

shout.

"Run!"

She remains at my side, her steps matching mine.

We burst out of the forest in a blur—straight toward the cliff, the scent of salt directing us through the trees. She flicks me a questioning look, breath ragged. I gesture ahead.

Then we're airborne—free-falling into the sparkling sea below. We sink deep until the water forgives our intrusion and lets us rise.

We break the surface laughing. Lyv's eyes, once gold, are blue again, twinkling in the rays of the falling sun. Her smile almost lifts it back into the sky. She is beautiful. Wild. And I love every part of it.

We stagger from the ocean and onto the beach.

She smirks. "I'm starving. Let's hunt."

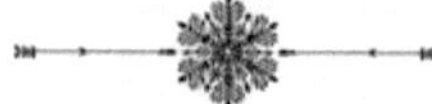

Olyvia

Just before disappearing back into the sea with a long spear, Karze decides I should handle the fire. I laugh—obviously, I'm the better choice for that task.

There. With the sand cleared, I stack the logs I gathered from a fallen tree and bring them to life with fire. The flames roar, then settle—radiant.

I hear him, then see him. "How about this catch?" And goddesses—what a catch. Several vibrant fish, shimmering in an array of colors, are stacked along his spear. Karze shakes the water from his silver hair, kneels beside me, and asks, "Did you have fun today?"

I smile but don't answer. The anger is gone, yes—but it's the secrets locked deep within that weigh me down.

"This is delicious," I say. "Reminds me of home. The fire on the beach. The simple food. We just need some drums." Sadness creeps in again.

Karze wraps his arm around my shoulders, pulling me close. "Lyv, talk to me. Please let me in. I'll never hurt you."

I lift my gaze to his, drawn to the firelight resting in eyes that stay steady and unguarded, and something inside me settles. He means it. Every word.

And nothing holds me back. I tell him everything—the truth I've carried alone for far too long, sealed from Myst by the curse.

Karze is silent. My secrets are heavy, and now he carries them with me.

A flutter of wings draws my attention. "Well, looks like there's a straggler," I say as a petite bat lands on a branch near the fire.

Karze huffs. "Of course she followed me." He looks at the bat. "Bree, switch."

The bat chitters at him, but nothing happens. She only flaps her wings harder, as if offended.

Karze rubs his forehead. "She never listens."

I watch the tiny creature, then look back at him more intently—his wings, the bite in the forest, the way he moves through shadows. This only confirms what I already suspected.

Karze stands and steps back, eyes lingering on me. "I should go before she causes trouble."

The bat swoops in a crooked loop, still chaotic.

Then Karze's form dissolves into a soft burst of inky shadow and wings. In a blink, a sleek black bat takes his place, gliding upward. Bree darts after him, flapping wildly. I watch them vanish into the night, a slow smile betraying my thoughts.

"That answers that," I confide under my breath, brushing a hand over the warm starfish at my neck before turning toward the path to the palace.

Who is Bree?

38

Crescere Moonz

Royal Blood Drips Black

Myst

A knock at the door brings in Krystelle.

"Krys! When did you get here?" The words feel forced. I'm not sure we're on good terms. Still, I tuck that thought away. "What brings you to Crescere? How is everyone in Arkaik?" I ask, noticing the slight shift in her demeanor. There's a thin thread of unease woven through her.

Finally, she answers, "The queen thought it would be a good idea for me to visit. She felt you might be feeling homesick and thought I'd enjoy seeing the crescents collide in the sky. Everyone is fine. Shadow misses you—she's doing more than necessary for me because of it."

We step into the open air, following a walkway bordered with bright flowers until the garden comes into view. Krys adds, "You'll be traveling back by ship—the same way I arrived—after the Crescere Solstice celebration."

For a moment, I drift into thought. This journey. New friends. New places. Even the nightmare named Iyce. And then I recall what Shayn and Garrett told me last night—the ships have come. The pieces fall together. Yes, I'm ready to go home. I miss Midnight terribly.

Krys continues, "Upon your return, the queen has planned a Masquerade Ball in your honor. Royals and nobles from Glaycyr

Falz and Crescere Moonz are on the invite list."

Another Masquerade Ball. I smother an eye-roll, remembering the chaos of the last royal gathering. A witch, of all things—will she be haunting this guest list too?

To keep the conversation alive—something that once came so easily—I bring up Olyvia, my handmaiden who slips through the festivities in costume, moving with ease among the dancers. She's not just present; she's thriving, in ways I never expected.

She is so much more.

Krys immediately stiffens. "How well do you know her?"

"What do you mean by that?" I surprise myself with how protectively I respond.

She turns her back and walks toward the lily pond, clearly trying to change the subject. "I wondered. I didn't mean anything at all." Then she steps back toward me, delivering a not-so-genuine hug.

What lay behind my mother's decision to send Krys?

"Finally, we're all together again!" Beatryx exclaims as we step into a steaming cleansing pool—one of the common baths meant for relaxation rather than the sacred waters we entered upon arrival. Around us, the kingdom thrums with celebration, the air thick with anticipation for the crescents' collision.

"This water is pure bliss." Beatryx sinks deeper, letting the heat envelop her as we all savor it, a ritual said to cleanse the body and set the blood humming. The scent of eucalyptus lingers, and the warmth settles deep beneath my skin, loosening everything wound tight.

Everyone is here at last. Krys arrived this morning, brought straight to the palace, while Blayze, Isabella, and Julian got in late last night.

Attendants wait nearby with thin linen robes before we move

to pools nestled among flowing streams and blooming flowers. A girl offers coconut water infused with mint. The taste is crisp and herbal.

Drink in hand, I descend the steps, fabric skimming the water as the others follow. The pool is only waist-high, which steadies me. I'm rarely in water beyond bathing, and it stirs something uneasy—especially after the lagoon.

Once we settle into the cool water, Krys glances at Olyvia and asks, "Olyvia, how have you enjoyed traveling with Princess Myst? I'm certain you've stumbled upon sights that must have seemed impressive enough… at least to you."

A flicker of irritation crosses Olyvia's face. I think Beatryx notices it too. Olyvia answers, "I have enjoyed assisting the princess during her travels."

Krys turns toward me but keeps her thoughts to herself.

Beatryx, ever direct, jumps in. "Krys, how did you enjoy traveling here by ship? Were the waters rough?"

"It was fine," Krys snaps.

Isabella is the quietest, keeping mostly to herself. A young mother, she carries a different kind of wisdom. Her white hair is stunning, plaited and piled high at Olyvia's insistence—too thick and heavy to wear loose.

Our chatter fades as a handsome man strolls toward the pool, drawing every eye.

"A deep massage with our finest oils is next on the regimen," he announces. "Who would like to come with me? It's incredibly relaxing. Don't be shy."

Beatryx moves first. She places her hand in his and glances back with a wink. We smile at her boldness.

"Blayze holds my heart in the palm of his hand. This is a treatment, ladies," she says with a grin.

As she walks away, I laugh softly. "I aspire to be just like her. That attitude is moving mountains." *If only I had even half her confidence.*

Aside from Isabella, the rest of us are escorted to our massages. She chooses to head back to be with Julian. She's protective, and after everything she's endured, she has every reason to be.

Later, as Olyvia and I return to the pavilion to dress, we step onto the veranda for ginger tea. There, we notice Veda whispering something to Laila, too quietly for us to hear. Laila covers her mouth and shakes her head, but Veda insists.

"Your dresses for the Crescere Solstice have been chosen," Veda says. "It's tradition. Everyone staying at the palace has their attire selected for them."

I glance at Olyvia, who smiles, and say, "That's charming. I'm delighted to see what I'll be wearing this evening. The garments are amazing."

Laila remains withdrawn. A long, unsteady sigh escapes her before she says, "The goddesses have decreed white attire for every heir of sovereign blood, across all realms."

Olyvia chokes on her tea. I place a hand on her back. "Are you okay?"

She nods and says she's fine, only tired from the day's activities. A pang of guilt hits me. Between the festivities and her still keeping up with our hair, I shouldn't have pushed her so hard today. Still, I'm grateful she's here. Her presence steadies me in a way I can't explain.

Olyvia rushes to her room.

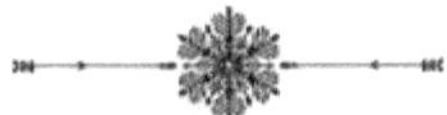

Krystelle

What exactly am I supposed to discover about Olyvia? So far, she's only a girl who braids hair, gathers little tokens from the gardens, and somehow won Myst's affection. *That's it. Nothing more.*

And Myst—she's simply herself, Princess Myst. She's made new friends, and when they left Arkaik Alpynz, I watched from my window with pure resentment. She gave me a single, fleeting look.

As I approach the Queen of Crescere's chambers, the two women guarding the iron doors strike a chime and swing them open in unison. It has been some time since I last saw the queen.

"Mother," I say softly as I step into the oasis.

She turns toward me, and for a moment I'm struck by how much she resembles her sister, Queen Frost of Arkaik Alpynz, though she is older and her features darker. Her white gown sparkles with diamonds, and I lose myself in the detail of it.

"It has been so long, my dear," she says. "You've grown up so quickly."

Four girls work on her hair, and I can't help thinking of Olyvia. She could do a better job than all of them combined. That much I know.

As if reading my thoughts, the queen speaks sharply. "I'll be quick. Time is running out. When you enter your room, you will wear a blue dress, not the white one that was chosen by the goddesses. Do you understand?"

I hold her in a cold, unyielding stare, then turn and leave the queen's chambers. The path to my quarters is short, yet each step carries the weight of my spiraling thoughts. I am tired of being hidden. *When will my secret be revealed? I hate the color blue.*

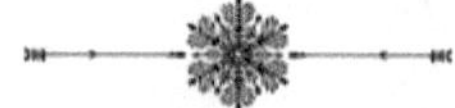

Myst

I already know the color of my dress, so that is settled. But the clothing here is beyond stunning. When I see Laila holding up my evening gown, I pause.

"Myst, this is richer in beauty than most gowns I've seen, and I've seen a few."

The lehenga is pure white, and its hem is adorned with an uncountable number of opals. When I take it from her hands, its weight is heavier than anything I have ever worn, yet its beauty overwhelms me. The choli is white lace, strapless, revealing a trace of my waist. Tonight, I am dripping in gold. The piece I cherish most is a thick cuff clasped high on my arm, blazing against my skin.

Then Olyvia steps out of her room.

I gasp.

Laila and Veda go still, eyes bright with disbelief.

Her dress mirrors mine in design, but it's raven black. Against her porcelain skin and golden hair, she looks like a beautiful dream held captive within a nightmare. Rubies glow across the dark fabric.

If royals are wearing white, what does black mean for her? Should I be concerned?

Olyvia and I join hands and walk toward the door, excitement stirring at the promise of the six crescents soon becoming one.

Before we can leave, Laila steps forward. "One last piece for you both," she says. "These are gifts from Veda and me. Serving you has been the most enjoyable experience we've had in quite some time."

The dupatta is stunning. I will keep it forever. Olyvia receives a delicate ring for her smallest finger. Warm embraces follow, and tears of pure joy spill freely.

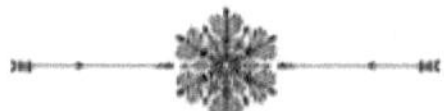

Blayze, Beatryx, Isabella, and Julian meet us in the royal courtyard, where guests hum with anticipation.

"The villages are alive with festivities," Blayze says, wrapping his arm around Beatryx's tiny waist and resting his hand on her hip.

Those two are stunning together, and I hope it lasts. Beatryx has changed since meeting him, in the best way. I love seeing this side of her. Her dress is a deep green, matching Blayze's eyes, and together they are fierce.

The royals are all dressed in white. Prominent nobles wear deep blue, green, or red. *I still have no idea what black means.* Olyvia is the only one wearing it—until...

"Hi!" she squeals as Karze joins our group.

He's dressed in black too, and Olyvia told me only moments ago that he's a vampyre. *Oh, goddesses… is Olyvia a vampyre?*

He introduces himself and his younger sister, Bree, who looks to be about ten. Long silver hair the same shade as his frames the young girl's face, her wide brown eyes taking in everything at once. There's a mischievous energy about her—playful, alert, and a little unpredictable. She stays close to him, clearly comfortable in his presence. Yet her quiet confidence makes me wonder what she's capable of.

Shayn

"She's beautiful poison. Conclusion reached," I say, looking at Garrett.

He smirks. "You just figured that out?"

We linger at the edge of the growing crowd around Myst, sipping potent drinks laced with heat and fragrant spices, handed to us by one of the attendants.

Garrett's voice thickens as the drink settles in. "Last time I crossed paths with Beatryx was during our trip to Glaycyr Falz. Afterward, I told myself never again. She met Blayze there. He's a good man. Perhaps he alone can tame her."

I raise a brow. "Blayze could use a leash." And someone willing to hold it.

Blayze

"Guards."

I extend my hand first. Garrett takes it, then Shayn. They are decent men—steady, disciplined—though I am not blind to their former interests in Beatryx. She offered that information freely. I allowed it, even after making it clear her past affairs hold no weight with me. Hopefully, we can all move forward. The goddesses seem intent on pairing me with the most devious mind-controller in the realm.

"Look!" Olyvia calls, pointing upward.

We lift our eyes to the luminous crescents, glowing softly as they drift toward one another. Behind them, the palace rises in still majesty, its white marble façade shimmering like silver. Here in the grand royal courtyard, we stand bathed in ethereal light.

Children dart past us, flying kites beneath silk banners that ripple in the breeze.

When I glance at Beatryx, she meets my gaze instantly. Beneath the lanterns strung from the trees, her hazel eyes gleam green—a familiar trick of the light. They shift like that sometimes. Not with anger, but with curiosity. With thought.

"Iyce was stopped at the gates," she says evenly. "The queen herself came out and told him to leave. No written request. No entry." She tilts her head. "So how did you get in?"

I offer a small smile.

"The queen and I share an understanding older than parchment—an unspoken accord. I need not reach for ink to request entry. She trusts I'll come with purpose, not presumption."

Beatryx nods slowly, absorbing that, then walks toward Isabella and Julian. She embraces Julian first—all smiles and giggles— before taking Isabella's hands in her own. Isabella leans in as they begin to speak quietly beneath the celebration, while Julian remains close, his attention fixed on the kites overhead.

I watch them for a moment longer than necessary.

Julian's voice rings out. "Mamá, I want to fly a kite too!"

Olyvia steps in. "Karze and I can take him, if you're okay with that."

Isabella agrees. Julian whoops with joy as Olyvia and Karze take his hands, swinging him between them on the way to the booth. Karze's young sister skips beside them, bright-eyed and thrilled.

Isabella looks the simplest tonight. She wears a cream lehenga embroidered with white roses and a long-sleeved white choli. At her wrist hangs a small drawstring pouch adorned with pearls. She has always been modest, and it suits her.

"Blayze, look," Iz whispers.

I haven't seen her since we arrived. But there she is, serving drinks. The ink is exactly as her father described. Green vines curl around a blue cosmos bloom, starting at her left shoulder and ending at her waist. She is the future queen of Vaitomo, the kingdom they all pretend doesn't exist.

Then something strange happens. She locks eyes with Shayn. There's something there. Very interesting. Shayn might be the key to returning her to her father. But I need more information.

Myst

Children weave through the courtyard, chimes and bells in hand, ringing them in perfect harmony. The moonz above have nearly aligned into a perfect sphere, and that, they say, is when the magic begins.

A striking woman with honey-toned skin and tightly curled black hair approaches, handing each of us a flute for the full moon toast. Just then, I hear the voice I've come to rely on more than I realized.

"Wait for us! No toasting without us, please."

Olyvia. She returns with Karze, Julian, and Bree, and the woman gracefully hands them their glasses. For the children, she offers small vessels filled with warm spiced milk.

Everyone is here—except one.

Where is Krystelle?

Isabella steps beside me, her voice soft with memory. "I do

believe the chanting will begin soon, and then the beauty takes place." She glances toward the moonz. "Blayze, Iyce, and I were brought here as young children and witnessed this occasion, but that was the only time. It was unforgettable, and afterward people were laughing, crying, and feeling every other emotion imaginable. True magic."

I take her hand and squeeze it as a rush of excitement overtakes me.

Garrett

The drums begin to sound deep and resonant, vibrating through our bodies. They're thunderous and commanding, yet sensual, weaving rhythm into a wordless story that speaks to something ancient in all of us. Cheers erupt, and the crowd's voices swell into song, rising with the crescents above. Their chant becomes a rhythm, a pulse that shakes the air.

What happens next defies description. Above us, the full moon shines, twinkling and glistening. Then, as if summoned by the crescents themselves, the kingdom's signature lights shoot across the sky in vibrant streaks. The entire scene is a wonder.

Our close circle gathers—Myst; Blayze and Beatryx; Isabella and Julian, who clutches his kite string as the bright fabric dances high above us; Olyvia; Karze and his young sister; Shayn and that mysterious companion of his; and me. We raise our glasses, lean in, and clink them together with a burst of unity.

And all I can think about is one person. Anabelle. I wish she were here beside me. When I glance at Isabella, I see the same look on her face, the quiet ache of longing for someone.

Blayze and Beatryx are lost in their own moment, and none of us saw this coming. The man drops to one knee. He's proposing, the stone so large it catches the moonlight like fire. Beatryx is on him faster than lightning.

Healing will be mandatory after this evening.

Krystelle

The blue dress lies at the edge of the river, its presence divine as I lean my head back and watch the crescents collide overhead. This kingdom is my birthright. I am the heir to the throne, yet once again I am not acknowledged. *How much longer must I remain unseen?*

"What bothers you, my powerful little crescent?"

His voice cuts through me, gentle and piercing, impossibly attuned. I turn to the one man who makes sense in this life and press my lips to his. Then he and I, and this river, become tangled. Away from the chaos, we are one.

And together, we will be destruction.

"I love you, Iyce."

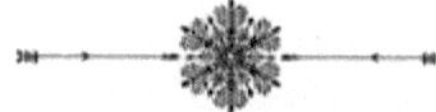

Myst

It's morning, and the ships are waiting. The crew moves across the deck, tightening ropes and checking rigging, while dockworkers roll barrels and crates up the gangplank. Families linger at the edge of the pier, pressing tokens into departing hands, and gulls wheel overhead, their cries mingling with the clang of bells. The harbor hums with the rhythm of preparation, but for my group, the moment of departure has not yet come. It lingers just beyond these final goodbyes.

Krystelle is already aboard. At morning meal, I asked where she'd slipped off to last night, but her answer didn't sit right. A river swim, alone, while everyone else was together. I don't know. I can't make sense of it. *Maybe I'm not meant to.*

I turn toward Beatryx. "You're engaged." I lift her hand, turning it gently to admire the stunning ring.

It's unlike anything I've ever seen—bold and elemental, unmistakably hers. Blayze had it crafted from volcanic rock, the kind that holds heat long after the fire dies. The stone is massive, dark as obsidian, but alive with copper and deep crimson glints that shift like embers caught beneath glass. It reminds me of the rare black fire opals I once read about, stones that seem to burn from within.

Its surface is raw yet polished, a perfect contradiction, just like their love. The turquoise band that coils around it in braided metal looks forged, not molded, as if it survived something ancient. It doesn't sparkle. It pulses.

She's glowing.

Selfishly, I will miss her not coming back to Arkaik Alpynz with us. But those two are practically inseparable now, and Beatryx will be an asset to Blayze in the coming days, whatever awaits them in Glaycyr Falz.

"Please visit me when you can."

Beatryx throws her arms around me in the most loving embrace, then pulls back—still holding on—and says, "Myst, we are more than friends. We're family. And I love you."

I close my eyes for a heartbeat, swallowing the truth in the ache.

I head toward the docks, where Shayn is visibly restless.

Then she appears—Kayin. Shayn crosses the dock in long, urgent strides, and they fold into one another as if their lives depend on it. He cups her face, rests his forehead against hers, and the moment seems to still around them. Only when he finally releases her does she leave something in his hand.

I find myself staring, the familiarity tugging until it clicks—small and precise. Arkaik Alpynz. The lamplit castle library, more than a year ago. The plaque on the ornate desk. The hushed circle of scholars. She'd been among them, part of the Antiquity circle, bent over copied texts and maps. The memory draws tight like a thread and settles within me, soft and certain.

Olyvia

The time has come. I have to say goodbye to Karze, and it hurts more than I expected. He's been something rare and steady in the middle of my sadness, a light when everything else felt dim.

He struts over with that familiar grin, lifts me off the ground, and spins me until I'm dizzy with laughter. When he sets me down, he keeps his hands on my shoulders, steadying me as I catch my breath.

"Before you go," he says, eyes narrowing playfully, "I've been meaning to ask. The goddesses choose white for anyone with royal blood. So how in the realms was your dress black?"

I smirk, leaning in just a little. "My mother makes the best potions."

His laugh bursts, warm and knowing, and he reaches for the starfish necklace he gave me, his fingers resting gently against it.

"I'm always right here," he says. "Just send your thoughts, needs, or wishes my way, and I'll hear you, Pretty Tears."

I wrap my arms around him one more time. "Until we meet again. I'm sure I'll need something. Please tell your sister, Bree, goodbye for me."

For a moment, he does not make some clever remark. He only holds me tighter, chin brushing the top of my head, and the silence between us says more than either of us would dare.

As I walk toward the ship, the wind carries his final words to me alone. "Goodbye, Fire Girl."

I send my own message back, a flicker of flame only he can see.

His laugh follows me up the ramp, echoing in my chest long after I've stepped aboard.

Standing at the edge of the deck, I look back at everyone. Julian is the last person I see. He waves his little hands, and I blow him a kiss he pretends to catch.

Cutie.

39

Arkaik Alpynz

Myst

Where are my beautiful Midnight, Sage, Shadow, and Hayze?

After we step from the carriage beneath the castle's looming archway, the two most at odds—Krystelle and Olyvia—flank me as we walk inside. Garrett and Shayn trail behind, both visibly distracted. I still don't know who the woman was—the one Shayn held with a fierceness I've never seen in him. I know only her name, nothing more, and he's clearly shaken.

Garrett is quiet, hands buried in his pockets as if he's reaching for something that isn't there. Even Olyvia feels distant, her usual spark dulled. The journey has weighed on each of us differently. Now we must readjust.

I sigh as we enter the great hall. My mother and father stand a breath apart, oceans between them, delivering a welcome polished by practice. The formalities are brief.

Practically running to the north tower, I turn down the long hall to my chambers—and there she is. Midnight, racing toward me on all fours, her eyes locked on mine.

"Midnight! Midnight! My beautiful girl…"

I rush forward as she leaps into my arms, and we tumble backward in a blur of joy.

"I love you so much. I missed you even more, my pretty girl."

When I finally look up, my guards are approaching, and Olyvia breaks ahead of them. She kneels beside us and cups Midnight's ears in her hands, smoothing them down with a soft touch. Midnight leans into her, recognizing and accepting her. "Did you miss Myst, Midnight? She missed you too, pretty girl."

Overcome with emotion, I reach for Olyvia and pull her into an embrace. "Thank you for being with me through these past twelve moon phases. I'll never forget the moments we shared, the experiences, the bonding, and the love that now lives between us."

Olyvia gathers my hands in hers and presses a kiss to one, then the other. "Love is powerful," she whispers.

Her blue eyes flash gold for a moment, and something inside me halts, breath slipping away before we embrace again.

Finally, I reach my room, where Shadow waits in her usual way. "I've drawn a lovely hot herbal bath. You must be utterly exhausted, my child."

I drop everything and run into her open arms. She holds me warmly, and the tightness inside me eases. A wave of relief washes over me.

"I have gifts for you, Shadow."

Shayn

"The path has carried us back to its beginning, and everything has changed," I say to Garrett, who's been quiet and distracted since we left Glaycyr Falz. Even Myst seemed distant when we left her quarters, drained in a way I hadn't seen before. It feels like we've all aged faster than expected, reshaped by things we didn't choose.

Garrett stares straight ahead as we exit the castle and move toward the stables. Just when I think I've got myself figured out, he says something that throws me off again. "So… are you ready to talk about the woman you held like you'd already decided she'd be the mother of your babies?"

I look at him. "Let's find a pub near the harbor."

Garrett carries the same hollow look I'm carrying.

The pub we find is dim and quiet—perfect for the mood we're in. We skip the bar and choose a table in the back.

An older woman appears out of nowhere, hair piled messily on her head, half of it falling in untamed strands. "Well, what are you having?" she asks.

"The stew and the coldest ale you've got," I say.

When she turns to Garrett, I cut in with a quick nod his way. "Same for him."

I slide six coins across the table, letting them clink into a neat little pile. She eyes each one like it might bite, then shoots us a long, suspicious look before scurrying off with the silver.

"She was peculiar," I say. Garrett only nods.

"It's nice to have this food again. Nothing like what you're used to."

The conversation drifts on, mostly carried by me.

I lap up every drop of stew with a thick piece of bread and finish it in one bite.

We're halfway through our ale when she returns, slams two more mugs on the table—foam spilling over—and tosses a linen over her shoulder. "Drink up, boys. You paid for it." She grabs my empty bowl and vanishes again.

The small wooden table wobbles every time one of us shifts. Annoying, but fitting.

Garrett finally speaks. "They should talk to Elke at the Rustic Barn. She's the best woodworker in the realm."

"Agreed," I say.

Then he looks at me, steady. "I'm ready to talk. Let's go somewhere more private."

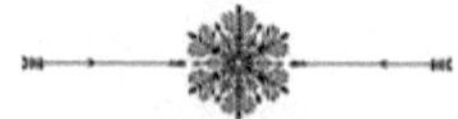

Garrett

The frigid cold of Arkaik Alpynz is brutal—especially after

leaving a warmer part of the realm. *I'm such a coward,* I think, for several reasons. Maybe once I tell Shayn the truth about Anabelle, I'll feel some relief.

We make our way to the town's library, and as we enter, bells chime. A little man appears—the same librarian who helped Myst. He's an odd fellow, though I've been thinking that about a lot of people lately.

Thankfully, Shayn steps in—because I'm not thinking clearly.

"We're here to research fighting techniques," he says smoothly. "Would you be so kind as to point us in the right direction?"

Shayn is so full of shit, I think as we follow the odd man to a back room.

Then Shayn carries the lie further. He taps the iron clasp on his cloak, etched with the soldier's crest. "This is extremely confidential. We'll need you to close the doors."

The librarian is taken aback but complies—helped along by the royal coin Shayn presses into his hand. Once both heavy doors click shut, Shayn removes his satchel and pulls out two glasses and a canteen of whiskey, filling each one to the brim.

With a grin that could split stone, he slides a glass toward me. "Let the truth pour."

I start from the beginning—how Anabelle and I met, how quickly it all unfolded. "I'm completely entranced by her," I say. "Her face, her skin, her hair—her kindness. I kissed the top of her hand once. That was as far as we ever went. But I saw the want in her eyes. I felt it too. Still... I want more than sex. We both know that can ruin something if it happens too fast."

Shayn raises an eyebrow. "I don't agree with you," he says, knocking back his drink. "But I get it. Continue." He pours himself another.

"We'd meet at that strange fountain—the one with the statue of the lost queen. She was always drawn to it, like it meant something. After that, we'd walk and talk about nothing. I don't even know much about her. Just her name. But I could feel her sadness. Still, we laughed sometimes. She told me she missed home, but I didn't press."

Shayn frowns. "How do you not ask questions? That's how you get to know someone."

He's right, I think, but it was simply how it was. "It felt like we had an unspoken agreement not to delve into each other's lives."

Shayn chuckles. "Maybe that's for the best. I'm picturing you telling her about your threesome with your best friend and Beatryx's hot ass."

I shoot him a look, and he gets the message.

He refills my glass. I lift it, swallow, and feel the golden burn settle in my chest. "Every time I close my eyes, I see her. She's always there. I can't think, eat, or get through the day the way I should."

Shayn's grin fades. He looks genuinely concerned, raking a hand through his hair. "Will you go back to Glaycyr Falz?"

I take a long breath, then reach into my pocket and place the delicate piece on the table. "If I want to return this to her—yes."

Shayn's eyes widen at the sight of the ring.

"I went back to the gallery where we first met—on the day we left the kingdom. It was lying on the floor, sparkling like it was waiting for me. I didn't have time to look for her. Blayze was rushing us out, apparently because Beatryx caused a stir with Iyce."

I pause, staring at the ring.

Shayn

Damn. He's not right in the head. Garrett's a sensitive man, but I've never seen him like this. I could tell him my own truth—how I'm falling for a woman I barely know—but he's too wrapped in his misery to hear it.

And Kayin… gods, I can still feel the weight of the letter she pressed into my hand. A message for her father. It's mine to carry now.

"Let's head back to the castle. We could both use a slice of Sage's cherry pie."

Garrett places the glasses and the empty canteen back into my satchel and fastens it before I toss it over my shoulder. My sad friend nods, and I ease the door open—stopping as a new visitor enters the library.

I'll never know how I know it's her, but I do.

I press a finger to my lips. "Shh. I don't want her to see us."

We stand in the darkness of the alcove and listen as she asks the librarian for books about Glaycyr Falz—and something else I can't quite catch. What is the cloaked, golden girl up to?

The librarian points. "I have no idea about a curse, but tomes concerning that kingdom are upstairs."

Olyvia thanks him and darts off.

My signal to Garrett is his cue, and we slip from the shadows, making straight for the main door—the bell chiming in the arctic wind as it closes behind us.

Then Garrett asks the question that's been on my mind. "How did you know who that was? We couldn't even see her face when you said something."

Still puzzled, I give a small shake of my head, baffled by my own words. "I wish I knew. I have this unexplainable connection to her—like she's familiar in a way I can't place. And yes, I know, it sounds strange."

Olyvia

"Look for the sign labeled Historia and Geōgraphia. Most of the books cover this kingdom, but I believe there are a few on Glaycyr Falz," he holler-whispers as I make my way up the stairs.

The section is easy to find, and sure enough, nearly every title centers on Arkaik Alpynz. But then—finally—I spot a few on

Glaycyr Falz.

Hmm. Glaycyr Falz: Past Rulers—no, don't need that.

The Powerful Glaycyrs—maybe.

I slide it from the shelf and carry it to a small table, ready to skim through the chapters.

A spell should hasten the process. I murmur, "Soli le fetuu," and the pages stir, fluttering like feathers caught in a summer breeze. Then, as if guided by unseen hands, they fall still—settling open on the very page I am meant to read.

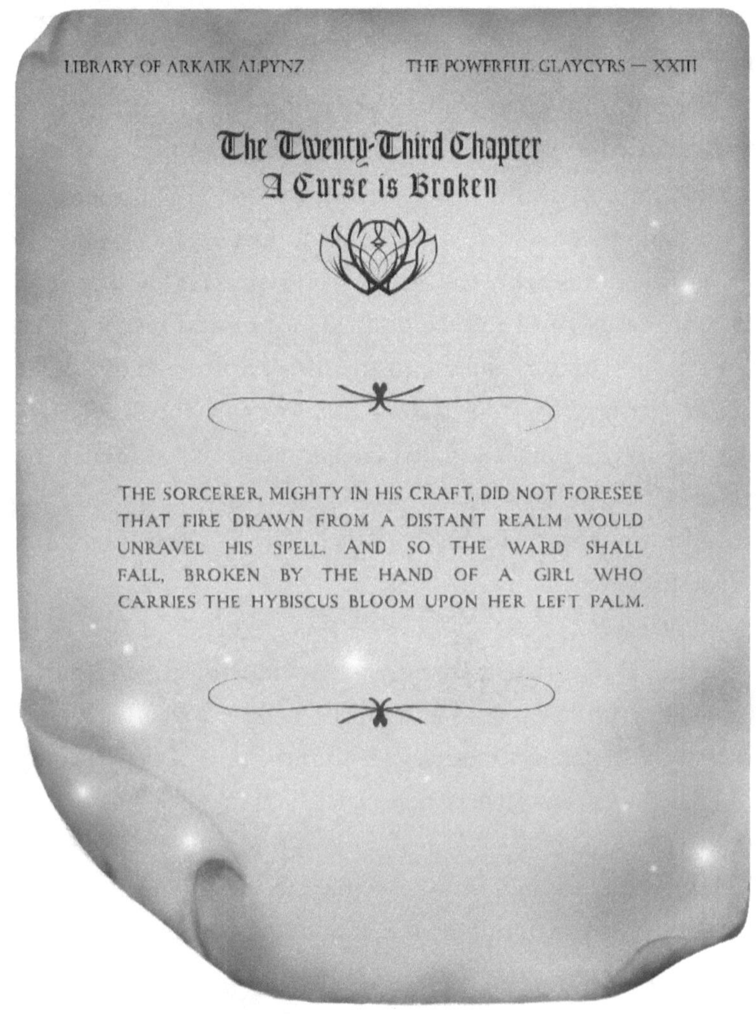

The Twenty-Third Chapter
A Curse is Broken

Open, close. Open, close. I flex my palm several times as beads form on my face. That's it? How?

Books—why are you not giving me more information?

Frustrated, I slam the book shut without bothering to return it. But then—it opens itself again, to the same page.

Not in the mood to play games with a book, I make my way down from the higher level, but as soon as I reach the landing, a shimmer of color demands my attention, pulling me forward before I even realize I've moved. The spell breaks only when a voice speaks behind me.

"For only one silver coin, you may look into it, and your future will be revealed to you."

My attention shifts to his well-rehearsed voice, then back to the intriguing piece of art. What could it hurt.

I pull a coin from my satchel and press it to the counter, holding it there until I release both the silver and his stare. Then I approach the structure, taking in the masterful wood, crafted from something magnificent. Intricate runes cover the surface—rare, unlike anything I've seen. Their meanings are so complex I can't begin to decipher them.

As I move closer, I whisper, "Please don't show me being wed to a toad."

I look.

Nerves fluttering, I place my eye to the crystal, and a burst of vibrant color unfurls, alive and shifting. As I turn the wheel, the hues knit themselves into shapes—until I see it, a depiction of me walking through icy woods near a lake, then up a hill shaded by towering trees.

Haunting sounds follow—so melancholy even the trees seem to shudder. The prism ring feels eerie but urgent beneath my fingers as I keep turning it, my slight tremble doing nothing to stop the images shifting into a future I can almost touch.

A thin wave of unease ripples through me.

"I'm… overwhelmed," I whisper, the truth exposing me. I close my eyes, fighting to steady myself as I wait for whatever comes next.

What is this place? A lost province, now nothing but cursed ruins? I plead, "Please show me what I need to do."

What I see next makes me gasp. I rush to where the strange librarian sits, pressing the library's crest into each book from a waiting stack. He glances up, annoyed.

"Where are the cursed ruins?"

He removes his small glasses and looks at me sternly. "Which ruins, exactly?"

Irritation spikes. "Is there not just one location?"

His expression tightens with disbelief. "There are several. Do you have any specifics about the ruins you're trying to find?"

Still unsteady, I blurt out, "Yes—harps were playing a haunting melody, and I heard unnerving crying from women."

At that, he looks relieved. "Ahh, very helpful indeed. You're speaking of the Balag ruins—south of Volcanic Lake, past the fishing town east of Glaycyr Falz."

As he draws breath to begin a long-winded story, I cut him off. "Thank you, sir!"

I hurry for the door, and as I step outside, I'm almost certain I hear him mention a dragon.

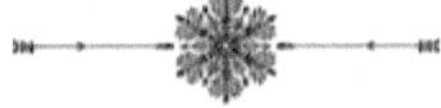

Myst

Seeing Shadow and my sweet Midnight has lifted my evening, and the bath eased more than tension—but I can't stay in this room. I need to find Hayze. There's too much I need to tell her.

Standing in my closet, staring at these gowns, feels strange after the clothes we wore in Crescere Moonz. They were bold and beautifully designed, and I felt incredible in them.

I choose white breeches and a pale tunic, perfect for blending into the snow. The boots feel great, and I wish Olyvia were here to braid my hair. Still, I manage my usual side braids, tying them back before throwing on a black cloak and pulling riding gloves over my hands.

Midnight lies by the fire, and when she sees me heading for the door, she gives me the most dramatic side-eye.

"Back soon, sweet girl."

I swing the door open—and stop.

No guards wait outside my room. The empty hall hits me all at once, a strange hush where their presence used to be. I've walked out unescorted before, but each time still feels like a stolen breath of independence.

My usual back staircase is waiting, and being alone has its advantages—I notice more than ever before.

Am I alone.

A prickle crawls up my spine. I feel watched. Slowly, I turn—and there they are. Massive paintings of my ancestors, noticing me as if for the first time.

Or warning me.

I still, studying each face, desperately searching for myself in them. My eyes, my mouth, my skin tone—anything.

Do I belong.

To avoid the main areas of the castle, I slip down a narrow service passage to the main level, then duck through the kitchen, grabbing a cookie on the way. Sage makes the best shortbread— and everything else, for that matter.

As I near the stables, my heart quickens at the thought of Hayze and the joy of seeing her again. The night sky is magnificent, lit with scattered stars. When I open the barn door, the horses greet me with soft, familiar neighs. I step inside and make my way toward the back where Hayze keeps her quarters—but then I hear something all too familiar.

The farther I go, the clearer it becomes. The door to her small room is ajar, just enough for me to peek inside.

Hayze is there—but she isn't alone.

She is pleasuring Jessye so wildly that the girl's moans could wake the dead. And against my better judgment, I watch—because Hayze is a skilled lover. Jealousy and anger rise in me as I see her tongue and lips move with precision. Hayze doesn't stop—she keeps going until you can't take it anymore.

I've seen enough.

I turn to leave—but trip over a damn bucket.

Great.

I'm instantly back on my feet, brushing bits of hay from my gloves as I move toward the barn doors. Once outside, Hayze catches up to me, and for a moment I stand there, trying to figure out what to say.

"Surely you heard the horn sounding from the ships as we came in. Hard to believe you could miss my return."

Hayze looks completely disheveled, and I feel vile. Yes, I knew she spent time with other women—but I've never had to see it.

Will we ever be together? No.

But she's always been that security for me.

I guess it's time I grow up.

She stands there and doesn't say a word, which is probably for the best. I turn from her and walk straight for the Whispering Woods—the one place that brings me comfort.

Beneath the low interwoven branches, heavy with snowfall, I feel my power rising, begging for escape. I tear the gloves from my hands and let the snow-blanketed ground take them, my fingers spreading wide—like a butterfly opening its wings—as the mist surges out on its own, thick and blinding, rushing to shield me before I can even breathe.

The woods have never shared their secrets. And yet, as I walk deeper, something ancient stirs—something that knows me.

I should've taken Aspen—my horse, my constant—but it's too late now. Grandpapá's cottage is too far in this unforgiving cold, and all I can do is walk—walk until the anger burns itself out or burns through me.

Once I'm deep enough, my screams tear free. *'Whispering snowflakes—whisper to me, please, anything!"*

Nothing.

The snow takes me, and I drive my hands deep into it, reaching for something to hold onto. I just want to feel something.

What is my purpose?

Who am I?

I don't even know anymore.

My eyes burn as tears fall, and then I collapse.

40

Arkaik Alpynz

Arrival

The Hidden One

The woods fall silent after Myst's screams—the innocent snowflakes seeming to absorb them. Now she lies gloveless and unconscious in frozen sleet and frost, the moment around her held utterly still.

Until—

Snow crunches beneath my boots, deep impressions marking the passage of man and beast as I move through one of the realm's most whispered-about forests. The trees stand in solemn watch beneath a mantle of white, streams threading under thin sheets of ice.

She lies nearly hidden in the drift, a black cloak fallen aside. I release the horse's reins and kneel beside her, brushing the snow from her cheek with the back of my hand. Even in this state, power hums beneath her skin.

I shrug off one of my heavy furs and lift her just enough to wrap it around her still body. My gaze lingers longer than it should before I force myself to focus. Her lips are pale, touched by frost, but as warmth reaches her, color slowly returns.

The snowflakes shimmer—as though acknowledging me.

I gather her into my arms and settle her onto the horse before climbing up behind, wrapping us both in warmth.

A small, abandoned cottage appears after a short ride. I guide the horse to the barn, then carry Myst inside and lay her on the sofa. The hearth is cold, so I stack logs and spark them to life. Flames catch quickly, warming the room. Out of caution, I cast a protection spell over the cottage. To anyone outside, it simply vanishes—its light dimmed, its warmth contained, its presence reduced to a veil of snow.

Removing the hood of my cloak, I look at her again. She cannot remain in those damp clothes—not in this cold. The frost will claim her if I do nothing.

I search the cottage for another presence. There is no handmaiden, no keeper—no one but me. If there were, I would step aside without hesitation.

So I act only as necessity demands.

I tend the fire until it burns higher, then hang her outer garments near the hearth to dry. From the armoire upstairs, I choose a woolen robe and return quietly.

She looks peaceful. Too peaceful. But the soaked layers beneath must come off as well. I turn my gaze aside, slide the robe around her shoulders, and ease the wet fabric free from behind— my hands careful, distant, and brief. Nothing taken. Only enough to shield her from the cold.

Once she is wrapped and warming, I step back.

I search the tiny kitchen for something comforting. Dried peppermint waits in a cupboard, so I brew tea and add honey generously. She will wake soon. This time, I cannot simply get her to safety and disappear. I will not leave her alone.

Maybe this is the moment to tell her the truth—that I am the one who walks in her dreams, who spoke to her in the barn in Glaycyr Falz, who pulled her from the waters of the deceitful lagoon in Crescere Moonz.

She truly needs to learn to swim.

At the window, I watch the snow thicken, drifting down harder than before. We will be here through the night.

"Do I know you?" Myst asks softly.

When I turn, something in her expression shifts. She inhales sharply, her hand falling to her side as she takes me in.

She recognizes me but cannot pin the familiarity. She never can. I always cover my tracks. And now, with her defenses lowered, her thoughts brush against mine—unbidden and fleeting.

How is he so beautiful? Those eyes... one dark gold, the other soft green. And his hair—messy in the best way. I can't look away. Maybe he's thinking the same, because it feels like he's staring straight through to the real me.

There is something remarkable about the way her mind moves.

Time to answer her question. "Not officially," I say. Not wise—but true.

Myst clutches the robe and fires off questions. "Where is Grandpapá? Did you hurt him? How did you get into his cottage? Who... who undressed me?"

I take one of the deepest breaths of my life. "Only what the cold required," I say, steadying my voice. "Drink the peppermint tea. You passed out in the snow. Your body needs warmth."

She tries to stand, but dizziness drops her back onto the lounge. "You used a protection spell? Why? What are you planning?"

"Break it if you have a problem with it," I say before I can stop myself.

She bristles. "You know I cannot do that."

Hearing her say that—believe that—ignites something sharp in me. "Never say that again. Never say you cannot do something. You can—and you will—when the time comes."

Fear flickers across her face, but she does not look away. She reaches for the teacup, lifts it to her lips, and sips—eyes locked on mine, filled with questions I am not ready to answer.

Fuck.

41

Arkaik Alpynz

Golden Butterfly

Myst

Once again, I stand alone in my chambers, gazing at my reflection in the full-length mirror. The mirror has become my confidant—listening to secrets, enduring my tantrums, watching me shift with each season and every passing year.

The gown is so brazen I can hardly look away—from it, or from myself. Winter reigns outside, and the gown echoes it in blue and silver, the colors of the kingdom. Shocking. Most of it is sheer, allowing the snowflakes etched into my skin to shine through delicate fabric.

Long translucent sleeves cling to my arms and taper to my fingertips. The intricate snowflake neckline plunges low, silver fabric covering my bosom and veiling my most intimate parts. Still brazen. Nude fabric glides over my waist and lower back, revealing more snowflake art. The bodice is gossamer blue, sheer enough to show the outline of my legs and the markings etched there—twenty now—one for each year I've carried the title of Princess of Arkaik Alpynz, beginning at birth.

The only jewelry I wear is the snowflake necklace Grandpapá placed around my neck so long ago at his cottage in the Whispering Woods, and it twinkles softly.

Thinking of that cottage pulls me back to the last time I stood inside it—only days ago—with the man whose name I still do not know. The next morning I heard the soft click of the door before catching a glimpse of him riding into the forest on a beautiful horse. I left soon after on Ginger, Grandpapá's patient mare, the barn quietly kept—fresh hay laid out, water clear in the trough. Who had been caring for her? I rode through frost-laced woods until the castle walls came into view. I haven't seen him since, yet the sense of him lingers.

Quiet.

Watchful.

Always watching.

His final words settle over me, and I draw a slow breath, returning to the present.

My hair is pinned up in the intricate braids Olyvia created for this evening. Tonight, my mother will adorn me with a crown I have never worn—meant only for this winter ball. Afterward, it will be put away again. And one day, when I have a daughter with Iyce—

Forget that thought.

The doors open, and Olyvia, Krys, Shayn, and Garrett step inside. Loneliness strikes at once. I miss Beatryx, Blayze, Isabella, and Julian. Because of the trouble Iyce and his father caused in Glaycyr Falz, they won't be here. Krys catches my eye—once so close, now slightly unfamiliar. It's been over a year since we've had any ease between us, yet tonight something in her presence eases. Maybe we're finding our way back.

Olyvia appears at my side. "Close your eyes. Slow your body. Think about your best memories. That's what I do when I'm uneasy—it helps."

I follow her advice. Flashbacks of Grandpapá and Grandmamá, laughter with Beatryx, Olyvia and me in Crescere Moonz, and the artwork the man without sight painted of us fill my mind. I hope to see it someday.

The others close in, joining hands with Olyvia to form a circle around me. Krys says, "On the count of three, we sprinkle magical glitter dust on Myst. One, two, three—"

Silver and blue butterflies fill the room as dust cascades like the sky weeping joyful tears. My mood lifts at once. Shayn opens the balcony doors, and the butterflies sweep out, leaving a shimmer behind.

Garrett grins. "Picked up that enchantment at the Snowflake Embers Charm Shop—Frost-Flutter. Seldom crafted. Butterflies woven from starlight and frost magic to lift spirits and mark special occasions. The shimmer? Pure lunar dust."

I clap. "Thank you, Garrett. I loved it."

Olyvia steps forward, glancing at Krys. "This next surprise is thanks to Krys. She convinced Queen Frost to let us crown you tonight—no doubt with reasoning, arguing, and a touch of charm."

Garrett approaches with an ornate wooden box. I know what rests inside—a crown worn by the princesses before me at the Winter Solstice Ball on their twentieth birthdate.

Krys hands me a small skeleton key. "Only you can open it. The Queen made that clear."

My hand trembles as I place the key into the lock and turn it. A faint click echoes. The lid lifts on its own, and all eyes fix on the crown.

A shiver runs through me—a faint mist escaping from my fingertips. I steady myself and move to the mirror. Krys and Olyvia gently place the crown upon my head, Olyvia careful not to loosen a single strand of hair.

The band is ice-blue, engraved with delicate patterns and royal insignias. Diamond snowflakes adorn the top, each gem rare and radiant. A black velvet lining ensures comfort.

Shayn smiles. "You are every bit a true queen—and more."

I glance at Olyvia and notice the shine of a tear. An unexpected bond tightens between us, and I embrace her.

Before we leave, Olyvia lifts a mask with a flourish. "I nearly forgot the most important piece. Now you look like an elegant golden butterfly."

Garrett drapes a white royal mantle around my shoulders, fastening it with a sapphire snowflake clasp.

Warmth swells in my chest. "Thank you for keeping me focused—and for standing beside me when I need it most."

We step from my chambers—Krys and Olyvia behind me, Shayn and Garrett following. As we near the ballroom, unfamiliar faces blur together. Olyvia whispers, "Smile. Focus on one object ahead." I rely on her more than I realized.

I take her hand with my right and Krys' with my left. Silence falls as we enter.

The queen sees me first, her eyes widening as she approaches, studying my attire as though seeking reassurance in it. My father stands nearby with a goblet, speaking with other royals and glancing toward Sage as she quietly steers the evening's rhythm from the kitchen. Without a word, my mother slips away, signaling to her attendants.

Trumpets sound and guards close in around me. My father approaches. I bow; the room follows. He extends his hand, and I place mine in his. Together we walk to the dais.

I search for Grandpapá. *Where is he?* His cottage was abandoned, and I won't relax until I see him. He was once king—until my mother stripped the crown from him and made my father her king.

Speaking of my father, he begins his elaborate speech, and I lean toward the queen. "Where is Grandpapá?"

Her answer offers nothing. "It was best he did not attend."

"Why?"

Her face curdles. "The last time he attended, the crown you're wearing was on my head. It would upset him." Her gaze drops to my snowflake pendant.

That makes no sense.

My father concludes, "The queen and I thank you for welcoming our daughter, Myst, to your kingdoms. Welcome to Arkaik Alpynz. Eat and drink until you're beyond satisfied!"

Music swells as laughter fills the ballroom. I leave the dais, still thinking of Grandpapá. I hate crowds—especially when I'm the spectacle.

The King of Glaycyr Falz has sent lords and ladies as representatives of the kingdom, which raises concern—I've been thinking of my companions there all evening.

Quite a few guests are here from Crescere Moonz, including the queen, who seems unusually fond of my mother. Krys lingers at her side, and a faint, oily unease settles over me.

Olyvia looks like a delicate flower this evening. Even though she's acting as a handmaiden once more, I insisted she wear a gown and attend the ball. She deserves to be seen.

Her dress is soft pink, with sheer sleeves that gather at the wrists, and braids woven throughout her hair. The colors complement the starfish necklace she never removes.

She offered to braid Krys's hair, but she wasn't interested. Of course she wasn't.

My thoughts are still swarming when warm hands close around mine, guiding me toward the side of the ballroom that leads to the kitchen. Then I realize who it is.

"Sage!" I close the distance and wrap myself around her, and she pulls me in without hesitation. She feels like the one place I belong. Like home.

When we finally pull apart, she looks at me with a growing smile. "You are radiant, my darling. I haven't seen you since you returned from your journey. How was it?"

We visit for a while, and then she gently tells me I should probably get back to the ball. I agree, but it's hard to leave the warmth of her company. I want to stay right here. She hugs me once more and says, "We'll talk again soon. Keep that head held high."

After several dances, small bites of Sage's lovely desserts, and a few glasses of champagne, I begin to feel bored. Too bored. And in that very moment, as I stand in the center of the ballroom with the celebration swirling around me, a sudden rush of cool air blows in.

With it, a golden butterfly flutters delicately through the air until it lands on the back of my gloved hand.

"Hello. Do you have a secret for me?" I ask playfully. Not expecting a reply, I glance around the room—but the butterfly indeed whispers in *his* voice, sending shivers across my nape. "Come to me. The balcony nearest the Whispering Woods."

Why am I obeying a butterfly?

Slyly, I slip through the crowd and disappear from the ballroom.

What if I'm deceived?

What if I'm not?

As I make my way to the north tower and finally to the balcony doors, I see a shadowed figure. Both doors fly open, and a cool breeze rushes around me, lifting my skirt, begging me to step outside. As if I could resist.

He turns around slowly, leans against a column, and speaks. "Nice gown. Are you cold, Snowflake?"

"You," I say, flat as glass.

He lets my questions from last night settle like crushed tea leaves at the bottom of a barrel before speaking again. "The crown is something to behold, but I appreciate the body etching more."

Flustered, I huff, "Goddesses above, this damn dress!"

He chimes in, "Yes, the damn dress. All those little secrets are out now. No more guessing for anyone." His gaze shifts to the woods and the falling snowflakes, as if he studies them.

The balcony rail is cool beneath my hands as I move closer and watch the snowflakes too, my thoughts drifting with his question. "Have you received your omen from one of them yet?"

Disappointment colors my voice. "No. And I was beginning to think I never would." I turn toward him. "But your little butterfly enchantment gave me hope."

His quiet laugh is rough and deep, igniting a warmth I don't trust. What is this man up to? I don't even know his name.

His beautiful eyes cut to me. "Tell me about your body art."

Heat rises to my cheeks. "I didn't choose this. A new one appears each year on my birthdate."

He looks back to the woods.

"I wanted to see one person tonight," I say softly, "someone who lives in those woods, and that didn't happen."

He turns back toward me again, eyes sharp. "Who did you want to see?"

Sadness traps me, and he must see it, because his attention is intent. Too intent.

"My grandpapá—the one whose cottage you took me to." My voice tightens. "He should have been here. I asked my mother about him; her excuse made no sense."

His expression shifts, thoughtful. "I've been roaming those woods for days. I've seen no one in or near the only cottage. I thought it was deserted. That's why I took you there."

My eyes widen. "She lied, and I hate her for it."

His voice moves with a calm, liquid steadiness, like water over stone. "You need to learn how to be strategic when you want information. Throwing a tantrum and demanding answers will get you nowhere. Ask the right questions."

Then, with a glance at my dress, he adds, "And you need to dress appropriately for this cold kingdom you live in. Just putting that out there. I have no patience for watching a woman shiver from the cold. Other reasons, yes—but not that."

I roll my eyes. Infuriating. "So, Mr. I-don't-know-your-name, how would you have questioned the queen about her father's whereabouts?"

He laughs again, then looks practically through me, pinning me in place.

"Mother, dear, I was thinking you and I could ride out to Grandpapá's cottage and bring him a nice lunch and some cobbler. Can we plan that? That's a strategic approach." Whatever excuse she gives, you keep pressing until she gets angry."

He steps back. "At that point, you've got her. Go ahead, Snowflake—try it with me."

I press my hands to my skirts to keep them still, flustered again by how easily he unsettles me. He has no idea my mother is the Queen of Lies and Evil.

Fine. I'll play. "Hello, man who roams random woods with a golden butterfly. I bet you have a lovely name. Care to share it with me?

His laugh is deliciously dark. Goddesses, control me.

"I have to get back to the ball."

As I walk away, I hear him call out, "Work on your strategy, Myst."

Olyvia

I remove my dragon-shaped mask and slip into the kitchen to see Mamá, giving her a brief update on our travels. So much has happened, but I keep it short.

With two plates of food in her hands, she gives a subtle nod toward her room, leading me away from inquisitive eyes and ears. We sit on her small bed, picking at the delicacies and sipping hot mint tea.

She seems most disturbed by what's going on in Glaycyr Falz and the information I uncovered during my research—information I'm still trying to make sense of myself. I don't tell her that I'm supposedly the kingdom's savior, the girl with the hybiscus bloom on her left palm mentioned in their historia books. That revelation might break her. It's already too much for me.

"Okay, darling, I'm glad we've had this opportunity to talk, because I've missed this so very much. On a separate note, how are you holding up?"

Unable to hide the sadness pressing on my chest, I answer honestly. "I'm getting by. But there are times I really struggle. I miss home, I miss Mykah, and I miss you." *More than I can say.*

My loving mother wraps her arms around me and holds me close. "As the youngest, you are so brave. You've lived through some traumatic things and have come through them so strong—and so beautiful."

She pulls back, keeping her hands on my arms, then places one gently at the center of my chest.

"Never forget the source of that radiance. It rises from deep inside you. True beauty is something you carry."

We embrace again, and as Mamá walks out with me, she says, "This will all be over soon, baby. I promise you that. You see, I'm not so beautiful anymore. I'm angry—and the realms are going to know that very soon."

She's serious. My giggle slips out. Hers follows—dark, unsettling. There it is.

That's my Mamá.

I make my way through the ballroom when a sharp pain shoots through my hand, so intense it sends a jolt to my head and nearly makes me stumble.

I flip my hand over. The hybiscus bloom is pulsating so strongly that its vibrant color glows through the fabric of my glove.

A nearby table holds a few untouched water glasses. I grab one and drink deeply, the coolness easing the ache only slightly. Not enough. I know I must leave—now.

I slip out of the ballroom through a back door, unnoticed, and find the nearest empty balcony. Once outside, I clutch the starfish hanging from my neck and whisper, *"Karze, I need you, now. Meet me at the town library closest to Arkaik Alpynz—and bring your favorite weapons." Please hear me.*

Now I need to find different clothes. *Fast.* But what do I tell Myst? I don't even know where she is. *Damn it.* I'll leave her a written message.

Finding a good pair of breeches and a tunic around here is nearly impossible—and I'm not about to take off across this realm in a dress. I head straight for the servants' quarters, wondering how I'll ask for what I need.

Think, think…

"Hello, is anyone here?" I call out.

Silence.

I walk farther inside and find myself in a decently sized kitchen, a large wooden table at its center for food preparation. Then a voice drifts in, "Can I help you, miss?"

Startled, I turn—and there he is, a boy about my age. Perfect.

"I'm desperately in need of a pair of breeches and a tunic for a friend… one a little shorter than you. Could you spare them?"

His smile irritates me—he sees straight through the lie. Of course he does. "We have breeches and tunics to fit you. Follow me, my lady. Are you running away from home?" he asks, smirking.

"That is none of your business. Why would you even ask me that?" I snap, yet I still follow him down the back staircase to a large laundry and mending area. I don't have time to argue.

Ignoring my question, he opens a door to a spacious closet filled with riding gear, and my eyes light up.

He smiles, curious. "I'll leave you to it." The door clicks shut behind him.

I find exactly what I need: riding breeches, a long-sleeved tunic, leather boots and gloves, a warm cloak, and a coat. I change quickly, leaving the dress draped over a chair in the corner.

I slip two gold coins stamped with the hybiscus bloom from the small pocket sewn into my gown and place them on the counter where the moonlight will catch them.

Cracking the door open quietly, I glance both ways and slip out through the back exit we passed earlier. *Breathe.*

As I round the corner, I hear the boy's voice behind me—muffled but clear enough to catch. "Holy goddesses, this is my lucky day!"

I smile.

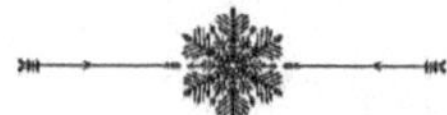

Back in my room, I open the small trunk and remove Shayn's weapons—the ones I borrowed the night I dazed him. They're all very nice, but the dagger carries a presence I can't quite name, something that lingers against my palm as if aware. I take it, along with a short sword, for whatever the fates have waiting in Glaycyr Falz. From the drawer of my bedside table, I take two small vials of potions and slip them into my satchel. I grab more coins from my stash and tuck them into a hidden pocket inside the lining.

Now I need to do something with my hair. I weave it into one long plait and pull it over my shoulder. "I'm as ready as I'll ever be," I tell the girl in the mirror.

Then I remember Mamá's words and press my hand to my chest. "Beauty will rise above evil," I breathe.

I slip out and head straight for the town library.

The air is bitterly cold, and a light drizzle begins to fall as my hand pulses brighter with each step. I feel a little crazed in this moment—that much is certain.

"Nice ass, Pretty Tears!"

My head whips around fast—and there's Karze, laughing hysterically. "I thought you were going to shake it into another realm for a moment there," he says.

I close the distance between us, my voice low through my smile. "Do not forget what I am capable of." We embrace. Then I continue, "Thank you for coming. I must go into the library, then we'll go to the stables and fetch two horses for the journey to the cursed ruins."

Karze slips into the bakehouse to gather what we'll need for the road.

Inside the library, I slap a coin onto the counter and wait, the toe of my boot tapping against the floor. The librarian lowers his glasses, eyes me with a slow shake of his head, then takes the coin without a word.

I cross the room to the magical kaleidoscope—its glass glimmering with invitation. Three deep breaths. I press my eye to the window of secrets.

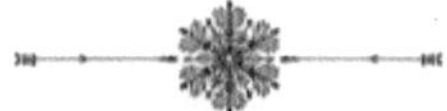

"What did you see? Tell me, Lyv!" Karze's voice cuts through the wind.

"I can't," I say, stepping back. "But we can't linger."

At the stables, we find two strong horses and begin leading them out—until a voice stops us cold.

"I'm coming with you."

Karze and I turn in perfect sync.

Garrett stands there, his face blank, as if the decision is already hollowing him out.

I plant my hands on my hips. "How do you know where we're going?"

His gaze flicks to the dagger in my boot. Shayn's dagger. "I just do," he says. "And I'm coming."

Karze steps forward. "You're abandoning your post. That's desertion. Treason."

Garrett shrugs. "I know."

I step closer. "You'll be hunted. Stripped of rank. You won't be welcome back."

He meets my eyes. "Then I won't come back. Unless Myst forgives me."

Karze studies him. "Why Glaycyr Falz?"

"I need to find someone." Garrett takes a step, like he's already halfway gone.

The hybiscus pulses stronger now. I look toward the stables. "Find a horse. We leave now."

42

Glaycyr Falz

Blayze

Beatryx and Isabella are in the kitchen, hands busy, laughter soft. Julian sleeps upstairs, worn out from an afternoon tumbling through snowdrifts. The women make full use of my oversized kitchen—this place feels like a home.

But something's off.

And so am I.

The thought lingers as I rise from the table and head upstairs, trying to make sense of the unease tightening in my chest. I've had these insights before, but this time they're sharper. Closer.

Through the hallway window, I spot Sasha on the north balcony, her wide eyes fixed on something unseen and her posture knotted with tension, drawing me outside.

"What is it, girl? Are you sensing something too?"

She coos in greeting, then turns back to the forest—gaze locked on the distant silhouette of the castle.

Iyce.

What is he doing?

I press my fingers to my temples, trying to quiet the ache building behind my eyes. It does nothing. The pressure lingers, dull and insistent, as light footsteps begin to climb the stairs behind me. I don't turn.

"Our secret's out, Sasha," I murmur, my voice low against the open air. "The north balcony isn't just ours anymore."

When I finally look, she's there—the woman who has completely claimed my heart. My friend. My love. My bride-to-be. My queen. She glances over, her eyes bright, that familiar smirk curling at her lips. "Well," she says lightly, "I had no idea you were hiding secret places within these walls."

I try to mask the pain clawing through me, but she reads straight through it. Concern softens her features—and I hate it. *I'm her protector. I'm faltering.*

She places a gentle hand on my cheek, drawing my gaze to her steady hazel eyes.

"Tell me what you need," she whispers. "I'll get it—whatever it is."

She's undone me completely.

"It will pass," I manage, my breath shallow, as her other hand comes up to cup my face. She kisses me so softly I barely feel it.

"Blayze."

Beatryx presses a final kiss to my cheek, acknowledges Sasha, and turns. I know she's going downstairs to speak with Isabella—and I understand. She's seen nothing but strength in me. What she saw just now frightened her. I read it in her eyes.

I glance into the room where Julian is still sleeping, likely out for the night after his day in the snow.

By the time I reach the kitchen, Isabella has already untied her apron. Beatryx glances at me—almost apologetic, but not quite.

"What's going on?" I ask, narrowing my eyes.

Isabella turns, clearly worked up. "You know exactly what's going on. And why you keep it to yourself—why you won't share that with someone who loves you—" She gestures toward Beatryx, who shifts uncomfortably. "—is beyond me."

She doesn't stop. "I have black walnut at home. If you can watch Julian, I won't be long."

"I'm going with you," Beatryx says.

I don't like this—not one bit—but I'm out of options. Without the walnut extract, I'm useless.

Isabella is already in the barn, readying the horse. Beatryx wraps her cloak around herself. I step toward her, tie the top ribbon, and take her hand.

"Take this."

She glances down at the small dagger, ready to protest, but I cut her off.

"Just take it. Use it without question, if need be."

She accepts it—but leaves something in my hand. At the door, she looks back and smiles.

"Gives me something to come back to."

Her delicate engagement ring rests in my palm. I close my fingers around it.

Olyvia

Garrett and Karze flank me as we sit atop our horses, staring down the path that winds through the Glaycyr Mountains. We've met those unpleasant rock soldiers before—immune to fire magic. The memory hits hard.

"Garrett, is there an alternate route? Maybe one that includes an inn?"

Both men remain silent, eyes fixed on the horizon, until Karze speaks. "What's the story with going this way?"

Garrett answers without turning. "Don't ask. And to answer your question, Olyvia—yes. Follow my lead. The forest is colder, but no harm will come to us there. No carriage could pass that trail, which is why we had to take the mountains last time."

As we approach, an older man steps forward. "Welcome to

Soldier's Rock Inn," he says in a slow, wandering voice, as if his thoughts take the long way around. "Wife's inside—best stew and beer bread in the realm. She'll fix you up, and I'll tend to your horses."

Garrett thanks him and presses a coin into his calloused hand.

Inside, the rich aroma of braised beef and herbs greets us. The inn is clean and oddly charming—dimly lit, with a kitchen at its center wrapped by a circular bar. We take a corner table where we can watch both the front door and the staircase.

A sturdy woman with rolled sleeves approaches, humming softly despite the tired set of her shoulders. She sets down three bowls—each with a thick slice of bread soaking in hot broth—then places a worn basket of more bread in the center of the table.

"Name's Helmi. Two questions: do you want ale? I presume you do. And do you need a room? I've got one left—tell me quickly or it'll be gone."

"We'll take it," Garrett says, placing a gold coin on the table.

She snatches it up, leaving a key marked **3N**.

Once she walks away, I speak up. "I am not sleeping with either of you."

Then I shove a piece of broth-soaked bread into my mouth.

Delicious.

The ale is good too, easing the throb in my palm. I glance at both men. "Come on. We need rest so we can leave as early as possible."

The room is modest. There's a small bed—which they tell me to take—and two cots are brought in, each with heavy quilts. The two of them drink more ale and scout the grounds while I wash up.

Earlier, I caught Garrett eyeing the dagger—he definitely recognized it as Shayn's. While they're gone, I try to etch new art onto the metal, coaxing flame along the steel to disguise it. But the blade resists me, refusing to take the shape I want.

Myst

Shayn escorts me back to my chambers. The ball was exquisite, and the man on the balcony… intriguing. I only wish he'd tell me who he is.

Inside, the lit sconces cast a warm glow across the room. Shadow lights them every night—I can only assume she kept the ritual even while I was gone. She never wants me to feel the dark closing in. She holds the light for me, always. And I love her for that.

When I hear Shayn closing the heavy door, I catch it gently. "Thank you, Shayn. Give Garrett my regards when you see him. Tell him I wish him a swift recovery."

He nods and leaves.

Hopefully, the evening holds no more surprises.

I sit at my dressing table and gaze into the mirror, eyes falling on the crown I've worn all night. At first it felt heavy—as crowns should, the weight of a kingdom pressing down.

But by the end of the night, I barely noticed it.

Maybe I am made to be a queen.

Am I?

I lift it carefully and return it to the open box. Soon it will be cleaned, polished, and tucked away in the royal vault… awaiting the next.

The bath was soothing. At the balcony doors, I crack one open, letting cold air settle in before I crawl beneath warm blankets.

Then I notice something on the table beside my bed.

I set the glass of huckleberry-infused water aside, my hand going straight to the parchment.

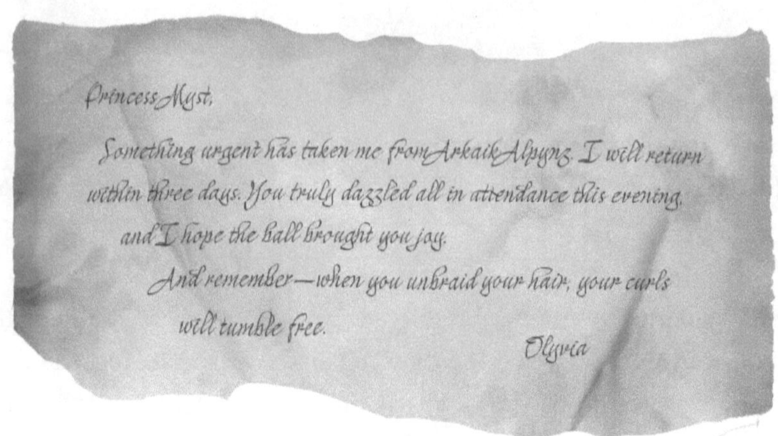

Where is she? This isn't like her.

"Olyvia, darling, I haven't the strength to undo the gorgeous braids. Maybe tomorrow," I whisper, as if she could hear me.

She cannot.

No one can.

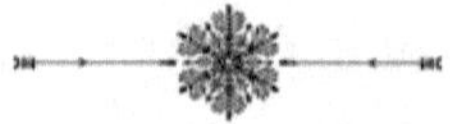

"Hi, Myst. Are you looking for a refreshment this evening?"

Sage sits at the writing desk, likely planning tomorrow's goings-on. I catch her off guard when I hold up the parchment.

"Do you have any idea where Olyvia has gone? And yes— shortbread, please. It's delicious."

She takes the script, reading as I choose the perfect square. Her expression shifts—strange, faintly worried.

"It sounds like she'll be back soon," she says. "Try not to worry."

Back in my room, I try. But too many strange things are happening. Beatryx is not here. Olyvia is gone. And Garrett… Shayn said he was unwell, but all I feel is that he's gone too.

Suddenly, I feel very alone.

A familiar knock stops my heart—the one that used to calm

me.

The door opens, and Hayze steps inside.

Tingles erupt across my skin. She is the only person who has ever touched me in a sensual way. But I'm no longer interested. Someone else has been unraveling me lately—*and I don't even know his name.*

Ignoring her, I turn and walk toward my bathing chamber.

In the dressing room, I put on a robe and loop the sash once before returning.

She's still standing there, and it stops me.

"Myst," she begins softly. I tilt my head as she continues. "I want the best for you in this life. And I will always love—"

"Hayze," I interrupt. "I'm past it. I'm not angry. I'm not sad. I feel nothing. I wish you the very best in this life as well."

I don't get another word out—she's suddenly in my space, hands gripping my arms. "Can you just listen for once, without getting so damn defensive?"

Shaking, I pull free and walk to my dressing table, picking up my ivory hairbrush. She follows, watching as I sink into the chair.

"Go ahead."

She takes the small bone I offer, and I allow her that much—listening.

"I will always stand with you," she says, "but you must allow it. There are few people in royal kingdoms you can trust, including some you place confidence in now. I see and hear many things in my position as marshal. And I am the one you can depend on—even at the cost of my life."

Her words crack something inside me. Tears slip down my cheeks as I turn my head away. Hayze steps closer and kneels before me.

"Myst, you are my princess and future queen. There was never a you and me written in any book. You know that, and I know that. Your one true love is out there waiting, and I have found mine. But you must allow our friendship to continue, because I swear to you on my dead parents' souls—hard times are coming. You stand at the center of it, and you will need me."

The tears overtake me. I drop to my knees and wrap my arms around her. She holds me, and we both cry.

And I do need her. The thought alone threatens to undo me all over again.

Finally, I lift my head. "You taught me how to love myself. And how to love my body. And for those things—I will always love you."

We embrace again.

Isabella

"Chaa!" I dig my heels into Blayze's powerful stallion. He surges forward into a sprint.

"Hold on like never before—we're moving fast," I warn Beatryx, who wraps her arms around my waist.

I've ridden this forest countless times but tonight it feels different—eerie, slick, wrong. The trees seem to press in as we cut through the dark toward town.

Beatryx senses it too. She leans in. "Do you feel it?"

I tilt my head just enough for her to notice. "Open your senses," I call over the wind. "What does the quiet hold?""

She takes a breath. "Only danger," she says softly. "Nothing clear. It could be anything."

She's still learning how her mind works—how it speaks in moments like this. The feeling may be real… or not. But I trust her instincts, even when she can't yet name them.

At the edge of the clearing, I dismount and extend my hand. Beatryx grips it, swings her leg over the beast, and slides down beside me.

"Inside," I whisper. "I'll grab the walnuts, then we leave—

unnoticed."

I go straight for the shelf where I keep my bottles. I skim labels. Normally everything is organized, but lately my life has been a beautiful disaster, and nothing is where it should be.

"Where are you, black walnuts?" My hands tremble. I'm so worried about Blayze that clear thought feels impossible.

Beatryx joins me, holding a small candle. We agreed not to light the interior—not with so much uncertainty outside.

"There." I snatch the bottle and shove it into my satchel, then turn toward Beatryx, speaking more to myself than to her. "What else? What else do I need?"

My mind spirals. Then she grabs me, pulling me out of it.

"Breathe, Isabella." She inhales with me, forcing me to match her rhythm. "Getting the black walnuts to Blayze is the most important task—no matter what waits in the shadows. Look at me. Do you understand?"

I nod, tears stinging.

We step outside and move toward the stallion. I throw the satchel over my shoulder, mount first, then reach down to help Beatryx up.

Just as her fingertips graze mine, everything crashes into the moment.

"Well, what do we have here?" Iyce sneers, his smile sharper than a blade. "My loving sister—our darling little princess whore— and her new friend, who poisons royalty."

Fury flares in Beatryx's voice as she lashes at him before I can stop her. "How dare you speak of her that way!"

She doesn't think—just moves.

The look in his eyes is enough.

Dangerous.

Beatryx whirls toward me, eyes wild. I catch her hand, but she yanks it away. "Go!" Beatryx cries.

One kick—and we're gone.

We both know the truth: without Blayze, we don't stand a chance against Iyce.

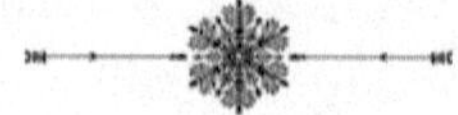

Beatryx

This isn't my first encounter with Iyce, which is why I know—without question—he's here to finish what he didn't have the courage to start last time.

His face hovers close. Too close. All beauty and venom.

"Do not go into my thoughts," he warns, voice low.

I laugh at the threat. The audacity. A man with a heart carved from ice.

With my hands behind my back, I slip off one glove and let it fall to the wooden floor.

He moves behind me and snakes an arm around my waist. I flinch as he yanks me against him, his words hot at my ear.

"You really want my pathetic coward brother?" he hisses. "Don't you feel this? Wouldn't you rather have this?"

The words that leave my mouth are sharp. "You have a dick. That doesn't make you one of a kind."

I summon every ounce of strength, reaching for his mind—and crash against a wall. Sealed. Blocked.

My hand flies to the dagger hidden in my corset. I draw it, ready to carve that smug beauty from his face—but he's faster. He catches my wrist.

Then—cloth pressed over my mouth and nose. A scent I don't recognize floods me.

The dagger clinks—sharp and final—

—and everything slips away.

Isabella

I've never ridden a horse so hard—nor dismounted with more force—than I do now. By the time I reach the top of the stairs, Blayze is already at the door, looking distraught, as if he knows something has gone terribly wrong.

I'm unraveling, held together by whatever threads haven't snapped. "Blayze. Iyce. Beatryx…"

He pulls me into his steady arms and begins stitching me back together, like he has done so many times. "Breathe with me, Isabella. Slow and steady."

We repeat the rhythm until my body begins to follow it, something inside me loosening as though searching for sanctuary.

When I finally tell him what happened, he's calmer than I expect. He leads me inside before asking, "Did you get the black walnut."

I pull the little glass vessel from my satchel. "Yes."

"Are you up to making the potion? What can I do to help?"

"We don't have a choice. They're harvested and dried, so the outer husks are easier to remove."

I tie on an apron and steady my hands.

"Julian?" I ask.

"Sleeping," Blayze says.

He cracks the husks with quick, sure movements while I locate his extraction press—then it becomes his task too. We heat the wood beneath the walnut meat to ease the process. By the time we finish, a third of the jar is full—enough to get him through this.

"Normally, I filter the oil once the impurities settle," I say, pressing the bottle into his hand. "But you don't have time. It'll taste stronger, but it works the same. I made hot tea—add a few drops."

Blayze shakes his head. "There is no time for tea."

He pulls on his furs, uncorks the bottle, and lets three drops fall onto his tongue. He grimaces, then nods. "Thank you. I'm going after Beatryx now. Stay inside, no matter what. I've cast a protection spell—for you and Julian."

"It's impossible to take too much," I remind him. "Use more whenever you need it. Stay ahead of the weakness."

He steps outside, pausing to take in the frozen forest. His lips—cold and soft—press against my cheek, leaving behind a trace of sorrow.

"I love you," he says.

"Blayze—wait."

He turns back to me.

"When we were separated, I touched her. I pushed a healing protection onto her. It wasn't much—everything happened so fast—but she has something on her."

His expression shifts—relief, worry, determination all at once. Then he nods and disappears into the trees.

I sink to my knees, the silence swallowing me. There's been too much—Myst saw our mother, I crossed paths with Youri, Julian's father, in a way I wasn't ready for, and now this.

I pray.

Blayze

"Where are you, my star?" I whisper into the frozen air, breath coiling like smoke as I ride through the forest toward the kingdom—my kingdom—that was stripped from me the moment I defended my sister's honor.

I close my eyes and open my senses, thinking only of Beatryx. I don't know where Iyce has gone, but I will find her. We've never shared magic, but she's learning mind persuasion—a gift she ignored as a child. If there's any thread to follow, I'll chase it.

The snow is packed, the forest silent. Only hoofprints mark the path behind us. We stop at a stream trickling beneath ice, and I dismount, letting my stallion drink.

Every moment matters.

I pull the bottle from my satchel and place three more drops on my tongue.

Then—I hear her.

My gaze sweeps the quiet landscape until a sound draws my eyes.

"Sasha!" I call, arm outstretched.

She lands lightly, feathers puffed, posture hunched. Her wings flare as she crouches, neck rotating in a slow, predatory arc as her keen eyes scan the surroundings. Then she blinks—knowing.

"What is it, girl? What are you trying to tell me?" I whisper, brushing a finger over the soft feathers on her chest.

She hoots once, then lifts into silent flight, rising into the frozen air. Her broad wings stretch wide as she glides, conserving energy for the journey ahead.

I keep my eyes on her as she soars above, then mount my stallion and guide us out of the Forest of Frozen Dreams—away from Isabella and Julian.

We reach the small town where Isabella's home sits among the others. Sasha circles overhead, buying time before we move on.

The moment I step inside, an aura of warmth and love hits me—memories of her in the kitchen, Julian laughing at her heels. But it doesn't last.

The air shifts.

I sense my brother's presence—and the aftermath of his rage. Glass shards glitter across the floor. Oils and herbs lie shattered. And amid the chaos, one thing catches my eye.

This is why I adore Beatryx—intelligent, alluring, always leaving behind a trace.

A smile spreads across my face, unbidden. She would appreciate it. And gods, I need it.

I will find you.

I bend and retrieve her glove and the dagger.

Outside, sunrise pierces the Glaycyrs, momentarily blinding me. Sasha spots what I'm holding. With a sharp dive, she snatches the glove from my hand, releasing a menacing screech as she veers eastward.

Using the glove to track Beatryx, Sasha guides us across the Polar Gardens. As we near the fountain that honors my mother—the Lost Queen—

The world tilts. My chest tightens as I falter.

The once-frozen water begins to trickle.

I tremble as hope takes hold.

You want to play games at Glass Lake, brother?

I'm on my way.

Olyvia

"Wake up, iron-hearted! We have destinations to reach and havoc to wreck! Join me downstairs for a bowl of spiced porridge so you two lovebirds can adjust to daylight." Chuckling at my own jest, I descend the creaky stairs and settle at the bar in the center of the room. Helmi sweeps between the tables, the bristles whispering across the floorboards. She leans the broom against a chair and greets me with a raised brow. "Where are you three headed?"

Lying has never been my strength, and I feel the usual tension creep in as I watch the innkeeper move behind the bar. I try to sound casual, but it still comes out stiff. "We're, uh… studying artifacts," I say, hoping the words land better than they sound.

Helmi pauses, eyes narrowing enough to make me brace for a follow-up question, but after a beat she nods and disappears into the kitchen.

Relief washes through me when she returns with warm porridge and a glass of fresh juice.

Garrett and Karze appear as I reach the door, both half-awake and confused. They each grab a cinnamon roll and fall in step beside me. "We've overstayed our welcome," I say quietly. "She's asking questions. Let's move." And with that, we leave—nothing but dust in our wake.

"I really miss Crescere Moonz," Karze groans as we enter the town just ahead of Glaycyr Falz. "These eastern kingdoms are freezing my balls off."

Garrett laughs. "You'd be surprised what your balls can sustain. Just keep walking." They both laugh harder while I shake my head.

"Garrett, did you hear anything about the lost ruins in Balag when we were here last? Did you or Shayn come across anything?" I shift the satchel against my hip, its familiar weight steadying me while I wait.

Blunt should be my middle name. Garrett's puzzled expression confirms it. He shakes his head. "I never saw or heard of any ruins during our time here."

His answer sends my thoughts spinning. *Damn.*

I can't simply walk into the castle and request the royal cartographer. There must be a monastery, a library, or a chart-house—someplace that caters to explorers and merchants.

I need guidance. I'm running out of time.

I glance down at my palm. The hybiscus pulses, a quiet reminder of urgency. "I need a map."

"Whatever goddess you pray to has already granted your request," Garrett says, voice lifting. "Look down that cobblestone road. It sits just beyond the market."

I turn, and sure enough, a mapmaker's hall nestles between a busy market and a blacksmith's forge.

As I step toward the door, Garrett places a hand on my shoulder. I turn just enough to face him. "This is where we part. I don't know what you're tangled up in, but let's hope we all make it out alive."

I press my lips together, steadying myself before turning back toward the quaint shop—but before I can step forward, Garrett catches my arm and whispers what I'd already suspected. Then he slips into the flock of people flowing toward the castle.

Karze opens the heavy oak door, its hinges groaning softly. I step inside first, him close behind. "What are we looking for exactly?" he asks. "And what did Garrett say to you?"

I spare him only a brief glance, already drawn to the sight before me. "We're going to the blacksmith once we leave here. I need to make a trade."

The shop is dimly lit by oil lamps hanging from thick wooden beams, sending a soft amber sheen across the vellum maps lining the walls. Some are framed in rustic wood, others rolled and tied with twine or ribbon, and some stand upright in heavy stone jars. The air is rich with aged paper, ink, and beeswax. A few men sit at large tables surrounded by hand-drawn maps—some local, others of lands I've never seen.

Curiosity tugs, but there's no time.

A weathered voice cuts through the steady scratch of ink on vellum.

"Welcome to Glaycyr Navigator Hall," the man says, rough but not unkind. "Name's Kaapo. Looking for something specific? We don't see many womenfolk in here."

Karze leans in, tone low and dry. "Well, you do now, old man."

My elbow finds his side, and he doubles over as if struck by a blade.

"We travel as scholars," I say, keeping my voice even. "Seeking knowledge of the province called Balag. I've heard—though the source is questionable—that it lies east of Glaycyr Falz."

Kaapo scratches his head, unease flickering across his features. He clears his throat, scans the room, then motions for us to follow.

At a smaller table, a map sits surrounded by tools—quills,

compasses, rulers arranged with impressive precision—but the shape of the realm unsettles me.

Steadying myself, I ask, "Who is this map being prepared for?"

We enter a private study, and Kaapo shuts the door before answering, "Iyce, Prince of Glaycyr Falz. Keeps my trade in business, he does. Pays handsomely… and expects the best."

Heat flares in my chest as he turns the lock. Without another word, he snatches a map from a cluttered table and unrolls it across a longer one. "Grab that side and use the weight there," he says, and Karze moves instantly.

Kaapo adjusts a glass lens set in a brass ring fixed to the table's edge. He positions it over a faded section, leaning close. "Balag," he reads, guiding a brass pointer to the mark. "No one goes there. Cursed since the princes fought their final battle and left ruin behind. Evil still clings to the fallen stones."

I know the tale. I've read most accounts. Good. These ruins are exactly where I need to be.

"Do you have a smaller replica for purchase?" I ask.

Kaapo brightens at the prospect of coin and leads us toward the front. Karze is already reaching into his pocket. As I trail behind, my elbow clips an ink jar—black liquid spilling across Iyce's commissioned map.

We leave quickly. Above the door, a wooden sign swings in the frozen breeze, etched with a compass and scroll.

"Damn," I mutter. "I meant to buy a compass. We don't have time to go back."

Karze pulls something from his satchel and tosses it upward. As it falls, I catch the silver compass, its weight steady in my palm. A smile tugs at my mouth. "You're good. Wait here. I'll only be a moment."

I step into the blacksmith's dusty but orderly shop and approach the counter. Setting Shayn's dagger down with quiet confidence, I ask, "What trade options do you have for this?"

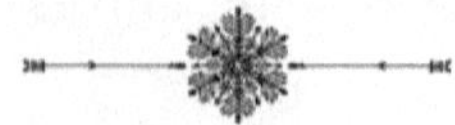

Later, Karze and I ride together on a single horse, hoping to draw less attention as we approach the busy gates. After studying the map, I lean back. "If anyone asks, we're here for a personal meeting about potential work at the stables."

I'm getting pretty good at lying.

Karze nods, irritation edging his voice. "You know, I can come up with some damn good nonsense myself. You don't have to make every single plan."

I ignore him.

As we pass through town, I notice places I missed before—an alchemist's shop, another blacksmith, and a scatter of small shops tucked between narrow alleys and stone archways.

Refocusing on the map, I direct Karze southeast. But as we pass the edge of the Forest of Frozen Dreams, my thoughts drift—Blayze, Beatryx, Isabella, Julian. I hope they are safe.

There are fewer common people now, but more guards and nobles. We must be careful.

"Karze, stop the horse."

My tone is enough. He halts without question, and I dismount, walking toward the fountain I first glimpsed from the library with Clarina. The sight stops me cold, shock flooding my chest. When I turn back, Karze is staring—confused—but he joins me. I place my marked hand into the water.

"And what's the story about this fountain?" he asks. "Because I know there must be one."

"It's flowing. Come on—we must hurry."

He mumbles, "Of course it's flowing. Isn't that what fountains do?"

I huff a laugh. "I don't have time to explain, but it's significant. The fountain's been frozen for years."

"Of course it has," he says. "I knew that."

We slip into the edge of the forest. Balag is close now, and I decide to give him more. "Do you remember the challenge we faced in the Timbers of Blood on Vampyre Isle? The one that led us straight to the creature?"

Karze slows the horse and drops to the ground, returning a moment later with snow clinging to his boots.

"Lyv," he says, voice low, "you don't have to stand alone in everything… Stop shutting me out. Let me in. What's the plan. How can I help you."

Guilt tightens my chest. He holds out his hand, and I take it, letting him help me down.

"The fountain stands for the Queen of Glaycyr Falz. They call her lost, but I believe her disappearance was staged. When she vanished, the fountain froze to ice. For it to be flowing now… something immense is stirring."

A few tears slip down my cheeks. Karze kisses the pulsing bloom on my palm. "Lyv, you are so strong. You've got this—and I've got you."

For a moment, all feels safe.

"And what I saw in the kaleidoscope the second time," I say quietly, "is a story for another time."

He sighs. "More secrets."

"We can't wait any longer," I urge. "I'll explain the first vision while we move."

I stand and breathe deeply. Fire spills from my fingertips, thawing a nearby frozen pond. Steam rises, blending into the cold air.

Karze's eyes light up, as they always do when I use my magic. "Now I'm ready."

His smile tells me he is too.

The trek uphill is steep, so we walk, allowing the horse its freedom.

"Go on, pretty lady. Get home quick," I whisper, watching her run back toward the kingdom.

Sadness creeps in, but Karze moves closer and takes my hands. Then, without warning, he begins to sing…

Once I'm steady again, he asks, "You ready to fly, Lyv?"

Before I can answer, he lifts me into his arms and shoots us into the cold sky—relief flooding our exhausted bodies.

He knows I need to save my strength.

And so does he.

43

Arkaik Alpynz

Myst

Half awake, my sight steadies as a chill settles through me.

One balcony door is ajar, welcoming the crisp winter inside. Shivering, I grab a duvet and pull it over my shoulders, holding it in place as I scoot to the edge of the bed. My toes touch the cold floor, and I pad to the door, easing it shut.

I almost turn—but the beauty of the Whispering Woods holds me still. Snow fell intensely overnight, each snowflake twinkling softly in the pale solstice light.

Grandpapá, I will find you. I kiss my fingertips and press them to the glass, the snowflakes beyond reflecting my promise back to me.

I move toward my dressing closet, slowly gathering myself as I change into riding clothes.

I have an idea.

Normally, I ride Aspen into the Whispering Woods. But this morning, I choose Shyanne to carry me to the Forest of Shadows, where daylight struggles to pierce the dense veil of trees. She is a powerful mare, black as velvet with a soft step.

She is the horse I need to take me to the witch—to Mairi.

I was thirteen the last time I ventured into this forest, where an unease seems to pulse through the air. Its trees rise tall and close, branches knitting together to dim the light so that even at noon the air feels dusk-bound. Mist writhes low across the ground, clinging to roots and stones. The silence is never complete—there is always the faint rustle of unseen movement, the whisper of leaves stirred by no wind.

Deep within the forest lies the River of Spells, its waters glimmering with an unnatural sheen. On the riverbed, stones shimmer faintly, each alive with promise. Some glow with gentle warmth, offering kindness to those bold enough to reach for them. Others pulse with darker intent, their risks too great for most to dare.

A crooked path leads to the witch's cottage, nestled in a hollow where shadows linger longer than they should. Smoke drifts from her chimney, carrying scents both sweet and unsettling. The forest itself seems to watch, as though every tree and stone knows the bargains struck within.

The horse stops near an old willow and I dismount, making my way through the trees to the gate—only to be stopped by something unusual.

A girl not older than me pulls weeds in a garden.

"Hello," I call hesitantly. When she turns, I am taken aback. Black hair, knotted and wild, veils most of her face, but her enormous green eyes break through.

"Veraminta! Hurry up, girl!"

Mairi's voice slithers through the garden before she appears, staring straight at me as I stare back.

Her cackle ripples through me, but I stay focused as she comes close to the gate. "Well, look at you. How brave you have grown to be."

I am not here for idle talk. "I need a favor."

"Do you, pretty one? A favor means I get something in return. What are you willing to give up? And what do you want?"

I hate her games. "I want to know where Grandpapá is."

Her smile begins to form as her eyes pin me in place.

One blink, and she's inches from my face—I never saw her move. She makes her demand. "Give me the necklace you wear."

My hand flies to the pendant and I step back.

Her laugh belittles me to my bones. "Clearly, you are still a child. Run back to your castle."

Instantly, she is gone, and a black cat slinks around a cracked flowerpot, its large green eyes blinking slowly—three times.

Iyce

Blayze will be distracted by what he finds at Glass Lake—he should have known better. *Why would I challenge him in a place where he holds power?*

Kicking both doors open, I stride into my chambers and drop the unconscious Beatryx onto the bed. I glance at the bitch and laugh low. "I need a drink."

At the serving table, I weigh my choices, then reach for the sapphire. It glides down my throat like liquid satin. I pour another—slower this time—lifting the ornate glass as I strut toward the balcony, but stop. Jasmine clings to the air.

Subtle.

Seductive.

I look again at the woman lost to sleep, absorbing every detail: thick lashes that flutter, lips like bruised roses, danger worn as easily as silk. Something inside me tightens. Now that words sleep on your lips, I see why my brother has fallen for you.

I drain my glass and press my palm to my breeches, willing restraint, but desire only coils tighter. Why deny the seduction of a woman scented with moonlight and peril?

I return for a third glass, cool droplets tracing down my face as I drink. My fingers find the leather laces at my waist and I tear them free, groaning as I brace both hands against the table. My control slips. I covet what belongs to my brother—and I hate him for it. I raise my wrist to my mouth, biting through the sleeve ties, then do the same to the other. With one hand, I pull the tunic over my head and cast it aside.

From my desk, I drag the chair close to the bed and sink into it. I stare, my hand restless. I trace her curves, the softness of her jaw, the quiet rise of her chest—all in my mind. I can't stop. My grip tightens and the rhythm builds. And when the release comes, it's not just lust—it's possession.

"The next time I do this in your presence, you'll be awake—fully aware of what's happening. And I will be inside you."

Her expression does not change. Lost in slumber.

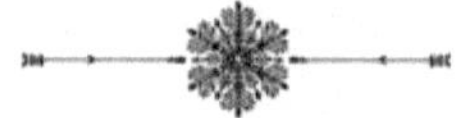

Blayze

Glass Lake comes into view, and I slow my horse.

Sasha perches high in a snow-laden tree, her eyes wide and unblinking. The last time I stood at this lake, Beatryx was with me. She loved it. Ophelia glides across the lake, elegant as ever.

The memory cuts deep. Fury rises in my chest as I dismount and move toward the water's edge.

Then—without warning—I feel her.

A low growl rises from somewhere ancient inside me. Primal. Unrelenting.

Iyce had better pray to every god and goddess—because this time, I will kill him. Even if it kills me.

Sasha doesn't move. That means something is nearby.

I keep walking, circling the lake as its surface mirrors the sky in shifting shades of glassy blue. The silence presses in, thick and watchful.

Then I see it—the source of her scent.

Half-buried in the snow, trembling in the wind, lie her mahogany ribbons.

The roar that tears from my throat shakes the trees. I crouch, gather the ribbons, and press them to my chest like a sacred offering.

She was here. This close. And he dared to touch her.

Sasha dives, talons flashing, and snatches the ribbons from my grasp.

I rise, steam curling from my lips, and shout into the frozen air, "To the castle! I know exactly where he is!"

Olyvia

Karze's grip tightens as we land hard, his wings sweeping wide to brace the impact before he pulls them in close. I'm still pressed against him, breath caught, staring at the silver sweep of feathers settling into place. He's myth and muscle and danger all at once.

Only then do I manage, "Did you hear that?"

He nods. "Sounded like a wild animal. This kingdom is strange."

A shaky laugh escapes me before I can stop it. "Well, we're about to be consumed by strangeness. Because… I'm beginning to hear it again. What I heard when I looked through the kaleidoscope."

Karze tilts his head. "Speaking of that—what did you see?"

A sudden roar splits the air.

Before I can answer, a deep red dragon slices over us, wings beating so hard the ground shudders. Wind slams into us, forcing me into a crouch as leaves whip past my face. Karze drags me under the nearest branch, both of us ducking instinctively.

My heart stutters. A warning. Or a promise of death. One more hindrance.

A sharp breath escapes me as the sky settles. "It wasn't just what I saw—it was what I heard. Can you hear it? That haunting melody."

He squints. "No." Then he reaches out, and I take his hand. His voice steadies me. "I'm in this with you all the way, Lyv. Don't be afraid. I'm right here."

My smile tells him I'm grateful.

We continue through the icy woods, passing a lake that gleams like polished silver. I tell him more. "These sounds—they're leading us to the cursed ruins, where harps whisper and ghostly women cry. Do you still not hear it?"

He shakes his head, squeezing my hand tighter as he speaks through the freezing wind. "I'm beginning to wonder if you're the only one meant to hear it."

I look at him, and he sees it in my eyes—I hear it more clearly now.

I grow serious. "Promise me something. You know who I am. If anything happens… find my mother. Tell her."

Karze lets go of my hand, and the loneliness is sharp. Then he turns, drops to one knee, and meets my eyes.

"Lyv, I swear on my life—nothing bad is going to happen to you. We're going into those ruins together. And you're going to bring back fire, because that's what the damn book said you do."

I fall into his arms, and he holds me tightly.

"I swear, Lyv. Let's fucking do this."

I force myself to match his energy, and we press forward, toward the haunting sounds that have been waiting for me like a promise kept. As we draw near, the air thickens with eerie silence, pierced only by faint melodies of unseen harps and the mournful wails of women echoing through crumbling stone archways.

The ruins, once a province of beauty, are overrun with twisted vines and shadows that seem to move of their own accord. We stand in awe, exchange a glance—and break into a full sprint up the fractured stairs to Balag.

At the heart of the domain, the harps and cries that once consumed me fall quiet. Karze grabs a glowing torch from the stone wall lining the old cobblestone road and tosses it to me. I catch it, and the flames roar. Fire magic serves us here.

He takes a second torch, but his flame flickers.

I roll my eyes and keep walking.

Fear no longer grips me. I have a duty to fulfill, and I will see it through—no matter the outcome. This is bigger than me.

We scan the destruction—ice scorched by Iyce's frozen magic, ash still smoldering from Blayze's fire.

"What were the brothers fighting about?" Karze asks.

"Their sister…" I begin, but before I can finish, an unnatural sound rises—growing closer.

Amid the turmoil, we stand shoulder to shoulder, bracing for whatever comes.

Karze's silver hair falls into his eyes as he draws his sword, ready to strike down anything that dares interrupt me—or the reason we're here.

We venture deeper into the ruins, and once again I hear the harps. This time, they're more than haunting.

They're hypnotic.

My heart pounds.

Karze sees it in my face and barks, "Lyv, stay focused, girl!"

Flames dance beneath my fingertips—a wild, rising urge to confront whatever hunts us. Karze stares, eyes wide. "You're glowing, Lyv. And your eyes—they're gold again."

Then something in him shifts.

The vampyre boy emerges—piercing eyes, bared fangs.

His presence radiates transcendent strength—a perfect balance of darkness and light.

Comforting.

Terrifying.

The next moments blur.

"Watch out, Lyv!" Karze shouts, grabbing me and shielding my body as we crash into a crumbling wall. Overhead, large birds flee in frantic flight.

The birds are always the warning.

"They're coming straight for us!" Karze sees what I see.

We leap to our feet, bracing for a full-on attack by creatures blurred in the darkness. The short sword on my back hums for release. I draw it, along with Shayn's dagger from my boot—the one the blacksmith examined before shooing me from his shop.

A war cry bellows from deep within me, raw and unrelenting. My eyes lock onto the looming nightmare. "Fight!"

My mind spins, but instinct takes over. I channel Mykah's maneuver and sprint toward the ghostly women—each one pale, hollow-eyed, their long hair flowing in different shades.

The golden-haired ones are mine.

There's only room for one girl with golden hair on this battlefield—and it's me.

I don't know how to kill them. Not yet.

But I choose the one whose hunger reaches for me.

The smile that spreads across my face is its own weapon.

I slash my sword across her neck, clean and swift. Her head hits the ground and rolls.

But she lives.

The headless ghost lunges toward me. I slice both hands from her body, and still she comes.

I glance to my side—Karze is holding off two redheads, blades flashing. "What takes them down?" I shout.

His voice cuts through the chaos, dry and defiant. "When you figure that out, let me know."

Then I see something pulsing deep inside her chest.

Her lifeforce.

She takes one step toward me, and I drive my sword straight through it.

All the golden-haired ghosts collapse.

I blink. That was… odd.

"The color of their hair binds them!" I scream. "Puncture the heart!"

"That was gross," Karze declares as he wipes his blades clean.

Then his eyes shift, refocusing on something ahead. It catches me off guard—until I follow his gaze and know exactly where we are.

Without a thought, I dash toward the remnants of the smaller castle, calling back to Karze as he runs after me. "This sanctuary was mentioned in the books. The queen loved Balag and its people and often came here for solitude."

"Then why didn't you know the Ruin's name?" Karze asks.

"The books never mentioned it by name," I snap, "but I know this is it."

The once-respected iron gate that guarded the courtyard lies on the ground, decaying. Karze and I step over its remnants and move inward, where paths are overgrown with weeds and grass. The air is thick with whispers of the past, and I can almost hear the laughter that once lived here.

When I look up, my heart stops. At once, I move toward a faint sound—too focused to register what I see next.

Water seeps from a crack along the side of a two-tiered fountain, its stone so weathered it looks ready to crumble, the rosework etched into its surface nearly erased. The basin holds little more than remnants of recent rain. The fountain itself stands silent—no longer flowing.

One last elixir remains in my satchel. I uncork the vial and pour its shimmering contents into the basin. The water hisses as it touches ancient stone. A faint glow pulses beneath the surface, as if the fountain remembers what I seek.

I place my left hand into the cool, now-enchanted water and close my eyes. Warmth coils up my arm, threading through me.

Magic takes hold.

And the fountain reveals the past: elegant men and women strolling through courtyard gardens, their voices soft with joy. Flowers bloom in perfect rows, and young girls weave blossoms into one another's hair. The iron gate stands tall, gleaming in the morning light.

But what comes next chills me.

Near the castle's entrance stands a woman with auburn hair, fiery red highlights cascading over her shoulders and down past her waist. A modest yet intricate crown rests atop her head, and as if sensing my stare, she looks directly at me and smiles.

Her eyes are identical to Blayze's—forest green.

Then I see a younger Blayze walking up the steps toward her, taking her hand and kissing it gently before hugging his mother, the queen.

Karze touches my back lightly, drawing me from the vision that shook me to my core.

"We are in the right place," I murmur. "Let's go inside. Be ready for anything."

We enter the great hall. It is spacious, with high ceilings and large windows covered in tapestries scorched and hanging in ragged strips. The fireplace takes up an entire wall, coated in ice. Once-magnificent leather furniture is torn and burned. Broken glass litters the floor.

It's destroyed.

Karze and I agree the kitchen isn't worth our time and go straight to the wide staircase leading upward. "Let's continue up, then work our way back down," I suggest. Now that we've reached the highest floor, the air feels eerie—heavy with silence—and I'm thankful Karze is here.

"Do you want to check the tower or balcony?" he asks.

I glance toward both. "You check the balcony. I'll take the tower. Look for anything unusual." Then I follow the narrow spiral staircase to the top.

I look out over what was once the vibrant bustle of life in Balag. Now the streets are empty, color drained from the land. In the distance, the massive castle of Glaycyr Falz rises—still imposing—but here we are surrounded by vacant countryside and rundown farms. The view unsettles me because I know it must have once been magnificent—a place where the queen could sit and gaze across the land she loved.

A fight this bad with a sibling is something I cannot imagine. It makes no sense.

I turn and go back down the stairs. "Find anything?" I holler.

"No. Not a damn thing. Let's go back to the first floor. There must be something in the heart of this castle."

We take the staircase down, and the hybiscus bloom on my palm begins to pulse intensely. I stop, wrapping my other hand around it, trying to soothe the painful throb.

Karze's expression hardens. "That's it. Let it guide you, Lyv."

I meet his gaze, eyes wide. "You're right. I'll check the library. You check the chambers and guest rooms."

This feels invasive, like I'm violating the queen's privacy. But I must find out what in all the goddesses' names I am supposed to be doing.

While searching for the library, a flicker of light catches my eye, and I veer into the armory. This seems to be one area untouched by the brothers' fight. Torches burn softly along the walls—and then I see what matters.

Weapons.

So many, each more incredible than the last: swords, axes, spears, daggers in every shape and size. Bowstrings, scabbards, quivers—finely made. I'm skilled with every one of them.

When I pull myself from the vault of blades, Karze is waiting. He slips into a silly voice. "My lady, I have a fine bracelet for you. Allow me."

After everything I've put him through, I let him fasten it around my wrist. Two stones gleam—one ice blue, the other fire red.

Gorgeous. If nothing else, we'll get it to Blayze. It has to mean something.

"Find anything in the library?" Karze asks.

"Haven't been yet," I say. "Let's go now."

When we enter the library—the heart of knowledge in this once-quaint castle—I'm struck again by the loss. More than half lies in ruin. What remains offers only the faintest hint of the wonder it once held. It was a place to read, to study, to dream. Now it's a memory buried in destruction.

Vaulted ceilings still soar overhead, and wooden shelves line the walls in quiet symmetry. But the air—once rich with parchment and polish—is now thick with dust, particles drifting through narrow shafts of light from the high windows. Books are scattered: some frayed at the edges, others sealed in timeless ice.

One time-softened book catches my attention. I reach for it, but the title is so faded it's difficult to read—*Tea with Enya*. Sadness wells up.

Julian has never met his Grandmamá. This is all so wrong.

Karze stands at a large wooden table positioned against the far wall, and I join him. Its surface is covered with maps, quills strewn about. The maps stand out, so I scan them until one captures my interest.

Tears begin to fall. Karze moves closer. He knows the realm beneath my hand is my home. His arm comes around me as he pulls me into his warmth and dries my tears with his fingertips, letting them soak into his skin as he murmurs, "You'll be home soon."

I exhale. "Thank you."

Turning from the map, I notice a stained-glass window. What it depicts is strangely specific.

Is this why he feels such a strong connection to her? Does she remind him of his lost mother?

The thought grips me as I move closer, captivated, studying the intricate blown glass of Sasha in flight—feathers etched in cobalt and gold.

The owl is as white as the snow she glides above, with powerful wings tipped in fire red and piercing green eyes. Looking at it feels surreal, and faintly I feel a buzz from the dagger in my boot—Shayn's dagger.

Without taking my eyes off the owl, I reach down and grasp the handle.

Karze starts backing up, pleading, "No, my lady, please do not sacrifice me to the glass owl."

Because of the bizarre connection between the dagger and the glass, I ignore him. Eyes wide, I examine the blade and ask, "Do you see this?"

A hybiscus is etched in fine detail along one side.

Removing my eyes from it seems impossible. The silence grows heavy with dark whispers from long ago. The books share their stories—sorrowful echoes of what happened here.

As if hearing them too, Karze locks eyes with me. Then he turns toward the glass, pointing—his face overtaken by shock.

I look.

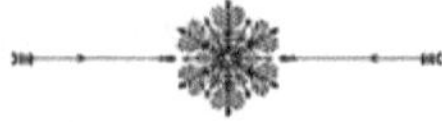

Blayze

At the docks south of the castle, the air is thick with the scent of brine and fish. Sailors bellow commands while merchants haggle over prices. Temporary stalls brim with barrels of ale, bolts of fabric, sacks of grain, and exotic goods from distant realms.

Children dart between the grown-ups and pause to watch, wide-eyed, as an impressive ship with flowing sails glides into the harbor. A young boy calls to a girl, "Tuuli, ye want some roasted nuts?" A stray dog weaves through the swarm, sniffing for scraps.

Amid the chaos, guards remain vigilant, ensuring no one flees with valuable goods. A loud shriek draws my gaze upward, and I see Sasha soaring above the docks, hunting her own rations.

Trees at the forest's edge shield me as I cast a quick spell to slip past the crowd. After retrieving what I need from my horse, I pat the beauty and speak softly. "Get home, stud. Be safe."

The stallion huffs, raises his head, swings his tail—then bolts toward the Forest of Frozen Dreams, where Isabella waits anxiously. Once I cross the pebbled path from forest into the kingdom's hardened territory, my powers will vanish.

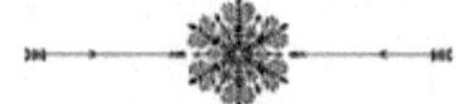

Garrett

I find Anabelle locked in a room in the royal wing. She reveals her true identity as a princess and explains Iyce's trap: Beatryx has been brought here to lure Blayze.

When I journeyed to this kingdom during Myst's travels, I toured the castle with two other guards. From that visit, I came to know the bones of this place. I close my eyes, recalling the map I memorized. I don't know the exact proximity of Iyce's chambers to the catacombs, but I'll do my best. Direction is half the battle.

Anabelle places her personal items into a small satchel and slings it crossways over her chest, and we leave quietly.

Once we pass the kitchen unseen, a narrow staircase hidden behind a shelf of barrels carries us into the catacombs. I glance at her. "Do you know how to use a weapon of any kind?"

"No. I was never taught." She seems embarrassed.

I hand her a small dagger. "Hide this on you. You never know what will go wrong. Throw it, stab someone, use it any way you see fit—if you need to."

Anabelle begins to shiver, and I wrap the cloak draped over my arm around her. "This is not fit for a princess, but it will keep you warm." It swallows her small frame, but I tie it, and we move through the damp tunnels.

Each step deepens the musk of ancient stone and wet air, even as torches flicker, faintly revealing the narrow, winding paths.

As we enter the crypts, crumbling tombs line the walls. Some bear family crests and ornate inscriptions; others remain bare. The air feels weighted, threat pressing in with every moment.

Anabelle is captivated by the tombs and steps closer to a smaller one. She raises her torch, illuminating fading engravings. "A child is laid to rest in this one."

"Princess Katriina, the youngest of four born to Enya, my mother," Blayze says solemnly, startling us. Then he continues, "What exactly are you two doing down here?" He looks directly at me. "Shouldn't you be in Arkaik Alpynz?" He turns to Anabelle, joking, "And shouldn't you be preparing for our wedding?"

Anabelle rolls her eyes. "One, we are not going to wed. Two, we are trying to find Beatryx."

Blayze chuckles low. "Sounds like we're on the same parchment on both accounts. Thank you. Follow me if you want to see an unfair fight that may leave me dead."

We follow him as hidden alcoves and secret chambers branch off the main passage, but he knows exactly where to go. Blayze shoots me a look, and then we both catch it—the one thing that always marks Beatryx.

Jasmine.

Blayze stops at a small door, and Anabelle and I crash into him. He turns, patient. "We need a plan. Anabelle—since you're wearing a maid's costume, and I'm not even going to ask why—would you be willing to go into Iyce's chambers from the main corridor? Would he recognize you?"

Anabelle grabs her head with both hands. I know she is having another vision. As I hold her close, I wonder who consoled her through these invasions of her mind before now.

Anabelle breaks free and looks directly at Blayze. "Iyce is going to try to get you to the balcony and throw you off. And no—he won't recognize me."

Blayze leads Anabelle out through another door that will take her to the corridor outside Iyce's chambers—the threshold to hell itself. If Iyce is gone, she'll slip inside and give the signal. Then we must move fast.

Anabelle

With my head down, I move quickly through the cold corridor and pray to Sekhmet, Goddess of Protection, because a war is brewing. Iyce's tantrums are something I've witnessed from afar since arriving in this kingdom. His maturity is the size of a mustard seed, with power larger than he deserves.

Iyce's doors stand before me—large, wooden, unforgiving. Hungry ears beg to listen. I place my ear to the thick wood and strain for sound. Hearing nothing, I carefully turn the iron handle and push the heavy door open.

Beatryx lies on his bed, her ankles and wrists tied.

What an awful man.

She isn't conscious, so I cough lightly—the signal to Blayze and Garrett that Iyce is not here.

Blayze appears through the small door near the bathing chamber. At once he is at Beatryx's side, hands on her delicate, doll-like face, checking her and cursing his brother under his breath.

Garrett and I wait for the next task—but then Iyce bursts into his chambers, both heavy doors threatening to come off their hinges. He must have sensed Blayze's presence. He charges.

This is my one opportunity to use the blade Garrett gave me.

The brothers wreck the room, towering over Garrett, who is no small man. Fully absorbed in cutting Beatryx's ropes, I hear Blayze holler, "Hand-to-hand combat, brother—no magic. Can you take me that way, you wretch?"

A blush floods my face, and I force my thoughts back into order.

Time stops when icicles begin to form on the ceiling—a sign of Iyce's rage. I glance down at the blade in my hand and realize it isn't sharp enough. I look to Garrett, who is trying to help Blayze by throwing punch after punch into Iyce's back, making zero progress.

I push harder against the ropes, sawing the blade back and forth until threads finally begin to rip apart.

Garrett, chest heaving, comes to me. "Let's get her out of here. I'm only slowing Blayze down, and he made it clear—nothing matters more than Beatryx's safety."

I nod. He lifts Beatryx, and we disappear through the trapdoor into the cold, dark passages.

My heart stays with Blayze. Please—let him survive this.

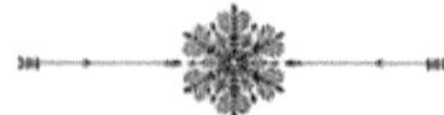

Blayze

I glimpse Beatryx for only a heartbeat before pure anger drives me toward Iyce. I must keep him distracted long enough for Garrett to get Anabelle and Beatryx to safety.

Iyce laughs, and then his words sever all thought. "You'll always have to wonder what exactly I did to her, won't you, brother?"

I launch toward him—but before we collide, he throws up a wall of ice. It shatters on impact, bursting into a spray of glittering shards.

My hands wrap around Iyce's thick neck as he exhales a stream of freezing air—sharp, deliberate—into my face. The chamber crystallizes into ice, sparing only the two of us.

I reach into the depths of my soul, pleading for fire.

Only disappointment answers.

Cold pins me to the wall as he speaks again. "Not only will I have Myst, but I'll make your wicked Beatryx mine, too. And when she sees how weak you truly are, she'll be glad to belong to me."

A guttural sound escapes me. Somehow, I force myself forward through his blizzard of madness, step by heavy step. When I reach him, he grips me with one hand, lifts me as if I'm weightless, and strides toward the balcony's edge.

I catch the handrail with both hands, slowing us—but what I see soaring through the sky shakes me to my core.

Sasha.

Iyce's eyes follow mine. When he sees her, he lets go, sending me over the railing. I grab the statues jutting from the pillar and cling with everything I have.

The next moment blurs as Iyce pulls a dagger from the holster across his chest and hurls it—hard and fast—straight at Sasha.

The dagger strikes true.

44

Glaycyr Falz

Olyvia

When I look back at the stained-glass window, I see a green vine and fixate on it as it swirls through the colored pane, winding toward the owl's left wing—where a white hybiscus bloom appears, intricately woven into the design.

The same bloom that marks my palm now glows in the glass.

Karze stares at me as I plead, "I don't know what to do. I see it, but I don't know what to do!"

Karze shakes his silver hair—always falling back into his face—and says, "Think, Lyv. Close your eyes and think about what you saw in that kaleidoscope."

I close my eyes and trace every detail, from the haunting harp notes that echoed through the ruins to all that followed. Then, cautiously, I move toward the window, where Sasha watches from within the glass. As I near it, a surge of energy pulses between the bloom on my hand and the one before me.

The moment is perfect—until I hear a frightening laugh. The one wicked being who would want to stop me.

The sorcerer.

I silently pray to Pele, my Fire Goddess. "Mother of Fire, guide me. Mother of Fire, guide me. Mother of Fire…"

And then I hear her words: "Only you hold the power of the fire etched into your palm as a bloom. To unleash its brilliance, command radiant heat from the glowing color, then align it perfectly with its twin. Speak your ancient words, and the owl will listen—forever breaking the spell."

I do as the goddess I trust commands. As I align my hand with the bloom in the glass, the sorcerer I knew only from books appears at my side.

But before he can stop me, Karze hurls himself between us, and their battle begins.

Karze shouts over his shoulder, "Don't stop, Lyv! I'll hold him back!"

I speak the ancient words I've recited in my mind since childhood, and a burst of fire magic strikes the glass, illuminating it in a blaze of color. The owl's wings seem to flutter, and the flower pulses with ancient power—

until pieces of glass dislodge, cutting through the air like a shrill song. Each shard glimmers as if alive, refusing to fall, refusing to rest. They circle me in a maddening dance, and within their chaos I glimpse the shape they once held—the owl, fractured, yearning to be whole.

I reach into the spinning storm, desperate to draw the pieces together, to sway the creature back from ruin. But the glass resists, splintering further with every touch, as though the curse delights in keeping the owl undone.

Karze

The sorcerer, dressed in twilight-colored robes, stands firm with dark, glowing eyes. Magic crackles around him, filling the air. With a flick of his wrist, he unleashes a wave of power.

Anger consumes me as I raise my wings as a shield and watch sparks erupt around me.

"Damn," I snarl.

I tower over the insidious being, wings of midnight unfurling as I bare my glistening fangs. I lunge for his throat, claws slashing through the air—but he chants, and a shimmering barrier deflects my attack, throwing me backward.

Lyv is within my sight, glowing brightly, her palm facing the glittering fragments of the shattered owl as they circle around her.

I have to stop him. I must keep him away from her.

Enraged, I soar upward, then dive toward the sorcerer, who watches me with fierce intent. But as I close in, he thrusts his hands forward and summons a blazing tendril of magic that strikes my wing, tearing through sinew and bone with a sickening crack.

I roar, pain searing through me—then plummet toward the wooden floor, my wing fluttering down with me, all but torn free. Fury burns in my crimson eyes, but the pain is unbearable. I fail to stand, hissing through agony.

The sorcerer stands over me.

This must be my end, I think, body shaking, as he leans down, pride in his voice. "This fight is over."

But something streaks past me, too fast to see—and her scream cuts through the air.

Olyvia

"You're damn right—it's over!" Madness echoes through the castle as the sorcerer looks up at me with a smirk, but the blade is already flying through the smoke-filled library. It lands in the center of his throat.

Mykah would be proud.

The sorcerer crumbles, and I rush to Karze.

He looks at me, chest heaving. "You did it, Lyv. You broke the spell. It's over now."

Tears fall through my anger as I force the words out. "Your beautiful wing…"

Karze looks at his wing, then at me. "It's just a wing. It's okay."

"It's not okay," I snap. "It absolutely is not okay!"

Karze's gaze shifts toward the stained-glass window. "Look, Lyv."

When I do, I can't believe my eyes. With the spell broken, the window is restored to its true form. I turn my hand upward. The hybiscus that once pulsed in my skin is gone, replaced by a silver gemstone that glows.

A gift.

I grasp it tightly.

The entire window pulses with magic, and the owl within it stirs. This time whole, it rises from the glass and spreads its wings, which flare into fire.

I pick up the dagger and extend my hand to Karze, pulling him to his feet. "Let's get out of here." He tucks his fractured wing tight against his side.

We run.

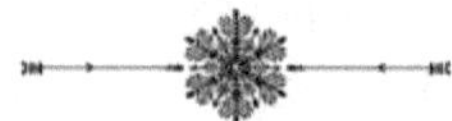

Blayze

Sasha's cry shatters the air—the dagger has struck true. Thought fogs as I cling to the statues jutting from the pillar, fury ripping through me.

In this darkness, fire brands my back as wings tear free, flames bursting from their tips.

I am airborne.

For a heartbeat, I hover—then land on the handrail like a savage beast, hunting my prey.

Iyce.

He is running, freezing everything behind him.

He will have to wait.

I'm in the air.

Isabella

Something feels terribly wrong, dread tightening its hold on me. Julian sleeps soundly while I pace the room. I am a healer, but the unknown is a terrible weight.

As the thought settles, a faint cry for help drifts in from outside—a woman's voice. I go to the door but halt, a warning rising in my chest. It could be a snare.

Blayze's spell keeps intruders out, but it never binds me inside.

Then the voice returns—a voice I have not heard in so long.

I throw the front door wide and descend into the frozen woods, my cry echoing. "Where are you?"

Someone lies collapsed in the snow, her bare body bleeding into the white silence.

Tears flood my eyes as I run to my mother, whom I have not seen since I was banned from the kingdom. I wrap my cloak around her frail body and hold her close, never wanting to let go.

"Mamá, please—stand with me. We must get you inside." She is so weak, and desperation grips me.

Once I have her settled in a room downstairs, I see the wound—something struck her neck, grazing the place where life itself flows.

Thank the goddesses it did not go deeper.

Who did this?

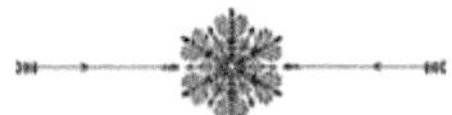

Blayze

Finding Sasha is my priority. She is wounded, and my heart aches with worry as I look back at the kingdom and see fire and ice restored to balance.

After a few blinks, my eyes adjust to the height. Gliding over the forest, I spot a horse bearing three riders. My wings beat faster until I overtake them, dropping in front of the horse and forcing it to halt.

Beatryx sees me first and cries out, "Blayze!"

The moment suspends. I cannot reach her fast enough—yet suddenly she's in my arms, and I hold her close.

After pointing Garrett and Anabelle toward my home in the woods, I tell them Beatryx and I will not be far behind.

Then I pull her into me. "Never again will I lose you. Did he hurt you in any way?"

She looks up and shakes her head. "Not that I'm aware of. I was in a spell-sleep, but I could hear things."

I slip my arm around her waist as we walk through the peaceful snow. *Sasha. I have to find her without delay.*

The thunder of running feet barrels up from behind. We spin to see Olyvia and Karze tearing toward us. They stop hard, gasping—Olyvia bent over, speechless.

Beatryx reaches for her and pulls her into an embrace. "Come with us. We can talk once we get to the cabin."

As we walk, Olyvia and Karze finally tell us everything that happened in the ruins—a place my mother loved deeply. I say to Olyvia, "You broke the curse, and I felt it the moment it happened. I grew wings."

Beatryx squeezes my hand, and I wrap both arms around her, holding her closer until the cabin comes into view.

The first thing I notice is blood in the snow—then more droplets leading to the door.

Panic hits. The others see it too, and we rush inside.

But all seems normal.

Garrett and Anabelle sit at the table with Isabella, who leaps up and runs to us. My sister wraps her arms around me, and we embrace as I say, "Everything is all right—except one thing. Sasha. Iyce threw a dagger that cut into the side of her neck, and I haven't seen her since. Did she come back here? Is that her blood I saw outside."

Isabella gasps.

Olyvia and Karze remove their cloaks and hang them on a hook near the entrance—hooks that have never been used.

Then Beatryx asks Olyvia, "Where did you get that piece? It belongs to my mother."

Protectively, Olyvia covers the two stones on the bracelet with her hand—when a familiar voice cuts through the room.

"Actually, it belongs to me."

My mother, Queen Enya, steps into the room and stands before us all.

Emotion overtakes me as I move toward her and reach for her hands—then I see the cloth wrapped around her neck.

And in that instant, I know.

My mother is Sasha—the owl who never forgot me, who watched over me in my darkest days in this frozen forest.

I fall to my knees and weep.

Beatryx presses both hands to her mouth, struggling to contain her emotion. Isabella is at my side, helping me up, and together we embrace our mother.

Isabella tells us how she found her. "She was clinging to life when she made it here."

I pull them both against my chest, holding them close.

Queen Enya

Olyvia removes the bracelet and walks toward me, and emotion surges as I begin to tell my story. "When Blayze and Iyce were born, I wanted to create something memorable to represent the power they each possessed."

I hold the bracelet up, the glow shimmering along its edges. "The blue stone stands for the frozen elements Iyce possesses, and the red stone signifies the balance of warmth Blayze always brings. On my last trip to Balag, I looked for the bracelet, and it was gone. I had no idea where it went—or why."

Olyvia asks, "How is that even possible, since we found it in the castle at Balag?"

Everyone is puzzled. Then Anabelle steps forward and holds out her hand. "May I?"

Carefully, I place my precious piece in her palm. She holds it close and closes her eyes.

We watch in silence as her senses return, and she begins to speak, voice low and steady. "I saw a dark-haired woman with hazel eyes. She wore a ring on her smallest finger, set with a blue stone encircled by rubies. Atop the stone rested the letter B. She spoke to a man—a powerful sorcerer—her fury unmistakable. She told him the bracelet held no magic, then hurled it toward what I believe is your chamber in the castle."

A tall boy with silver hair speaks up, pleased to contribute. "That sorcerer won't be telling anyone anything else—Olyvia handled that. As for the bracelet, I found it on the floor near a large chest, on one of the higher levels."

Anabelle hands the piece back to me, and it glows again.

Then Beatryx speaks. "That woman is my mother, and she is a horrible person. The ring you described is a ring my father gave me, and she took it when she left us. As a matter of fact, she is in Glaycyr Falz now, and I have no idea why. I traveled there with Princess Myst and saw her."

I look at Beatryx. "I wondered what the king and your mother were up to myself."

Blayze speaks instantly. "I intend to find out exactly what is going on."

I lift the cloth at my neck, and Blayze guides me to a chair. "When you and your brother let wrath take hold, I did my own prying and saw the king speaking to the now-silenced sorcerer." I look over at the tall boy and wink. Then I continue, "I knew I needed a way to end this curse, and Olyvia was the girl with strong fire magic. Olyvia, I believe this bracelet protected you once Karze placed it around your wrist. Its power is sly—just like me."

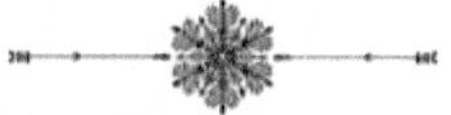

Olyvia

The gem in my hand warms, and *I know what I must do.* Slowly, I step to the queen again. "I'm not sure if you know the end result of breaking the curse—beyond restoring balance—but a small gift was left in my palm."

I open my hand, exposing the shimmering silver gem. The queen is taken aback. Tears well in her jewel-like green eyes as she recites a spell that lifts the stone from my palm and fastens it to the bracelet. She places the bracelet around her own wrist; it clasps on its own.

"This silver stone represents someone gentle—my precious daughter Isabella—who uses her pure heart to heal, but also to love. Only one more stone, and the bracelet will be complete."

Anabelle whispers one name: "Katriina."

Next, the queen takes my hand and blows a light fire onto my left palm, leaving the outline of the hybiscus that had disappeared.

Seeing it, I beam. "I love it. Thank you!"

"No one will ever forget who you are and what you did for Glaycyr Falz!"

The next voice jolts us all from our haze.

"Mamá!" Julian shouts, running down the stairs.

I can't help looking to Queen Enya, who longs to go to her grandson—whom she has never cradled or sung lullabies to. She begins to rise, hesitates, then eases back into her chair, longing written across her face.

Isabella takes Julian's hand as they walk toward the queen. "There is someone I'd like you to meet."

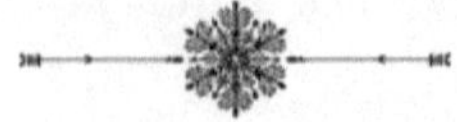

In the kitchen, Blayze and Garrett discuss something serious while Beatryx and Anabelle prepare tea and gather refreshments.

Karze has been resting since Isabella tended his broken wing. Meanwhile, I stand in a daze, missing home and family more than ever.

I grab my cloak and slip out, craving a walk in the snow. But before I get far, I hear my name.

"Lyvy! Lyvy!"

Turning back, I see Julian on the porch, bundled up. My heart swells with love—and the friendships I'm finding here. I scoop up a handful of snow and toss it his way, making him laugh.

When I reach him, I take his outstretched hand, and together we walk back inside.

Everyone sits at Blayze's table, enjoying cherry brandy and conversation. This family has a lot to catch up on.

Peeking around the door, I see Karze sleeping. He stirs and, despite the pain, says, "Isabella assured me I'll be back to perfection in no time."

"You definitely will be." My smile tells him I believe it.

A light knock brings Anabelle in, her expression anxious. "Olyvia, do you have a moment?"

"Yes." I pat Karze's hand. "Rest."

Anabelle leads me to a quiet corner of the sitting room, away from the others. She confides that she has just seen a powerful vision—one that includes me, unlike any she has known. She takes my hands in hers.

"Olyvia, I've had countless visions, but none have carried the urgency of this one."

"Tell me," I plead.

What Anabelle reveals next cuts to my core, and I know I must return to Arkaik Alpynz at once.

I thank her and find Blayze, pulling him aside to relay what she told me.

Frantic, I say, "I must get back to Myst."

Blayze studies me. "I have not done this with anyone in a very long time, and it requires at least two people with fire magic. If we include my mother, the fire will answer with greater strength."

My eyes search his face as he asks, "Have you ever gone through a portal?"

45

Arkaik Alpynz

Sage

"Sleet, Sleet, my Sleet…" I moan—breathy, raspy.

Heat glistens across my ivory skin, pale hair spilling past my waist as I move over the king. Sleet grips my hips, guiding my rhythm, his gaze fixed on the rise and fall of my body.

We crest together.

He rolls me onto my stomach, pressing slow, lingering kisses along my back. For a moment, he studies me—then eases onto his back.

"Use your lush lips to clean up the mess you've made, lovely one."

I obey, tasting us as he begins to harden again. His fingers trail down the center of my chest, pausing at the hollow of my belly and stealing the breath from me.

Then he rises, takes my hand, and leads me toward the vast bathing chamber.

Wax drips from the candles in a steady rhythm, striking stone. Walls of carved granite enclose a sunken tub at the chamber's heart. Above us, stained-glass depicts entwined figures frozen in winter light. With sunlight, they would come alive. The fireplace murmurs along the far wall, cedar smoke curling through clove and sandalwood.

Sleet stands taller than I, sculpted and immaculate—steel-blue eyes, hair dark as a starless sky, every movement precise. Gentle—until he isn't. And I love him most when I quiet the storm within him.

Do not let your mind wander there.

It does anyway.

Each time I see him, memory follows—the love that was torn from me, taken by Frost. And she wasn't finished. She took Myst, too.

He lifts me effortlessly into the steaming water. My head falls back as his lips find my neck, each kiss lingering longer than the last. I straddle him, fingertips tracing his chest before my lips follow.

He gathers my hair from my face, framing me for a moment before drawing me close, his breath warm at my ear. "I love you."

I answer in a whisper.

Sleet begins to fall, shimmering lightly around us, dancing across our skin—and I hold my power tight. If even one hybiscus petal slips, he will know.

He uncorks a glass bottle, pouring a measured blend of primrose and gardenia oils into his palm before smoothing it over my shoulders. The scent blooms between us as his hands move deeper with each slow glide, unmaking the tension in my body until warmth gathers low within me. His gaze never leaves mine.

He undoes me every time.

Sleet steps from the tub, hand outstretched. I place mine in his, and he wraps me in linen before lifting me to the basin's edge.

From a dish, he selects a blackberry, dips it in cream. His fingers part me, smearing sweetness before he claims the fruit with his mouth.

He draws up a stool and buries himself between my thighs, slow, deliberate, reverent. My legs fall across his shoulders.

"When will you get your fill, my love?" I whisper through breathless sound.

"Never."

His fingertips tenderly part me as he strokes my blossom, his tongue worshiping me until I gift him once more with sugar love.

He rises and pulls me close, claiming my lips. His hands roam with familiar certainty, but when he speaks, his voice softens.

"You are not leaving my chambers today."

I smile into his fading kiss.

He carries me back to the bed and lays me down with a gentleness that feels foreign on him before slipping beneath the blanket beside me.

"Sleep, my beautiful love. I'll hunger for you again when we wake."

I believe him. I surrender to the warmth beside me, eyes closing, aware of his gaze even as sleep takes me.

Sleet

She cannot conceal her scent—or the memory of her taste.

I'll always remember.

I'll never forget.

46

HEILALA

Hybiscus Kingdom

Mykah

"It's time. Wear leather and fur. The alpynz ahead are cold as winter's wrath."

Beneath the ancient wooden rafters of the barn, lantern flames sway in the draft, casting long shadows across straw-covered dirt where my hybryx is tied to a sturdy post. With urgency, I yank my tunic over my head and run my hands over her thick chest, speaking softly to steady her as her warm breath turns to steam against my wrist. "Easy now. You'll need all your strength for what's coming."

One of my companions laughs low. "Careful, Elestria will be jealous."

Instinctively, I hurl a dagger at his face. He shifts aside with silky ease, the blade left quivering in the beam behind him.

I secure the harness, checking each strap and buckle. "Time is short. We move ready for anything."

A small calf nudges my leg. I crouch, running my fingers through his soft fur. "You can come on the next adventure. You're too small for this one—and yes, I'll take care of your mamá." *If we return.*

Kai sits on a bench sharpening enchanted daggers, their blue aura pulsing faintly. "Each one is sharp enough to pierce whatever stands in our path." He slides them into the leather belt crossing his chest.

Jabarri—tallest, broadest—packs a satchel with healing elixirs and dried rations. "The cold will be our greatest enemy."

Kai hollers over the beasts' restless calls, "We aren't riding to your grandmamá's villa, you witless mule." More daggers fly.

I pull on a long-sleeved tunic, fasten my weapons, then shrug into a heavy leather overlay with crossed straps, sliding two short swords into place. We gather around a map spread across a crude table. I trace our route. "We follow these stars to the forest. From there, it's a straight flight."

Small hands push the barn door open. Honey-brown eyes peek through. "Papá!"

My attention snaps to my daughter. I lift her into a tight embrace, then set her gently on her feet. This is why I return. Always this.

Elestria steps inside—dark curls, steady gaze—the mother of my child and my wife. She reaches up and tightens the strap across my shoulder, her lingering touch saying more than words. "Are you sure you do not need my help?"

She is a warrior beyond measure, but I need her here—with our daughter, Nala Veya, and with our kingdom. I kiss her deeply. "My love, I won't be gone long. Keep things calm here, because when we return, chaos will follow."

She nods, takes Nala's hand, and steps back.

Taking the reins with a firm grip, I mount first; the others follow, settling behind me. Our beasts spread their massive wings, and the barn fills with the thunder of feathers.

"We ride!"

Lantern light fades behind us as we soar into the night sky, ready for whatever waits beyond the cold.

47

Arkaik Alpynz

Amethyst Hybiscus

Myst

Six moon phases ago, during the summer solstice, I turned twenty. My marriage to Iyce has been meticulously planned—every detail accounted for—and is set to take place in one week.

Tonight, I ride into the Whispering Woods, seeking solitude.

Aspen radiates heat beneath me, steady as we settle into our familiar rhythm before he surges forward, his hooves barely grazing the ground. Wind lashes my face, my hair whipping like ribbons until he slows again, easing into a trot and then a walk, allowing me to sink into the rise and fall of his movement.

He carries us to the stream he favors, and we veer from the path that leads to Grandpapá's cottage—because he is not there.

I lean into his warmth, my ungloved fingers sinking into his thick mane as snowflakes drift down, brushing my cheek and catching in my lashes, soft and fleeting. In the hush, something feels… different.

We step into the forest's heart, where everything has transformed into a frozen wonderland. Branches bow beneath fresh snow, and when I peer into the depths, my breath clouds before me, mingling with the mist unfurling from my fingertips. It coils around my hands, glowing faintly—familiar, as though it has always belonged to me.

The woods stir beneath my magic—awakening slowly, as if

remembering me.

I let my fingers move, releasing shimmering strands that weave through the falling flurries, an opus of winter that drifts and shimmers in the quiet.

Aspen slows, his hooves crunching softly into the snow, and I lie back along his spine, looking up at the night sky where the stars twinkle above me.

"Hello, twinkling beauties. Do any of you have a secret for me?" I murmur, my breath turning to frost as I laugh softly, half in jest, half in longing.

These woods hold ancient secrets—my own included—and something in me feels ready now in a way it never has before.

Aspen shifts beneath me as the snowfall thickens, the forest no longer still but aware—watching, listening. I straighten and guide him toward the brightest star, the flurries drifting as though the woods themselves are observing my every step.

"Honestly," I say under my breath, "it's probably a myth."

But the words no longer feel certain.

We move deeper into the dark, enchanted woods until, at some point, I dismount and continue on foot, the silence deepening around me. The stars seem lower now, glowing like lanterns guiding my path.

Then it hits—not gradually, but all at once.

Raw, powerful magic thrums through the air and into me, stealing my breath as something inside me answers.

Snowflakes whirl so fast they hum.

And then I see it.

The amethyst hybiscus glows against the snow, its petals rimmed in frost, waiting.

My breath catches as I kneel before it, the world falling quiet around me.

"I've been looking for you."

A whisper cuts through the stillness.

"Find your mother."

The sound settles deep within me—not foreign, not frightening, but achingly familiar, like something I was always meant to hear.

The whispers have waited twenty years for me to hear them.

They finally have.

I turn, searching for Aspen—only to realize I am no longer with him, and before fear can take hold, a second voice follows, softer this time, closer.

"Go to the beach."

My hand rises to my chest, pressing against the rapid beat of my heart as the truth settles in.

I have to find my mother.

Aspen finds me, and I am once again on his back, leaning forward into his warmth as we surge through the woods. He moves as though my urgency is his own, reading me with every stride, my fingers tangled in his mane as we glide through the snow—almost flying.

The castle towers rise ahead, looming through the frost. I dismount before Aspen fully stops, boots striking stone as I run. Hayze appears, instantly taking in our breathless state, the frost clinging to us—but I am already moving past her.

"Please take care of Aspen!"

My body moves faster than thought, my mist trailing behind me in thin, restless strands as I race through the doors, up the wide stairs, east toward the queen's chambers. A guard calls after me—"Princess, how can I assist?"—but I do not slow.

I reach her doors only to be blocked by her guards.

"What business do you have here?"

Ignoring them, I throw both hands up. Mist floods the hall, swallowing their sight as I push past and burst inside.

Empty.

The word lands harder than it should. I spin, scanning the

chamber, the silence pressing in.

What are they guarding?

She isn't here.

Heart pounding, I step onto the balcony. Beyond the railing, the Forest of Shadows stretches into darkness—the place where Mairi lives. A pull grips me, stronger now, undeniable.

Maybe she's there.

There is no time to think.

I leave her chambers and race back through the castle, the distance collapsing beneath me until I reach the barn once more. Hayze turns, bewildered. "Myst, what has gotten into you? What is wrong?"

"I don't have time to explain," I say, already moving.

Then I surge toward Twinkling Sands Beach—

fast as storm winds.

Olyvia

Garrett, Anabelle, and I stand in the garden outside the castle gates, shaking our heads as we try to regain balance after passing through the portal. Garrett steadies Anabelle with an arm around her waist as she sways. We're all disoriented. Then Anabelle lifts her gaze and asks, "Olyvia, where is the beach? You must go quickly."

Her words strike straight through me.

I nod, wrap my arms around the tiny woman, and say, "Thank you—not only for coming, but for sharing the vision."

I hug Garrett next, pressing Shayn's dagger into his hand. "Let Shayn know he was right. The dagger holds magic."

Garrett's eyes brighten.

I'm already turning, already moving toward the beach when I call over my shoulder, "I will see you both again one day."

A sudden gust sweeps through the garden, carrying Anabelle's voice. "Where are you going, Olyvia?"

I don't slow.

"Home."

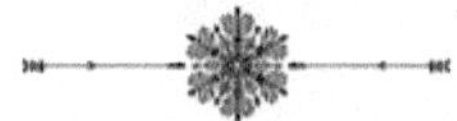

Myst

The beach cannot come into view fast enough. I run until the shore opens before me, and the sky darkens into something unfamiliar. Amethyst hybiscus blooms begin to fall like sleepy butterflies—the same flower from the card I saw two years ago, the very one I just found blooming through snow in the woods. They drift downward, opening fully as they settle into the sand.

I move toward the ocean, wind rising as it whips my hair and tugs at my gown, forcing me to clutch the skirts in both hands.

What I see next stops me.

Sage stands at the edge of the shore, bare feet wading into the water.

She looks peaceful. Beautiful. Radiant.

The wind howls as I struggle to stay upright, watching three immense, mystical creatures descend toward the beach, each bearing a rider dressed in black. Their wings glide through the amethyst petals, scattering them in soft, drifting spirals before they land with fluid, controlled power.

Sage notices them—then looks back at me.

I recognize those beasts. The same ones Iyce took from the faraway isles, only larger.

Are these men here to take the younglings home?

The snowflake necklace brightens, turning cold against my skin. I press it into my chest, thinking of Grandpapá.

Then I look up at the lead rider—

and I am staring into my own eyes.

Sage moves toward me, hips swaying. "You are precious, like a hidden kingdom that needs you."

My voice betrays me. "Where is my mother?"

The wind surges. Sage steps closer, shouting through the storm, "Please trust me."

I do. I love her. I always have.

She reaches for the pendant.

The moment her fingers touch it, she screams and is thrown back.

The riders do not move.

Sage forces herself up and tries again, but the force drives her back once more. "Myst, you must remove it yourself!" she pleads.

Grandpapá fills my mind.

I clutch the pendant. "No!"

"Do you not believe in the whispering snowflakes, Myst? Please—you're the only one who can remove it. Please believe in me, baby girl. I would never hurt you."

And when she calls me that—

something fractures.

Memories strike hard: my mother's coldness, the arrow grazing my cheek, the gowns forced upon me, the absence of touch, of warmth, of anything that felt like love.

She never chose me.

Then Iyce—his claim, the marriage I do not want, the life already written for me.

If I keep this on, I disappear.

The wind fights me as I release my skirts and lift trembling hands to my nape, fingers fumbling with the clasp.

I choose myself.

The necklace slides free, slipping down my body before falling into the pink sand.

Let it go.

Something inside me breaks as it leaves me.

"About fucking time," the lead rider says, dropping from his beast.

He walks straight toward me, tilts his head, and speaks a single word in the ancient language.

Darkness takes me.

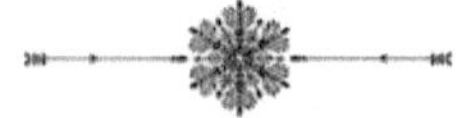

Mykah

It is something I hate doing, but Myst must be under a spell to survive this flight. As gently as possible, I lift her onto my shoulder and carry her to my beast. With one foot in the stirrup and an arm around her, I haul her up and settle her before mounting behind her.

The air tightens around me, wind whipping sand and snow into a furious spiral that claws at the sky. I fucking hate this frozen kingdom and its fucking people.

Then I hear—

"Mykah! Mykah!"

The familiar voice cuts through the storm—and then she appears.

"Lyv! Over here!"

Once again, I am on the ground as my baby sister—stronger than all of us—crashes into me, and the winds falter, circling us instead of tearing through.

Where in all the hells is my mother?

"Mamá!" I shout over the gale. I spot her on Jabarri's beast, already taking the lead. Then I see Jabarri riding Kai's beast, with Kai behind him. She never sticks to the plan.

Silently, I pray to all the goddesses. I lift Lyv by the waist, guiding her onto my beast and steadying her as she settles behind Myst. With the reins in hand, the three of us rise into the air, the storm surging beneath the beast's wings as it carries us higher.

Beautiful chaos unfolds before me.

The beach is blanketed in amethyst hybiscus blooms—silent, powerful.

And finally, we are bringing Myst—our sister—home.

The wind stops.

Sage

Ahead of the others, I glance back, taking in the sight of all three of my children together—for the first time.

But this is only the beginning.

EPILOGUE

Arkaik Alpynz

Queen Frost

Amethyst petals lift, stirred by a haunting breeze searching for what lies hidden beneath.

Until…

A shimmer catches my attention, and my eyes focus on what twinkles, causing a chill to scrape across my body. I bend, my fingers brushing the petals before closing around a familiar shape— a snowflake pendant, half-buried, its chain cold.

"Chanteel," I hiss, fury reaching my eyes. "She was disguised as a castle steward—right underneath us."

A large presence casts a shadow that swallows me as he presses against my back, arms encircling my waist, hands settling on my upper thighs, steadying my fury as he speaks.

"We'll get her back." Iyce says calmly. "Their kingdom and realm are weakened—and that began over twenty years ago. A fleet can be readied by morning. I will lead it, if you wish."

I turn within his hold, eyes alight as I study his face, kiss him fiercely, then pull back, shaking my head.

"No. Let them do it for us."

Iyce stills.

"We'll lure her back," I say, venom coiling through every word. "And when we strike—" my smile sharpens, "—it will be against their precious Heilala."

Iyce's eyes turn savage.

"There is brilliance in your mind, my Queen."

Hidden Hybiscus
Book II
Hybiscus Snowflakes Series

ABOUT THE AUTHOR

Elke Chantil is a debut fantasy author whose stories weave mythic landscapes, emotionally layered characters, and magic touched by legacy, identity, and longing. Her love of storytelling began in childhood, nurtured by nightly tales read aloud by her mother, and has since blossomed into the Hybiscus Snowflakes series, beginning with Whispering Snowflakes.

Born and raised in Texas, Elke infuses her worlds with a touch of twang and a shimmer of myth, inviting readers into realms where identity and legacy bloom beneath the ice. When she is not writing, she finds joy in family, her pets, woodworking projects, and the ritual of preparing Sunday meals while music and football fill the background.

elkechantil.com
Instagram @elkechantilauthor
TikTok @elkechantil